Fourth Edition

5 7 9 10 8 6

Saint John's, Antigua
West Indies

First Published Sept. 2nd, 2022

Revised May 31st, 2026

ISBN: 979-8-9868910-0-2

Visit the author's website at
https://lmsanguinette.wordpress.com

DEDICATION

This book is dedicated to my siblings Madison and Conor, as a reminder that with a little faith and hard work, dreams really do come true.

WELCOME
TO
VISANTHE

L. M. SANGUINETTE

OTHER WORKS

VISANTHIAN NOVELS

Welcome to Visanthe   (Book 1)
Visanthe in Ruin   (Book 2)
Visanthe Rising   (Book 3, coming soon)

Of Arrows and Roses   (standalone, coming soon)

POETRY COLLECTIONS

The Days I Dream of Coffee
The Days I Dream of Chocolate
The Days I Dream of Chardonnay

CONTENTS

YOZORA
OSIIR
MIDD
CAMP
SAAR
RED
DESERT
ARALDIN
FIELDS

HAIZEA
ILISO
ODLE ISLE
SOLIA
IDUNE

PROLOGUE

"GET UP!"

The woman's screech dragged her from the deepest, darkest depths of whatever dimension dreams live in. It could have dragged a demon from Hell. She tossed and turned in her bed, hoping to cling to the last hours of peaceful slumber. But no. The curtains were drawn, the sun was high, and time crept ever forward.

"Today is the day," the woman reminded—again. The tired reminder provoked only a roll and a groan as she nestled herself deeper into the blankets.

People were always reminding her of things. *Don't slouch. Don't speak. Remember to smile. Remember your temper…* And the worst, and probably most frequent, *remember your birth.* That last one irritated her most of all because it was the one thing she couldn't actively change. Postures, expressions, tempers, yes. But birth? That was a sentence. One with no chance of bail, no chance of probation. A sentence that ended only when your life did.

As were the events of today, she thought.

Today was nothing more than a sentence, marked by a symbol on her wrist that, from one day to the next, appeared without warning, without remorse, without the simple passage of time that turns seeds into trees and hair grey. It simply appeared where it had not been before—where it wasn't wanted. She should feel lucky, or proud, like most of the children her age would under such circumstances, but looking at it now, the pesky symbol happily nestled in the centre of her wrist, all she felt was sick.

She almost got away. The countdown to her birthday began only two weeks before, and her mother had been on edge about her mark—or lack thereof—ever since. After all, everyone in her family had been marked. Why hadn't she? And then, on the eve of her twelfth birthday, much to her mother's triumph—and her own dismay—it came.

Some would have rejoiced. To them, it was a mark of dignity, a mark that branded you special, *divine* even.

Not to her.

Instead, she sat alone in her bathroom crying, attempting all manner of painful ways to wipe, scratch, and eventually burn it off, but to no avail. To her, it was a branding, like the one given to cattle sent to slaughter.

She rolled over reluctantly. It made no sense to prolong the suffering. Out of the corner of her sleep-encrusted eye, she spied two others standing expectantly at the door. One bit his nails, the other bit her lip.

"You brought an entourage," she mumbled in reply.

"You're being difficult," scolded the woman as she ripped the sheets from the bed. "You know how important today is."

"Yes ma'am." Her apathy shone through the words.

"Your mother is waiting."

"Yes ma'am," she repeated with a moan.

"And stop with the sarcasm," the woman growled as she wagged a wicked finger.

The automatic "Yes ma'am" caught in her throat. It wasn't worth picking fights today. She nodded silently instead, watching as the woman rummaged through her wardrobe at the other end of the room.

The woman tugged at dress after dress, shaking her head disappointedly with each flutter of dark cloth.

"You know, most children wouldn't have slept a wink last night," she added bitterly. "You should try showing a little more gratitude."

The woman was right, of course. Birth aside, most children would've been thrilled to be in her position. Again, she wasn't most children.

"This will look lovely on you," the woman announced finally, turning back to her with dress in hand, looking positively chuffed at her choice. As she spoke, she paid more attention to the awful, ruffled, yellow tulle dress than to the young woman who would be wearing it. "And please try to remember your behaviour is a reflection of the entire kingdom, Your Grace."

The young princess didn't need to be reminded of what today meant, she couldn't forget, no matter how hard she tried—which she did actively. It nagged at her, every hour of every day since that pesky symbol appeared. She wished she could give it up—the symbol, the title, the need to abide by protocol—all of it, but the woman glowered at her again.

"Get dressed. Now," her caretaker reiterated with a finality to her tone that stopped any further replies dead in their tracks.

The young princess didn't bother to comment that the dress would sallow her skin. It would only lead to a lecture neither of them had time for. Besides, the other two were still waiting at the door to wash her and tie her hair in knots.

She stumbled from her bed to the balcony, heart burdened by the mounting festivities below, feeling as though she was trading one prison for another. Somewhere beyond the horizon, Middle Isle, the birthplace of all powers, was waiting. Whether she liked it or not, soon, all eyes would be on her. Her intestines bunched themselves into something the size of a pebble. At least by tomorrow, the nagging would be over. By tomorrow, there would be no more wondering or worrying. By tomorrow, she would have her powers.

* * *

THE FIRST FIREWORK to light up the night sky made even the sun look dim. It was as much a political statement as it was celebratory commencement. Everything about this day was. The air vibrated with excitement, nervousness, and a touch of something magical. It whispered through the crowds in a language long forgotten yet ever-present, lurking just beyond the realm of sense. This year, however, something else accompanied it. Something sinister tinged this magic, imperceptible, save to a lucky few—the kind of people who saw ominously moving logs for what they were: crocodiles.

Stone bridges bubbled up from the turquoise depths of the ocean on its command, connecting each nation to the land between lands, the neutral ground, Middle Isle. These bewitching gates opened of their own volition, as they always had, and always would. Through them, separations fell flat. Five nations—earth, water, fire, air, light—became one people, even if only for a few hours.

Thus, began Divination Day.

The Harri, people of earth, crossed through the first gate, one made of granite and embellished with flowers and iron ore. The Ur, people of water, owned the second gate, one of glimmering blue ice, lined with dagger-like icicles and intricate carvings of fish. The third gate belonged to the Argia, people of fire, and was made of glowing amber with a fiery lava core. Gate four belonged to the Zerua, people of air, and stood imposingly from a sea of low-lying clouds, made of the purest white marble. The fifth gate, that of the Izar, people of light, was a mass of moonstone and quartz.

Off in the distance stood a final gate that caused no awe and hummed with no life—a neglected gate. Shrouded in shadows and mystery, it blended seamlessly into the background. This sixth, now darkened, moss-covered gate stood abandoned, reclaimed by nature like a monument to a long-forgotten past.

But left to their own devices, forgotten pasts have a curious way of repeating themselves. Wrapped in the mounting joy of the festivities, not a soul paid notice as the sixth and "forever sealed" gate budged.

The crowds climbed into the ancient amphitheatre, awaiting the night's festivities. This year's lucky twelve-year-olds trembled on the edges of the stage, waiting patiently for their names to be called off the list. Energy radiated from some and only fluttered in others, but no matter. A lot or a little still meant special, chosen. The mark on their wrists still branded them divine.

Tonight, they would become *kanala*, wielders of one of the six powers that governed Visanthe. Tonight, the magic claimed them.

Amidst the commotion, five leaders took their respective spots around a six-pointed star in the centre of the amphitheatre. At the heart of the star stood a final pedestal holding six gold rings, each with an engraving of its nation's emblem: a leaf for earth, a droplet for water, a flame for fire, a cloud for air, a star for light, and circle for something none remembered but all feared.

A great fire rimmed the arena, lighting it up like an earthbound sun. At the stroke of midnight, and not a moment sooner, the proceedings began.

"We welcome you, one and all, to the 775th annual Ring Divination Ceremony," boomed the seasoned voice of the Harri leader. He clapped his stubby hands together, sending a rippling echo through the arena. The crowd stifled cheers and held their tongues. The voice had come from a man short and sturdy. He stood firm like a boulder, stroking a salt-and-pepper beard with sun-browned hands. His different coloured eyes—one moss-green, the other a vibrant, almost glowing jade—looked proudly out at his people.

"On this day, our children become *kanala*," spoke a voice as cold as the one who wielded it. With frosty white dreadlocks hanging from her head and skin so dark it glowed blue, the queen of the Ur looked like an ice sculpture, only twice as firm and infinitely more cold. She jabbed a sharpened sceptre into the stone floor, unmoved by the festivities. Her frost blue eyes scanned the crowds like a polar bear out for its next prey.

"This year we are proud to divine twenty children, originating from each of our five nations," chimed a voice as sweet and rich as fine golden honey. The words left her delicate lips like notes strummed on harps by angels. The air around her was warm like the afternoon sun. Golden curls bounced just above her broad shoulders, and eyes that sparkled like crystallised amber glowed against her sand-coloured skin. Framing her figure was a cape of delicate white fire. The queen of the Argia brandished a dazzling smile, drawing attention to a steady face, rather than the stream of flames she fidgeted with between her fingers.

"Blessed be, spirit, he who brings light to our darkness, air to our lungs, blood to our bodies, fire to our hearts, and flesh to our bones. Welcome, Iturri," said a voice that rolled like thunder to the heavens above. The king of the Zerua coughed from behind a fluffy white beard. He stroked it lightly as his cloudy grey eyes scanned the amphitheatre, stopping on the face of each child apologetically. "After today, you will become channels for one of the six powers that govern our land. You will be bound to them, and them to you."

"Honour them, respect them, and they too shall do the same," said the final leader. Her delicate voice seemed to resonate deep within the souls of all who heard it as if she were speaking to a light somewhere far beneath the skin. Though youthful in appearance, legend said she—princess of light, leader of the Izar—was as old as time itself, and somewhere in time, gravity lost its charm over her. Blinding white waves of hair hovered around her petite body. Two especially wide sapphire blue eyes sat perfectly nestled in her ageless, caramel skin. "But be warned. Iturri, and Iturri alone, chooses its host and its form. From the moment it settles, there is no turning back."

Each year it was the same speech, yet each year it garnered more applause. Possibly because the people to whom it referred were now a small minority. The *kanala*, wielders of power, had steadily been decreasing for years but never had the number been so low. Compared to last year's two hundred and thirty-seven divined, this year's twenty was nothing more than a sick joke. One more reason why this Divination Day felt wrong.

Silence fell over the crowd as the first child stepped up to the platform. One by one, she placed each ring on her middle finger before waiting patiently for her judgement.

Suddenly, the girl let out a shriek. The Zerua ring began to glow and burn. An energy like no other surged through her spine, turning her moss-green pupils a cloudy grey. The ring grew tighter and tighter until it had sunk into her skin completely, leaving a plum-coloured bruise in its wake. This power binding had left a small, almost invisible cloud shape in the centre of the bruise. The other once strong, metal rings broke off as if made of nothing more than sugar. Under her feet, the floor shifted outwards to one of the points of the star.

"Welcome, my child," said the elderly man with the fluffy white beard in a tone of practised melancholic monotony as he baptised her with a sprinkling of cloud dust. She bowed politely and joined her new cycle, gently rubbing the new scar on her finger.

The next child followed suit, stepping up to the platform and placing the rings on his finger. This time the surge was less prominent. His pupils remained a light blue. The floor beneath his feet shifted to the leader of his home cycle.

"Welcome home," said the icy Ur leader. She wasn't the smiling kind. The most she could muster was a slight lift to the side of her mouth, exposing teeth like glowing pearls against a crushing ocean of darkness. But the attempted smile wasn't for him. Once again, it was political. Her nation gained a *kanala*, and with it, power. She showered him with a light ocean mist and let him run back proudly to his parents.

By the later hours of early morning, nineteen children had been divined. After each, tumultuous applause, and of course some tears. But now it was time for the last child. The usual respectful silence before each child was replaced by murmurs and confusion as the last child took her place on the platform. Some were surprised to see their rumours confirmed, others were just surprised. The child that stood nervously before them on the star-shaped platform was none other than the young Argia princess.

* * *

THE YOUNG PRINCESS stared blankly at the sea of gossiping people, intimately aware of their whispered comments and judgmental glares. She was the first royal to be divined in almost three decades, and it seemed people had forgotten the precariousness of such a situation. Her mother claimed there was nothing to worry about, that their blood was always divined Argia, but not even her mother could deny the eerie feeling of wrongness that accompanied this divination.

Her mother watched from the Argia pedestal, fidgeting with a stream of flames between her fingers, a charming smile plastered across her face. If her mother was nervous, she hid it well. She was not gifted such grace and poise. The pair of them, last heirs to the house of Orrin, true leaders of the Argia, were as different in appearance and mannerisms as night and day.

Staring up at her mother's eager face, she couldn't help but recoil. Standing before the massive crowd, their eyes held her captive, their tentative scowls restricted her breath. Sounds blurred as they hit her ears. Dizziness took over. Her eyes lost their focus… and distance. Too much distance… from the stage… from her body…

She was surrounded, and yet, so *alone*.

With a deep breath, she waited for the sensation to pass, knowing she couldn't falter, when, through the spell, a single face took shape. This face which had never shown any expression other than blank disinterest now looked unequivocally sad. The leader of the Izar tilted her head, scrutinising the Argia princess with a sobering frown. Her floating hair seemed to droop as though gravity had regained its hold on her.

Unlike the others—the stubborn Harri lord who was said to have once cracked a mountain with a single fist and always smelled of sandalwood, the icy queen of the Ur who froze the hearts of traitors and drowned her foes on dry land, the quiet king of the Zerua who hovered rather than walked and reshaped clouds for her on boring political visits—she knew nothing of the Izar leader. Her mother had once remarked that being so old meant nothing fazed her, but it didn't seem that way now. Now, she looked worried, and the young princess couldn't help thinking if the Izar ruler was worried, she should be too. Suppose it was all a mistake, her being here…

Iturri doesn't make mistakes, she thought. *Only messes.*

A great boom brought the world back into focus. Reality cut in like a strike of lightning. *The Harri leader must have clapped again.*

Before her, the rings appeared. Around her, the crowd waited. Inside her, something tensed.

The young princess hesitated momentarily before sliding all six rings onto her finger. The world held its breath as everyone watched in nervous anticipation…

CHAPTER 1

A HOME AWAY FROM HOME

HE BLINKED.

For a second, he was there, wandering the halls he'd once called home. For a second, he'd done it, returned to the lands he'd once ruled. For a second, the world opened, the magic welcomed him home. But in the next second, he blinked.

He was back in his study. Back in the creaky villa overlooking the Caribbean bayside that he'd come to call home. The salt-tinged sea breeze sauntering around him reminded him that this was his reality. Whatever he'd seen in those brief blissful seconds was only a dream—or something like it.

The morning light filtered through the ceiling-length panes of glass. Specks of dust caught in its rays glittered as they fell to the floor. One even came so close as to fall into his hand. It never touched. He didn't let it. It hovered above his wrinkled palm, trapped in an orb of captured sunlight. Not even the breeze could move it.

He contemplated it with a sad smile before releasing it back into the morning air.

At least I still have that, he thought. *Even if just a little while longer.*

"Hyrum!" she called from below. "Hyrum! It's time for breakfast."

Ms Short was exactly that. A stubby English woman in her late forties, who had worked in the household for quite some time now. She was irritating but efficient. More importantly, she didn't ask after the things in the house that weren't quite "normal." She was a simple woman, to her credit, and Hyrum had grown quite fond of mocking her lack of curiosity in the many years she'd worked for him.

Hyrum smelled her flowery perfume long before she reached the top of the stairs. He walked easily, despite the density of the air—the density of his bones. He had grown accustomed to it, though he played up aches and pains every once in a while. People might have gotten suspicious otherwise.

He met her at the door, her hand poised to knock just as he opened it. His cold eyes scanned the landing before falling squarely on her.

"Oh, Hyrum. Sorry, sir, 'bout the screaming and all. I assumed you were ignoring me."

His lamppost figure towered over her, supported in part by his favourite cane—glazed black wood topped with a golden gorilla head. He held tight to it, how one might a good luck charm, but his reasons were not so light-hearted or frivolous. His were something of a darker persuasion. Hyrum glowered at her from behind a neatly trimmed white beard and tiny copper spectacles.

"I don't ever ignore you, Liz. I simply choose to acknowledge you at later moments." His voice was deep like a chasm and equally as cold.

"Oh, Hyrum, you shouldn't be so uppity at your age. Why, imagine if I took offence one of these days and up and left. Whatever would you do?"

"Replace you," he replied with a smirk. "I plan to outlive you either way."

"You should do, bitter as you are. Always the spiteful ones that live the longest."

"And you, Liz, should make a will."

"Sounds like you know something I don't, Hyrum," she said with a chuckle.

"Possibly," he replied, "but you know how deals with devils go… I am still waiting for a good offer on your soul."

Ms Short shook her head. Thankfully, this was her response to anything that seemed to veer from the lines of "normal," but that didn't stop him from having a little fun with her. In truth, it surprised him that she stayed on and endured it, seeing how readily she clung to the rosary around her neck.

Of all the people that had come to work in the house, she was the only one that lasted more than a decade. As irritating as she was with her boisterous laugh and her whisper that no library would accept, he'd grown somewhat fond of her. If he had intended to die before her, he might have left her something; might have even left her the house. The years had made her family, not blood like the child—far as it might be—but family all the same.

"Where is the child? Not getting into trouble again, is she?"

"No, sir. I sent her for bread this morning," she said as she descended the stairs. "Though I had to drag her out of that little shoppe of horrors you call a library earlier. I have no idea what she is so fond of in there. All seems like voodoo and black magic to me. Not the thing a respectable woman would be into, if I may say so."

"Voodoo? Black magic? My little library has you so frightened, Liz?" he mocked as he clunked gracefully down the stairs behind her. The tick of his cane and the *clunk* of his shoes on the wood echoed through the house like a slow waltz—heavy and graceful, and somehow unequivocally sad.

"I may not believe in them things, sir, but that doesn't mean I can't fear them." She poked out from the kitchen and wagged a finger at him. "Mark my words, that child is too curious for her own good."

Hyrum smirked. "And I was afraid you had nipped it all out of her."

The ends of her wrinkling mouth curved into a frown. "Curiosity is a dangerous thing, sir."

"So is ignorance," he countered.

The truth was, they were both right. *Ignorance vs. Curiosity,* a battle he knew all too well. It was the reason he was here, and the reason the child was. But he made a promise—more than a promise, he'd bound his soul, and thus, he too was responsible for the child's current state of ignorance. He argued with himself many times about if he should break it, what consequences it might have, and whether he even could. So many in fact, that the taste of the rum he'd used to silence this incessant argument appeared on his tongue out of memory alone. He wrestled with the thought at least once a day, and each day, at the bottom of a glass of this well-aged rum, he came to a single conclusion: his drink needed refilling.

He pushed the thoughts back into the depths of his mind with a sigh and made his way to the dining room. As he took his seat, he thought back to the day the child was first placed under his care.

How she's grown these past few years. How much she still has to grow...

She reminded him of himself—her passion, her vibrance, her energy—but for her sake, he hoped the rest of his traits were lost in the gene pool.

At some point during this train of thought, Ms Short entered the dining room. He knew the distant mumbling in his ears was her lecturing him on the upbringing of the child or complaining about the "presence" in the library or something that had gone missing only to reappear where it shouldn't be. But those were other demons, and he'd long since stopped listening to what she had to say. His mind had drifted as it usually did at these hours of the morning to another time, in another place, in another world. To a feeling in his bones that spoke of change.

"Liz," he announced, interrupting the day's lecture. "I shall be expecting company at around three. I would like some coffee and rum sent up to the study three minutes before, and not a moment later."

With a resigned huff, she added, "Yes, sir, I'll see to that."

He turned his gaze to the bouncing young figure at the foot of the garden fiddling with the padlock on the gate. His fingers automatically went to a ring on the middle finger of his right hand as they always did when such thoughts arose. He twisted it absentmindedly, remembering a time when another ring occupied its place.

"I should like not to be disturbed," he added.

"No, sir," she replied and retreated into the kitchen to finish the breakfast preparations.

CHAPTER 2

NEW SENSATIONS

SAVARA WOKE TO the light of the full moon drenched in a cold sweat—again. The same dream that had haunted her for the past month had, once again, robbed her of a peaceful night's sleep, only this time, it was worse.

"It was only a dream," Savara told herself, though she'd been telling herself the same thing for so long that, at this point, it was more mantra than consolation. Her fingers trembled as she ran them through her sweat-soaked hair, trying in vain to rid herself of the image.

The dream was always the same.

Shadows, whorls of them, swarmed her like moths to a flame. Next was the fire—there was always fire. It would start as a spark from within the darkness before becoming an all-consuming blaze. Sometimes she'd catch flashes of colour between the flames—a hint of blue, a streak of green, a smattering here and there of silver and gold—but she never had time to stare too long. Then came the screams, high-pitched and desperate. But the worst sound was always the laughter. It curdled her blood even in her waking hours.

There were days when she could've sworn to have heard it on the wind. Real or not, her heart quivered, nonetheless.

The same screaming voices would then begin pleading with her to stop. Over the past month, the only saving grace she'd had was that she never recognized the voices. Last night's dream was different, which made it all the more terrifying.

Despite her attempts at altering the dream, her own movements were always the same. Her gaze would drop to her hands only to find them covered in blood. Whose? She never knew. Tears would fall hot and heavy from her cheeks to a scorched stone floor. Then, just as the fire would begin to grumble, she'd raise her hands and…

Savara never quite knew what happened at the end, only that she felt as though she were being torn apart from somewhere deep inside herself. That was usually the point at which she'd wake up, sometimes screaming, always drenched in sweat, and questioning what she'd seen. She'd heard of lucid dreaming before, but this was something different.

This felt *real.*

Savara gazed out the window as she waited for her pulse to steady. The night was clear, stars twinkled in the open sky, and off in the distance, boats bobbed on the waves. To anyone else, it would've been perfect sleeping weather. Yet here she was, trembling in the gentle sea breeze and afraid to close her eyes.

"Only a dream," she repeated, hoping this time she'd believe it. Though the dream was already slipping from her mind, the tingling in her palms remained.

Savara focused on the moon outside, unwilling to stare down the shadows behind her. Twilight would soon give way to dawn, and she'd have to be up to fetch the bread from the bakers anyway. Between the whisperings of the creaky old house and the beckoning sensation from her uncle's strange library, it was a wonder she ever got to sleep at all.

Savara wriggled out from her bed and yawned as she made to shut the window. She briefly stared out at the empty garden below. Something about it gnawed at her. The air seemed charged with something other than sea salt and spray. Things she'd seen many times in the past decade no longer looked familiar. The streets, the shrubs... even the ocean seemed different. As though the world reset during the night, and she had been left behind.

Savara debated whether she should attempt sleep again, fearing it would be marred by the same visions, before ultimately deciding against it. At least this way, she could poke around the library.

* * *

THE BARNYARD DOOR in the kitchen slammed open. Waves of dark brown hair and the scent of freshly baked bread blustered through the door before she did.

"Is Uncle Hyrum up yet, Ms Short?" Savara asked as she nibbled on the end of a warm baguette, last night's dream already a distant memory.

"Yes, he is, dear. Ready and waiting in the dining nook. We will have breakfast in just a minute," Ms Short replied, scrambling the last of the eggs.

"Not again," she groaned.

"You know they're his favourite."

"Yes…" Savara let out a defeated sigh. It wasn't a battle for today. "I wanted to ask him about a book I found in the library," she added, coming back to the reason for her curious spark.

"Now Savara, you know better than to go sniffing around that dusty old library of his," Ms Short admonished. "The things that man keeps in there… Not what a—"

"—respectable woman should be occupying her time with." Savara rolled her eyes as she finished the one phrase that seemed to mark her adolescence.

"Hmm," Ms Short said with a frown. "You know what they say about curiosity killing the cat."

"That satisfaction brought him back?"

"Yes, dear, but you're not a cat."

Her uncle's library, which she had only recently been granted access to when she turned seventeen, was just a large, musty room with lofty ceilings and blackened oak floors, in theory. In practice, however, the number of books and paintings and displays that jumped out at the eye caused it to seem much more matchbox-sized. Lining the walls were bookshelves that went on forever upward, filled with large, leather-bound volumes that had collected dust from every century known to man. Large glass displays sat scattered across the floor, containing everything from weapons to rocks, cups to craniums, and any other oddity that should more rightly belong in a museum. Unlike any museum she'd been to, however, she swore the library was alive.

Savara hadn't admitted it to anyone—not even Jasper, her best friend—but each time she visited she noticed a low pulse emanating from the room that she could only rightly call a heartbeat. During the daytime hours, all was quiet, but during the nights she heard it whispering, beckoning her to find it. Night was for the dark and demons, Ms Short would impress upon her, but then, Ms Short was always trying to impress upon her things she refused to learn.

"But Ms Short," Savara began, once again pleading her case to the matronly woman who believed only in the things she could see with her own two eyes and touch with her own two hands. "Haven't you ever wondered what might be out there? The world can't just be this island and these people."

"You have a good life here, my dear. This island and these people have treated you well. You shouldn't knock it."

"But there has to be more out there…"

"Would you prefer to be shipped off to Europe or the Americas, where people work twice as hard and live half as well?"

"Maybe. Those places are old, filled with history, personality…maybe even magic…" Savara smirked.

"Magic? Is that what this is about?" she scoffed. "Magic? My goodness, child. You need to stop rummaging through your uncle's things," Ms Short replied irritably. "Magic is for heretics and people who aren't content with their place in life. It doesn't exist, child. There are no dragons, no witches, no pixies, faeries, or monsters under the bed. The sooner you get that through your head, the happier you will be."

Savara sighed. She never understood Ms Short's aversion to the unknown. She relished in it—thrived in it. In the earlier years of life with her uncle, he'd told her stories of far-off places and distant worlds. Of creatures that science could hardly describe. Of people who walked hand in hand with magic.

Savara was well-studied. Grown. She knew that these kinds of stories were just that. Stories. For a long time, they only occupied her passing thoughts. The ones that follow raindrops down windowpanes. And they might have stayed that way had she not found the library.

"Why are you so afraid of it?" Savara prodded, hoping to find a flaw in Ms Short's argument.

Ms Short dropped the spatula, sending bits of scrambled egg to the floor. "That is no concern of yours," she replied nervously. "That library of his should be burned, along with the rest of the undesirable, heretical memorabilia that he keeps in it." Ms Short bent down to clean up her mess, unsettled and still rambling. "No wonder your head is filled with such fantastical nonsense."

"What about all the stories? You can't just dismiss them."

"I can, and I do. That is not the world I have chosen to live in, Savara, and if you had any sense, you'd choose the same. Now, go wash up and get ready for breakfast. I'll have no more of this *magic* talk."

"Fine…" Savara mumbled, giving up on yet another battle for the morning. "Oh, and would you mind setting out an extra plate for breakfast?"

Ms Short craned what little neck she had and raised her curious brow. "Who for?"

"Jasper. I crossed paths with him on his way back from visiting his grandmother in the home."

"Oh…" Ms Short grinned knowingly.

"It's not like that. We're just friends."

"Right."

"I told him to come in for breakfast," Savara said as she nicked some cheese from one of the cutting boards. "Maybe poke around the library and," she mumbled just low enough for Ms Short not to hear. "Then head to Skully's for my birthday."

"I know that look anywhere, you're up to no good."

"I do not have a look," she replied indignantly.

"You'll get yourself into real trouble one of these days." Ms Short pursed her lips. "You are just lucky your uncle has immeasurable patience with you."

"Or immeasurable indifference…"

"Now, you know that's not true," Ms Short said, her motherly tone softening.

"We are only having breakfast because he feels he must show face on my birthday. That way, he can ignore me the rest of the year."

"Your uncle is a piece of work, but he means well. Besides, you two are more alike than you think."

"I doubt it," Savara replied, reaching for another handful of cheese.

"And stop munching," Ms Short scolded, swatting her hand out of the way. "Now, go wash up. We'll be having breakfast soon." She scraped the pan clean onto a plate, taking care not to burn herself. Savara found herself wishing the rest of the eggs had ended up on the floor, that way they could be replaced with something slightly more appetising.

Something had been bothering her all morning. The day felt like any other in the small island town, and yet, like none before. Savara washed her hands distractedly, her mind hitching on the book she'd found during her insomnia rather than if she'd already used the soap—which she had, twice. The leatherbound volume, like everything else in the house, was ornate, old, and, strangely enough, seemed to whisper when opened. The script inside glittered as though wet but refused to smudge when touched.

Maybe Jasper would know what to make of it, she thought.

A frigid wind blustered through the window, bringing the unavoidable shivers that prickled the hairs on her neck. Accompanying it was an eerie feeling of being watched. Savara peered out at the back garden—just in case—but found everything in its place. She frowned, hoping that closing the window would close the tap to those sinister feelings, but they had already pooled themselves within the pit of her stomach.

Savara splashed her face with cold water and scanned it for signs of a new year. Little cracks in her lips would remind her to drink more water and her button nose was allergy-free. Other than that, she was the same. Her dark hair still curled at her temples and her charcoal eyes were still flecked with all the colours of the rainbow.

Maybe this is what eighteen feels like... she thought. The shadows you inherently feared as a child become feelings of being watched, the voice in your head now says you're unequivocally the same—but different.

Still, something felt wrong.

CHAPTER 3

OLD FRIENDS

JASPER HAD NEVER been special. Never been chosen, never been idolised. He had never been anything but plain old Jasper. He even looked plain in every way imaginable. Plain brown hair, falling over plain brown eyes, covered by plain black glasses.

Plain, but familiar, he reminded himself.

Familiar, reliable, and classic were the words most often used to describe him. Words which he tended to take as passing compliments. He had better things to occupy his time with than feeling plain, the stars above and the bones below being two of his favourites. In fact, he hadn't even noticed his own plainness—and might never have if he hadn't met her.

Jasper remembered it like it was yesterday. Somewhere around the cove, in a spot he'd claimed for himself when he was just a boy—a spot that no other soul had reached because it involved a lot of climbing and was rewarded with very little beach—he caught a glimpse of the most enchanting creature he'd ever laid eyes on, his soon-to-be best friend.

The night sky expanded infinitely above. It was the perfect place to stargaze, secluded, unpolluted, with only the sound of the rolling waves for company. Jasper had been waiting all week to come out to see a forecasted meteor shower. Of the only two routes to this hidden sanctuary, he chose the one through the water. The other was barred by jagged and shifting rocks that were unfriendly at best. He swam part of the way and hoisted himself up the rest. It helped that in his fourteen years he was lanky and agile, as his arms could reach the stable edges and his body was still light enough not to be a burden. He climbed over the last rock gracefully only to fall flat on his face out of sheer shock.

She sat on what little beach there was, stroking the back of one of the largest nesting sea turtles he'd ever seen. Somehow, she'd managed to get right up close to it. Jasper blinked the water from his eyes to make sure he wasn't going mad. She was petting its back as though it were a house cat and… talking to it? He cleaned his glasses with his shirt and replaced them high on his nose, staring incredulously at the scene, all but entranced by the strange, beautiful creature, and the turtle she talked to.

The girl paid him no more mind than that which it took to press a finger to her lips before she rambled on to the sea creature. But he couldn't take his eyes off her. In a town as small as theirs, you either knew everybody or at least had seen them around. She was neither, yet there she sat. Not more than a year or two younger than him. Talking away to… a turtle.

She glanced over at him again, nodded her head, and tapped the sand beside her. Her silent command to sit won him over. The rest of the night was spent in equal silence, save for her occasional murmurings and the sound of the waves against the rocks. And it was this friendship, which started in silence next to a nesting turtle under a sky full of stars, that first alerted him as to how plain he really was.

Even now, as he sat answering questions made to judge the content of his soul, he couldn't help but think that his soul, compared to those of the people of this household, lacked value.

The man's gaze was predatory. His eyes glinted like those of a hawk as they homed in on its unwitting prey: Jasper. His stony face was almost impossible to read, save for the occasional involuntary twitch of disgust betrayed by his lips.

"I like your…ring." The words came out feebler than Jasper had hoped. "That's the symbol for the third eye, right?" Luckily for him, the topic seemed to pique the man's interest.

"It is," he replied, leaning in closer. "And what *exactly* is it that you do, boy?" Coming from anyone else, the question might have been casual, friendly even, but Jasper knew it wasn't a question at all. Marked by the stiffened emphasis on the word "exactly", it was a statement meant to intimidate and belittle without sounding tyrannical. One that subtly meant, *tell me you're not useless*, to which there were many wrong answers, and even the right ones could be wrong depending on the mood of the person asking.

"I'm an archaeologist, sir," Jasper replied, making a conscious effort not to look away, though his stomach recoiled.

"Hm…" The sound was not entirely of disinterest. That was good.

This disappearing-reappearing uncle of Savara's who had taken her in under a decade ago was the subject of most of the town's gossip. Stories circulated throughout the island of a shadow man who spoke to spirits, because even in the disbelieving modern world, talking to spirits distinguished you, ostracised you, or as Savara put it—in her uncle's words—earned you some god-damned peace and quiet.

One glance at this frail old man made anyone question the gruesome gossip. Those delicate, veined hands couldn't have strangled goats and summoned storms. His off-kilter gait couldn't have taken him further than the back fence, let alone across deserts and abandoned isles. But something in him seemed false… Almost restrained.

It's his eyes, Jasper realised. *Those sapphire blue eyes.*

Their glow spoke volumes. Of pride, deceit, will… They looked as though they'd seen more than all the historians in all the lands. And his manner… It was too perfect, too well-studied to be true. Almost as if he was an actor lost to his scene. Even the wrap of his fingers on the table seemed practised.

On a second glance, this frail old man didn't look so frail after all.

The man stroked his beard lightly. It seemed the two men had reached their conclusions about each other at the same time.

"Uncle, I told you to behave yourself," Savara admonished. "Jasper, I'm sorry about that."

"It's fine." He laughed, nervously trying to hide his relief. "Happy Birthday, Sav."

"I have been perfectly civil with your friend," Hyrum replied. "Happy Birthday, my child."

"Thank you both." Savara smiled and took the seat next to him. "I hope my uncle didn't scare you too much," she whispered.

"No," Jasper replied, scratching the back of his head. "We were just picking each other's brains," he added, but he let out a soft sigh of relief all the same.

"No more brain-picking," said Ms Short as she laid out the last of the plates. "Eat before it gets cold."

* * *

BREAKFAST WAS QUAINT. Conversations were kept trivial, for the benefit of Ms Short. She often admonished conversations with words that took more than a breath to say should be left for the study—anything that ended in "ology" fit under that category nicely. But as at ease as everyone was, even Jasper, the newcomer, could tell there was something noticeably off about the esteemed patriarch of the household.

The fire in his eyes had been replaced by something devoid of feeling but not quite empty. A hollowness in his voice told them he scarcely registered the conversation. His eyes were fixed on the window, looking past the shrubberies and the fence, well past the neighbours' houses below, towards the open ocean.

"Uncle, are you alright?" Savara asked.

"What?" he scoffed, shaking himself out of a trance. "Of course I am." It was a lie.

"I was just saying, I think it's time for me to move out. I'd like to explore the world—"

"No." The finality in his tone startled everyone.

"But Uncle, I'm eighteen and this house has become a prison."

Jasper thought he saw the old man tense at the word *prison*, but he shrugged it off with a soft huff.

"Sav," Jasper chimed in barely a whisper, not wanting to incur the wrath of the stately gentleman opposite him. "Maybe it's not the time."

"Stay out of it, Jasper," she growled.

"No," Hyrum repeated, no longer fazed by her comment. "I believe your fate lies closer to home."

Savara clenched her fist at the word *fate*. Clearly, the two left much unspoken. Jasper sipped quietly on his tea, wishing not to be part of whatever argument ensued. It hurt him slightly that she hadn't told him of her plans to leave, but when he noticed the nervous quiver in her lip, he realised there was more to her sudden drastic decision.

"Uncle, you don't control fate," Savara continued. "No one does."

"Savara, I am not asking you."

Savara stood up forcefully, rippling the tea in her cup, and turned back to her uncle. His gaze had returned to the window, as though finished with their conversation. "I'm eighteen now. I will find a way to leave, whether you fund it or not," she huffed before storming off to her room.

Jasper stood awkwardly and inclined his head towards Ms Short. "Thanks again for breakfast," he said, before running off behind Savara.

***

HYRUM HARDLY NOTICED them leave.

"Another successful breakfast," Ms Short said anxiously as she began to clear the table.

"For once, Liz, I believe we agree." Hyrum fiddled with the ring between his fingers, gazing out past the garden once more.

CHAPTER 4

COFFEE FOR ONE

HE LOVED COMING here. The tether pulling at his soul seemed weaker when he crossed over, as though iron chains had been switched out for simple ropes. He knew it was all an illusion—that it was simply the distance—but he liked to pretend it was more. He enjoyed the feeling of freedom, even if feigned.

He pulled the collar of his coat up a little higher and dipped the brim of his hat down a little lower, sheltering himself from the winds of the Caribbean seaside. The act was automatic. If having lived most of his life this way, avoiding eyes and stealing away in shadows, had taught him one thing, it was this: the less of you people saw, the less of you they noticed, and given the current situation, going unnoticed proved ideal, to say the least. Even the woman at his favourite café barely registered him as he ordered his usual coffee and banana bread.

Over the years, he had grown to see it as a gift. The gift of invisibility, if ever there were such a thing. What he had yet to realise was that nothing in this world—in the vast expanse of the universe—was invisible. Eventually, all unnoticed things are noticed.

He sat down as he always did at one of the tables off in the far corner of the café and pulled out something that looked extraordinarily like a pocket watch—but wasn't. The waitress who brought his order acknowledged neither him nor the strange artefact. Some might say this was a charm of his, but he knew no charms were necessary, only precautionary. People saw only what made sense in their own world, and his presence in this one didn't. Aside from two other patrons—a sleepy fisherman and a young professor entranced by her book—the place was empty. After a brief and unsatisfactory glance at its face, he placed the object into his pocket once more and moved for his breakfast.

The coffee smells better here, he thought with a deep inhale. He brought the mug to his lips. The taste wasn't great, but that's what enticed him. The metallic taste of the pot mixed with the organic taste of the beans. Unlike in his world, the people here used machines to do things. The result wasn't perfect, but somehow the imperfections felt *real*. As he was about to take a bite of his banana bread, someone caught his eye.

She was a vision, more beautiful than she'd been in her painting. He paused, letting his eyes follow her up the street to the window beside him, hardly noticing her companion. She couldn't see him; he was confident of that. For once his precaution proved well, though part of him wished he hadn't been so diligent. Part of him wished to drop the enchantment, just long enough to meet her eyes, but he knew better. In his heart, the thin glass separating them felt as wide as the ocean beyond.

Their eyes met like opposing magnets. He shivered under her gaze. Somehow, she sensed his presence, her eyes shifted in and out of focus, trying to hold onto his vanishing image as though he were a trick of the light. Slowly, she lifted her hand to the glass. He mirrored her with the hand that longed to touch hers. Where their palms met, separated only by the windowpane, their energies danced and fogged it, collapsing what once felt like an ocean between them.

But then the tether pulled short.

He waited just long enough to see her seated—a risk he knew he shouldn't take but did anyway. The thing inside him was waking up. A second longer and there might have been trouble. He stood, taking a final sip of coffee before leaving behind most of his breakfast and half of his soul.

He stepped through the doorway, disappearing entirely from the world before his foot met the ground.

The door shut, ringing a singular hanging bell as it closed; though by the time anyone heard it, he was already gone, the world already behind him. The door once again kept the outside cold a mere pane of glass away from the patrons inside.

CHAPTER 5

A LAST TEA

AS THE CLOCK marked ten to three, Ms Short hobbled up the stairs, balancing a tray of coffee and glasses for rum. Though Hyrum was an avid believer in teatime, *as any self-respecting person would be*, she thought, this particular request bothered her.

It had been quite some time since he'd received company. On the days when he did, she was always forewarned. She'd be given notes about their albeit peculiar tastes and how and when she would greet them. Today, however, there was nothing. The request came shrouded in the kind of secrecy that ate at her nerves—and which already had her planning to listen at the door.

Ms Short slipped into the study quietly and set the tray down on the desk. The early afternoon sun sauntered through the large windows, casting shadows over everything in the room. He gazed out of them, looking more forlorn than usual. The light seemed to highlight the many marks that time had traced on his face. He seemed much older now, though his appearance remained the same. As if he'd lost his fighter's spirit. She contemplated him in the glow of the afternoon sun and thought, *time moves slowly for some people.*

"Thank you, Liz," he announced, but the sound of his voice and the distance in his eyes troubled her. This was not the Hyrum she knew.

"Will you be wanting anything else, sir?" she asked, twirling the edge of her apron around her finger.

"No, no. That's quite alright." He waved his hand carelessly in the air. "It's such a nice day… I'd go for a stroll if I were you. Shame to be stuck in the house on a day like this."

"Yes, sir. Maybe you'd like to go for one later?"

"I'm afraid the town wouldn't rest if I decided to walk." He shot her a melancholy grin before returning his gaze to the window.

"As you wish," she said, slipping out of the study and closing the door behind her.

The moment she crossed back into the hall, her concerns vanished. She'd entirely forgotten her plan to listen in at the door. She'd somehow even forgotten that Hyrum was to have company. The only thing that concerned her now was a long stroll through the town. There was a beautiful porcelain teapot she'd been contemplating buying from one of the shops in the centre, and for some reason, today seemed like the day to do it.

Ms Short hobbled down the stairs again and stopped briefly to fluff up her hair in one of the mirrors. By the time the clock struck three, she was nearly out the door when a sudden thud from the hall stopped her.

Company, she remembered, *Hyrum is having company. How could I have forgotten?*

She doubled back towards the staircase only to find herself suddenly impaled, having walked straight into the blade of a sword. Confused and fading fast, she gazed into the most frightfully sad eyes she'd ever seen.

Death, she thought, *is a curious thing*. Of all the final thoughts to have, her last was utterly ridiculous. *Old Hyrum was right*. He'd outlived her, though not for much longer, she imagined.

She blinked slowly. The eyes were gone. The world around her was going. Fading into the blackness of a world she thought she knew, feeling everything so intimately, before feeling nothing at all.

Her lifeless body slid easily off the end of the sword and hit the ground with a thud. Her blood trickled down into the crevices of the hardwood floors, staining them darker than any polish could. That would have bothered her immensely to clean… if she were still around to do so.

CHAPTER 6

A CURIOUS PACKAGE

THE RAIN WAS coming. At this point, it wasn't a matter of if but when. Savara gazed out at the cobblestone streets, letting her eyes follow as far as the roads would lead and out to the ocean beyond. The royal palms danced in the breeze along with the occasional stray paper and leaf. The salty air hung densely in her lungs with a tingle to it that rattled her bones.

Not a grey cloud in sight, and yet, she knew without a doubt there was going to be one hell of a storm.

As she'd hoped, she and Jasper found themselves at Skully's, a small hole in the wall at the edge of town that served a decent coffee and better cookies. She'd been looking forward to it all day. Something hers on a day that felt anything but.

Savara rested her hand on the glass, fogging it beneath her palm, and peered through the window. As expected, save for two others, the place was empty. Jasper had walked ahead, but she lingered, watching as her handprint disappeared.

Normally, she wouldn't have worried about the fogged glass—or have stopped to check the window—but that shifting feeling from earlier nagged at her again. She stared at her palm, fixating on a tingling sensation where it had touched the glass.

"Are you coming?" Jasper called, holding the door open for her, the book she'd found weighing down the satchel on his shoulder.

Savara looked back at the disappearing fog on the glass. The feeling—whatever it was—had subsided. She turned to Jasper and nodded, wondering if it hadn't all been in her head.

The warmth, the smell, their seats, a bell. Everything was in its place at the little café.

Jasper went to order as she saved the table. Outside, a man walking his dog crossed her line of sight. Her eyes were drawn to the creature, and its eyes to her. She watched it pause mid-stride to take her in. The brutish, impatient man yanked at the dog's collar. She raised a hand to her neck as though she too were being tugged at, but her hand met only skin.

"Something wrong?" asked Jasper, attempting to make himself known. He slumped himself back into the uncomfortable booth chair in front of her.

"What?" Savara replied, snapping back to reality. Her eyes fell on the plate and widened. She let the scent saunter up her nostrils as her mouth began to salivate.

"Your neck," he pointed out as he munched down on a cookie. "Does it hurt?"

"Oh, no." She figured there was no use explaining what had happened. She couldn't. "Mosquito," she lied instead.

"How odd," he replied between chomps. "Can't imagine why. It's the dry season."

"The rain is coming."

"Sav. I don't think we are seeing the same skies."

"Trust me," she said, unsure of how she knew it, but she was certain. "It's coming."

"Yeah, alright. Five dollars says it doesn't rain 'til next month." Jasper laughed as he stretched his arms over his head, his body relaxing into their usual rhythm. His eyes, like always, were fixed on her. Normally, she'd be able to relax alongside him. Today, she couldn't even hold his gaze. "Hey, you aren't still mad about what your uncle said this morning?" he asked, noticing her distant gaze.

"No… I mean, I'm not mad. I just feel like I need some time alone to figure things out."

"What kinds of things?"

"Life…" Savara stared out the window, wanting to avoid the uncomfortable prodding. "I had that dream again…"

"The one where the dinosaur uncovers you?" Jasper asked, once again trying to make her laugh. This time, she chuckled. "No? Alright, just me then," he added, smiling. But she had already returned to the window.

She couldn't fault him for the joke. He always tried to make her smile. Today was just… different.

"It's just a dream, Sav."

"I guess…"

"Seriously, Sav. What's going on? You know you can tell me anything."

"I know," she sighed, thinking of how best to explain her dilemma without sounding ridiculous. "Do you ever get the feeling you don't entirely know yourself?"

Jasper reached over and brushed a stray curl from her eyes, tucking it neatly behind her ear. "I don't think anyone really knows themselves, Sav."

"It's just… I've felt like this for as long as I can remember. Like a part of me is missing and I need to find it or else…" She trailed off, unwilling to speak the words that made her heart wince.

I'll never be whole.

Jasper fixed his glasses on the bridge of his nose. "Life doesn't come with meaning, Sav. You have to make it meaningful."

"That's all well and good for you to say, Jasper. You know what you're supposed to do, and you're good at it. I've got no talents. I'm not exceptional at anything. I'm just… Me. I can hardly even remember my childhood."

"Sav, you're being a little too hard on yourself. Nobody really knows what they're supposed to do. We react to the world around us and hope for the best." He reached over to take her hand. "I only became an archaeologist because that's what my parents did. That's all I knew."

"So, you never felt…" Savara thought of the whispering book in Jasper's bag, the strange dream that had been haunting her for the past month, and today's off-kilter feeling. A word appeared on her tongue, one that did little to temper her nerves and rather raised goosebumps on her arms. "…*called?*" she whispered. "To go somewhere you've never been? To do something you don't fully understand?"

Jasper furrowed his brow, rubbing his thumb over the back of her hand as he asked, "Is that why you want to leave?"

Suddenly, a slither of sadness trickled up from her palms. It was faint, almost unnoticeable. But it wasn't hers. She pulled her hand back, and almost immediately the feeling died. He may not have said it, but he hadn't needed to. He could smile all he wanted, but that sadness was his.

"I don't know," she replied, focusing on her palms and the spot where the sensation had been, unable to unfeel his sadness. "I don't feel I belong here anymore."

"Whatever you need, just know I'll be there for you," he said, and though she knew she could trust his word, she couldn't see how he could help.

"Savara?" The cheery, heavily accented voice startled them both. The waitress stood beside their booth, holding a package wrapped in brown paper and twine. "You are Savara, yes?"

Savara looked from the package to the woman sceptically. "Yes…?"

"For you." The waitress rested the box on their table and smiled. Content with her good deed, she returned to the bar, disappearing before any questions came her way.

"Strange," said Jasper, staring at the package as he munched on another cookie. "What is it?"

"No idea," Savara replied, turning it over in her hand. She furrowed her brow. When she looked up again, the waitress was nowhere to be seen.

"And what is… *Vi-san-thee?*" Jasper asked, sounding out the word.

Though it was mostly garbled, thanks to the chunks of cookie in his mouth, the sound of the word sent shivers down her spine. Savara sensed the beginnings of a headache coming on. For some reason, the word had brought back an image. A fleeting one. Little more than a place of white walls. But the more she tried to bring it into focus, the more her mind hurt.

"Sav?"

"What?"

A plate crashed somewhere in the back. The hanging bell chimed over the closing door. Up above, thunder boomed. The cotton-candy clouds were quickly replaced by menacing grey ones.

Savara looked up as a streak of sheet lightning rolled through the darkened skies. Her heart began to race.

"Looks like I owe you five dollars," Jasper said, reaching into an empty wallet before blushing. "Or… dinner at Mauro's after I get my next paycheck?"

"You're ridiculous," she said, forcing a smile despite her lingering confusion.

"But seriously… Visanthe? It's written on the side, real small," he remarked, sending crumbs from his lips to the table as he spoke.

Savara turned it over, a deep frown settling on her face as she contemplated the words, *Remember Visanthe.* They were written in a sparkling silver which, much like the pages of the book she'd found, looked too wet to touch yet never smudged. As she passed her fingers over the words, she noticed a strange pulse in her palms. She swallowed hard at the sudden emotions building in her throat. She couldn't let Jasper see how troubled she was. Her fingers recoiled, unconsciously rubbing at a scar on her middle finger as her mind went elsewhere.

"I think it's a place…" she replied, unable to explain how she knew or why.

The word had stirred something in her mind like the remnant of a dream. *Visanthe.* It tasted of metal and cold, and, like a witch's spell, it brought her mind back to a place of fantasy.

Elegant marble floors. Laughter bubbled like the sparkling champagne flowing from the fountain. Glittering ball gowns, twirling like Russian tops. Flames that took on lives of their own. Courtiers, jesters… even a dragon.

She reasoned whatever it was must have come from a story, one of those childish wishes she had abandoned when she found out that the world no longer held mystery and magic. She shook her head, casting away the strange sensation.

"Are you going to open it?" Jasper asked.

"I don't know…" Savara ran her fingers over the coarse wrapping.

There it is again. A low thrum of power.

Savara found herself tugging at the twine, wondering what secret the mysterious box held, all the while not convinced that it should be opened. She shifted in her seat, deciding to wait as she gazed at the length of glass again.

The first few droplets of her expected storm clung to their spot on the window like the little tree frogs in her garden. Soon, the sky grew dark. Some of the droplets had taken to racing down the glass. The clouds, swollen with rain, seemed to be holding back. Savara reckoned it was a good idea to leave now before they decided to burst. Besides, thanks to the strange events of the morning, the café no longer felt like a sanctuary.

Savara tugged at her coat, the strange package nestled close to her chest in one of the pockets. The damp air howled through the streets, whisking flowers off branches while the palm leaves rustled in chorus. The wind licked her cheeks in its haste. No matter how hard she tried, she could not stop the cold from seeping into her bones. Shivers wracked her body, yet she knew not all of them came from the shift in weather.

The little package nagged at her, and not in the way of pleasant surprises. Part of her wished to open it, to reveal its secrets. The other part wished to cast it off the nearest dock and let it sink to the bottom of the ocean.

CHAPTER 7

DUPLICITY

THE BREWING STORM reminded Savara of a similar one many years ago, the last great storm, the day she first arrived at the house. Even now, with each close of her eyelids, she pictured it as clear as the day it happened.

Thunder rolled through the blackest of clouds as lightning spliced the heavens. The downpour flooded the roads, creating waterfalls on most of the hills. The winds howled agonisingly through the streets, plucking trees from the ground in its wake.

People spoke of it as a once-in-a-lifetime kind of storm, something almost *supernatural*. It wasn't a day Savara chose to remember but, walking up to the eerie house with the mounting wave of darkness behind it, flashes of it forced their way into her mind.

Someone cradled her, trudging through the rain and mud up to the house. Blink. Ms Short appeared at the sound of the doorbell. Blink.

Someone was yelling as she waited in the hall. Blink. *Dripping wet and catching a fever, she stood shivering before her estranged uncle. Moments later she was showered and in bed.*

Her childhood, aside from those flashes of jumbled memories, was a blur. All she knew was that, after that night, she'd been left alone in the world.

Despite the mounting downpour, the house looked jarringly still from the street. The only lights she could see were those of her uncle's study, high on the second floor. Savara could just make out a shadow shifting around through the window.

"Looks like Ms Short went out for the evening and forgot to leave the lights on," she said, looking around the gardens for any trace of the woman.

"We must be in for one hell of a storm…" said Jasper with a quiver in his voice. "The wind seems to have ripped the lock right off the door."

The wooden barn door swinging restlessly in the breeze summoned her like an outstretched hand, reeling her towards it. "You'd think my uncle would have heard it…"

Savara didn't even realise her feet had taken to following it when Jasper shot a hand out and tugged her back. "Sav, something doesn't feel right," he said as he eyed the gate behind them longingly.

"You said yourself the wind must have broken the lock." She tried tugging her arm free, but he tightened his grip.

"It's not just that. Haven't you noticed the power is out in the other houses on the street?"

"Maybe the outage hasn't reached us yet…" she countered, though part of his worry was beginning to get to her too.

"Sav, I don't think that's it. I can't describe it but I'm getting a bad feeling."

"Oh, so now you've decided to believe in bad feelings?" she replied, unwilling to relent to the fear that was creeping into her heart.

She didn't want to admit it but she felt it too. What started that morning as an inkling, a little buzz in the back of her mind, had blown into a howling gale as vicious as the one around them. The house felt different too. Charged, as though it were sucking energy from everywhere else and pulling it to the study. Her heart began to race. If she could've gone somewhere else, she would've. But there was nowhere else for her here, and the weather showed no signs of letting up. It was either brave the house or get caught in the rain, and at this point, she'd grown too cold to fight the weather.

"Besides, the rain is picking up. You can either wait here in the rain or come with me." Savara pulled herself free and made for the door. Some of her nerves disappeared immediately after pulling free, as though they hadn't been hers to begin with. The sensation only stopped her for a second, only long enough for her to question what had happened. But then, lightning ripped across the sky, and she found herself running once more, concerns all but forgotten. Over her shoulder, Savara spied Jasper following close behind—reluctant, but following all the same.

Life in the garden was out of commission. The little yellow butterflies that usually danced between the grasses were gone; the chirrups of the tree frogs silenced. The sounds from the rest of the town, few as they were, had faded too. Everything was a blur of raindrops and white noise, except for the slow, repetitive *bang* of the door in the wind. Savara ignored Jasper's disapproving glare on the back of her neck as she entered the darkened kitchen.

The room looked as it always had, but the evening light that distilled in from the windows cast shadows over everything, adding unfamiliar duplicity to an otherwise familiar world.

"I think I've seen enough," Jasper whispered and tried to make for the door, but Savara caught him by the collar. "Nope, of course not," he mumbled to himself. "Because my completely rational fear of the dark means nothing to you."

"Jasper, shut up and come here," she chided him, though she knew better than to call him irrational.

Savara had spent the better part of six years in the eerie old house, listening to the creaking floors and the wafts of sea breeze that moaned like ghosts through the halls. Objects here disappeared and reappeared in unconventional places almost on a regular basis. If there were any house in town to be afraid of, it was this one. It had always been a dark and spooky place, even on the best of days. But this dark was different.

Suddenly, a thud sounded from upstairs.

Jasper shot her a terrified glance. "I'm leaving."

"No, you're not."

"Sav, did you not hear that?"

"Do you want me to go up on my own?"

"I don't want you to go up at all! I want you to come with me. Outside. Up the street. Possibly to the police station."

"I need to check on my uncle, Jasper." She dug around for a weapon. "It would be helpful to have a big, strong man at my side," she mocked to hide her apprehension.

"Very funny, Sav. When have I ever claimed to be big? Or strong? And if it helps my case, man can be up for debate too."

"Shut up and take this," she said, holding out a wooden spoon.

"For what?" Jasper replied in an agitated whisper. "To cook dinner for whoever it is before they kill us?"

"Jasper, don't be ridiculous."

"Me? Ridiculous? *I* am not the one waltzing up to a bad feeling with nothing more than a spoon—" *Smack!* "Ouch," he moaned, rubbing the lump appearing on his forehead.

"It works just fine."

"Fine, Sav, and on your head be my funeral." She picked up a rolling pin for herself and made for the hall. Jasper followed hesitantly, still rubbing the growing bump. "Can we at least turn on the light?" he whispered irritably.

"Let's not. Just in case…"

"Of what?" he growled fearfully, but she decided it best not to answer. "In case of *what*, Sav?!"

The hall didn't receive any of the light from the other rooms. Savara gulped down her fears and followed the wall to the base of the staircase. Footsteps too swift to be her uncle's sounded overhead. Curiosity pulled her forward as the fear in her body and Jasper's fought it. She knew the house well, imagining the layout in her mind and avoiding the occasional side table and coat rack. Jasper bumped into them all.

"JASPER!" she hissed.

"Sav, help…" he whispered. "I'm tangled in something. I beg of you, turn on a light…"

"Fine, but hurry…" She slid her fingers around the wall at the top of the staircase until she heard a satisfying *click*. "I think I can hear someone shifting around in my uncle's study…"

"S-S-Sav…" stuttered Jasper.

"What?!"

Savara imagined that Jasper had tripped himself up on the carpet or knocked something over or, being Jasper, a combination of the two. The last thing she expected to see was Jasper tangled in a lifeless body. Not just any body… The world paused. Her heart skipped a beat—or three.

Ms Short.

Savara put a trembling hand over her mouth quickly to keep herself from screaming. Everything inside her wanted to bring the house down. Her knees buckled. She clung to the banister, it was all she could do to keep upright.

"It's a body," Jasper began with a high-pitched crack in his voice. "It's a body, it's a body, it's a…"

"I know…" Savara squeaked. She needed to get down there, she needed to help him, but her feet were glued to the ground.

"Help," Jasper prodded, already turning pale from the shock. "Sav!"

"I'm coming…"

Silent tears raced down her cheeks, and yet, in her heart she felt nothing. Not even the wood beneath her feet as she crept down the stairs. The shock had taken everything from her. Every thought, every sensation. Jasper continued his audible panic, but Savara heard nothing except the sound of her own shallow breaths. Even her voice sounded like an echo as she spoke.

"I'm coming," she repeated after only two rungs, and then again on every other rung until she reached the landing. All the words in her vocabulary had been replaced by those two. "I'm…" she sniffled as she helped him up from the floor and stared down into the terrified glossy eyes of the woman that had been like a mother to her for the better part of her adolescence.

Ms Short had a certain feel to her, like a leather coat against the howling wind, suffocating but protective. Now she felt like nothing—less than nothing. A chair warmed by its last occupant felt more alive than she did.

"Sav, we need to leave," Jasper hissed. "Now." The hand that still held tight to the wooden spoon had gone white under his force. "Sav," he repeated when she made no move to follow. His voice sounded distant. "Sav!" he yelled as he shook her, trying to snap her out of her daze.

"She's…"

"Dead," he urged when her lips wouldn't form the word. "We need to leave."

"I…" Savara bit back the tears that had already stained her eyes red. "We can't."

Jasper's entire face blanched. "You're insane."

"My uncle," she pleaded, still unable to form a coherent thought longer than two words.

"Is probably in the same state."

"Please," she said, the word more breath than sound.

"Shit." Jasper paced about the landing, punching the air with trembling fists. "Shit, shit, shit, Sav." If he was about to cry, he held it in, but the pallor in his face shifted into frustration. "You can't be serious."

Swift footsteps above brought her world back into focus. She looked away from the corpse; afraid death might leap into her eyes and drag her down next. Savara turned back to the staircase and began her climb.

She bit down on her breaking heart and whispered, "You work with dead things all the time."

"No, no, no…" Jasper hissed, wagging the spoon in the air. "I work with things that have been dead so long they don't look like they've ever been alive. I saw her alive and well this morning!"

"Jasper," she pleaded. "My uncle is the only family I have left." Jasper eyed the door longingly, but finally consented when she added, "Please."

Savara knew it was a bad idea. She knew she'd probably condemned them both, but her uncle was her only blood relative left. She couldn't just leave, especially not after hearing footsteps that *might* be his. If he were in trouble and she could've helped but didn't, she'd never forgive herself. With the rolling pin in hand, she crept upstairs, again avoiding the creaky rungs. Jasper followed close behind, the spoon in his hand only moments away from snapping.

The sounds grew louder as they reached the door. Shifting papers, opening drawers, swift footsteps. At least it meant that whoever or whatever it was hadn't heard the raucous downstairs. The element of surprise was still on their side.

With shaky hands, she managed to twist the handle. Her muscles contracted when she heard the release of the lock. She exhaled softly, opening it wide enough to peek through without being seen.

Uncle Hyrum's dainty veined hand dangled limply over the side of his favourite armchair. *Move,* she thought, willing his skeletal fingers to twitch. *Get up. Please get up…* But all her willing was in vain. Memories of long nights in empty houses flashed before her eyes.

In her mind, she was fifteen again, her uncle had disappeared, leaving her at the mercy of the house as it whispered its sinister stories, only this time she couldn't hide under the covers 'til morning.

The time between each second stretched on eternally as she waited. Waited. Eventually, it became clear her uncle wasn't the source of the noise—and wouldn't be anytime soon.

Still, the stepping continued.

Savara knew she should've run, but the ripe concoction of fear and anger coursing through her fixed her in place. She nudged the door open just wide enough to slip through, managing to creep behind the settee unnoticed. Jasper had tried to pull her back, but her body was on autopilot. Finally, her teary, terrified eyes turned to the intruder.

He could have been a tower in another life.

Swathed in a dark, hooded cloak that had long since been in fashion. His calves forced themselves against his lower pant leg. His boots looked like they could kick through concrete. He himself as though he were built from cinder blocks.

She no longer thought of Jasper behind the door. Her uncle's corpse gave her the strength to stand, but her feet didn't carry her out. A strange power took over, sending her tiptoeing towards the man, rolling pin in hand, arm raised to strike.

CHAPTER 8

STRANGER COMPANY

SHE DIDN'T SEE him turn.

She didn't feel him grip.

The next thing Savara's disoriented brain knew was that her feet were dangling inches off the ground.

In the blink of an eye, the man had caught and hoisted her singlehandedly off the ground like the catch of the day. Curious eyes stared back at her with a stillness that made the night tremble. His movements, both cautious and predatory, matched his lion-esque reflexes. Face to face with the mysterious figure, she found he almost looked like one too.

Scratches on his squared jaw might have been made by some sort of creature. Ferocious strength and restraint left their marks on him. Everything about him spoke of caution, of dominance.

Everything but his eyes.

Irises a shade of blue just shy of indigo glowed beneath heavy brows. Looking into them, she glimpsed an open savannah sky full of stars. A lion on the outside, possibly, but on the inside, something else entirely. A spark of recognition flashed through his eyes.

Savara shivered under the force of his gaze.

He tightened his grip on her wrist, making her drop the rolling pin before pushing it far from reach. His movements were swift. Decisive. She didn't doubt he could've incapacitated her with the same crushing grip. It was a wonder why he didn't. The pressure snapped her back to the present, sending a rush of adrenaline through her veins. She came back kicking.

"I'm not going to hurt you," he said calmly in a voice that could still seas. "Stop squirming before you hurt yourself."

"You've killed two people already." The words left an unpleasant taste on her tongue. "I can't imagine you'd think twice about a third." Savara tried to wriggle free, but his grip was too strong.

"That wasn't me."

"Liar!" If words had bite, this one matched a wolf's. It came out with half a snarl and left her growling. A fire burned inside her as the world outside drowned in the storm.

"Calm down, Savara."

"What did you say?" she whispered, blanching as she wondered how her name came to be on the stranger's tongue.

Before the man could reply, Jasper came at him from behind with a thwack to the head that did nothing more than break the spoon. The stranger dropped her instantly and pinned Jasper to the ground.

Savara propped herself up enough to meet his eyes. Jasper's arms jut out awkwardly from behind him as he squirmed in vain under the force of the man's knee.

"Let him go," she hissed. The demand came out with less ferocity than she'd hoped. Savara moved for the rolling pin, but an invisible force sent it rolling out of reach and clamped her to the floor.

"Let me explain," the stranger replied.

"Let. Him. Go," she tried again.

The stranger nodded cautiously, as though he were the one afraid of her. With a final warning push of his knee, released Jasper. Savara too was freed from whatever force kept her in place. The man stood excruciatingly slowly and raised his hands to the height of his cheekbones as Jasper got to his feet and stepped towards her, clenching his shoulder.

"I mean you no harm," the man said, glancing back at the pair of them. His voice cut through the tension in the air like a smooth knife through warm butter.

Savara and Jasper exchanged a nervous glance but held their tongues.

"I assure you all is as it was when I arrived," he continued.

"How do you explain your rifling through papers then?" Jasper growled as he rolled his shoulder back into place. "Sav, he's lying. I can feel it."

Savara scrutinised the hooded stranger, still replaying the sound of his voice speaking her name in her mind. She frowned as his eyes fell on hers once more. Energy surrounded him, one she surprisingly hadn't noticed before, one that seemed to engulf the room. It almost felt as if *he* was the source of the strange power outage afflicting the street. Without realising it, her fingers danced over the base of the middle finger—the spot she always touched when things didn't seem *right*.

The man raised an eyebrow irritably. "If I had intended to kill either of you, *human*, I would have done so when you were waiting behind the door."

"Human? What do you think—" Jasper began, but Savara cut him off.

"That doesn't explain what you're doing here and why my family is…" she trailed off again, unable to voice the word. The thought alone brought more tears to her eyes that she refused to let fall. The man was either a murderer or a graverobber. He would be joining her late family, regardless. Savara balled her fists, readying herself to lunge at the man when Jasper, with his one good arm, pulled her back. He squeezed her tightly into his chest as the murderous rage bubbled inside her.

"Sav," he said softly. She knew he was only trying to help but all she wanted to do was scream. She wanted to tear the house down with the stranger still inside. "Sav," Jasper repeated, waiting for her to stop shaking.

"But Jasper," she whispered into his chest, still trying to process the world around her, "they're…"

Dead. Glassy, fear-ridden eyes, dried blood, pallid skin, all the things that would haunt her nightmares—and only six years after her parents.

"I know," he replied before she could get the word out. "I know," he repeated in a soft comforting voice, but none of it stopped her trembling. "Explain yourself," Jasper commanded the man, fearful still, but strong. She knew it was for her.

Savara pried herself from Jasper's arms as the man removed his hood. Despite her mistrust and whatever she'd imagined of him, he did not look like a killer—not totally, at least. Nestled in the shadows of his face was remorse, possibly borrowed to be worn like a mask on occasions such as these. But there it was. The curve of his mouth, the clench of his scarred jaw, and the furrow of his brow, all seemed earnest, though it did little to console her.

"I was called." His eyes moved down the point of his chin and across the room to the frail old corpse in the armchair.

Even in death, old Hyrum looked as stately and extravagant a gentleman as ever. His beard remained in perfect shape, hovering over the gilded sword embedded in his chest. An expression of plain serenity plastered his wrinkled face. His suit, despite the puncture, held not a single crease. Hyrum was his own brand of being, without a doubt. Even as they looked upon the blood staining his crisp white shirt, no one could truly say they were surprised to find it not red like the corpse below, but a deep, inky blue.

"Talk about a true blue-blood," commented Jasper.

Releasing some of the pent-up energy, Savara whacked him on the shoulder. Now was not the time for those types of comments. She couldn't pull her eyes away, but the more she looked, the more her stomach churned.

"It's the air here," the stranger remarked, without further explanation.

Questions littered her mind—nagging, preying, tormenting. Words rose and fell like the tide, getting caught at the back of her throat only to be swept down again into the depths of her conscious mind. So much left to say, but none of it seemed to matter. Her uncle, gone, Ms Short, gone, and here she stood, wondering what would become of her now that she was officially an orphan.

"Who are you?" The words strained her vocal cords as they forced themselves from her lips. "And what are you doing here?" Hot tears carved around the apples of her cheeks. Savara held her nose up high, pretending they weren't there even as they pooled at her chin and dripped to the floor. The two men were respectful enough to pretend along with her.

"My name is Captain Griffin Conroy of the Royal Izarian Guard, and leader of the Ris." He placed a heavy hand over his heart and bowed.

Savara understood about half of the words that spilt from his mouth. She figured they were words to be proud of, seeing as how his posture stiffened. Savara had never been fond of pomp and pretence. This man, Griffin, seemed to represent that and more—all that she had rebelled against for more years than she could remember.

"And I have been sent to bring you home," he added, noticing the ever-deepening crease between her brows.

"Home?" she thought aloud, the word forcing more tears to fall. "What on earth are you talking about?"

Savara had never quite felt at home anywhere, but she figured that was just a testament to teenage angst rather than the fact that she wasn't *actually* home. Sure, there were times she'd noted things didn't feel quite right, the way a shelf looks incomplete with a book missing, but in this case, she was the shelf, and the missing book had long since been on her radar. *Take me home…*

She looked over at Jasper, fiddling with something of her uncle's that he probably shouldn't. He'd been her one and only friend ever since she'd arrived here. *Home is where your friends are,* Savara thought, remembering all the memories she'd made with him as clear as a bright summer's day. Glancing around the room, this feeling only grew. *I'm already home,* she reasoned. *This is where my family is—was. This is the house I grew up in, the town I've terrorized ever since...*

A sharp pain appeared at her temples. Violent shivers wrapped her shoulders. Memories of the day she first arrived at the house burst into her head yet again, as though actively seeking her out. Savara squeezed her teary eyes shut until the images in her mind—the wind, the rain, the dark—disappeared. When she opened them again, she found his eyes locked on hers once more. The blue of his irises pierced her with all the qualities of a scalpel, dissecting each expression.

Suppressing whatever weakness she'd betrayed during her episode, she flared her nostrils and scoffed, "I'm already home."

"Is that what you believe?" Griffin countered.

"*Believe?*" she hissed.

"You mean, you don't know?"

Savara finally wiped the tears from her eyes. Sadness had taken a back seat to shock. Shock to anger. Now, anger and intrigue played a vicious game of ping-pong between her heart and her mind. Much to her dismay, intrigue was winning.

CHAPTER 9

A DISCOVERY OF NEW WORLDS

THE MAN WAS irritating, to say the least. His arrogant stance, his deep voice, especially the way he looked at her. Jasper hated when men looked at her like that—like she was something to behold, something to claim, and on occasion something to break. Even worse was how they'd traipse around as if they were kings when, in fact, they probably were worth less than the soles of their boots.

What they didn't realise was, Savara played her own games, by her own rules, and cat and mouse wasn't one of them. She could've gobbled all of them whole if she'd been a different person. They were mice coaxing a tiger into play and expecting it to work out in their favour. Though Jasper despised their looks, he found Savara's unconscious shattering of their egos to be a diverting source of entertainment. None of them ever stood a chance.

This one was different.

This one had a quality about him that ground at Jasper's nerves. Jasper, though not prone to believing in bad feelings, found this one especially hard to ignore.

This one is going to be trouble.

Jasper sought out something less nauseating in the room to watch, still rubbing his shoulder from where Sav had whacked him—*unnecessarily,* he thought. His keen eyes surveyed the damage, pretending he was on one of his digs. Something in the room wasn't sitting right with him—and not just the irritating presence of the six-foot-tall stranger.

His eyes fell on the corpse. The blank, lifeless eyes he'd seen sparkling with mischief only hours before stared back at him. Their hollowness reminded him of the mummies of the old world. Those eyes looked as though they'd seen more than seventy years would allow—seventy being an estimate based on the texture of the skin and typical age spots. A doctor might have said the same. After having met the man, however, Jasper didn't believe he was that *young* for a second.

"Can you believe this guy?" he whispered to the corpse. "Who does he think he is, waltzing in here like this?" He crossed his arms and growled. "I mean, it's like she hasn't even noticed that I've left her side. We raised her better than this… I mean… you did. Of course. Not stepping on any toes here." He tapped his foot irritably while nervous fingers rapped on his arms. "I helped though. Little bit…" Jasper soon realised he'd said more to the corpse in those few minutes than he had in the whole time the man was alive. "I bet you wouldn't stand for this… not that you're going to be doing much standing, but… you know… life of a pincushion and all… or should I say afterlife?" He imagined the man's scowl. "You're right, I'll stop."

Unable to watch any longer, Jasper's wandering eyes eventually caught on the hilt of the sword: jewel-encrusted, old, and unlike anything he'd ever seen or studied before. Its beauty was unparalleled, as was its lethality. The rubies jutting out at its hilt looked as red as the blood it must have spilt. The blade as black as the death it must have caused.

As he followed it into Hyrum's chest, he found himself in alignment with those strange copper spectacles. He furrowed his brow as he contemplated them. Something was off. He knew he shouldn't disturb the corpse, but he needed to be sure…

"Sorry about this," he whispered to the corpse before removing them. He turned them over in his hand, his curiosity only deepening. *I must be crazy,* he thought, replacing his glasses with Hyrum's.

Suddenly, the world before him transformed.

Symbols and markings written in a fading blue light, emanating from beneath the skin itself, trailed across the corpse's body. The wooden floor beneath his feet transformed into an ocean of stars. The books lining the shelves suddenly gained life—holographic titles, shifting figures, some even breathed. The room around him became a marvellous, fading midnight sea.

Jasper turned back to Griffin, noticing the same markings across his skin. He scowled.

He's going to be twice as annoying now…

Everything his eyes fell on was bathed in blue… everything except the sword. It stood out against the rest like a gash, the light reflecting off it a menacing, blood-red.

"Yikes!" He fumbled the spectacles from his eyes, catching them before they hit the ground. The world without them—and it saddened him to admit, the world he'd grown up in—now looked painfully grey.

"What is it, Jasper?" Savara and Griffin had both turned to him, only just realising his absence.

"Sav, I think you should see this."

"Not now," she called back irritably.

"Yes, Sav. Now."

"Jasper, they're just glasses."

"I don't know what they are, Sav, but they're not glasses."

The man peered over at Jasper and raised an eyebrow in contemplation. "What a curiously intelligent human you are."

"It's hard to take that as a compliment when it's worded so insultingly," Jasper growled.

Savara walked over to inspect them as Griffin trailed a pace or two behind. She shot him a glance that said, *stay where I can see you.* To his credit, he stepped left into her line of vision, clasped his hands behind his back, and nodded. Jasper shot him a quick sneer before turning back to her. Savara nudged him forcefully in the ribs and scowled.

"What?" Jasper knew he was being childish, but the man set him on edge.

"Not nice, Jasper."

"…because nice is high on my priorities list…" he grumbled. "I don't like him, Sav. And I don't care if he knows it or not," he added just loud enough for the man to hear.

"Jasper, my family is…" She prickled. He squeezed her shoulder, acknowledging the word she wouldn't speak and the pain he knew she carried. "And the only person who might know anything about what happened is standing about three feet from us and probably listening, so forgive me if who you like isn't high on my priorities list either."

It didn't change how Jasper felt about the man, how the sight of him prompted a scowl, but she raised a fair point. In the end, it wasn't his family splayed out like cutlets at a butcher's shop, but if she needed this, he'd support her. He'd have to put up with the guy a little while longer, but he'd always support her. It wouldn't kill him… *hopefully*… but he didn't have to like the smug look the guy had on his face. Jasper glowered at him again. *He's definitely eavesdropping.* The man raised a tentative eyebrow at him. Jasper narrowed his eyes in response.

"What did you want me to see?" Savara nudged him again, reminding him of the manners she knew he had, and he knew he didn't owe the stranger. "They're just glasses," she added with a frown. She spoke a little too loudly to cover up their whisperings, but Jasper didn't care if the jerk heard him.

"Here, let me help," Jasper said as he tucked her hair gently back behind her ears and rested the coppery wiring on the bridge of her nose. As his plain brown eyes met hers, in all their rainbow-splotched glory, he blushed. Jasper placed a hand over his mouth and coughed lightly to cover it up. Then, he guided her eyes over to her uncle's dangling wrist.

Savara's jaw dropped. "What is this?" she gasped. Savara turned around the room, curiosity sparkling in her eyes. She looked exceptional like this. Her eyes devoured everything in their path, and Jasper's devoured her. He could have watched her for an eternity this way. But then, his heart sank.

Her eyes fell on *him*.

Though she'd tried to hide it, Jasper had caught her blush. He wanted to throw up.

"Do you still think you know everything there is to know about the world you live in?" Griffin's voice was more condescending than Jasper would've liked, especially as it was directed at Savara. She glared at him, but Jasper knew she wasn't mad. Worse. She was interested.

Jasper faced Griffin with a glower that held all the annoyance that Savara's should've, and then some. He studied him—the scuff of his boots, the strange, out-of-fashion cloak, even the way his hair was tied. He looked like a mercenary. Too shady to be a soldier and too restrained to be a thug. And the scars on his cheek looked suspiciously like knife wounds.

Nothing but trouble, he thought. And yet, intrigue was starting to get to him too.

Despite his dislike of the man, the prospect of a new world was too incredible to ignore. Even now, Jasper found himself desperately wishing to understand the puzzle they'd been forced into. How did the strange man appear in the house? What was Hyrum? Why was he killed? And most importantly, what did all of this mean for Savara?

His poor Savara. As he watched her in that moment—her little lip bite, her furrowed brow—he knew he'd never leave her alone. No matter what it meant for him.

Jasper thought back to the morning's conversation about feeling *called* to do something or go somewhere. Savara, he realised, was his calling. He'd go to the ends of the earth for her; he'd jump worlds for her if it meant being there when she needed it. And to think, he might never have noticed it if it weren't for Griffin.

Jasper watched as she studied her hands, mesmerised by the markings that only the glasses could show. He'd seen them too: a spiral on her thumb, a cluster of rings on her wrist. Her light was a beautiful violet.

"Jasper, do you—"

"No," he said before she could ask. No, he didn't have any markings. He was *human*… He stared at the ground, consciously avoiding her gaze. He hadn't said it, but knowing that they were different—having proof of it, broke his heart.

Savara turned to Griffin once more. "Who called you?" she demanded.

That's my girl…

"Him," Griffin replied, pointing his chin in the direction of the corpse.

Suddenly, out of nowhere, he froze. Griffin's ears pricked, listening for something in the apparent silence. Jasper looked around for the source of his worry, but he heard nothing. Yet, Griffin's eyes narrowed, focusing on something far beyond the room. The fists at his side began to tremble. Something was very wrong…

"I don't think it's safe here," Griffin added in hushed tones. There was an edge to his voice that hadn't been there before. An urgency that Jasper couldn't place—or unhear.

"I need to know, why did my uncle send for you? And why is he…" Savara asked, her voice cracking as she spoke.

Though she tried to keep it together, Jasper noticed how she kept her gaze as far as possible from the corpse. He placed a hang on her shoulder, his heart lifting as she rested hers over it and squeezed. She still needed him, and that was all the consolation he needed.

Griffin's brows knitted together. "That sword is not of this world," he told her.

Which means, neither was the person who did it, Jasper realised, a heavy frown settling in on his face. Judging by the way Savara shivered beneath his touch, he knew she'd realised it, too.

He was at an impasse. Part of him wanted to take to the mystery, uncover every potential secret that this new world had to offer. The other wondered that this all wasn't a hoax. He could go home. He could forget this all ever happened. But that would mean he'd have to forget her. Between the corpses, the spectacles, and the man before them, Jasper knew this world would take her from him, whether he wanted it to or not. He could already see her turning the stranger's words over in her mind. If he did nothing, he would lose her.

"You have questions," Griffin added to Savara. "I'm sorry to say I don't have all the answers, but I know where you can find them. I know this is too much to take in at once, and I can imagine how confused you must feel, but it is imperative you come with me."

"Worded like that, it doesn't seem like she has much of a choice," mumbled Jasper.

"Your opinion is of little consequence," he retorted, taking too much pleasure in his adding of the word, *"human."*

"I'm quite done listening to yours too," Jasper replied, picking up the cane to strike.

CHAPTER 10

THE JUMP

"NO MORE FIGHTING!" Savara yelled. There'd been enough violence for one day. She was angry, tired, and confused by how the day had turned out. Not to mention the mourning that would eventually kick in when the shock wore off. She innocently hoped every grey cloud really did have a silver lining, but she found it increasingly hard to keep that hope alive.

Savara wasn't ready to make peace with this situation. She'd rather be rid of it as soon as possible. She wished to drown her sorrows in something violently alcoholic, something strong enough to erase the day from her memory entirely. But that choice was a luxury she didn't have. Perhaps, one day, she'd find the person who did this and maybe even return the favour. Not now, though. Now was the time for grieving, the time for saying goodbye to the source of her troubles. Hopefully, there was something better waiting for her a world away from this one.

"I'll go," she announced, holding back a wave of tears.

"Sav, you can't be serious," said Jasper irritably.

"Time is of the essence," chimed Griffin.

Jasper took her hand with pleading eyes. "Sav, I won't let you put yourself in danger."

"It's not your choice, *human*."

"And you think it's yours, *soldier boy?*"

"You are not her keeper," Griffin scoffed.

"And you are not her saviour," Jasper hissed. "I'm the closest thing to family she has left."

Their bickering further pushed her decision.

"You're right," she replied. The words felt heavy as they left her mouth. With the wound of her parents' death newly refreshed and the gale outside in full force, her desire to leave—to flee—only grew.

The two men looked at each other and then at her before replying in unison, "Who?"

The world she thought she knew turned out to be as fleeting as a shadow and just as surreal, like waking up from a dream she hadn't realised she was in. Hazy, groggy, and still adjusting. A part of her had always known there was something off about this world—or at least her presence in it. She was a puzzle piece from a different box. By the sound of things, any clarity she wanted surrounding what had happened and why lay elsewhere. Her mind was already made up. It had been, long before she'd seen the marks. Long before the gruesome murders. Long before him…

"Both of you. Jasper, I don't have family here anymore, but you're not my keeper, and I won't ask that of you either.

And you…" She frowned at Griffin. "I'll go, but not as a favour to you. I still don't trust you. I need answers." She softened as she returned to Jasper and added, "Answers I won't find here."

He glowered at Griffin before speaking again. "I'm coming with you."

"Jasper, I can't ask you to do that."

"Respectfully, Sav, you're not."

She knew he didn't trust Griffin either, but that didn't mean it was a good idea for him to come. Savara forced her eyes to look again at her uncle's corpse. He was a man of that world and still ended up skewered. Jasper wasn't even that. He wanted to make sure she was safe; she didn't want to put him in danger.

"Hey," Jasper said softly, cupping her face in his hands. "I would never let you go alone. I know what it means to you. And… if I'm being honest, as much as it pains me to admit, I can't say I'm not curious."

"What if it's dangerous?" she whispered.

"If I had to choose between danger and losing you, I'd choose danger any day. Besides, I don't trust grouchy over there as far as I can throw him."

"Which, judging by your stature, *human*, isn't even a measurable distance," Griffin commented.

"Oh good, you eavesdrop too. At least now, I won't have to pretend to be civil with you," Jasper hissed in reply.

"Stop!" Savara yelled. She knew it would be a bad idea to leave them together. She'd have to play referee through every interaction. At least she wouldn't be alone. Savara wagged a warning finger at Jasper before turning to Griffin. "He's coming."

Griffin was visibly annoyed by her decision, but he wasn't in the position to argue. "If he must," he sighed. "But I repeat, time is of the essence."

Savara cast hesitant glances between the two. Jasper clung tightly to the cane, two pairs of glasses dangling from his collar, as he slung his bag over his shoulder. The cloth satchel was weighted down by the strange book she'd found that morning. He'd decided. She hoped he wouldn't come to regret it. Griffin, whose presence still gnawed at her, had an unsettling look in his eyes that he tried to mask, that of an animal who sensed an earthquake.

Questions littered her mind. Thankfully, they drowned out the reminders of loss and proddings of grief that were all too ready to send her spiralling. Griffin promised her answers. She'd see to it that he kept that promise.

She took a last look around the room, trying to take it in its entirety in her memory. Would she ever be back? Could she? And how would she ever bury the corpses? All good questions which would keep her up at night. The more she thought about them, the more she needed to leave. She could no longer bring herself to look at her uncle's corpse slumped gracefully in his favourite chair.

She nodded to Griffin, pulling her coat tight against her; not because of the sudden draft that burst through the windows, but to make herself as small as possible, hoping that her feelings would shrink too.

"Are you going to tell us where we're going?" Jasper pestered.

"No," Griffin replied dryly as he pulled a satchel from his side, dipped his hand in, and retrieved a handful of black dust. With a hefty puff, he enveloped them in a cloud of this sparkling dark powder. The world around them disappeared as though they'd fallen into a dream.

* * *

THE VICIOUS STORM outside subsided, giving way to an empty sky and a blinding moon. The remaining airborne specks of dust floated gently to the ground, glinting in the newly risen moonlight. There were no traces of the three people who stood there moments before.

Heavy, leathery paws padded gracefully on the wooden floor, stepping over the bloody corpse at the base of the stairs without so much as a glance. Giant nostrils sniffed the air, following the scent of what anyone in this world could only describe as magic. The last of the night's creatures trailed the scent up the stairs and into the study. It rested its head under the limp hand of the corpse in the armchair and purred. It sensed the slowly fading presence of the newly vanished souls.

It had just missed them.

It spread its wings, shedding a single glossy black feather as it stretched its claws. With a great leap and a blink of its ruby-red eyes, it too vanished into nothingness.

The two corpses disappeared. The doors and windows all shut simultaneously with a loud clatter. All was quiet once more in the house; not a soul stirred.

CHAPTER 11

THE FIRST STONE

THE APPRENTICE SKULKED around the bodies of the palace guards like a tiger in hunt. The shouting and screaming from outside were silenced as the great doors slammed behind him. Not even the spirits protecting the Argia palace were a match for the thing inside him.

Shadowy dust slithered around the hot, sticky patches of freshly spilt blood before settling on the marble floors. He trod carefully.

No sense in soiling good shoes with bad blood.

His eyes were as empty as the hollow halls of the palace, glowing the colour of the darkest depths of space. Every so often, they'd flicker the colour of blinding blue lightning, but the void would always reclaim them. With one hand, he summoned an orb of light which illuminated only the patch of ground he trod on. With the other, he brushed his fingers sacrilegiously over the portraits of kings and queens of old that lined the walls.

He had never been a fan of royalty, even before his crusade. They sat high and mighty on gilded thrones, basking in the light of their own fires while their people's magic faded. Despite what anyone else would say, he knew his actions were just.

The Apprentice stopped.

The echo of his previous footfall faded in his pause. His hand hovered tentatively over the last painting, hidden shamefully at the end of the hall. He with eyes that saw all had almost missed it. *Almost.* The Apprentice raised his hand higher, casting the melancholy light over the portrait.

The bottom left quadrant had been scorched in a fit of anger that still lingered around the painting, but the figure remained mostly intact. He stared up at the eyes of the girl, sensing things he'd long forgotten—fear, loss, pain. For the first time since his crusade had begun, his heart skipped a beat.

The Apprentice questioned his actions for only a moment before something else began calling him back. Reminders of a debt, a soul, of necessary action. His spine prickled with its message. It told him to push ahead and not look back.

He brushed off the chills and continued walking. The further he got from the painting, the further away the emotions faded, until there was nothing left but the memory of feeling, and even that would fade, eventually.

He continued his search, following the streaks of magma that lined the walls to the grandest room of the palace. Warm white light seeped through the crack beneath the gilded door.

He took a deep breath, put out his light, shaded his eyes, and pushed it open.

The chamber was ablaze; the light from the sconces and tracings of magma reflected on every surface imaginable. It took a second for his eyes to adjust. There, he spied her.

A draping white nightgown danced in the chilly morning breeze that sauntered through the open windows. Golden curls hung loosely at the side of a symmetrical face, hiding the stifled rage of her rosy cheeks.

The last queen of Osiir.

She looked resplendent and strong on her golden throne. Despite being a queen of fire, her gaze had all the piercing qualities of ice. The Apprentice bowed in her presence, a sentiment which went unreturned.

"I know what you've come for," she said firmly.

"Good," he replied. "That will make this much easier."

"As easy as wiping out my entire palace?"

"Necessary action."

The reigning queen of the Argia pressed her lips into a thin line. The depth of his voice betrayed no trace of remorse or regret. It angered her. Part of him enjoyed her rage; the other was unable to voice its opinion.

"You speak as if you were prohibited choice, but here you are, alive, whilst my people lay strewn through the castle like autumn leaves," she hissed, her fury bringing flames to her fingertips.

The Apprentice sighed. "I am sorry, My Lady, that you and he do not see eye to eye—"

"I do not meet eyes with cowards," she scoffed. "You come here after the fact, having stained my soil red with the blood of my people, having invaded the sanctity of my palace, and claim it is over nothing more than a difference of opinion?" The queen of the Argia stood firm, regally marble-esque, with a glower to scorn generations. "He has trained you well, but a creature of no remorse deserves no forgiveness. You are a *monster*."

"It seems cruel of you, My Lady, to call me a monster and a coward when we both know what you did to your last child—"

"That's enough!" she roared, a blast of fire spewing from her lips like a dragon. "Speak of my spawn once more and you will be turned to ash, the very kind your master manipulates."

"I suppose, then, you do not plan on cooperating."

"With *Him*? The pretend king on his presumptuous throne? No."

The Apprentice had predicted as much. "I am afraid you have no choice."

"Tell me," she began softly. "Do you take pleasure in being his attack dog? Do you relish in the suffering?" Foul hatred tainted her melodious voice.

"I take pleasure in knowing that my work is just."

"You are no better than the wild animals of the forest looking for their next meal, their next fill of blood. Someone should cage you."

The Apprentice frowned. "You mistake me, Majesty. I am not in the business of murder. I, like you, have a part to play in correcting this world." His voice was steady as he spoke. It ground at her nerves. "In this case, I simply offered Your Highness the more civil option."

The queen of the Argia thrust her hand forward, creating a ring of white flames on the floor around his feet that burned hot in the open air. "Come no closer," she threatened, closing her fingers slowly; a movement mimicked by the dancing flames.

The Apprentice muttered under his breath and enveloped himself in travelling dust. When he reappeared at her side, part of him was happy to see her pride shift unequivocally to fear.

"Now then… I came for something important, and sadly, I am not allowed to leave without it."

He cast his hand in the direction of the queen, casting a rope of blue light around her hands and feet—and mouth, *for good measure*. She thrashed around violently on the floor, but he paid her little mind now that she was incapacitated. On the throne behind her, he found what he had come for: a small glass orb, nestled in the ornate golden fretwork, containing a flame from the time before time itself. Carefully, he worked it out of its holding place and turned it once over in his hand.

"An inextinguishable flame," he announced, gazing upon it thoughtfully. "You should be more careful with such valuable objects, Majesty." He stooped low over her and rested his hand on her shoulder. An image flashed from her mind to his. "Oh?" His eyes turned to the glass pendant that hung from her neck. "He will be pleased indeed," he added as he ripped the charm from her and rolled it around in his palm…

THE APPRENTICE STROLLED casually out of the dimmed palace and into the brilliant hues of the sunrise. He wiped a smear of fresh blood from his cheek as he gazed out beyond the horizon. The queen hadn't been entirely wrong in her judgment of him. He had much blood on his hands. All would be worth it, in the end, to see Visanthe as it was— as it should be.

Just then, a creature of the night appeared at his side, popping into existence as this creature typically did. The large black panther, with wings that spanned the length of a full-grown adult, purred in a rumble that shook the stairs beneath them. It waited by his side, watching the sun creep slowly over the town. Glints of light caught in the bubbling fountain beyond and cast shining ripples over their faces.

"Tell *Him* I have it."

The panther took a step forward.

"And…" The Apprentice paused, fighting with himself over whether to divulge the interesting piece of information he'd uncovered. One part of him begged his lips to stay shut. The stronger part of him silenced it. "That I found her, the child."

The panther yawned and stretched its wings.

The Apprentice stared down at the charm in his palm. A low pulse emanated from within. Half of him fought to protect it, the powers of the missing child. The other half won. He tightened his grip, cracking the glass and releasing the tiny ball of lavender light. It flew up into the sky and, in a flash that spanned the length of the heavens, disappeared, seeking out its true owner.

"It will find her," he said to the creature, keeping his eyes on the horizon. "Follow it."

The panther took off in one great leap, disappearing from the world in the next beat of its wings.

Alone, The Apprentice sat quietly on the stoop and watched the remainder of this pink and orange sunrise, the broken glass still clenched firmly in his fist, a puddle of dark red blood forming beneath it. *You won't forget this,* he thought to himself, pressing the shards harder into his skin.

A wicked smile grew on his face. "Neither will you," he replied aloud.

CHAPTER 12

NEW FACES

FOREIGN EYES WATCHED over her like the guardians
to unpleasant sleep. They were a new addition to her dream.
The shadows, the menacing laugh, the screams; they all
played out as they had many times before, except for the eyes.
The eyes—deep as space and mournful in their gaze—were
new.

Savara's eyes shot open.

A dream, she thought. *Just a dream.* The beating of her heart
echoed in her ears. She took a breath, feeling a dull pain in
her spine against something soft. *Where am I?* She scanned
her memories for an explanation but came up blank. Her
body was slow to wake. Her mind still reeling. She peered
around for something to save her from the darkness.

A tiny gas lamp stood on the table beside her, illuminating
only as far as she could reach. Savara unhitched a breath and

rolled over, finding a similar lamp on the bedside table next to her. Its gentle glow cast shadows on the familiar face of a snoring young man, whose two pairs of glasses rested on the table. She tried whispering to him to get his attention, but he was sound asleep. There was no telling what lay just beyond the bounds of the lamplight. She hesitantly stretched her hand over and turned up the flame.

The room had the distinct qualities of a hospital, from the beds to the odd bits of medical equipment resting on every available surface. Behind her, Savara found that the wall was made of thick cloth akin to that of the tents used on a battleground. The discovery did nothing to soothe her nerves.

Savara made to stand when a sharp pain shot up her left arm. She slumped back down, clenching fast to it until the pain subsided. She almost tried again when, out of the darkness, an unfamiliar voice spoke up.

"Slowly," it said. It was a man's voice, deep and spiced, reminding her of cinnamon. It had a soft, grainy texture that was pleasing to the ear. Listening to it made her stomach yearn for something sweet.

Savara scanned the darkness beyond for some sign of life or movement but found nothing. "Who's there?" she finally called back.

A light breeze sauntered around the beds as a man stepped into the light. She spied his eyes before his body, despite appearing at roughly the same time. They shone like twin moons on the darkened canvas that was his face. He was short and trim, with a head that gave her the distinct impression of being carved out of pure chocolate, with symmetrical proportions, soft angles, and a reflective shimmer where his hair would be.

"It is good to see you awake," he replied in the same seasoned voice. "I was beginning to worry."

"Where am I?" she asked apprehensively. Her question was punctuated by Jasper's snoring in the bed beside her.

"Camp Saar. Refugee camp on the outskirts of the Araldin Fields. We are in Argia lands, if that makes you feel better," he added, noticing her confusion.

Savara furrowed her brow, more lost than before. She began to wonder if she wasn't still dreaming.

"How did you sleep?" he asked as he approached. Her skin prickled as he neared. Savara decided it best to keep her mouth shut. When she didn't answer, he placed his hand to his heart and added, "I mean you no harm, I am the camp medic."

"Fine, I guess." The air around her felt different; lighter. Her lungs fought to keep it in. "My body hurts."

"That is normal. You were already unconscious when you got in last night. I patched up any superficial wounds. You should be good as new in a few hours. The jump between worlds is both physically and mentally taxing."

Jump. Savara might have written off the strange, fading injuries as having fought with herself in her sleep, but that not-so-innocent word *jump* forced her to remember what she'd done, where she'd *jumped* from, though, she was hazy on where she'd *jumped* to. Her eyes made their best attempt to adjust to the scene as her mind tried to stitch its memories back together. Static consumed her brain. Each time she tried to focus she was met with a sharp pain around her temples.

"You have questions. Is it okay if I ask a few first?"

In the dim glow of the fire, her eyes shifted over to where Jasper lay sleeping. His features took on a softer quality under the lamplight. The bags under his eyes had subsided. The stray curls that fell over his face reminded her of a sleeping baby. Unlike her, he could sleep and sleep well. It didn't matter where or when; if his body needed it and his mind allowed it, he was asleep.

Stay sleeping for now, until I figure out where we are and what trouble I've managed to land us in this time, she hoped of him as she gazed upon his resting face.

Savara turned back to the man and dipped her head in a singular, tentative nod.

He returned a sympathetic smile. "Do you remember your name?" he asked.

"Savara," she replied easily. "Savara Clarimonde."

He furrowed his brow. "And your companion?"

"Jasper. Harrow."

"How much do you remember from before you woke up, Savara?"

"Not a whole lot."

"Anything will do."

Maybe it was the air itself, or maybe just his cinnamon-kissed voice and gentle manner, but one of the two had managed to charm the memories out of her. The mental static cleared just enough to take her back to a storm on the horizon, a darkened house, two corpses, and a cloaked figure.

Savara followed the strange thread of coincidences that had resulted in her jumping, all the while searching for a conclusive end, or possibly, a beginning that made sense. Some of the details were hazier, while others were all too accessible: the image of the door flapping in the breeze; of

Ms Short splayed lifelessly across the floor; of her uncle's corpse, complete with all the strange markings; and a pair of hauntingly blue eyes.

"I'm not dreaming, am I?" she concluded.

"No," he replied. "Though, it seems your memory is intact. That is a good sign."

Neither response consoled her in the way she figured he had intended. Savara bit her lip, remembering that talking to strangers in unknown places, however gentle they appear to be, might not be the best of ideas.

"What am I doing here?" Speaking the question aloud, Savara realised she'd posed it to herself as well. She remembered why she wasn't home—if she could even still call it that—but her heart constricted at the lack of judgement she'd shown in blindly following a stranger, especially across worlds. What would her uncle have said? *Nothing, he's dead,* she reminded herself. Even thinking the word sent shivers down her spine.

"That, I cannot say."

"Is there a way back?"

"I would not know."

"You're not one for words, are you?" Savara grumbled.

He grinned knowingly. "Depends."

"Figures." She exhaled heavily. "Is there anyone in this place that might know anything at all?"

"The captain."

"Is he as great a wordsmith as you?"

"Not at all," the man replied with a laugh that flowed through the room, filling the air with warmth. "But he will have your answers." Somehow, she knew he meant more than just the where's and the how's. Her heart didn't know whether to steady itself or stop. "He is waiting for you in one of the other tents. We can leave whenever you are ready."

Savara contemplated a still-sleeping Jasper. She wasn't ready to wake him. Not until she knew he'd be safe. "Will he be okay?" she asked softly.

"He is in good health. I imagine he will be up in a few hours. His body systems are a little different to ours."

Ours.

She frowned, remembering his pained look when she was about to ask if he too had markings. Deep down, Savara had known she was different. The way she sensed into others' emotions was not something she could ever explain, as though she could feel the little flutters of their souls. She'd always believed she was crazy. She never would've imagined this... Yet perhaps the truth had been there all along.

When she was younger, her uncle used to tell her stories. Tales of fantastical beasts, fires that lived, oceans that sang, people who moved like gods... She'd always listened with rapt attention. Sometimes she even wished to be one of them, one of the people who could move stones with their minds, summon fire at the twitch of their fingers, create gigantic waves or powerful winds with the flick of their wrists, or even steal the light from the world around them.

"My uncle used to tell me stories," Savara began, her voice was distant, her mind lost to the past. "I think they were about this place. About the creatures that call it home, and what they're capable of..." Back then, his stories seemed to resonate with something inside her, which she mistook for longing. Now, she wasn't so sure. Considering how her mind had painted them with such detail, it was almost hard to believe it had been imagination alone.

When the man didn't reply, she added, "They weren't *just* stories, were they?"

His pause felt eternal. The flickering of the lamp's flame filled the space where words should've been. Finally, the man sighed.

"No."

Savara frowned deeper this time. If they were in fact true, this world was a dangerous place. More so than she'd anticipated. Perhaps more so. From what she remembered, none of his stories had ever ended well.

"They weren't *happy* stories," she continued.

"Not all stories are happy, no matter the world."

Thinking back on all the strange tales her uncle had filled her head with over the years, she realised that part of the pleasure in stories is that they are just that, stories. Things to imagine without facing consequences. No one gives a second thought to the monsters that lurk in the shadows so long as the hero is safe at the end.

But hearing a story is different from living it. She couldn't simply close the book when she got scared or skip to the end to know everything would be okay. Savara didn't like the new sensation taking root in the pit of her stomach, the one that left her wondering what exactly it meant to *not be human*, and in Jasper's case, to be one in a world that wasn't.

A world away, Uncle Hyrum's corpse was probably collecting cobwebs on the plush armchair by the window, rotting in peace. What would he think of her now? Falling headfirst into all that which he'd tried to protect her from. He along with Ms Short, the only family she could remember, were victims of the monsters of this world, and he'd known of their capabilities. Savara was woefully ignorant, and Jasper even more so.

Jasper slept peacefully, unplagued by the monsters of her memories. Savara imagined him squaring up against the beasts she was told of as an adolescent. Guilt trickled into her stomach.

What have I done?

"Is he in danger?" Savara asked. "Since he isn't like…us?"

"His appearance might be passable for Argia, the people of the southern desert are generally more tanned. His eyes might give reason for concern, as they are quite strange in colour."

"And what about the powers?"

"There are many in this world without powers, your friend will pass for one of them." The man turned back to her with a small vial in hand. "Here," he said, offering it to her. Savara looked upon it apprehensively. "If I had wanted to kill you, I would have done so while you slept. This is for the pain." He rested the vial on the table beside her.

Savara picked it up and sniffed it before gulping it down. Every muscle in her body tensed as the vile liquid burned its way down her throat and into the pit of her stomach.

"Yuck!" She gagged.

The man smiled. "I never said it would taste good."

She trembled, waiting for the fire in her body to dissipate, and as it did, the numb throbbing in her back and legs subsided with it.

"Thank you," she replied, curling her toes.

He nodded. "You are all set," he said, pulling clothes from an old chest elsewhere in the tent and resting them on her bed. "Put these on and meet me outside."

"Wait," she called out before he reached the door. "I didn't get your name."

His smile beamed in the darkness. "They call me Brass."

"Brass." Savara smiled back, taking in that eerie glow of his again. He reminded her of the shiny metal and the instruments made of it, charming and warm, and incredibly unique, like a saxophone. She imagined he played his own tune and moved to his own rhythm. Still, there was something in his air that seemed almost melancholic, cold like the metal of the instrument.

"It suits you," she concluded. Brass flashed her a brief smile before slipping out into the sunlight. Savara waited for the mesh to drag shut and began to undress.

CHAPTER 13

THE RIS

SAVARA STUMBLED OUT of the tent and into the blinding sun. Its orange glow kissed her skin. The fresh air brought life back into her paled eyes. She felt the steady pulse of her own heart in the soles of her feet, the tickle of the dewy grass between her toes. She scrunched and released them, enjoying their movement. A chill filled her lungs with each breath. With each soft exhale life swirled inside her.

The forest expanded around their clearing, distilling the sunlight from high above. Rows of low-lying tents extended out on either side, curving back into a giant circle. Wisps of smoke and ash from a crackling fire rose above the tops of the tents to her left. Everything was quiet, save for the low chirpings of sparrows in the distance.

"Better?" Brass asked.

"A little," she replied as she stared at him under this new light. His silver eyes glinted under the sun's rays. His skin was a shade of deep oak brown that blended in with the forest. A sleeveless grey tunic with shimmering gold buttons at its front exposed three pristine white tattoos along his left arm: a sun, a moon, and a star.

"Shall we go find the captain?" he said as he clasped his hands behind his back.

Savara nodded, following two steps behind to take in the world around her. The colours were more vivid than any she had ever seen. The constant sensation of grasping onto and losing memories tormented her. As though the world was trying to speak to her, remind her of the part of it she once knew, but each time she tried to remember, her mind went blank. She likened the feeling to the remembering of a song's melody but not the accompanying lyrics—and it ground at her nerves.

Each crunch of gravel and grass beneath her feet hummed, as though something flowed from within the ground itself, gently pushing against her soles. Savara contemplated the ease in Brass' steps, wondering if he too felt this strange energy when realised his feet never once touched the ground. Little pockets of air formed under them, supporting each step before flowing onto the next.

No wonder his stride was utterly silent.

Noticing the pause in her footsteps, he turned. "Is something wrong?"

"Your feet..." she replied as a blush crept into her cheeks.

Brass let out a rich, warm laugh into the chill of the morning air. "A habit of mine I can't seem to kick from a previous life."

"Is it… magic?" she asked, regretting her childish choice of word.

"Nothing so fantastical but, I suppose to someone who has been in the human world for so long, you have no other explanation for it."

"I must sound foolish."

"Foolish would be not to ask. What you are is ignorant, though I imagine not for much longer. Still, it would be best if, for the time being, you kept as low a profile as possible. You are somewhat of a rare commodity around these parts, and that kind of ignorance might attract unwanted attention." He paused, noticing her apprehension. With the kind of smile you reserve for precarious reassurances, he added, "You are safe with us."

Savara inclined her head, but something in the quiver of his smile told her that he wasn't entirely sure of his words. This world played by other rules, ones she couldn't remember and probably never would. Safe means little in the face of ignorance, which left her wondering, *Safe from what?*

Somehow, she knew that even if she could voice the words, she wouldn't get an answer. They walked a little further in silence before another question breached her lips.

"You mentioned before that this was a refugee camp. Refugees of what?"

Brass' airy steps faltered. His sole hit the ground with a soft crunch. This time, he did not disguise his frown.

"Things here are not as they used to be," he began. "People have suffered much, especially in the Argia territories. Within the last decade, this region has witnessed the rise of militants in the form of organized crime syndicates. Not too long ago, there was an attack on the royal house of the Argia which left no survivors and effectively ended the monarchy. When the dust settled, the mafia claimed the kingdom for themselves, using whatever control they had gained from within the underbelly of society to manipulate the masses. They forced lower leaders of the townships to relinquish control to them, removing anyone who disagreed."

The entire dreadful scene played out in her mind—a queen losing her crown, pools of blood staining sandstone streets, a city plunging into darkness. "How awful," she whispered, unaware and unsure as to how the images had gotten there, to begin with.

"Those who could afford to move lands did so, while those who could not, ended up here." Before she could speak, he placed a finger to his lips and lowered his voice. "This world is on edge, Savara. Squabbles are becoming wars. Hatred is taking up root where compassion once grew. People are past the point of reconciliation, preferring now to cast blame, and sadly, to shed blood." Noticing the fear she'd let creep into her eyes, he sighed. "I apologise if this has upset you. I am not sure if I should have told you all of this, but you have the right to know what you might encounter."

At the end of his tale, Savara noticed a different energy rippling from him, a longing for peace that seemed years in the making. Brass dipped his head before walking again, taking with each light-footed stride that feeling of longing further from her. Neither spoke for the remainder of the walk.

They stopped at a relatively small tent just beyond the campfire where all energies seemed to be replaced by one low thrum of power. Brass glanced around to make sure they wouldn't be overheard.

"Before you go, there are a few things that you should know that the others might be hesitant to tell you," he whispered, forcing her to move closer to hear properly. "Dark forces are playing with things they have no business playing with. Stay alert and be careful with whom you trust. Not all is as beautiful as it may seem."

Savara frowned. "I understand."

"You don't, but you will in time." He tried to reassure her with a friendly smile, but what resulted was something of a more sombre and melancholy nature. Before she could reply, he gestured to the half-open fold of the tent. "May this bring you comfort."

"You're not coming?" she asked, disheartened. Savara was beginning to enjoy his company.

"I must see to your friend. Besides…" He paused, considering his next few words. "This is something you must take in on your own."

"Hmm…" She sighed and took another tentative step towards the door.

"Oh, and Savara," Brass added with a smile. "Welcome home."

A cold shiver ran down her spine. His words burrowed themselves deep into her mind. *Welcome home,* he'd said, but she knew they weren't welcoming at all. They were a warning. She turned back to say something in reply, but he had vanished into thin air.

CHAPTER 14

NEWS FROM THE EAST

THE WINDS DIED in the small area surrounding the tent, setting it apart from the rest of the camp. The feeling of springtime dissipated somewhere between the main path and the entrance, as though it were something separate. A low pulse emanated from within, beckoning her forward.

Savara missed Brass' calming presence as soon as he'd disappeared, but she knew he was right. She needed to see this through alone. She placed her hand gently on the mesh, afraid something might jump out and bite her. *It's just a tent,* she reminded herself, and yet, her chest rose and fell faster in its presence. Behind the mesh lay real answers. *I need real answers,* she affirmed, taking a deep breath before forcing herself inside.

The mesh closed with a heavy sweeping noise behind her, blocking all light from seeping through. It took a few moments for her eyes to adjust to the new darkness. Savara blinked until the picture became clear, breathing a wary sigh of relief as she noticed the small precipice not more than two steps in front of her. She scanned the room for any other precarious pathways when she stifled a small gasp.

The outside of the tent had done little justice to its contents. The floor had been carved into the form of a rectangular pool to create the effect of grand, lofty ceilings. On every wall, shelves, and shelves of books, each one yearning to be touched by those who dared seek their contents. Savara likened the room before her to a darkened chapel. Until she noticed the stars above. They shifted and danced with all the grace of fireflies in an open field. Real stars. Galaxies even. No roof in sight.

Surely this had to be magic.

Savara managed to free her eyes from the enchanted ceiling and cast them downwards to a small trail of steps to her right that led down into the centre cavity of the tent. There, bathed under the light of floating blue orbs, sat a large table that reminded her of the story with the knights. Maps of all shapes and textures were strewn across it haphazardly, along with figurines and antique measuring equipment. The whole tent buzzed with an energy that made the feeling she'd noted earlier of the grass beneath her feet pale in comparison. Lost in wonder, she hardly noticed the three figures debating nearby.

* * *

"TRADESMEN FROM THE east bring word of trouble within the Ur provinces," she said coolly. Her fingers rapped

98

on the hilt of her sword, something Griffin noticed she did when things felt amiss.

Judging by how his friends positioned themselves on opposite ends of the table, Griffin knew the two of them had gotten into some sort of spat while he'd been away. *They always find something to argue over.*

"Great, more parties," replied their other companion sarcastically, picking ashes from his nails. "And who would be at the receiving end this time?"

"The Harri," she replied, directing the answer to Griffin, ignoring him entirely.

Definitely a fight, Griffin reasoned, but even without looking at Sebastian in the dim light of the room, he knew his friend's eyes were on her.

"They seem to be rekindling old hatreds," she added.

"They have too many of those already," Sebastian mocked. "They collect them like Simon collects pets. I mean really, they can't be serious."

Griffin noticed a small purple mark under his left eye. *Either she's hit him, or Simon has, and knowing him, he probably deserved it. He is always looking for attention in the wrong places.*

"It's not a joke, Sebastian," she scolded. "The Ur claim their feuds with the Harri should have been settled the old-fashioned way…" She softened her tone but gripped tighter to the hilt of her sword. "They are preparing for war."

"That's ridiculous. Even they know they can't take on the Harri. They'd be crushed as soon as they crossed inland." Sebastian tried to make light of the situation, but doubt tugged at his words. "Didn't they learn from last time?"

"They think that last time wasn't settled the way it should've been… That the Izar should have stayed out of it."

She lowered her voice. Griffin knew what she was about to say before the words left her lips, but it didn't make the blow any less wounding. "And they're probably right."

"That kind of brooding is dark and stormy even for you, Stormy my dear. Don't your people try to avoid confrontation?" Sebastian replied, raising a flirtatious eyebrow, tired of dancing around her attention. "Sitting high and mighty on those clouds of yours…"

"Test me, Sebastian. I'd slit your throat in a heartbeat."

"Oh yeah?" Sebastian replied, a provocative smile growing on his lips.

Griffin ignored their current spat. He was more interested in the ramifications of a war between the Ur and the Harri than yet another quarrel between two people who somehow couldn't keep their hands off each other's throats but never quite managed to kill each other.

Sebastian is right, he thought. *The Ur stand no chance against the Harri troops on land, and they know it, so why the risk? Unless they think there's some way they could win…*

A stray insult snapped him back to the meeting at hand. Griffin realised it was time for him to intervene before they mucked up his floors with blood and ash. "That's enough," he called, still unfazed by their bickering and death threats.

"Grif, I don't think you truly appreciate the irony of your moderating," said Sebastian.

"Oh, believe me, Sebastian, I appreciate it, but Izar or not, I'm still in charge of your sorry carcasses, and I'd rather not have to clean your blood from my floors," Griffin replied with a soft smirk.

"Who said it would be my blood?" Sebastian scoffed, but a simple glance in Storm's direction, at her murderously cold glare, made him relent.

Griffin rested a pensive finger over his mouth and chin to stifle a proper smile. "That's why."

"That's fair." Sebastian shrugged.

"Now, if the two of you don't mind, I'd still like my report," said Griffin as he gazed at the maps in front of him.

Sebastian picked up from where Storm left off. "The Ur may have ties to the Argia mafia, meaning they wouldn't stand alone, but anything that comes close to Zerua territories would bring them in, and your Izar friends in Yozora would jump at the chance to assert dominance. Let's face it, Grif, if they do decide to make good on their threats, the entire world will go to war."

"The world is already at war, Sebastian," Storm growled. "Or maybe you Argia don't see much from behind your pint glasses."

"Very funny, Stormy my dear. Tell me, did the wind decide to ruffle your feathers today?"

"You forget, Sebas, that the uprisings began after what happened at the palace, by no fault of my own or my people."

"*Forget*, Storm?" He stood up forcefully. "You *forget* that it was *my* people whose homes were destroyed, whose crops were burned, and whose palace was laid siege to…" As he counted them off, little flames shot from his nostrils with each forceful exhale.

"Don't get hot-headed with me, Sebas," she threatened, hand ready on the hilt of her sword.

He ignored her and continued his rant. "Or were you Zerua too high up in the mountains with your heads in the clouds to notice?" A bright burst of yellow light appeared, and from within it something twinkled. Sebastian shot her a coy grin under the new and shifting light. His accusatory tone became provocative. "Drop it, Anika. You don't want to start something you can't finish."

Storm had drawn her blade. The refined piece of metal glinted under Sebastian's throat, reflecting in the cloudy grey of her irises. The movement was as quick and natural as a bat of an eyelash.

But he too was quick.

Sebastian had drawn a dancing yellow flame that burst into life in the same instant she'd moved. It hovered gently above his right palm, illuminating their faces: hers, as though begging for a reason to let the blade slice through him; his, egging her on with yet another unnecessary smirk.

"Sebastian, so help me I—" she began.

"If you two have finished your lover's quarrel," Griffin interrupted, his voice mildly irritated. Storm snarled at the words, but he ignored her. His tone sliced easily through the tension of the room, silencing the war being waged before him, as it had done many times before.

Storm pressed the blade a little deeper into his neck in warning. Sebastian winked, teasing her efforts. They both knew that Griffin would not allow spilt blood in his room. Storm rolled her eyes and stowed her sword. Sebastian's flame evaporated into nothingness, taking the light with it.

"Good," Griffin continued. "I apologise for having kept the two of you in the dark, but I had to take care of this business on my own."

The two shared a glance of irritation.

"We aren't stupid, Griffin," Sebastian pointed out. "There had better be a good reason you didn't want us involved."

Griffin nodded. "I got word from an old contact of my father's claiming he was in possession of something that might explain the current state of the world. I couldn't be sure it wasn't a trap, so I said nothing. I managed to get my hands on some travelling dust and crossed…"

Smack!

Griffin raised a hand to his throbbing jaw. He smelled the sharp, metallic tang before he saw the red droplets on his hand. *At least she's as quick a hit as ever,* he thought, knowing both his silence and his actions had earned him Storm's strike. One of the rings on her fingers had drawn blood—the same finger she now wagged disapprovingly at him.

"If you ever try something like that alone again, you'll be lucky if all I do is break your jaw," she hissed.

I know, he thought, holding back a smirk that would've earned him another whack to the face. He cast a glance over to Sebastian, who only shrugged.

"If she didn't, I would've."

"I know what the consequences would have been, but I didn't cross *entirely*," Griffin clarified.

"Do you mean to say there are still gates?" asked Sebastian. The little flames in his eyes glinted in the darkness. "I thought they were all sealed up."

"Not gate. A prison of sorts, belonging to our world, residing in theirs. Fair game for jumps, though, technically, still illegal."

Sebastian took a seat, staring up at him concerned and intrigued, while Storm continued to brood silently.

Griffin knew it would be hard to convince them of the necessity of his actions. Expecting their resistance, he pulled a glistening dagger from his coat and embedded it easily into the wooden tabletop. The blade was made of hardened shadow, the white-gold hilt bedecked in blood-red diamonds. Storm and Sebastian held their breaths as they stared at the glittering marker of death.

"I believe there are other players in this game. Thankfully, my efforts were not in vain. Sadly, I lost my contact," continued Griffin, ignoring the luring calls for attention from the ornate dagger. Trinkets like this one—the ones from the old world—played their own games, conduits for Iturri that lusted after blood.

"*Them?*" asked Sebastian tensely, pulling his eyes away from it. "Are you sure?"

Griffin nodded.

"How can that be?" asked Storm. A frightening realisation crossed her face. "I thought *they* were a myth."

"I thought *they* died out…" added Sebastian.

"Neither I'm afraid," Griffin replied. "*They* are very much alive. From now on, we must be twice as vigilant. I don't know how they managed to escape, or why, but I can't help feeling they are responsible for the recent massacres."

"Grif…" Sebastian began cautiously. "What exactly did you retrieve from the other side?"

Storm nodded in agreement and added, "What was so important that you'd risked your life in crossing?"

"I," he began, but paused, finally noticing her lingering presence near the entryway. *How long has she been here? And what has she heard?* Griffin wondered. "Not a what, a who," he said finally, still ruffled by the fact that he hadn't noticed her

CHAPTER 15

UNCOMFORTABLE TRUTHS

SAVARA CROSSED THE shadows and stepped into the light, noticing the heated stares from Griffin and his companions on her skin. She'd been listening in on the conversation as much as she could, but from Griffin's stifled surprise, she could tell that it wasn't meant for her ears.

"Fine," she replied with a bite of her lip. "Sorry for interrupting... I can come back later."

"No." He forced a half-smile that looked too stiff to be earnest. "We were just about done anyway," he added with a sharp glance at his companions.

"Brass told me you wanted to see me?"

Griffin wasn't the only one that made her nervous. Neither of the voices she'd heard before sounded particularly inclined to friendliness, and if there was a war to be had enter. Griffin recomposed himself and inclined his chin towards the entrance. "Nice to see you're up and walking. How are you feeling?"

As the three of them turned to face Savara, he rested a steadying hand on Storm's sword, advising her that the girl in the doorway was a friend—or, at the very least, a guest. He knew Storm would be hard to sell on the idea of a newcomer, but that wasn't a battle for now.

between them, the last place she wanted to be was caught in the middle.

"Yes. Please, come in." Griffin raised his hand slowly, and in turn, the lights in the room came to life.

She caught the gasp in her throat as she remembered Brass' words, *keep a low profile*, but there it was again—the rush, the electricity in the air, that feeling of magic. The hairs on her arms stood on end. Savara wondered whether they could all feel it as she did, if they had simply grown accustomed to the sensation, or if her time in the other world had made her more sensitive to it. Like a sobered alcoholic drinking after many years of abstinence, the sensation was intoxicating… dangerously so.

It didn't take her long to realise that the room contained no lamps, candles, torches, or light-emitting devices of any kind, only glowing orbs hovering around it that seemed to brighten like little suns and dim into extinction. The gentle blue glow that cascaded over everything reminded Savara of the times she'd spent snorkelling by the reef, but the three sombre-looking figures at the centre of the room reminded her less of the playful turtles she'd swum with and more like the predatory barracuda.

The light shifted hues. The watery blue faded into a soft turquoise before settling on a relatively cold white. Shadows bounced around in the darkness, and under the new light, she recognised the calculating glint in Griffin's eyes. The feeling of being caught in a lion's den nagged at her again. It suddenly dawned on her that, whatever these orbs were, they came from him. It didn't take her long after to realise that he was one of those people her uncle had cautioned against in his stories, the ones who stole light. She hoped the slight upward curve in his lip meant he was happy to see her, but something told her it may have just been a calculated charm.

In the newly illuminated room, her eyes caught the figures of the two voices she'd heard earlier. Savara would've hardly believed that the rather petite woman with a whip-like braid of deep red hair had brandished the threats she did if it weren't for her piercing glare now. Her narrowed eyes, rimmed to a catlike point with charcoal, irises a storm-cloud grey, looked as sharp as the blade at her side—and equally as deadly.

Savara didn't need to feel the strange attacking energy to know the woman distrusted her. The woman's gaze said it all. Her hand gripped tightly to the hilt of her sword. The only thing stopping her from launching an attack was Griffin's hand. He might have stayed her hand, but he didn't take the glower from her face.

Savara shifted her gaze over to the final companion, having to raise her chin slightly to meet his eyes.

He was taller, much taller than the woman. A mostly well-groomed sort of man with curling blond locks that fell just above his shoulders and a matching beard. Amber-coloured eyes glowed against sandy skin, reminding her of a bronzed Viking—and only slightly better dressed. He stood proudly, crossing his muscled arms over his broad chest, playfully aware of his good looks. Warmth emanated from him like that from a fire. This set her on edge. Savara knew better than most that there were two kinds of fire: the one that crackled merrily on a cold winter's day, and the one that wiped out forests. His eyes consumed her, as though she were kindling feeding his fire.

"Storm, Jakaus," said Griffin, dismissing them both.

"But it looks like the party's just getting started," said the Viking with a not-so-casual curl to his lips. A new warmth prickled over her skin. The temperature of the room raised slightly. A sensation hardly noticeable to most, but then, Savara sensed a fair bit more than most. He was playing at the border of the two types of fires, she just couldn't tell which side he stood on.

"Out," commanded Griffin, leaving no room for debate on the matter.

The two people bowed to him and made for the door. The woman left without so much as an acknowledgement of Savara's presence, while the man made a point of stopping before her.

"We'll be seeing each other again…" he said as he placed a light kiss on her hand. "…soon," he added with a wink, dipping his head to her as he left. She regarded her hand hesitantly. The feeling of his lips on her skin made her think again about the kinds of fire she'd experienced in her lifetime, finally reaching a single conclusion. Fire is fire, whether it warms you in the winter or burns down the woods, both leave ash in their wake.

Her eyes followed the two of them out of the tent where she caught a glimpse of them whispering heatedly to each other before the heavy mesh dragged itself shut. She could've sworn that they'd both looked back at her in the last instant.

"Please, sit," Griffin called to her from below.

The same feeling that had beckoned her inside called to her now. Savara descended the trailing staircase with stiff, hesitant steps, avoiding his gaze but keeping him in sight. He'd traded the cloak for a long-sleeved leather tunic, the scar on his chin in full view.

I am not leaving without my answers, she told herself, muting the expressions on her face while her hands trembled behind her back.

Savara settled into a stiff, old armchair that used to belong to someone much bigger than her. Her eyes danced around the room, actively avoiding his own. She felt the heat of his gaze on her skin as it brought a fluster to her cheeks. He studied her, scrutinized her in silence. Inside her, the pressure of her anxiety was building. She looked around for something else, something which might take away her nerves.

That's when she saw it. The dagger.

It glittered eerily in the dark, more at home in this world than in hers. If she listened closely, she could almost hear it whisper, gentle and soft, like the final sounds of a lullaby. Where had it come from? And why did it call to her?

"Water?" Griffin asked, snapping her out of her daze. He held out a glass towards her, stopping the questions from forming on her lips. The sounds disappeared as she turned to face him, but deep in her bones, she knew there was more to it. And that more had something to do with her.

Savara nodded, taking a firm hold of the glass. The water flowed like silk over her sandpaper lips. Not even the purest spring water back home could compare. She finished it in one go with her eyes closed, weak to the taste, down to the last drop. When she opened her eyes again, she found him still taking her in from beyond the rim.

"More?" Griffin offered her the pitcher.

Too embarrassed to answer, Savara shook her head.

"I owe you an explanation." His voice was calm in a way that shouldn't sound threatening but did.

She rested the glass gently on the table, taking him in with sceptical eyes. "Where are we?" The words she'd wanted to demand came out feebly. He played it off as though he didn't notice, but from their last meeting, she figured there was little he didn't.

He raised an eyebrow in challenge.

She heard a call, a faint voice from the depths of her mind. "…Visanthe?" Savara felt something click inside her, like pieces of a jigsaw snapping into place.

"You remember nothing of this place?"

"What is there to remember? I've already told you; I grew up on a small island in the Caribbean. No magic, no powers… Nothing out of the ordinary." Savara held on to the base of her middle finger as she recounted her story. "But… This place feels familiar, for some reason. I…" She was grasping at fragments of the past, but none of them consoled her. "Why?"

"In time. Have you always done that?" Griffin asked as his eyes dropped to her hands, watching as they danced around her middle finger.

"I—What?" Savara looked down at her hands and nodded. She hadn't even noticed she was doing it until he pointed it out. "I think so…"

"Curious."

"What is?"

"That particular spot holds great significance for Visanthians. It would be an uncanny coincidence for you to latch on to it in such a way were you not one of us. Don't you agree?"

"I don't understand," she replied, sitting on her hands to keep them from fidgeting—and him from watching.

"Here in Visanthe, there are six nations. The *Harri*, people of earth, can manipulate it to their liking. So too can the Argia, people of fire, the Ur, people of water, the Zerua, people of air, and the Izar, people of light. There are limitations, of course, and not all those who belong to these nations can… But you can consider that a basic explanation of the powers. Then again, enlightened people will always find new, unorthodox uses for their powers…"

"And the sixth?"

Griffin tensed. The lights around them dimmed as he frowned. "As a rule, we don't talk about *them*. What little is known speaks of them as creatures of shadow, of nightmares… of blood."

The cold word slipped with finality from his lips. Though she wished to press him for details, she could tell there were none to give.

"The abilities we have are not innate, they can between birth and the age of twelve in the form of a small mark like this one," Griffin continued as he searched for something on one of the many makeshift shelves in the room. He returned with a palm-sized lens which, when placed above his hand, illuminated the markings that branded him Visanthian. The one he referenced was about the size of a fingernail, nestled in the centre of his wrist, and made of seven overlapping circles. It glowed white under the lens.

"At the age of twelve, the children with this symbol are gathered in a ceremony we call Ring Divination, which activates their powers and leaves a scar—a mark of the cycle you are bound to, and thus, the powers you receive." Griffin offered her his hand, which she took cautiously. He raised the lens over her middle finger. In the exact spot she touched when the world didn't seem quite right, a small, violet circle appeared. "There is no question. You are from here."

He rested the lens on the table beside them and glossed over one of the scattered maps.

Savara craned her neck to get a better glimpse of it. The map was old, worn, browning in parts, and torn in others, but for the moment it held up. It covered the grand expanse of the world, even going as far as to colour the regions by what she assumed to be power cycles. Initially, Savara counted only five marked regions, or so she thought.

At the topmost centre of it, a portion had been purposely covered by dark, swirling clouds, hiding whatever lay beyond that point. Five regions and a whorl of shadows. Whoever created the map must have wanted to mark the danger of the zone. If the map was even half as old as it seemed, she imagined that generations since its creation had been equally as puzzled by—and fearful of—what lay beyond as she was.

"The small isle in the middle is a place where time stands still. There are no seasons and no changes in weather. And yet, the day the world began to change, it rained," continued Griffin, grazing the map with his fingertips, "and I don't believe the two are unrelated."

"What does all this have to do with me?"

Griffin opened his mouth only to close it again, seemingly at a loss for words. The veil of knowing lifted from his face, softening his features, and revealing someone just as in the dark as she was. Savara preferred this new face, a face that didn't withhold schemes. *This face*, she thought, *might be worthy of trust. Might.* Sadly, it meant he didn't have the answers she needed. Savara let out a defeated sigh, beginning to regret having come when he spoke up again.

"How old are you?"

"Eighteen."

"In theory, you must have been divined six years ago."

"Why in theory?"

"I remember every divination from the last fifteen years." The full intensity of his gaze rested on her now. "I *should* remember yours. I do not."

"So, you forgot. I don't see what the big deal is."

"The *big deal* is, I don't *forget*."

Savara furrowed her brow. "I don't follow…"

"That year, twenty children were set to be divined. I only remember nineteen. For a long time, I'd just assumed I'd heard wrong, but now, I'm not so sure…"

CHAPTER 16

FAKE MEMORIES

"SO, YOU THINK I'm some mythical, missing child?" she hissed. Nothing about the story consoled her. Not his insinuations, not his calculating gaze.

"It would at least explain what a child from this world was doing in that one," he said. "Something which I can assure you is not common."

"But it doesn't explain why I can't remember anything at all."

"No… It does not." His brows knitted together. Even he seemed troubled by the idea. "Though I can't speak to your loss of memory, I might know where we may find if not answers, at very least clues."

"I still don't understand why I would've been sent away when my parents died. And to an entirely different world?"

Griffin avoided her gaze. Savara sensed his guilt rippling in the air around him. "Your parents weren't dead then. At least, not both…"

She blinked. It took her a moment to process what he'd said. All this time, she'd grown up thinking she was an orphan. What if she wasn't? What if she was just unwanted?

"That doesn't make sense. Why would parents send away their child? Did they not want me?" Savara recoiled, pushing herself further back into the chair. Her face grew red, holding back the pressure of anger and tears. She turned away from him, realising she could no longer meet his eyes without wanting to cry.

Griffin reached over for her hand again, this time patting it gently between his. "Your mother did it for your protection." He pulled a letter from under one of the maps. "Here," he said, resting it in her hands. "It explains why. Why she thought you needed to be protected, and what she thought may become of this world if not…"

"Protected?" she whispered.

Griffin nodded. "It also mentions what should be done if something should happen to either of you there. Hyrum was aware of his task."

"Has everything in my life just been one lie after another?" she growled. The words tasted foul on her tongue. "Why make me believe I was all alone in the world? Why send me away?"

"You were twelve, Savara. There were things you didn't know—couldn't know. If you had stayed, you would've been killed, or worse. Sooner or later, someone would've come for you. Is that the life you would've chosen for yourself? You should be happy." The softness in his voice turned to bitterness while a vein pulsed steadily at his temple. "You were sent somewhere you could grow. Somewhere you could live unaffected by all of this. You were *protected.*"

"I didn't ask to be protected!" she yelled. Somewhere in the darkness of the room, a bird ruffled its feathers. "Let's stop pretending. I've heard enough lies to last a lifetime… And imagine, in my case, that's not just a figure of speech." Savara rolled her eyes and began to storm off when he caught her firmly by the wrist. She flared her nostrils furiously at him.

"I apologise," he said, releasing his grip. "They were wrong to have left you in the dark." He searched for the words to ease her pain. "I would have given you the choice like I did when bringing you back."

"Maybe Jasper was right. It wasn't a choice at all." Savara wanted her words to sting, for him to feel as rotten as she did, to hurt as she did. She knew it wasn't his fault, but the people who made the decision in the first place were no longer around and she needed to take it out on someone from this world. Some vicious part of her hoped it would make up for the anger, the frustration, the emptiness. It didn't. It only hurt more.

"Savara, you don't believe that."

"Who are you to tell me what I believe?"

"No one," he replied with a sigh, "but I do know what it is to hurt. To let hatred fester and consume you. Whatever you may feel now has nothing to do with how you felt then, and back then, I saw a panicked girl with very few options. Be honest with yourself, knowing what you do now, would you have chosen differently?"

Savara didn't answer. She didn't want to give him the satisfaction of being right, but in her heart, she knew he was. He could've told her she'd be made to work picking up animal waste and she'd still have said yes if only to escape that house, the corpses, and the life that no longer existed.

"Why am I here, Griffin?" Her eyes had grown red holding back tears of anger that she wouldn't let fall. Savara had no idea how much time had passed since she'd entered the tent, only that her very soul ached.

"Unlike what you must imagine, you weren't unloved. Quite the contrary. Your mother was too smart, too cunning to have sent you away on the mere threat of an attack."

"How would you know?" She scowled at him. "What do you know?"

"I knew her, once," he said, though she could tell he was holding out on her. "I knew you all…"

Savara could tell there was more to his involvement in her story than he cared to share. She didn't press the issue, but she didn't trust him either. He was a man of his own convenience, always looking over his shoulder, always planning his next steps. He was dangerous, and she'd followed him blindly. Savara felt her stomach recoil. Everything she'd known, everything she thought she knew, was a lie.

"Why then would she send me away?"

"I was hoping you might know."

"I've already told you, Griffin, I don't remember anything."

I do, called a voice from somewhere across the room. The sound was so faint that Savara almost mistook it for the rustle of the tent walls. *I do*, it whispered again. Savara's eyes fixated on the glittering shadow blade embedded in the table.

How easily it had pierced the wood, how easily it would pierce other things, she thought, though it worried her that such a morbid thing should cross her mind. It didn't entirely feel like her own thought, but it had happened in her head. The rage in her cooled, replaced by curiosity as the same sinister voice rang in her head, *I see you, I feel you, take hold and I'll heal you.* Savara blinked, wondering if she'd truly heard it speak when the voice came again. *I know you, I'll show you, take hold and see what I do.* Savara reached out to touch it, entranced by its strange calling, but Griffin stepped between, staring back at her with a furrowed brow.

"I know," he whispered. "I hoped a trip to your homeland might jog your memory," he replied. "To *your* home." The whisperings stopped abruptly. Behind his back, the knife disappeared.

"Again with this home thing," she groaned, trying to peer behind him to get another glimpse of it. He made irritatingly sure that she couldn't see past him, that *he* should be the focus of the conversation. "How can you even be sure there's anything to find?"

"I'm not. But it's the only lead I have. It's the only way you'll truly get your answers."

Savara met his eyes again. They looked sincere, as did his frown. He was just as in the dark as she was. The little part of her soul which had wanted to click in to place hadn't. There was still something out there for her to find, something more to know. Her feelings of not belonging had not entirely gone away, and in part, this gave her hope. Maybe she had been called. All she knew for certain was that here, wherever here was, she was on the right path.

Still, there was one thing she needed to know if she ever had the slightest hope of trusting him. It hadn't sat right with her from their first encounter, and it didn't sit right with her now.

"Tell me one thing first. The day we met, you called me by my name. How did you know it?"

A smile tugged at his lips. "I said I didn't remember your divination. I never said I didn't remember you."

CHAPTER 17

SCAR TISSUE

IT WAS ONLY the abridged version of the tale, he assured. He was alone in the woods and hadn't noticed the creature stalking him. When it pounced, claws met skin. She arrived out of nowhere. She intervened. Somehow, she'd talked it down.

Savara had thought the entire story unbelievable until he showed her the scar.

Three long ridges streaked across his back where claws had torn through a leather tunic. Grazing her fingers over them, the energy of a fresh wound fluttered under her touch, as though beneath the uneven skin the original pain still bubbled.

A picture formed in her mind of a creature—a horned wolf with golden brown eyes—snarling at a bleeding young boy. Savara imagined how she would've approached it; three times her size, the putrid scent of its warm breath blowing over her in huffs. She imagined what it would've felt like to pass her hands over its plush brown fur, her tiny fingers disappearing into its coat, and finding them guided to a lodged arrow. She imagined the strength it must've taken to pry it from the beast's neck, and the sound of it clattering to the ground, surrounded by droplets of warm blood. In her mind, the beast huffed forcefully in her direction, turned on its heels, and raced back into the forest.

But she hadn't just imagined it, had she?

Savara was sure the image would stop there, but then a man appeared, outrage and fury plastered across his face. At his side, another boy, who looked around the same age as the young Griffin, trembled. A thin gold circlet sat atop his brow.

Griffin prickled away from her touch, realising she was not just imagining things; she was seeing them. Somehow, Savara had tapped into the memory held within his scar. A vein pulsed at his jaw as he looked over her again, as if seeing her for the first time… and somewhat frightened at what he saw.

"Was that… a memory?" Savara asked, still reeling from the strange sensation.

"Yes," Griffin huffed.

Her fingers recoiled from his back and the buzzing in her palms began to fade. "How?"

"I don't know."

"What was about to—"

"Nothing," he growled. "Get out."

Savara tried to meet his gaze. He'd cleared his face of all emotions, but she could sense apprehension rippling from him.

"Griffin… Are you okay?"

"Get out, Savara."

Savara had no idea what she had done or how. Judging by his sharp shift in mood, she could tell Griffin didn't either.

"Right," she said as she bit her lip again, realising that this was the end of her visit. "I should check on Jasper anyway."

"Just go."

Savara shuffled nervously to the door, taking one last glance at him before crossing into the blinding sun outside. She waited just outside the tent, staring at her palms, remembering how it felt to tap into his memory. It had seemed so real, almost as if she were there—but then, she was there. Wasn't she? Maybe she was able to tap into it because she'd lived the same moment, only, she couldn't remember it.

The tent walls rippled behind her. Savara wondered if she should go back and apologise for… whatever had happened, but she didn't know where to begin. For the time being, she decided it was best to leave it be, at least until she figured out what she'd done and how…

***

IT WAS ONLY the abridged version of the tale. Griffin hadn't meant for her to see the rest. All he'd wanted to do was give her a glimpse—a brief snippet of the memory—to prove he was right. He stared at the flap in the tent where Savara had just been.

The whole thing came back as though it were yesterday, pouring from him like blood from a fresh wound. Griffin bathed himself in the solitude of his room.

Am I that weak?

To his great disgust, he could almost hear his father's voice say *yes*.

* * *

HE NEEDED SPACE, needed to breathe. After the argument, he couldn't stand to be in the same room as his father. Trying to be the perfect son was not enough—had never been enough. He'd stormed out of the building, walking as far as his legs would carry him. In his heart he knew not even that would be far enough.

Griffin was respectful, quiet, and, having devoured every book in his father's vast library—and more—no one was more studied. Adept in every fighting style originating from Yozora to Iliso, he was the perfect soldier, hailed by his father's old war buddies. He was even divined Izar for Iturri's sake! And still, his good-for-nothing father was sending him away.

The swarm of thoughts had taken him further than he'd imagined. The palace gardens enclosed him in a world of green. Beyond lay the darkened hollow of the forest. He didn't usually wander this far out, but it was as good a place as any to sit and think. Far enough away from his usual haunts that, if someone came looking, they wouldn't find him. They might even panic for a bit. *If they came looking,* he sulked. Who would come looking for him?

Griffin plopped himself down on the grass, unsheathed his sword—the ancient piece of glowing steel the only gift his father had ever given him—and began to sharpen it. He glowered at his own sorry reflection in the shining metal of the blade. People said he had his mother's eyes. If only he could've seen them in real life. Many a time he'd imagined what life might have been like if she'd lived.

A loud *crack* sounded from somewhere within the woods. Griffin froze.

"Who's there?" he called, jumping to his feet. With a relaxed grip on the hilt, he pointed the sword towards the sound and called out again. "I know you're there!"

If there's one thing his good-for-nothing father had made sure of, it was that he could defend himself with a sword. He gripped the hilt firmly but kept the slack in his wrist, easing into the weight and feel of the blade as he waved it before him.

Hand too tight would make you slow, hand too loose and you let go, he remembered, hearing his father's voice in his head even now.

A large shadow stretched out along the floor in front of him. A low growl and a slow crunching of leaves followed it, emanating from the dark depths of the forest. Its snout appeared first; slobber-coated fangs bared. Next appeared a heavy brown paw, each claw a blade protracting into the moist soil. The rest of it stalked into the light. The horned wolf was twice his size, its horns alone were about the length of his leg, and almost as thick.

"Stay back," Griffin said nervously. A flash of steel cut through the air in front of the beast. It retreated a step but came back stronger. It swiped at him, knocking the blade from his hands. Maybe he'd held it too loose. Griffin scrambled over to it. He was fast, but not fast enough. The beast landed its attack. Sharpened claws met tender flesh as they tore open his back and part of his chin. *This is it,* he thought. Who would hear if he screamed? Who would mourn if he lost? Who would miss him?

Lance, he reminded himself. *Lance would.*

As if remembering that gave him strength, he rolled over just in time to dodge another thrash of claws. He wouldn't be so lucky twice. He forced himself to stand and looked around for the quickest escape when, out of nowhere, she appeared.

Not just any she. Her speckled eyes glistened like those of a doe caught by lamplight. She held her hand out in front of her and hushed the beast, lulled its rage, and stayed its paw with only a look. Whispered words fell from her lips into the creature's ears. It growled threateningly at him. To her, it paid no mind. Her gentle hands managed to stroke its side, getting lost entirely in its fur.

After agonisingly slow seconds of her whispering, she ripped something from its neck and sent it clattering to the ground. *An arrowhead.* Lodged in its side and restricting its breath. Griffin stared blankly at the discarded piece of bloodstained metal.

The creature had come looking for help…

It huffed a warm breath and turned on its heels, galloping back into the darkened forest. She looked back at him and smiled innocently, as though none of it had happened.

"You're hurt," she said with a frown, watching the spot where the creature had disappeared as she spoke. "What were you doing out here? Did you get lost?"

"No, your grace," he replied with a low bow, made painfully difficult by the slits in his skin. "And it's nothing," he lied. The wound was deep. The curl of flesh rubbed against whatever scrap of tunic remained on his back.

She gasped at his open back. "You need help."

"Thank you, Your Grace, but no."

"Please. Call me Savara. I… don't like the title."

"I apologise, your grace, but it isn't done."

The young Savara sighed. "I know."

"What have you done?" shouted the hardened, disgusted voice of his father. Griffin held his breath, waiting for the barrage of insults that he knew was coming. His father never held back when it was time to attack, verbally or physically. "You sorry excuse for a soldier. You are sliced through."

From behind, Griffin spied another boy, long and lanky with a mass of rippling strawberry blond curls held steady by a golden circlet. His amber eyes looked troubled. *Lance.*

Griffin wouldn't meet his friend's eyes—he couldn't, not even for a second. His father's anger he could take, but the expression on his friend's face—the fear in his eyes—hit with more force than any of his father's lashings. Griffin stood at attention, keeping upright through the pain as he waited for his punishment. His father was about to dole out another metal-plated slap when he finally noticed his son's company. A white-hot fury boiled in his father's eyes that Griffin had never seen before but knew to fear above all else.

"You endangered the princess," his father hissed.

"No, sir, he didn't," Savara interjected.

"Pardon, Your Grace." His father bowed respectfully at the child, but there was no hiding his fury. "But this is not your place to intervene. Your life was put in danger by my foolish son. I apologise for the error of his ways."

"Your son saved me," she lied as she looked up at him. Griffin's heart skipped a beat. *She lied.* A *royal* lied to save him.

"Without him, I might not be here, sir." But they both knew it was the other way around.

"Savara, come here," called Lance, looking to protect his younger sister from the tyranny Griffin's father was about to inflict.

Savara frowned. "No."

"Now," he replied and glowered at her in a way that meant she too was in trouble. The two of them peeled off and headed back for the palace, leaving Griffin alone with his father.

Griffin held his breath, refraining from moving even the smallest muscle. Nothing that would make the punishment worse. His father made no movements either for an excruciating length of time. He simply glowered at his ward—glowered and calculated. Finally, after minutes of silence, he spoke up.

"You are leaving. Tomorrow. And that's final." With that, he was on his heels, following the two children back up to the palace without so much as waiting for his son's response.

* * *

…THE OWL COOING somewhere in the darkness of the tent cast the horrid memory from his mind.

Griffin knew he shouldn't have snapped at Savara the way he had. It wasn't her fault. All the tentative trust he was building with her had crumbled. At least she'd agreed to visit Osiir. It would've been impossible to get into the palace without her.

Griffin waved the thought out of his mind and turned back to the table. He twitched his fingers, bending the light around him and bringing the menacing dagger back into view. Its glittering rubies and shadow blade mocked him. It had been a long time since any such object had surfaced, and it was hardly a good omen. The secrets it held could prevent wars, but there was a good chance uncovering them might start others. It was a risk he had to take, especially now that his fears were confirmed.

It could have been worse, he thought as he contemplated its blood-red glow. *She could've found out who she was before time.*

CHAPTER 18

A RIFT

SAVARA'S STOMACH GROWLED. It might as well have been eating itself with the noise it made, but she didn't register this growl—or the five others it made since leaving Griffin's tent. Her mind was elsewhere; lost in the idea of the memory she'd seen but didn't own. Staring at her hands, she wondered what exactly she had done, how she could repeat it, and whether she should.

The scent of food snapped her back to the present. It sauntered around her, leading her to a half-opened tent that buzzed with activity. As she pushed through the mesh door, she was immediately assaulted by the most exotic and delectable smells to ever grace her nasal cavity.

All around, people laughed and drank as they shared some of the most tantalising meals Savara had ever seen or sniffed. As she pressed on further into the tent, she spied the man and woman from Griffin's tent, surrounded by a small group of people who seemed to be sharing jokes.

"Sebastian," called one of the men. "What do an Argia and a shot of bad whiskey have in common?"

Sebastian grinned. "They both burn all the way down," he said winking at his friends. "Isn't that right, Storm?"

"Not interested, Sebas," Storm growled.

"Just wait, I've got a good one. Why can't the Zerua stay in one place?" Storm scowled at him, but Sebastian paid no attention. "Because they're always gone with the wind!" The entire table erupted with laughter, but Storm was not impressed. When Sebastian finally noticed her unease, he tried to make amends by adding, "You can laugh too, Storm. It's just a joke."

Storm tossed an entire stein of whatever she'd been drinking on him. "You laugh, Sebastian," she hissed, tossing the empty glass to the ground. The crowd fell silent as she stormed out of the tent, fuming. Once again, the table erupted at the sight of a dripping Sebastian. He barely registered them. He smiled politely and promised more jokes tomorrow but worry lined his face. He breezed past everyone, including Savara, and out of the tent after Storm.

On another table, Jasper poured over the book she'd taken from her uncle's library as he shovelled food into his mouth. His brown, mousy hair spilt over the front of his glasses in messy curls. Occasionally, he'd flick his head to move them, only for them to fall in the same place.

"Jasper," Savara called, beaming at him.

Jasper almost dropped the book onto his plate in shock, but his smile was as bright as ever when he caught sight of her. "Sav!" He jumped to his feet and pulled her in for a breath-restricting embrace. "I was worried about you."

"I was more worried about you," she replied in short huffs. Her stomach rumbled between them.

"You sound like you haven't eaten in days," he said with a laugh, sending her off for food and demanding she not return without a three-course meal.

When she did return, plate piled high with multi-coloured meats and vibrant vegetables, she found him, nose deep in the book, eyes flitting quickly from one end of the page to the other, engulfed, entranced, and unaware of his surroundings.

A smile crept across her face as she remembered the many times he'd done this before. Back then, he was just a boy with his books and she, a girl pretending magic existed. *Those were easier days.* Her smile evaporated as the memories of her uncle's stories resurfaced. Images of Jasper facing off against people who might freeze him or burn him alive flooded her mind. Suddenly she wasn't so hungry anymore.

Sliding into the bench and depriving her stomach of sustenance for a few seconds longer, Savara contemplated her friend and the effect this world was already beginning to have on him. His skin glowed a richer hue under the light of the Visanthian sun. An air of excitement surrounded him.

Maybe him being here isn't all that bad, Savara concluded. Hesitating to make herself known again, she tucked in quietly, but the taste of the food woke her soul, making it impossible to stifle the "mmm" that arrived on her tongue.

"It's good, eh?" Jasper grinned from over the edge of the book.

Savara laughed. "It's like…"

"A hot bowl of granny's lentil soup on a cold day?"

"Like jumping from the rocks at Windward beach."

"Good one! Or what about coming home to a made bed after a twelve-hour shift."

Jasper didn't realise how right he was. *More like coming home after years*, Savara thought, unwilling to continue the comparisons. She took another bite to hide her growing frown.

"You look good, Sav," Jasper said, a blush creeping under the bridge of his glasses. "Not like that... I mean... you always look good, but..." He exhaled defeatedly. "Rested. I meant rested."

"Thanks," she replied half-heartedly, but after her dizzying conversation with Griffin, she felt anything but. "What about you? I left you sleeping." She took another bite and added, "What have you done all day?"

"I woke a little while ago. I got worried when I didn't see you, but I met this guy who said you were out and safe, and that I was safe and should get out. Nice guy. Few words but speaks volumes."

"Brass." Savara giggled, remembering her similar encounter with the curious medic.

"That's the one. Anyway, he showed me around the camp, and we got to talking..."

Jasper recounted the conversation in detail, feeling that it was, thus far, the highlight of his day. He explained how he'd taken the book from the house and how Brass had asked him about it when returning his things. Apparently, not many people could read those books. The old language had been out of use for centuries and few could translate it.

"But I can," he concluded, grinning vivaciously. "I cross-referenced it with a few other ancient languages, and I found some promising similarities. I think I can translate it."

"Who would've thought…" Savara replied.

With the raucous in the background, there was little chance of being overheard, but Jasper leaned in as though he had the secret of the century to tell. "I know what I'm about to tell you is going to sound crazy but, hear me out," he whispered. "The book *called* to me. Voice and all."

Savara didn't know what exactly things from this world could or couldn't do, but if the knife in Griffin's room was any measure, the idea of a book talking didn't seem so far-fetched. That book was the last tangible memory of her uncle and their life together. Even if it had all been a fabrication, the time she spent there felt real, more so than this did anyway. Savara hadn't realised she'd stopped eating, or that she'd taken to pushing sweet peas around her plate with the end of her fork.

"How are you doing?" Jasper asked softly.

"I've been trying not to think about it all day," she admitted.

"You know, Sav, you're allowed to feel sad. Hell, you're allowed to bawl your eyes out if that's what you want," Jasper said as he reached for her hand. "You miss them. It's only human to feel sad."

But I'm not human, she remembered. Her fingers recoiled at his touch. "I'll be fine…" she mumbled, but tears had already begun to lace her lower lashes.

"You know you can talk to me about anything," Jasper assured her. "Talking might help——"

"Jasper, I don't want to talk about it."

"Well, maybe we could take a walk in the forest instead? Take your mind off things? Like old times."

He didn't get it. Nothing was like old times. A wave of anger she hadn't realised she'd been suppressing burst from her. "Drop it, Jasper. I said I'm fine!" she yelled. It came out louder than she had expected. A silence fell over the room. People started to watch them.

"I'm sorry, I didn't mean to…" Jasper let his words trail off as he removed his glasses to wipe the lenses. It was a façade; they were already clean. "What did you do today?" he asked, attempting to change the subject.

Savara kept her eyes on the plate, unable to meet his eyes after feeling the guilt ripple from him. "I met with Griffin," she replied softly. She knew she shouldn't have snapped.

"Oh yeah, him…" Jasper mumbled.

He began rambling about his apprehension towards Griffin and the bad feeling he gets around him, but Savara had zoned out of the conversation. She dragged the fork through the remaining sauces on the plate, drawing spirals and circles, hoping their twists and turns would replace the whorls of anger inside her. At least it gave her an excuse not to look into those big brown eyes again and discover she was becoming someone unrecognizable.

Monster, an airy voice hissed. A cold chill ran up her spine as she glanced around the boisterous room. Nothing but stray glares met her alert eyes. Several things in the room could've made the sound, the sweep of the mesh door, the rustle of feet, or the flap of tablecloths.

I'm imagining things, Savara thought, though not fully convinced.

"Sav?" Jasper stared at her, waiting for a response.

"Sorry, I… What did you say?"

Jasper sighed. "I asked if you got any answers."

"Oh…" Savara blushed. "Well, Griffin seems to think I lived here until I was twelve, and that I was sent away for my *protection*…" The word irritated her. What did she need to be protected from anyway? Jasper seemed to frown each time she said Griffin's name, which she found odd as Jasper wasn't usually the kind of person to hate without cause. For some reason, he'd taken an instant disliking to Griffin. "I mean, I guess the timing fits, it's just…" She shrugged. She was going to need a lot more answers before everything would start to make sense.

"What's wrong, Sav?" Jasper urged. The worry in his voice made her feel worse. It was exactly what she'd been trying to avoid.

She had never kept secrets from him, not once in all the time they'd known each other. If she admitted how troubled she'd been by everything—the deaths, the dreams, and now, a possible threat to her life—he'd fight to take her back. But she couldn't go back. Not anymore. There was nothing waiting for her there. Whatever was looking for her made sure of that.

"It's nothing, Jasper. Besides, everything Griffin suspects is based on memories I don't have. He wants to take me to the place I was born to see if anything clicks into place."

"Is that what you want, Sav?"

She didn't necessarily want to unearth the ghosts of her past, now that she knew it was darker than she'd previously imagined, but what choice did she have? The words poured from her in her frustration.

"I've been living a lie, Jasper. I don't know who or what I am. I don't know where I came from. I don't even know why I'm here now. I've been looking for answers that I don't know if I'll ever find, following this voice in my head that… I'm not even sure is mine anymore." Savara sniffled, feeling the welling of heated tears in her eyes. "I can't go back. Not even if I wanted to."

"Your life wasn't all a lie, Sav," he said, attempting to console her. "Your relationship with your uncle and Ms Short was real. Our friendship is real… I understand how you feel but—"

"How could you understand, Jasper?"

"I mean, I sympathize with you, Sav. I just don't want to see you get hurt, and you have this habit of not thinking things all the way through before diving headfirst—"

"Is that what you think? That I'm being careless?"

"I'm just saying, it wouldn't be the first time you got yourself into trouble because you didn't think things through. Besides, we don't know anything about this world, and that asshole is pushing you right into the middle of all its problems."

"It's my world too, Jasper, and so are its problems."

"As of when? Five minutes ago?"

"I don't expect you to understand."

"It sounds to me like he's using you, Sav."

"He's helping me, Jasper. Which is a lot more than I can say about you."

"Why do you think I came here in the first place?" Jasper replied, raising his voice. "This has nothing to do with me, and quite frankly—"

"You're right, this has *nothing* to do with you."

"Sav, that's not fair. All I've ever wanted to do is be there for you, to help you."

"I never asked for your help!" Savara yelled. The room quieted around them again. "And I never asked you to come." Before Jasper could reply, she got up from the table and stormed out of the tent, leaving him jaw-dropped and alone.

Help, a vicious little word. Everybody seemed to want to help, but Savara knew it wasn't worth the cost. Her parents' help got them killed. Her uncle's help got him skewered. Poor Ms Short had no idea about any of this and ended up the same. Jasper got himself trapped in a world that just might eat him alive. All of this was because she had no idea who or what she was. Now more than ever, she needed answers, if not to protect the last person she had any affection for, then because now, more than ever, she was alone.

CHAPTER 19

A CHARMER AND A SNAKE

THE SUN OUTSIDE had begun its slow descent across the evening sky. Forest creatures scurried back into their burrows to hide away from the night's evils. The wind let out a brief yawn before awakening to its full howling potential, rustling branches as it whistled through the trees.

Savara regretted the entire miserable conversation. Jasper was right: she didn't think things through, not even the words she spoke before they left her mouth. *No one asked him to come along and put his neck on the line for me*, she thought, trying to convince away the guilt of having snapped.

"You're quite the little hothead, aren't you?"

Savara jumped, startled to find the man she'd seen in Griffin's tent standing beside her, cross-armed with a smirk on his face and a towel in his hand. His blond locks drifted elegantly in the breeze. Parts of them were still damp from whatever shower he'd crawled out of. His movements were gracefully subdued, but his eyes sparkled with mischief.

"You heard?"

"I think my grandmother heard and she's in a cushy coffin the next town over."

"I'm sorry, I didn't mean to… It just—"

He raised a hand to stop her stuttering. "I don't think it's me who needs the apology."

"I know," she admitted softly.

"Meh, what do I care? Besides, he seems like a good guy. I'm sure he's already forgotten it."

Savara stared at her feet nervously. It was the first time she'd shouted at Jasper, the first time she'd raised her voice and wanted it to hurt, but it didn't feel right. For that split second, as the words burst from her mouth, she didn't feel like herself at all.

"Sebastian Jakaus," he said, extending a hand. "We crossed paths briefly, but I never introduced myself."

"In Griffin's tent, I remember," she replied as she took hold. "You're Argia, right? I saw you holding fire."

He laughed a low, intoxicating laugh. Savara found herself staring at the curl of his lips, wondering how many people he'd charmed with that laugh alone. He tied his hair back slowly, making a clear show of brandishing the muscles in his arms. His movements seemed practised. He was too aware of each flex for it to be casual. It irritated her how cocky he was, and more so that it was working.

"Correct you are. I am Argia," he replied with a ceremonious bow. "That's why I empathize with your little show back there."

"Why do you say that?"

"Some people like to say us Argia are hotheads. I prefer to consider myself more… explosively expressionistic."

"Do you make a habit of twisting insults into idealised compliments?"

"Only when it helps my chances with the women doing the insulting," he laughed. "Not that there haven't also been attempts from the masculine hemisphere."

Savara rolled her eyes, unsure of whether to scoff at him or laugh with him. He was more self-absorbed than anyone she'd ever met, and yet she didn't feel the usual disgust at it. She figured he could talk glowing volumes about himself to a rock and convince it to fall in love with him.

"Has anyone ever told you you're incredibly full of it?" she asked.

"I tell myself that all the time," he said with a shrug. "I like to play hard to get."

"…With yourself?"

"Constant adoration can be tedious and no one else is capable of resisting my charms."

Savara rolled her eyes, finally reaching a limit on the amount of cockiness she could reasonably endure. She was about to march off in the opposite direction when he caught her by the arm. "Woah, slow down, Little Miss Serious. It was a joke, and those I do happen to be full of."

Savara could feel his vivacity crawling up her arm from where his hand met her skin. It felt as pleasurable as a warm day at the beach. She bit down the smile growing on her lips.

At least he's honest about how self-obsessed he is, she thought.

"Good," he said when she made no attempts to leave. "Now, you got a name, Sunshine? Or shall I just keep finding ways to remind you of your bright and cheery disposition?"

"Just Savara is fine," she replied.

"Hmm. Just Savara? I like it." He grinned as he turned her name over on his tongue. "So, Just Savara, where were you going?"

She hugged her shoulders. "Anywhere but here, I guess."

Sebastian turned from the dining tent to her, understanding blooming on his face. "If you're up for a bit of a walk, I can take you to the stables. I'm off to see my brother and I wouldn't mind the company."

Savara looked back at the dining tent, imagining the earful of questions she neither wanted nor knew how to answer. Sebastian seemed decent. At least if he managed to take her far enough away, she wouldn't feel as compelled to go back. She hoped the guilt would subside too.

"We don't even have to talk if you don't want to," he added.

"You won't ask questions?"

"Not unless you want me to."

Good. She nodded.

"Follow me," Sebastian beamed, extending his elbow in promenade, and waiting for her to take it. Savara raised an eyebrow at him. "Haven't met many gentlemen where you've been, huh?" He lowered it and began down the path. "Oh, and the grandmother thing? That was a joke."

"She's not dead then?"

"No, she is, but we cremated her," he laughed. "Traditionalists."

"Right," she nodded, pretending to understand what he meant.

Savara followed him along the twist and turns in silence. Occasionally, she caught him looking over at her as she admired the grounds. The curiosity sparkled in his eyes but, to his credit, he kept his word. No questions.

"This used to be my family's farm," he said when he'd clearly grown weary of the silence.

"You're a farmer?"

"Not anymore." A coy smile appeared on his face. "Though, if that makes me more attractive in your eyes, I'm happy to amend my statement."

Savara giggled.

"So, she does know how to laugh," he joked. "Progress."

"Charming," she replied sarcastically. She was grateful for the excuse to forget her troubles.

Sebastian shrugged. "Sometimes I can't help my natural magnetism."

"Do those lines ever work?" she asked, hoping to hear he'd struck out more times than not. Sadly, it was all too easy to imagine multitudes of women falling for the glimmering flames in his eyes and his tensed muscles—especially when he pulled back his hair. They might even flutter their eyelashes at his pearly white smile. Savara wrapped her arms across her torso, adamantly refusing to believe those things were working on her too. The blood creeping into her cheeks said otherwise.

"You'd be surprised," he replied with a wink. A stray curl fell from his hair tie. As he brushed it from his face, she caught him staring back at her with a look that meant he knew his charms were working. Embarrassed, she looked away as fast as she could, but that only made him laugh. "Don't worry, you won't have to suffer through my stunning conversational skills much longer. The stables are just ahead."

Pride alone kept her from admitting she was enjoying it.

THEY CAME UPON a large clearing beneath even larger trees, fenced in by stones that appeared to have sprouted from the ground into the shape of a corral. Under the dense canopy, it was hard to see without a light.

Sebastian snapped his fingers. A dancing yellow flame appeared above his palm, pulsing like a little heartbeat as it lit up the space around them.

"It still amazes me to see you control it," Savara said as she stared at it. "Can all Argia do that?"

Sebastian grinned. "It's like this with all the other elements. Any *kanala* Argia can control fire, but only a select few know the secret to conjuring it." He winked.

"Modest."

"Always." His lips parted into that fiendishly charming smile of his. "Though I do wonder sometimes where the fun in modesty is." He held the flame out in front of them to get a better view. She breathed a sigh of relief as she felt the cold shadows cover the blush on her cheeks.

Her idea of a farm and his idea of a farm were vastly different. Savara had imagined the typical farm animals, horses, pigs, cows, maybe even a few sheep, but was pleasantly surprised to be wrong. The stable itself seemed to be more like an enormous terrarium than a stable, with fences made to keep people out rather than animals in. At first glance, at least thirty-odd creatures shifted about beneath the canopy, but Sebastian assured her that many more were in hiding.

Savara stopped to admire a group of twig rabbits (jackalopes with twigs for antlers) as they pounded their feet on the ground, instantly creating large holes and darting through them. Sebastian insisted that many of the creatures had elemental powers of their own, explaining those of the few they could see before whistling into the distance.

The sound echoed through the cavernous space beneath the many intertwined branches. Curiously, Savara thought she saw a tree move towards them in response. As it entered the light, she realised it wasn't a tree at all, but rather a large moose-shaped creature with skin as rough as bark and moss growing in select patches around its neck, back, and head.

"This is Taffy. She's a moss-elk," he said, patting it on the side of its sturdy back legs.

The creature bowed its head. For a split second, Savara imagined she'd heard a voice say *hello*.

"Taffy," he said to the creature, laughing as it chuffed over his neck and nibbled his ear, "go drag Simon here, please. There's someone here I want him to meet."

The creature bowed once more and trod off slowly into the distance.

"She understands you?"

"When she wants to. We'll see what she brings back and then decide," Sebastian joked.

Savara rested her arms over one of the stone fences and stared up at the bioluminescent birds. Their nests in the branches looked like stars in an endless sky.

"Not even animals can resist your charms," she commented.

"You make it sound like that's a bad thing," he replied, leaning next to her. His voice was suave. She could almost hear the grin in it. "I'll admit I have an easier way with interaction than most."

"Again with the modesty," she mocked.

"No, that was honesty."

"So you assume," she said as she turned to face him, eyebrow raised in challenge.

"I never assume," he replied, returning the advance.

She leaned her head in closer. "You're a narcissist."

"I'll take that as a compliment," he grinned. His next words held on his tongue as complaints and insults began firing in his direction.

Taffy reappeared, holding a man by the shirt collar between her teeth. Sebastian pulled away from her and turned to the man and the moss-elk, leaving Savara to wonder what might have happened.

"Sebas, you could have called," the man grumbled.

"Yes, but this is more fun." Sebastian laughed with the lightness of the afternoon sun. Each time the warm sound left his lips, Savara noticed his skin sparkle. "Taffy, you can drop him now, thanks."

The elk opened her mouth and the man fell to his feet. As he straightened himself, Savara was surprised to find he looked almost exactly like Sebastian, aside from a neat pair of glasses perched delicately on his nose and a slightly different haircut.

"I'm going to give Flot your treats from now on," the man said to the creature. It chuffed and walked back into the distance. "Sebas, you almost got me bitten. I was devenoming the vipers. What do you want?"

"Defog your glasses, Si. We have a guest," Sebastian added, nudging him in his side. "Savara, meet my brother, stammering nerd and probably the best zoologist this side of Middle Isle, Dr Simon Jakaus."

He wiped a dirty hand on his shirt and extended it towards Savara. "It's an honour to make your acquaintance. And please, call me Simon."

Unlike his twin brother, Simon's smile was shy and friendly, as though he was unaware of his own attractiveness. Where Sebastian burned loud and strong like a firework, Simon glowed softly like the rising sun. He was less charred and scarred than Sebastian but kept fresh smears of dust along his forehead and arms. His golden curls were trimmed relatively neatly, sitting as though in a basket on the top of his head, dipping occasionally in front of his eyes. His tentative smile and hesitant nature reminded her of Jasper.

"Savara," she said, taking his hand. "How exciting it must be to be twins."

The two brothers exchanged horrified glances and then glared back at her. She wondered where exactly the insult lay in her statement.

"Sure, we might share a birthday," began Sebastian.

"...but we look nothing alike," added Simon.

"I mean look at him. He's hideous," said Sebastian, absolutely flabbergasted.

"Calm down. At least I have mum's eyes," Simon said, rolling minutely more tangerine eyes.

"Yeah, well at least I have dad's nose."

"...for trouble."

"Boys," she interrupted. Savara bit down hard on her lip to try and keep herself from laughing. She couldn't tell whether they were joking but, if it weren't for Simon's glasses and clothes, she would hardly be able to tell them apart.

"That's right, Simon. Behave. There's a lady present," Sebastian mocked.

Simon groaned and straightened his glasses again. "Why did you feel the need to interrupt me?" he asked his brother while rubbing a purple slash on the back of his hand. It looked deep and like it needed a good cleaning. Savara winced, making a point of keeping her eyes elsewhere.

"Griffin says to get Taffy and Flot ready. He wants to leave for Osiir tomorrow," replied Sebastian.

"Oh… It's been a while," said Simon disappointedly. Sebastian nodded, sharing in an understanding that she knew nothing of. After a long pause, he added, "They'll be ready at dawn. I've got to clear off some termites from behind Flot's ears, or else they'll get into the supplies." He sighed and pinched the bridge of his nose beneath his glasses. "I guess I'd better get started. It was a pleasure meeting you, Savara. If there's ever anything you need, my brother and I would be happy to help." He cast a knowing glance at his brother and added, "I have a feeling help will never be too far away."

Sebastian rolled his eyes. "You should get some rest if we're leaving so early," Sebastian said to her. "Come on, I'll show you to your tent," he added, ignoring his brother's comment.

Savara decided it was best not to get involved in sibling rivalries. She waved goodbye to Simon and turned back down the path. Sebastian turned with her and snapped his fingers in the air, grinning as his ears were met with the satisfying echo of his brother's chastising voice.

"What was that?" Savara asked.

"Nothing."

She stole a glance behind her and giggled as she saw Simon stomping out the blades of grass that had caught fire beneath his feet. Sebastian was trouble.

The walk to her tent from the stable was too short for any deep conversation, so they mostly talked about the people of the camp.

According to Sebastian, Griffin kept everyone in the dark until they needed to be involved in his plans—though, he made a point of noting Griffin's genuine care for those around him, and that his plans always had everyone's best interests in mind. Savara still wasn't entirely convinced but figured it was something she'd need to see for herself to believe. Brass, he noted, was a quieter soul whom he'd never gotten the chance to talk to at great lengths but assured her that any ailments she had—from the slightest cough to a gash down her chest—Brass could work miracles on. She decided she didn't want to know how he knew this and hoped she'd never have to find out.

"Sometimes I wonder if he isn't a witch in disguise," Sebastian remarked with a grin, provoking a giggle from her.

Simon, the twin who, in his mind, looked nothing like him, was too soft for things like war and violence but knew his way around almost every creature known to man. He was also the foremost expert on toxins, occasionally even using his brother as a test subject. Savara blushed, commenting that he'd probably deserved it. He nudged her in response.

Admiration twinkled in his eyes as he spoke about each of his companions. Savara sensed the love he carried for each one of them, like siblings in an unorthodox family. Through his words, she began to understand each one better, the way their different personalities fit together and the bonds that defined them. But his admiration turned into something more as they came to Storm…

"She hates me," Savara remarked.

"She's… cautious. Doesn't take well to new people."

"You mean, to people in general."

Sebastian shrugged.

"She's a bit of a bitch, and I don't know what I did to deserve it," Savara added.

"She can be a bit bitter," he agreed. "Slightly cold."

"About as slight as a snowstorm." The two of them laughed, but Savara caught a glimpse of longing in Sebastian that she couldn't quite place.

"Okay, so she's not the friendliest of people, but she's good people. Loyal to a fault. Brave too," Sebastian said with a slight bite to his lip. A faint blush crept into his cheeks and over his nose.

"Yeah, well, I'd still rather not be on the wrong end of her sword," Savara pointed out with a smile. Sebastian laughed, the sound crackling merrily from his lips and warming the cool night air. He made no effort to contradict her, and she doubted anyone who knew Storm would either. When Savara realised he wasn't going to make any further comments, she decided to change the topic. "You kept your promise," she said, poking at the embers in their conversation.

"I'm sorry?"

"You didn't ask any questions."

Sebastian smiled. "You asked me not to."

"You're not what I expected."

Arriving at her tent, he held the mesh open for her. "Maybe you shouldn't expect as much."

She swept her hair behind her ears, revealing the blush that had been festering inside her. "Thank you."

"Goodnight, just Savara," he bowed his head and strode off into the night. His blond curls swung behind him in tendrils like fading rays of sunshine as the shadows of the tents engulfed him. *About time too.* Sleep had caressed her eyelids for the better part of the past hour.

Inside she found a neatly arranged cot, a small writing desk, and a great wooden trunk that was just about hollow, spare for an extra set of clothes. Resting neatly on the top was the package, still delicately wrapped in its brown paper packaging and twine.

Savara sat on the bed and stared at it for a long time, imagining what it might contain, and who might have left it. After a while, she decided it was best to leave it tucked away and unopened. For some reason, she hoped keeping the mystery alive would keep her memories of the other world alive as well. When she couldn't keep her eyes open any longer, she blew out the candle at her bedside and huddled up under the covers.

Sleep consumed her. For the first time in a long time, despite the storm, the deaths, and the ominous clue to her past, her dreams were pleasant.

CHAPTER 20

THE PALACE

THE NIGHT'S PEACEFUL dreams felt like the break in a storm. Something new was on the horizon, and even her subconscious knew it. The morning sun broke easily over the tents, but Savara had not fully woken, even as she was ushered into the carriage.

Griffin hadn't given her much of a reason as to why they had to leave at the crack of dawn, only that it would be best to arrive under sleepy eyes. Whose? She didn't know, but if it were truly necessary for her to know, Griffin would've told her… at least, that's what she now hoped. His irritating habit of dealing in half-truths and secrets had been confirmed by Sebastian the night before. Somehow, it felt like he was keeping dangerous secrets from her, ones he really shouldn't.

The dawn sky and stillness in the air lulled her into a state between dreaming and waking. Her imagination ran free beside the carriage. Savara pictured stallions flying in flaming strides beside them. Each whip of their necks sent sparks into the air. She smiled at their frolicking. Suddenly, the angelic glow of dawn gave way to grey clouds. Thick tendrils of smoke slithered across the grounds beneath them. One by one, they snapped at the stallions, plucking them mid-motion from the clarity of day, ousting their flames. Out of the restless dark, a voice called to her.

Where are you hiding…

THE CARRIAGE HIT a stone in the road, jolting Savara awake with a small scream.

"Sav, are you okay?" said Jasper, reaching over to steady her from the seat opposite.

She blinked, finally wide awake. The shimmering rays of dawn had returned. There were no signs of shadowy tendrils or eerie voices. "I'm fine," she said as she waited for her heart to calm. "What happened?"

"You fell asleep," he smiled. "You glow in your sleep," he added with a blush as he pointed to the spots on her hands where the invisible symbols were. She hadn't noticed before that he wore her uncle's spectacles. He fixed them on the bridge of his nose and returned to the window. "I think we're here."

Savara pushed herself upright in the chair and looked outside. The rolling hills gave way to rooftops and sandstone streets below them. Under the warmth of the bright, orange sunrise, something cold lined the city, palpable from their ever-diminishing distance.

Cold, but familiar, she thought. *I've been here before…*

She slumped back against the seat and looked over at him again. He'd traded his clothes for a white cotton tunic and brown pants. He adapted quickly. More so than she had. Jasper gazed in awe at the world beyond the carriage, oblivious to her stare. He looked happier than she'd seen him in a long time. Some of the guilt lifted from her chest. The rest gnawed at her as she watched him look on in ignorance, unaware of the dangers this world held, especially for him.

"Jasper…" Savara began, unsure if to bring up their argument. She knew she should at least apologise, something along the lines of "sorry for snapping," but when he turned to her and smiled that lackadaisical smile of his, she knew he'd already forgotten.

"Yes?" he replied, his large brown eyes twinkling more than they ever did back home.

"Promise me you'll be careful."

"So long as you promise the same." He rested a hand on her knee and squeezed gently before returning to the window again, caught up in the charm of the new world.

Savara stared at him a little longer. He looked heroic under the shifting light; like the men dreamed up in fairy tales. In the back of her mind, she remembered what Brass had said about him. Whether or not he could read their language and learn their pasts, he still was noticeably different. And somehow, she didn't think different was a good thing.

The carriage slowed. Her smile faded. She looked outside at the sprawling streets below them, noticing a familiar pulse beating somewhere at the city's core. The feeling might have been familiar, but the place was not. All the thoughts that had taunted her over the years of not fitting in came back to her in an overwhelming succession. She may be from here, but she was just as much an impostor as Jasper was, only, she knew to fear it. Now, back in the city of her birth—the city she'd forgotten—she scarcely felt at home.

Something in the wind itself spoke of tragedy as it swirled through the expanse of the ruined town. It roamed where it pleased, blustering through open windows and doors, making curtains float like the ghosts of their owners. The back alleys were noticeably darker. Shadows had been taking up residence ever since the attack on the palace. This newfound darkness gave way to darker dealings and shadier slums.

Where are you hiding… the voice in her mind whispered again. The hairs on the back of her neck stood on end.

They were to part ways when they reached the outskirts of the city. Jasper and Sebastian were to look for supplies to bring back to the camp, while Savara and Griffin went to seek answers. She knew that Griffin had only agreed for Jasper to come along to keep him from doing something stupid—which is also why he urged Sebastian to babysit him. Griffin assured her that Sebastian would be the hardest person for Jasper to pick a fight with, seeing as he could singe his lips shut if necessary. Savara wasn't sure if that was his idea of a joke, but if it was, it needed serious work.

SAVARA AND GRIFFIN managed to slip through these slums mostly undetected. Griffin expressed his surprise at finding so little resistance and hoped that Jasper and Sebastian were having just as much luck as they were. Strolling through the vacant streets and hollow alleys, Savara sensed the eyes of the underbelly watching closely—that word of the arrival of cloaked strangers was moving quickly from house to house, making its way to unfriendly ears.

"It feels broken…" she whispered as she stared at the crumbling buildings and charred roofs. Everything around them was made of either sandstone or wood. In her eyes, it all looked like tinder.

"It wasn't always like this. Osiir used to be a beacon of light and hope when the monarchy was in power. It was smaller then," Griffin admitted. "Keep your head down," he added as they approached a man leaning against the wooden porch of a little ash-stained house, watching them intently.

Savara couldn't help herself. She sensed his glare on her skin. The man pulled a cigar from his back pocket, placed it in his mouth slowly, and sparked a light with his fingers. The small flame from the cigar cast grim shadows over the squinted, citrine-coloured eyes that sized her up. Griffin must have noticed the man too. He pulled her in close and quickened his pace. Behind them, the man exhaled a deep red cloud of smoke before vanishing behind a corner.

Each slow step brought them closer to what Savara could only describe as an off-kilter fairy-tale palace. Towers of marble traced by veins of ever-burning magma stood in such a way that, if the wind hit at the right angle, a melancholy song poured from their empty windows. The gardens had grown since the last inhabitants graced the premises. No more galas or banquets to require their trimmings. Weeds had become kings to kingdoms of rock and mud, hailed by the fallen petals of many springs. Stone by stone, grasses swallowed the paths, hungry to reclaim spaces they once owned. Ivy climbed the colder walls in a slow battle between earth and fire that earth was beginning to win.

"They say this palace was built on hallowed grounds," said Griffin as he approached the door. "An ancient power protects it, allowing only those with the blood of the House of Orrin to enter. It cannot be breached, invaded, or destroyed."

The emptiness around them hinted at the truth in his words, yet they were intruders. They dared step where kings and queens once strolled. They could've easily come to pluck the riches from the troves inside.

"Then, how did we get through?" Savara wondered aloud, but Griffin was already two strides in front of her and far out of earshot. The overgrown hedges and rusting iron fences guided them away from the darkened city and closer to the somehow more ominous palace. The word alone intimidated her. Griffin had promised answers from Osiir. She hadn't for a second imagined they'd be rummaging through palaces like high-class thieves. What was she expected to find there anyway? City birth records seemed too common to be kept in a palace.

"Are you ready?" asked Griffin, waiting expectantly with an orb of blue light hovering just above his palm. Though his body remained calm, his eyes brimmed with intrigue.

No, Savara thought immediately. She wished to run back to the comfort of her too-springy mattress in the stuffy, old room of the house that kept as many secrets as it did cobwebs. *How could anyone be ready for this?* And yet, a small part of her found itself battering against a cage in her chest she hadn't known existed. Her heart beat heavily for each doubt that filled it, thumping like a stallion against its corral.

Whether she'd wanted them to or not, the intimidating doors opened, beckoning them inside. If she'd been waiting for a call, this was it. If she ignored it now, everything—including her family's death—would've been for nothing. Savara gave in to the lure of the mysterious palace, finding a certain déjà vu in the silent swing of the doors and the hum of the air inside.

A faint, triumphant smile curled at Griffin's lips as he slipped through with ease. Savara took a deep breath and followed hesitantly, ushered further in by the echo of the door closing behind her that reverberated through the dark.

One by one, sconces came to life, illuminating the walls with blinding white flames. Savara shielded her eyes until they could adjust. At the far end of the hollow hall, a spiralling marble staircase led to the upper levels of the palace. To the sides, other halls led to darker chambers. Austere portraits lined the walls. Faces both old and terrifying stared back at them like guards at attention. The shifting light of the sconces brought life to their acrylic cheeks.

"Maybe there is some truth to those rumours after all." Griffin dropped his hand and let the little orb of light fade away.

"What do you mean by that?" she asked, letting her eyes wander around the room as she went about grazing every portrait gently with the tips of her fingers. The ones closer to the entrance were older; their figures, shadowed; their paint, dull but cared for. The ones in the middle were newer, envisioned by younger eyes, painted by younger hands.

She stopped suddenly.

Her hand hovered over one of the last portraits in the succession. The occupant of the glistening golden frame stared off into the distance, but nothing was too out of range for her glowing amber eyes. Under the tips of her fingers, movement stirred from within the portrait.

"Griffin," she called into the emptiness of the hall. "Who is this?" Something about the painting seemed familiar, like a forgotten tune resurfacing one note at a time.

Griffin appeared behind her and gazed up at the face in the painting. "You don't remember anything, do you?"

Savara shook her head. "That's what I've been telling you."

Griffin sighed. "This is the Queen of White Fire... your mother."

Mother... She slid her fingers over the woman's rose-painted cheeks. A wreath of gilded flames sat atop a head of blindingly golden curls. The woman in the painting was fierce and regal. A queen. *And I'm just... me.* Somehow, touching the painting created more distance between the person she was supposed to be and the one she felt she was.

The idea itself was ludicrous. Savara could barely organize a room, let alone a kingdom. Perhaps that was what Griffin wanted from her and her missing memories. To re-emerge from the mental fog and reclaim her place among the royals. To lead these people out of the dark.

He's got the wrong person, she thought. Her fingers recoiled. Her mother's eyes gazed on, but with shame bubbling away inside her, Savara could no longer meet them.

She followed the rest of the paintings down the hall, running her hands over their delicate brushwork, unaware of the similarity between her actions and those of another some weeks ago.

Arriving at the base of the staircase, she almost missed the final portrait. Under-lit and scorched through in places, the youngest of all the painted faces glared down at her with sorrow-tainted eyes. She imagined the child had been forced to sit for hours, enduring the dullness of having her portrait painted.

This painting lacked the gilded frames of the others, scorched and torn in an act of fury so great it emanated from the ripped curls of the canvas. But it was the way those weary eyes looked out at the viewer—searching—that made her bones quake.

She need not search her memory for this figure; the charcoal eyes and their rainbow-coloured splotches told her enough.

Savara stared up at the portrait, wondering how long ago it had been painted, and why she looked so…sad. "Griffin, this is…" she began, but as she turned back to him, she found she was all alone in the empty hall. "…me."

CHAPTER 21

HIDDEN THINGS

THE DANCING LIGHT from the sconces cast shadows across the floors. Given the scene, Savara had almost expected to hear the strange voice from her nightmares. Thankfully, the room was empty. Despite the light surrounding her, a chill caressed her shoulders. She didn't want to admit it, but it reminded her of Death's cold grasp on the corpses she'd left behind. Ever since then, she'd begun to picture Death as a person, seeing as she could feel it with all the intimacy of a soul.

A warm glow flickered to life on one of the upper mezzanines. She couldn't tell if it was Griffin, but at least it was an escape from the hollow room and hollower gazes. She decided against placing her hand on the railings, should she incur the wrath of unknown bugs or spirits—or both—and began her ascent.

The palace might have been beautiful in its hay day—chandeliers made of sparkling crystal hung above reflective marble floors and opulent objects commanded attention at every turn from their various displays around the halls. There were libraries, studies, bed chambers, rooms for entertaining, war rooms—she passed them all. It was the kind of place you had a hard time forgetting. But she had.

The next corner she rounded brought with it a familiar scent of lilies and peach cream. It hung in the air just beyond one of the chambers. The room, elegant and teeming with grandeur, was a whale's length and twice its breadth. The master bedroom. Towering pillars of white marble on either side of the bed encased it in draping silk, making it look as intimidating as the palace itself. At the end of the room, she spotted a large armoire filled with billowing gowns of the finest silk and satin, all smelling of the same lilies and peach cream. It suddenly dawned on her that the smell she was so intimately acquainted with must have belonged to the mother she could not remember.

Savara pulled out an airy white dress with gold embellishments and cape sleeves that draped off the shoulders. She looked around hesitantly before stripping down and slipping into it. It was all too wide at the hips and slightly loose at the shoulders. Slits at either side made her feel exposed, naked. Her mother must have been a force to be reckoned with to don something so open with any kind of confidence. The dress itself felt like a hug, a hollow one, but a hug, nonetheless. Her reflection in the mirror looked hauntingly false, like a ghostly reminder of what might have been had things turned out differently. Swathed in silks whose luxury she couldn't have dreamed of, from a world she couldn't remember, Savara felt like nothing more than a house cat in the shadows of lions. She switched back into her tunic and travelling cloak and returned the dress to its tomb.

As she exited, she spied the door at the end of the hall, slightly ajar, though, she could've sworn it was closed when she'd first arrived. This new room was entirely vacant save for covered paintings that hung like ghosts from the walls. Particles of dust floated gently in the air like snowflakes that refused to touch the ground. Savara tried her best to not think of how much the dust smelled of ash—and not the kind left behind by burning wood. The room had a stagnancy about it that made her skin prickle. She thought of leaving when a light breeze wafted through the open windows and lifted the edge of one of the sheets free. She had no idea why she was compelled to fix it but, as she drew closer, part of her memory lit up. Instead of replacing it, she pulled back the sheet with the grace of a matador.

Had it not been for the experience with Griffin's scar the day before, Savara might not have believed it when the energy caressed her fingers. A flash of memory sparked through her mind like lightning racing amongst the clouds, just enough to make her re-evaluate the vacant room. She looked around at the rest of the paintings hanging under the ghostly sheets, stripping them down one by one until she found herself standing in the middle of the answer to the question she hadn't dared ask.

My room.

In a house that all would remember, her room begged to

be forgotten. Why? She wondered what it must have been like to live here. Would she have been treated well? With more food than she could ever eat, more clothes than she could ever wear, and servants to tend to her every need, would she have wanted more?

I'm the girl with the scrapes on her knees and the knots in her hair, she thought. *The people who lived here were cut out for royalty. Maybe that's why I was cut out.*

Had it not been for a shout of despair, she would have forgotten about Griffin entirely. Savara followed the lingering sound of the echo down the stairs, through another hall, and past an indoor magma garden until she came to a room lined with dancing white and yellow flames. The same magma from the gardens trailed up and down the walls, streaming through the cracks in the marble. Despite the fire around her, the room felt cold. The streaks in the walls felt like bars on a cage. She wondered how the royals of Osiir must have felt in such a room, whether they were truly the keepers of flame or its captives. At the opposite end of the room, a gilded throne sat between two grand windows. Griffin knelt before it, muttering something like a prayer, unaware she'd entered.

"Is everything okay?" Savara called to him, surprised at the way her voice carried through the room. "I heard you yell," she whispered.

"I didn't mean to startle you," he said, dusting the ash from his pants as he stood. He wore the same face as when he sensed something wrong back in her uncle's house. "I've just had my worst suspicions confirmed."

"Griffin, I know you're hiding things from me. Either you

tell me the whole truth or—"

"I will," he interrupted. "I just had to be certain before I made accusations…" He gazed around the room as he beckoned her forward.

Superstition, she realised. He'd told her before that something guards the palace, blocking entry to those without royal blood. And yet, something had managed its way in— managed to start a massacre under divinely protected ceilings. Maybe whatever protected the palace had changed sides, but if so, why were they let in? In any case, Griffin looked as though he feared the walls had ears.

"I am sorry I didn't tell you who you were before. I wanted to be sure we could get into the palace first. It never would have let us enter if you weren't her… the missing princess."

"You speak about it as if it were alive."

"I'm not going to repeat the mistake of thinking something this old isn't." Before she could prod any further, he launched into another one of his explanations. "It was important too that you came to see the place, in case it brought back memories, but after seeing you with the portrait, I think your memory loss is something more… purposeful."

Savara had never given much thought to the gaps in her memory. She'd wrongly assumed it had something to do with trauma, only the trauma she referred to had been nothing more than fiction, carefully woven into her head with just enough detail to keep her from wanting to remember. Now, standing in the place she'd spent her childhood—the one she imagined very differently—she was ashamed for having never questioned it.

"I believe your memories, and those of everyone at your divination, were taken, and I am almost certain it had to do with the rain." Griffin pursed his lips, straining his mind for a non-existent memory. With a heavy sigh, he added, "In the letter your mother sent, she said the shadows have awakened, and that they would hunt you down if they knew you were still alive. She'd taken your inner light so your nature wouldn't manifest outside of Visanthe. It was stashed somewhere safe, supposedly."

"Is that why he died?" The words strained her throat. Nothing about her uncle's death sat right with her. Thinking back, she remembered him looking out of touch on his last day. It seemed silly to think he might've known, but then, stranger things had happened since. "My uncle... because they thought he had my light?"

Griffin frowned. "That, or because they thought he had you."

Savara wished she'd been more surprised. Ever since the voices appeared, deep down she knew she was at least part of the reason. It might have been her fault he'd been killed, but she didn't wield the sword—she hadn't impaled him. She still needed to find whoever did it and repay the favour. Simmering anger woke something inside her. After all, revenge is a cruel but effective motivator.

"What did she mean by *the shadows have awakened?*"

Griffin's forehead crinkled, confirming the fears she didn't want to acknowledge. "She was talking about *them*, the sixth race," he whispered.

"The Arima?" The name sent shivers down her spine.

Griffin too had paled as the word left her lips. The same tingling feeling inside her nudged itself forward at the sound of it.

He nodded. "She must have feared they would come looking for her too…" he whispered as he gazed up at the throne. "She was right. It took them a while, practically six years, but I guess the shadows finally managed to breach the palace. They slaughtered her and the rest of the inhabitants. I didn't want to believe it, but after seeing the broken throne, I knew they hadn't come only to kill."

Savara followed his gaze to where the throne stood imposingly on a marble dais. The intricacy of the fretworked backrest made it hard to focus on any one spot.

"It doesn't look broken at all," she said.

"Trust me, it is. There used to be an orb at the heart of the throne, placed so that no one could see it when the king or queen sat wearing their crown. And before you ask," he continued, as if reading her mind, "No. It couldn't have fallen out. Nothing short of forceful prying would have moved it from its resting place."

Savara followed the intricate fretwork until she spied a notch at the heart of it that looked like it used to hold something small and circular.

"What was it? And why does it matter so much that it's gone?" Savara asked, looking back at him with eyes that had grown weary from taking in a past she'd never remember and a man who couldn't give her the peace of mind she needed.

In typical Griffin fashion, she saw the cogs in his mind turning the question around in his head. He squared his jaw, frowning as he searched for the right words, but it appeared there was no right way to say these. "It means the attack on the palace was just a distraction."

Distraction? Savara braced her arms around her torse, containing the shivers that ran incessantly up and down her spine. She couldn't even begin to imagine how soulless a person would have to be to commit such an atrocity. "They did all of that for a marble?"

Griffin furrowed his brow. It looked heavier now, laden with the weight of this new understanding. "Not a marble. Each nation, at the time of its inception, was given an orb to guard and protect. As is the case with anything of great power that disappeared, they became legends, but that doesn't mean they didn't exist."

"What's so important about them?"

"Each orb holds a primal energy," Griffin replied, processing the information as he explained. "Like infinite batteries. This one was the original fire, given to man by Iturri, the spirit of all power, and which was then used to light the bonfire of Osiir. In theory, the orb could be used to control the element without being divined."

"They want to control other elements?"

Griffin shook his head. "All this trouble for a little extra power? I doubt it." By the way his skin prickled, Savara could tell it was more than a little.

"I don't understand what this all has to do with me. They found their battery. You said they attacked long before they came for me." She could tell he was on the fence about explaining the problem to her, so she tapped her foot adamantly. "If something is after me, I have the right to know."

"They must have found wherever your mother stashed your inner light as well. Otherwise, we wouldn't have seen it when I collected you."

"I have powers then?" Savara's heart fluttered in her chest. "Like my mother? Like Sebastian?"

"I don't entirely know…"

"What do you mean?" Savara knew he was hiding something. She wondered what could've ruffled him so when a dangerous thought occurred to her. Part of her had suspected it, ever since she saw the glistening dagger in his room, ever since she began hearing the voices in her head.

Why else would they have sent me away? And why would someone be looking for me now, unless…

In his avoidance, she found her confirmation.

"I'm one of them," she whispered, afraid that saying it aloud would bring on a curse. Griffin maintained his downward stare as he pursed his lips. Doubt rippled from him. "I'm one of them, aren't I?" she repeated. "That's why you need me…"

"Why would you say that?"

"Answer my question, Griffin."

"Yes." He stared at her. "I believe you are."

"And you brought me back because of those powers; because you want to see what I can do, to know what you're up against. Right?"

"Savara, it's not like that."

"You want to use me as a weapon. Is that it? Your secret weapon," she growled. The anger swelled inside her, its heat throbbing below her skin. "Jasper was right, wasn't he?" She stepped away, needing to put distance between them.

"You're using me," she scoffed. "That was the plan all along! How could I have been so stupid?"

"Savara, I swear to you, I wasn't sure… I couldn't be sure until just now that you were one of them. I brought you back for your prote—"

"Protection?" she barked. The palace rumbled around them. "Don't you dare say protection! Not after keeping all those secrets. Look how many others tried to protect me— kept secrets from me—and look how well it turned out for them. What makes you think you'll end up any different? Besides, if my powers are so fearsome, why do I need your protection?"

Savara waited for an answer that would never come. She knew this of him already and yet she still hoped some part of him would give up this game. Maybe he was incapable of telling the full truth. Maybe his demons forced him to always seek the upper hand. Maybe he was right to do so, living in this world that played by other rules. Griffin was the one who'd promised her answers, and yet, of all the people she'd met, his were the least satisfying. Thinking back on all the people she'd met, Savara finally realised what had him—and her family—so troubled. The anger inside her subsided, replaced by something of a darker persuasion. She lowered her voice. "You're protecting everyone else from me."

He confirmed nothing. "If I had told you what I thought you were outright, you might have sought the information on your own… You might not have liked what you found."

"I don't like it now any more than I would've if I'd found out before."

Griffin rested his hands on her shoulders gently and

gazed into her tear-filled eyes. "I am not using you, Savara," he began softly, not necessarily ignoring the comment, but keeping the distance between it and him very much alive. "Nor am I afraid of you hurting anyone."

That makes one of us, she thought.

"The world is out of balance, and I think there's a good chance you have something to do with it. If they are back, you can be sure a war isn't far behind, and I will not let you become a pawn in their sinister game. So, like it or not, I am protecting you, and everyone else, from what I see as a threat to this world as we know it."

This truth brought her little comfort. Not being a pawn in their game meant becoming a pawn in his. Savara began to wish she'd listened to Jasper the day they made the jump. Maybe now they would've been at Skully's, passing the time with a plate of cookies and convincing themselves that just as much adventure lay in their world—no, not *her* world. *This* was her world. Savara shivered. Either way, if what Griffin said about people hunting her was right, she probably wouldn't have made it through the night.

"What is it that they—I—we—not that I'm like them…" She wasn't like them. She rejected the idea of being lumped into the nightmare that was *them*, but the question remained. "What can the Arima *do*?"

For what felt like the first time in their conversation, Griffin's words held no secrets. "Nobody knows. The ghost stories say they could reach into people's souls… Control their minds… Manipulate their humanity…"

But his words were marked by a questioning tone. He needed to know if she had been able to do anything similar.

Savara shrugged. Other than sensing people's feelings, there was nothing that seemed *extraordinary* about her at all.

"Griffin," she whispered, still processing the strange twist of events as a single tear slid down her cheek. She couldn't tell whether it fell because of her lost family, the world she'd inadvertently ruined, or for her own horrible sense of self-loathing, but she made no move to stop it. "You said that people were afraid of them… that they were evil." He raised an eyebrow. The question left a foul taste in her mouth. She could see the thought playing out in the back of his mind. Maybe that's why he didn't tell her outright. Maybe he'd already asked himself the same question. She pulled away. "What does that say about me?"

"You're not like them," he reassured her, but the sudden stiffness in his tone and shoulders told her that he wasn't so sure either. This new face of his—the hesitant purse of his lips, avoidant stare, furrowed brow—was by far the worst. She saw it most clearly in his eyes, the look of a gambler beginning to question his flush. "It's time we get back to the others. We must tell them what we've found here."

They retraced their steps, weaving back through the network of overgrown vines that used to be the royal gardens, Griffin with a swift-footed prowl, while Savara stumbled multiple times trying to keep up.

Their conversation had run dry after her question, but the silence didn't bother her. She was too ravelled up in her thoughts to notice.

Griffin's answer didn't comfort her, nor did his demeanour since. He and the rest of the Ris had built up the image of shadowy, bloodthirsty creatures in her mind, but

after finding out what she was, she wondered—no, she
hoped they were wrong…

CHAPTER 22

THAT FIRST WHIFF OF POWER

THE EDGE OF the garden bled out onto abandoned streets. The occasional shadow bounced around the edges of the houses in the shifting light of the residual bonfire. There was something unsettling about this town. *Her* town.

Savara could feel eyes on her skin, even if she couldn't see the faces they belonged to. Once upon a time, she would've been hailed the second she stepped onto the pavement. Now, she wondered if anyone would spare her a passing glance. One shifty back alley after another, she pulled the cloak she wore tighter, trying to become invisible.

At the edge of the final street, the same man from earlier leaned up against one of the ramshackle buildings. A little yellow flame danced around his fingertips, illuminating the fiendish curve of his mouth. Griffin tugged her in close and kept his head down, but the man called out to them just the same.

"What are two strangers like you doing in Osiir?" His eyes rested on Savara as he smirked. She retreated further into Griffin's guiding embrace. "It seems to me like you're looking for trouble."

"No trouble. Just passing through," replied Griffin calmly. "Don't look at him," he whispered to Savara. "He's mafia. Stay close."

The man thrust his hand out, sending flames from a flickering streetlamp towards their feet. A discarded piece of wood beside them caught fire. "We don't take too kindly to strangers passing through these parts," he said, the grin wiped clean off his face.

The smoke from the flames filled the air. The rising heat curled the hairs on Savara's arms. She turned to Griffin for guidance, hoping he could read the worry in her eyes without her having to speak it.

"Just keep walking," he whispered reassuringly. "I won't let him hurt you. Besides, the mafia only attacks when provoked."

"He is doing the provoking," she replied nervously.

"Just keep walking, Savara."

The man growled at them. Their ignoring irked him to the point of setting a nearby bin on fire. Savara linked her arm around Griffin's, keeping her face hidden under the shadow of her hood. The man's seeking gaze sent shivers down her spine. The grin returned to his face as he called out to them again. "It's funny, there's nothing in that direction but the palace, and as I haven't seen the two of you for some time, if I had to guess, I'd say you managed to get inside."

The coy hiss of his words meant he knew he'd made an important find. Two strangers with access to the long-sealed house of royalty, the constant reminder to the thugs and ruffians who claimed themselves the new kings of a dying kingdom that there was still someone greater than them. It didn't take a genius—which this man clearly wasn't—to know that this kind of information could fetch a hefty price on these streets. Griffin knew it too, which is why his grip tightened on her arm.

The man shot an arm out in front of them. No fire this time. No pleasantries either. "And ain't nobody gets into the palace unless they're some kinda important."

"You must be mistaken," Griffin growled.

"I don't make mistakes, Izar rat. You're not going anywhere," the man said, brandishing an evil grin as though unsheathing a sword. With a deep breath and a sweep of his hand, the man summoned the flames around them and set the rest of the path on fire. "An old acquaintance of yours wants you to pay him a visit. He's got two friends of yours waiting. The wimpy one didn't put up much of a fight, but you should've seen what we had to do to your fiery friend—"

Before he could finish his story, Griffin's temper exploded as Savara had never seen it before. Sebastian's words came back to her, describing his loyalty to his friends, and Savara got a first-hand look at what that meant. He launched a series of glowing orbs in the man's direction. Each one hit the ground with an echoing blast, sending dust and pebbles into the air. The man jumped like an acrobat, twisting in the air, and landing on a crate in the distance. He cracked his knuckles and grinned viciously.

"Come at me, you starry-eyed waste of light," he goaded. "I've been itching for a fight." The man sent bursts of flames out at their feet as he dodged each of Griffin's attacks. Flashes of orange and blue collided. Each blow hit something new—crates, windows, awnings—enclosing them within an ever-shrinking cage of fire. It was only a matter of time before the entire path went up in smoke, and them along with it.

Savara pressed back as far as she could without getting burned. One of the wall lanterns exploded above her head, sending her to the ground with a hard thud. Her vision blurred. She lifted her chin in time to catch the man grinning at her. He could've torched her then and there, but he saved his fire for Griffin.

Despite a ringing in her ears, Savara pushed herself to stand as fear coursed through her veins. She looked for something to help fight back, but anything loose was already alight. The world around them burned, and she was useless to stop it.

"What have you done to them?" Griffin demanded.

"I'd worry more about your fate than theirs," the man snickered with another elegant dodge. "It's her he wants. You'll go in dead or alive."

The dance continued. Windows and shutters around them crackled in the fire. With another blast, a pagoda crumbled on top of her. Charred wood rained down from above. The scent of ash filled the street.

Savara closed her eyes and threw her arms up in a panic, feeling the intimate caress of heat as she waited to be crushed by the burning rubble. The flames glowed red through her eyelids.

It was only a matter of time, she thought, giving in to the eventuality of her fate. In the fear of the moment, she hadn't noticed those seconds of silence. *Savara…* a voice called out. She couldn't tell whether it was real or in her head. *Savara…* it repeated with a nervous edge.

"Savara!"

Her eyes shot open. The fire crackled around her. Griffin lay propped up on an elbow calling out to her. Debris hovered around them, suspended in space, but it was the man who startled her. He hung like a puppet in the air, bent unnaturally, gaping like a fish on land.

"Please," the man whispered, the shifty slant in his eyes gone, replaced by fear. "Let me go," he pleaded. "I'll tell you anything!"

Griffin pushed himself to stand slowly and walked over to her. The sound of her own breath drowned out all the other noises as he neared. Dodging the hovering charcoal and broken glass, he rested a hand on her trembling shoulders, squeezed, and whispered tentatively, "That's enough, Savara."

The world came back into focus. Her palms buzzed. Suddenly realising what had happened, she dropped her hands. The man crumpled to the floor. Around them, the suspended debris finally hit the ground, sending a cacophony of shattering glass and crumbling stone into the air.

"What the hell are you, lady?" he said between coughs.

"I…" Savara stuttered. *Was that me?* The word *monster* echoed through her head, as though it had just been shouted to the world.

Griffin loomed over the man like the Grim Reaper himself. "Get up, you worthless piece of charcoal." He grabbed the man by the collar. "Now, you better start talking before I have her finish you off."

Finish him off? Savara recoiled. The sounds of the man's gasps etched themselves into the crevices of her mind, along with Griffin's words. *He promised he wouldn't use me as a weapon…*

Sweat beaded on the man's troubled forehead. "Alright, alright…" Fear swelled in his eyes as he glanced between Griffin and Savara. "Keep her away from me, and I'll tell you everything I know."

If Griffin had looked back at her at that moment, he might have seen her falter, might have noticed the pallor in her face or quiver of her lip. He'd practically called her a monster. Luckily, the man didn't look back either, or else he might have realised her secret: she was Arima, *Blood Daemon*, and she had no idea what her powers were or how to use them.

"We caught you two entering the palace earlier and sent word back to Big Tog. He sent us for you. He said if we couldn't catch you outright, we take the others as collateral."

Savara noticed Griffin prickle at the name the man had mentioned.

"Where did they take them?" Griffin demanded.

"You trying to dig me a deeper grave?" the man growled. "Look, it ain't my business to be telling you anything. If the gang finds out I told you any of this, they'll be on my ass hotter than a forest fire."

"I don't see how that is my problem," Griffin replied. With a flick of his wrist, a blade of blue light appeared in his hand, aimed at the man's neck. "Remember, light burns just as well as fire…"

"Okay, okay. Put that thing down," he replied, fearfully eyeing the light energy in Griffin's left hand. "They—"

But before the man could finish his sentence, the next attack came. First came a fizzle, a little spark somewhere in the distance. Fizzle turned to flame. Suddenly a great blaze whistled through the air.

Griffin jumped back just in time to avoid it. The man let out a bloodcurdling scream that echoed through the hollow streets as it landed on him. His body caught fire, burning as easily as paper. He pleaded to the invisible shadows of the city—begged his case, promised he didn't say anything of value—but it was no use.

In the violent commotion, two figures jumped down from the rooftops and grabbed Savara. They reeked of ash and old cologne. She tried to scream. They gagged her as soon as she opened her mouth. When Griffin tried to fight back, three more pinned him down. A thick cloud of grey smoke filled the alley. Through the dark, she heard Griffin cough and cough until he dropped. Savara squirmed as much as she could against their grips and bindings, but it was no use. The scent of ash curled the hairs in her nose, bringing angry tears to her eyes. Fear forced her to breathe in more smoke and fall prey to the mercy of the foul-smelling strangers.

Everything before her faded in and out through the haze as she slowly lost consciousness. The last thing she saw was the charred corpse of the man who'd attacked them settle on the empty street, as she and Griffin were dragged unconscious into the underbelly of Osiirian society.

CHAPTER 23

BIG TOG

WHERE ARE YOU hiding…

The voice whispered from the same dark crevices of her mind. It had called to her ever since she stepped foot in Visanthe. Savara began to wonder if it had something to do with her missing memories. Was it possible someone from her past was trying to reach her? To break through the seal on her mind? But the uncomfortable sound of the voice only curdled her blood. Memory or not, she couldn't imagine anything good coming from it.

Where are you hiding… It hissed again, dragging her back to consciousness.

The thick scent of black coffee filled her nostrils. It smelled like Death. The beans must have been burnt and the coffee over-boiled to produce such a pungent smell. It kick-started the rest of her body, speeding her resting heart as if she'd drunk it herself. She wiggled her bare toes over something plush.

A carpet? she wondered. *Where am I?* The last thing Savara remembered was the street erupting into flames and a writhing corpse, charred beyond the point of recognition.

With another heavy breath, she blinked open her eyes. The warm glow around the room burned in the back of her eyes, a headache not far behind. She tried to lift her hand to shield her eyes to no avail. Something tight ate into her wrists, locking them at her sides. No matter how hard she struggled, her arms wouldn't budge. As the haze in her vision began to clear, she spied the coil of ropes that bound her to the chair. She then remembered the capture.

Griffin sat beside her, stewing irritably about the metal clasps around his wrists.

"Griffin?" Savara whispered, still woozy from the smoke. "Where are we?"

"Don't worry," he replied. "I'll get us out of here."

"You'll do no such thing," said a deep and heavily accented voice from the other side of the room.

"Big Tog," scoffed Griffin, clearly acquainted with their captor enough to name him by voice alone. By the tone of his voice, she knew no love was lost between them.

"Griffin, my boy, how long has it been?" The man appeared from the shadows. He wasn't big in any respect—at least, not anymore, if the portraits on the wall were to be believed. The man in the paintings was as wide as an ox, with no accounting for height. The man before them was average-sized and more on the thin side. Two thickened braids of hair curled on either side of his head like the horns of a ram. His eyes glowed a vicious yellow.

"Not long enough." Griffin raised his brows. "You look like you've been through the wringer."

The man he'd called Big Tog cackled heartily. In his gaping mouth, Savara caught a glimpse of golden incisors.

"Wife has me on diet." He showed himself off like a butcher brandishing meat. "I told her no one would take me seriously without the weight."

"I'm sure you're more than capable of making them," Griffin snarled.

Big Tog grinned. His walk suggested he'd lost the weight in little time and hadn't quite adjusted to the new posture his body fell into.

"Too right you are, my boy. I'm sorry about the rough greeting, it seems my new boys have no class." He nonchalantly picked the remains of his dinner from his teeth. "Not like you used to."

"How about we skip the formalities? Tell me what you've done with our friends."

"Ah yes, them." Big Tog sat himself down at a wooden desk, kicked his feet up, and twirled a dagger that had been resting on it in his hand. "They will be returned to you once I get what I want."

"And what is it you want?" asked Savara nervously.

His eyes consumed her greedily like a starving wolf watching fattened sheep. "Funny you should ask, my little duck. My men spoke volumes of you. They seem to think you entered the palace. But that would be impossible… unless you happen to have Orrin blood running through your veins."

"She's none of your concern," Griffin warned. His fists clenched between the metal bindings.

"Griffin, my boy, I had great patience for you once, but you have long since used it up. I will thank you now to keep your mouth shut, or I will shut it for you." The scowl disappeared from his face as he turned back to Savara, replaced by a look of growing intrigue. "It seems you also scared them with your little display of power earlier."

The man in the alley, she remembered. The pulse of the man's heart, the shrivelling of his lungs in his chest. The sensations crept into her palms out of memory alone. The tingle of power prodded her to try again. It begged to be used. She wasn't surprised that the men were scared; she'd scared herself. Savara closed her palms, stifling their murderous tendencies.

"I will see it now," Big Tog added.

Savara furrowed her brow. "What do you mean?"

"You will give me a demonstration."

"It's not something I can just turn on and off when I please."

He stalked towards her with his hands clasped behind his back, scrutinising her every feature, taking a noticeable interest in her eyes. The smell of black coffee leached from him so much so that she wondered if he'd bathed in it.

"Who are you, child?" he said under his breath, squinting at her as though searching his memory for a face she knew he couldn't place. "No matter. You will show me now."

"Don't," Griffin growled, trying to pry his wrists free.

"You will be quiet," he snarled. "And there is no use struggling. You will not get out of those bindings unless I say so." With a snarky grin, he added, "You will find I learned my lesson from last time."

"You have no idea what you are getting into," Griffin replied.

"Precisely, my boy, why I must find out."

"She's not one of your cogs."

"No," he replied, running his tongue over the gold on his teeth. "I believe she is something of a much more interesting persuasion." Big Tog strolled over to Griffin, still twirling the dagger behind his back. Savara watched him wearily. It soon occurred to her that, if she could see the blade, that meant Griffin couldn't. Big Tog acknowledged her realisation with a smirk, loosening his grip on the dagger. The sharpened edge glinted in the candlelight as he raised it high in the air. It swung down, aimed at Griffin's heart. Griffin hadn't even processed the strike before it was inches from his chest.

"Stop!" Savara screamed.

It should've cut straight through his skin. There should've been a river of blood. The knife and the hand holding it hitched in mid-air an inch shy of Griffin's heart. Big Tog was caught in the same curl of power that she'd used on his lackey. Unlike his lackey, he fought back, pushing against her control. She felt it, the prodding of his soul against the contours of her power. His heart raced, intimately aware of her grasp on it. Big Tog grinned, the light around them distilled as it caught on his golden incisors. He released his push on the knife. In turn, Savara released her hold on him. With a theatrical flick of his wrist, he tossed the knife, embedding it in the wall opposite them, and stalked over to her once more. His yellow eyes sparkled with curiosity.

"Exhilarating," he breathed.

Savara refused to answer, knowing all too well what he meant. She'd felt him—all of him, every muscle, every vein, every heartbeat. He may have kept a straight face, but there was terror in him. The kind of terror that must have built up after many years of inflicting death and knowing one day his time would come. His time had come and gone; his life spared by no merit of his own. It lit a different fire in his eyes. Savara sensed it. Something new had woken inside him, something devious that reminded her of hope—but wasn't.

She couldn't bring herself to admit how much the feeling enticed her too. How it tried to coax her into using more—into taking his beating heart and stopping it, just because she could. If he wasn't afraid now, he was a fool. Savara had never been more afraid of anything in her life. Her powers had a mind of their own. They were bloodthirsty. It frightened her to think that, maybe, part of her was too.

"When they told me what they saw, I couldn't believe it. Naturally, I had to see for myself." He paced up and down, plotting something wicked. When the sinister grin returned to his face, she knew her fate was sealed. "I am a man of my word, child," he began. "I promised your companions would be returned to you once I got what I desired."

"Why do I get the feeling the demonstration wasn't *all* you wanted?" she mumbled.

"Smart you are, my little duck," he replied, pushing a stray hair back into his braided horns. "It is not much I ask, only a simple retrieval. You bring someone to me, I give two someones to you."

Griffin shook his head firmly. Savara was told not to trust, let alone make deals with, people here, but she saw no other option. Big Tog was cruelty and malice wrapped in a recently downsized bottle. She'd rendered him powerless, almost killed him, and yet, she knew he could still murder the pair of them before she batted an eyelash. After what she'd done, the power she'd shown, it was either help the devil or remain his prisoner—and even that would be a stroke of luck.

Savara frowned. "You swear you'll return them?"

"I'll do one better." Big Tog licked his golden incisors and grinned. "I'll take you to them."

"Why?"

"Don't think I'm doing you any favours, girl. It just so happens that our interests align for this *brief* moment in time." He turned up his nose. "So, do we have a deal?"

She ignored Griffin's protests. Big Tog was one problem she'd rather be rid of sooner than later. Jasper's life was in danger, and to her, that was more important than any favour she would have to repay. She closed her eyes and nodded, ignoring Griffin's disapproving glare on her shoulders.

"And so pretty boy here doesn't kill me later…" He strode past her. The casual clunk of his wooden heel on the plush carpet and then on the marble floor behind them made her shudder. He returned, twirling the dagger loosely in one hand. He took her face in the other. As he leaned in, she got another whiff of coffee accompanied strangely by a lavender oil he must have patted on his neck. Savara's jaw tensed in his hands. This made his smile grow.

"Such a gentle face…" He contemplated the youthful curves of it before pressing the blade into the top of her cheek. Savara tried to pry her chin from his grip, but he held firm, letting the blood trickle from the thin line onto the dagger. "It would be a shame to leave a greater scar." With great showmanship, he sliced through his palm with the other side of the dagger. He turned the bloody incision to both her and Griffin before waving it over a candle. "I, Andreus Tog

Larsen," he began. The flames jumped from the candle to his hand consuming it in a deep red blaze. "…vow to return you," he waved his other hand at her, asking for her name.

"Savara."

"Savara…" he repeated, the sound curdling her blood.

"And Griffin," she added.

Big Tog rolled his eyes. "…and this traitorous wretch, to your companions, unharmed, and without hindering in any way their rescue or safety, in exchange for your hand in my vendetta against the dark."

"She will not help you with any further power grabs," Griffin snarled.

"Some things, my boy, are worth more than power." The flames surrounding the wound glowed bright red then orange, flickering every colour of the rainbow until they burned black. When they disappeared, the blood had crystallised in the wound, catching the light like sinister rubies. "My soul, little duck, is bound to our promise. This wound will remain until the promise is fulfilled—or one of us is dead." He smiled and whistled for his goons. "Now, I must make good on my part."

The same scent of ash and old cologne wafted through the door before the men did. The brutes that had attacked them in the alleyway appeared at the door, toying with different ropes and blindfolds between their fingers. They dealt with Griffin first, covering his mouth against his violent petitions until all his struggling ceased. Savara watched him go limp in the chair as the men proceeded to exchange one set of chains for another.

She was next.

Big Tog stood up from his desk and placed a damp cloth over her nose. Coffee-ridden breath clouded around her as he leaned in close and parted her hair at her ear. As her vision blurred, he whispered, his voice a soft string of dulcet tones, his words less so.

"Don't you worry about the soul bond killing you, my little duck," he said as he brushed his finger over something hard on her cheek. "Because, if you don't make good on your part, I'll kill you myself before it even gets the chance." The softness disappeared. His wicked cackle accompanied her as the world faded to black.

CHAPTER 24

REGROUPING

WHERE ARE YOU hiding…
Where are you…
Where…
The wind rushed in cold waves around their trembling bodies, a harsh contrast to the warmth of the mafia boss' study, and yet, both were equally unsettling. The dark of the night had settled in around them almost an hour before, leaving them prey for all its evils. Once again, they'd found themselves tied and gagged. This time, however, the bindings were feeble, made to be broken with relative ease.

By the time Savara woke fully, Griffin had already set to work struggling against his bindings. A swift flash of blue light appeared at his fingertips, splitting the fibres of the rope behind his back. He worked on her next, his fingers dancing over her wrists carefully. She felt the occasional lick of heat on her skin as he sawed at the rope.

When freed, Savara's hand instantly drifted to the slice on her cheek. Instead of soft skin, her hand met hard stone. It was as though the scab itself had been forged from gemstones, sprouting directly from the skin. She tapped them, nudged them, and scratched them. They wouldn't budge. They were affixed to her cheek, permanent jewellery, harder than rock and the colour of blood.

Bile rose her throat at the thought. She remembered Big Tog brandishing his own matching slit, that thin line of blood-red stones, and the wicked smile on his face after the fact.

A tear slid from her waterline, around the stones, and down her chin. How would she fix things now?

"Griffin?" she whispered through the dark. "Is everything alright?"

Griffin stooped down in front of her, a small orb of light hovering just above his palm. He assessed the stones, with each passing second, his frown deepened.

"You bound your soul…" he replied. "Souls are not things to be messed with, Savara. Especially not to be bound."

"He had Jasper and Sebastian, I had to get us out—"

"You don't understand. When you bind a soul, you are obligated to fulfil whatever promise was made," he explained as he helped her to her feet. "Since you didn't specify your part of the promise, it's up to him to release you."

"What do you mean, release me?"

"I mean, if we get out of this mess alive, we have a whole other set of problems."

Savara was going to be sick. The stones weighed on her, as did their promise. She felt her powers prodding at them, as though recognising their foreignness. Perhaps she'd precipitated her decision. Maybe Jasper was right to call her out. But this one she hadn't made out of selfishness. That had to count for something. Besides, if she couldn't control her soul, who's to say anyone else would be able to either? All that mattered now was finding Jasper and Sebastian and getting back to camp safely before anyone else got their hands on them.

"Where do you think we are?" she asked, swallowing hard at the bile in her throat.

"Maybe a few miles from camp," Griffin replied as he gazed up at the stars. "Not more than two hours walk. If we start now, we can be there before daybreak."

Suddenly, Savara caught wind of something through the dark. A low, whimpering sound drifted into her ears. If she focused a little, she could almost make out a slow beating sound. Had it not been for her murderous powers, she might have missed it altogether. But the longer she paused, the clearer it became. It called to her the same way the wolf had in his memory. Anguish had reached out for something to hold. The thing inside her reached back.

A heartbeat.

"Griffin, there's something out there," she said.

"Savara, it's not safe," he replied, but her feet had already started away from him.

Pressure built inside her. A feeling of wrongness flooded her chest. Something was out there, calling for her. It needed her. She picked up the pace, brushing past trees and bushes. The feeling of anguish grew stronger, familiar too. Hints of pity and fear joined. They screamed at her, getting louder with each step. Whatever was out there was hurt, dying.

Suddenly, the forest let up. Savara found herself at the edge of an ominous clearing. There, the sensation exploded. Her heart dropped.

She'd found them. Beaten and bruised, Jasper and Sebastian sat, bound to each other, in a bucket of water that had turned both of their skins an icy shade of blue.

"Jasper!" she cried as she raced towards them.

Jasper lifted his head at the sound of his name. His swollen cheek forced his left eye closed, but his right eye sparkled as it settled on her.

"Sav," he whispered. "Where have you been? And what happened to your face?" Jasper's brow crinkled where it could at the sight of the bloodied gems on her cheek.

"Don't worry about my face," she replied, covering the slice with her fingers. "You should see your own," she joked as tears lined her eyes.

His breath was uneasy. A purple bruise bloomed from beneath the rips in his soaking shirt. They'd been tortured. Her trembling fingers hastened over the knots, but the ropes had swollen under the water.

This is all my fault... she realised, fighting back another wave of tears.

"Griffin," she yelped. "Help." Her voice was weak. The cry had barely left her lips, but it was enough for Griffin to come running.

Anger bloomed on his face as he caught sight of them. In an instant, his light had reverted into a knife. He set to work on their bindings, his worry tangling with her own.

"Sebas? Sebas?!" he repeated, catching hold of his friend as his bindings slipped away from his wrists. Sebastian fell limply into Griffin's arms. Griffin's grip tightened around him, his body shaking with anger. "They put him in water so he couldn't conjure," he said, his voice teetering on the edge of violence. "What else have they done to him?" he growled.

"They beat him up pretty bad," Jasper replied as he let his body fall into Savara's arms.

His skin was freezing. His heart was weak.

Savara helped him out of his shirt, cringing when she spied what looked like burn marks across his back. She averted her eyes, draping her cloak over him for warmth.

"Jasper, what exactly happened?" asked Griffin as he rested Sebastian on the damp ground.

"We went out looking for Simon's potions and some extra weapons. While we were waiting for you guys in one of the local pubs, someone came at us from behind. Next thing we knew, we had sacks over our heads, chains on our wrists, and knives at our throats."

"Do you know who did this to you?"

Jasper shook his head. "I'm not sure, but we ended up in a camp of some kind..." He reached into his pocket and pulled out his old, faithful glasses—the ones with the beautiful black rims that Savara hadn't realised she'd missed. He winced as he settled them on the bridge of his partially swollen nose and tried his best to recount everything that had happened. "There were other people like Sebastian in cages. I didn't catch everything they said, they spoke in a heavy dialect, but from what I could pick out, they'd said they were being shipped off somewhere. Something about a fight? I'm sorry, I didn't get much."

"What kind of fight?" Griffin urged.

"I'm not sure, but it's going to be big. They looked scared." Jasper himself had begun to tremble again. "I don't know if it helps but, the bandits, or whatever they were, were heading east."

"East? That would take them into the Harri provinces." Griffin frowned. "You said these people were like Sebastian? You mean, they could control fire?"

Jasper nodded. "But only the ones in cages. The others seemed normal—like me," he corrected himself. "Except for their leader. He wore these thick, leather gloves, which I thought was weird given the heat of the place, but he took them off once when he was talking to Sebastian." Jasper's voice went quiet as he stared over at the scorch marks on Sebastian's back. "He had lightning in his fingers."

Griffin blanched. His breath hitched. Savara was sure he knew the man that Jasper had spoken of, and judging by his reaction, they weren't on friendly terms.

"Oh, and there was something else." Griffin frowned. "They kept mentioning these…living shadows? Big red eyes and smoky bodies. Does that mean anything to you?"

Griffin was silent for a moment. His face was a mask of calm, but Savara sensed his heart miss a beat. "No," he replied, his word putting an immediate end to their conversation.

As Griffin tended to Sebastian's wounds, Jasper turned to Savara, shivering under the cloak. "Sav, you don't think those things exist, do you?"

Savara knew there might be something to the stories, even if she hadn't encountered any herself. Between castles that guarded themselves and objects that talked, she doubted there was anything this world didn't have to offer. Jasper was all hope. Innocent hope. She didn't want to be the one to break him, but she couldn't let him go on thinking there was nothing to fear. She shrugged. She walked to the edge of the clearing to wring out his shirt.

I don't know what to think anymore.

Another hollow gust of wind rounded her shoulders. The hairs on the back of her neck stood up. She had almost forgotten the thing that had called her over in the first place. When she first saw Jasper and Sebastian, she wondered if it might have been them, but no. This thing, whatever it was, was darker. It wore suffering like a tattoo. This was the anguish and pain she'd sensed. They danced in the air around her now. She sensed them the way a shark smelled blood in the water. And right now, it had her on high alert. Whatever it was lay just beyond the bushes. Its presence was overwhelming and—to her surprise—almost *human.*

"Sav, are you okay?" Jasper stuttered.

Savara narrowed her eyes in the direction of the sensation, but she was unable to make out anything. Eventually, she turned back to the group. Sebastian was slowly coming to. Griffin worried about how they were going to make it back in the condition they were in. She thanked the stars above that they were all alive, knowing it could've easily gone down another way. She made to return to them, but the tug of the strange presence gnawed at her. She was too focused on it to notice the curling of shadows beneath her feet.

The forest grew cold. The twinkling stars above them disappeared. The clearing darkened. The voice from her nightmares rang loud and clear in her mind as it said, *I've found you.*

CHAPTER 25

THE SHADOWS

"SAV!"

Jasper's scream pierced the air.

Shadows crept from between the trees. Humanoid figures with beady, red eyes made of living darkness stalked towards them. They were just as Jasper described. Their breath reeked of rotting corpses and ash. Their fleeting forms went from human to cloud and back again as they circled the group.

Savara's heart began to pound. All the fears she'd known as a child came flooding back; of being left in the darkened corners of the rickety old manor, trapped between shifty shadows.

A shadow can't hurt you, Ms Short used to say. *It can't see you, hear you, or touch you, Savara.* She would chastise Savara into a restless sleep. For all her high-horsery, Savara knew Ms Short would roll in her grave if she ever encountered these kinds of shadows.

A low hissing sound reverberated around them. The shadows transformed into curling fingers that stretched through the forest.

"Jasper!" she yelled. With trembling knees, she took a step towards him, freezing again as the shadows blocked her path. They formed a curtain in front of her, barring her from her friends.

Flashes of light bounced around behind it—the blue of starlight, the yellow of flames. None broke through. She was trapped. Alone.

A single creature began to take shape from within the curtain. Eyes as red as the bloodstones on her cheek, hands as spindly as spider's legs, an otherwise featureless figure stepped from the whorls of ash. The whole of its body was fluid, shifting from human to cloud with each second that ticked by. Savara didn't wait for an attack. She dropped the shirt and ran into the bushes as fast as she could. The sounds of her companions faded into the distance until they were nothing more than the tail end of an echo.

Tendrils of darkness traced the floors beside her. She hurled herself over a rotting tree trunk. They chased. She dipped under vines that hung like a hangman's noose. They gained. She weaved through the trees to escape their path, but each time they drew closer. Within minutes they were at her feet, snapping at them, taunting them. Their lick was icy against her overheating skin. She stumbled. They found their opening. Tendrils shot out, catching her mid-stride, and dragged her to the ground. Her scream sent birds flapping into the open night sky above, far away from the horrors of the earth below.

The darkness slithered up her leg, coiling itself around her like a snake, encasing her in the foul stench of burning skin. She struggled against it, trying to pry herself free, but her fingers caught only handfuls of black dust. Hot tears streamed down her dirtied cheeks. She tried to scream again, but the black dust covered her mouth and her ears. The cold smell of the damp forest floor faded into that of wet charcoal. The sensation of stones digging into her back disappeared. She caught a final glimpse of the twinkling stars above before the dust rushed over her eyes. For an instant, all was silent.

* * *

THE ECHO OF her heartbeat startled her. It consumed the emptiness of the space around her. Savara opened her eyes. The forest had disappeared. The trees, the ground, the sky, gone. She lay alone in a void.

Once, many years back, she remembered drowning. The sensation of leaving the world behind, slowly fading from it the way a film fades to black. She remembered struggling against crashing waves and the feeling of losing herself. She felt like this now. Beneath her, a cold, black stone. Above her, emptiness given form. A faint silver mist circled her as she pushed to stand.

"Hello?" Savara called into the void. Muffled voices echoed around her in reply. At first, it was impossible to distinguish any single one, but as they grew louder, the sound became clear.

"*Daemon*," they called in chorus.

"Who said that?" she called back, her voice echoing in the silence until it faded into nothingness. The horrible choir started up again.

"*Blood Daemon.*"

"This is… just a dream," she told herself, attempting to ignore the hunger in the voices that surrounded her. Their words grew louder. They repeated themselves, over and over, singing out the horrible word: *Daemon.* "I…" she began with a faltering voice. Salty cold sweat pooled on her upper lip. From somewhere deep inside her, a purple light began to glow. It traced the veins down her arms and covered her hands like spiderwebs. Savara felt a power she'd never known rush into her body, an intoxicating sense of strength. But then the light shifted.

Lilac turned to harsh red, taking with it her new strength and more. Savara tried in vain to shake it off as it trickled into her palms and down to her fingertips. Her veins burned as if they'd caught fire. She struggled to be free of the glow, fearing her skin would melt away.

The evil chorus continued to sing.

"No," she pleaded meekly. The light became bondage, severing connections between her muscles and her brain. It held her in place as something inside her took over. She tried to push against it from within, but it was no use. She was trapped like a ghost in a shell, clinging desperately to a physical sensation that no longer existed. She strained against the cage her body had become. If her heart were still her own, it would've sunk. If her eyes could still cry, they would've flooded. She let out a wail of exasperation into the void, expecting no answer. One came regardless.

A sinister laugh echoed, low and rich, not like the howling chorus before, but rather the voice she'd heard in every nightmare. Its hunger grew as it drew closer. A heated breath crossed the nape of her neck as the voice whispered longingly, *"I've found you…"*

Savara couldn't say whether it was fear or anger that pulled her back, but she dug down deep inside herself and clenched a fist. "I am not a daemon," she hissed, willing her own lilac light back into her body.

"You don't know what you are," the voice goaded. "It's killing you…"

"I know I'm not your pawn." She jutted her hand out in the direction of the voice. A wave of power rolled from the top of her head to the tips of her toes and then fired out from her palm into the void.

The world stilled.

Savara's hand trembled as she watched for the repercussions of whatever it was that she had done. Her heartbeat echoed once more. Away from the cues of the natural world, time stretched on. Not even her uneasy breaths told her how long she'd waited before something called back in agony. A yelp, innocent and fearful.

What have I done?

Someone called out her name, muted and distant. This voice, unlike the wild chorus, had no echo. It spoke softly, begging and pleading for her to wake. *Wake? I am awake…* Though, slowly but surely, the darkness began to shift.

Her vision grew hazy as she became acutely aware of other sensations. The damp, moss-tinged air filling her lungs; the pebbles digging into the odd crevices in her spine; the throbbing in her head that she knew would turn into a migraine.

Finally, with a brutally painful thump to the chest, she woke.

* * *

TWINKLING STARS ABOVE, plush forest moss below. The still of an easy night embraced her. Each detail came with a sobering kind of calm. All was quiet again, but this time, a peaceful kind of quiet that perforated all around her… except for the eyes staring back at her.

Savara blinked.

They hovered above her judgingly, those haunting midnight blue eyes. Unlike the shadows that had attacked her, this figure had a heart, faint as it may have been. Savara opened her mouth to speak when she heard her friends searching for her beyond the trees. She lolled her head to one side and spotted them.

"Here!" she croaked.

Griffin and Sebastian made their way towards her. When she turned back, the man was gone.

"Savara!" Griffin called. "Are you hurt? What happened?"

Savara sat up hesitantly, searching around for the figure that had disappeared into the night, but he—whoever he was—was nowhere to be found. He'd left without a trace, not even a footprint on the ground to show he'd ever been there at all. "Did you see him?"

"Who?" Griffin urged, tension lacing his voice. "Did someone hurt you?"

"No, I must have imagined it." Her attention turned to Sebastian as he moved through the brush to meet them.

Something large and limp hung over his shoulders. With a sinking feeling in her chest, she looked around. "Where's Jasper?"

Griffin and Sebastian exchanged a worried look, but it was Sebastian who spoke the dreadful words. "You lashed out…"

Nothing in the world could have prepared her for the sight of Jasper's body dangling over his shoulders. All her fears, all the nasty little words the shadows had filled her head with, had come true. Her body shook viciously. "I didn't… I couldn't…" she stuttered, reaching out for his limp hand.

"He's alive," Griffin assured. "But we must head back to camp. Brass needs to see to him as soon as possible."

She nodded, accepting his hand as she got to her feet. Savara didn't know how her trembling legs managed to march back through the woods. Each step left them closer to breaking. She was ready to let them, but she knew she had to press on. She had to make sure that Jasper was okay.

They walked in silence. Soon, the canvas tents began to peek through the bushes. Griffin assured her Jasper would be fine, that he'd just sustained light head trauma, but it wasn't the trauma outside that worried her.

When he wakes, what will he think of me? she wondered. *Will he even want to see me? Or will he have learned to fear me like the rest?*

CHAPTER 26

A STRANGE PROPOSITION

JASPER WOKE TO the sharp smell of tea tree oil and shooting pains down his arms and spine. White bandages covered his wounds, but red patches were beginning to blossom from beneath. His tongue scratched like sandpaper in his mouth. It ached when he pushed it against the inside of his cheek. He raised his hand to the side of his face and winced.

So, it's still swollen, he thought. He noticed a glass of water on the table beside him, along with his black horn-rimmed glasses. They'd been snapped in two, the lenses cracked beyond repair. He sighed but figured it was for the best anyway. *They might be too conspicuous in a place like this,* he thought, reaching over instead for the glass of water. He let out a strained groan as he stretched his arm.

"Let me help," Brass said, appearing at the door.

"Thanks," Jasper replied. He gulped it down quickly despite the pain in his cheek. "Have I been out long?"

"A few hours. They brought you back just after midnight."

"Alright," he replied, straining to sit upright. Brass twirled his fingers and sent an air current beneath him to ease the strain on his muscles. "Thanks."

Brass inclined his head. "How are those bandages? Too tight?"

"No, they're fine," he replied, his mind elsewhere. He glanced around the empty room disheartened.

"She's not here," said Brass.

"Who?" Jasper lied, but the sorry look in Brass' eyes told him there was no use in pretending. Jasper sighed. "I know." Had he really expected she would be? That she would be sitting at his bedside with tears in her eyes, ready to hug him when he woke? *No, that wouldn't be like her,* he thought, no matter how much he wished it were. "Is she okay?"

"She was shaken. Guilty about what happened, I believe." From his casual tone, Jasper gathered he wasn't fully informed about the night's events, but that he didn't want to be, either. "Very worried about you, but I told her and everyone that came asking that you needed to rest."

"Who else came looking?" he asked. But the smile on his face disappeared as his least favourite person waltzed through the door.

"Good, you're up," Griffin said as he pulled up a chair beside the bed. "Brass, go check on Sebastian and make sure he isn't straining his wounds."

Brass looked as though he were about to comment before simply bowing out.

"What do you want?" Jasper asked apathetically. He wasn't going to hide his disgust. Captain or not, Griffin still irritated him. It was *his* fault they were all in this mess in the first place. Savara fell for his promise of escape and now they were both worse off for it. As far as Jasper was concerned, Griffin deserved to be reminded of it at every possible moment.

Griffin didn't answer. He looked over Jasper's wounds and his swollen face. There was no remorse in his voice when he finally said, "You've changed."

"What's that supposed to mean?" Jasper replied irritably.

"You're less of a man-child than the person I arrived with." Griffin's face was stoic as he spoke. "There's still room for improvement, but…"

"Is there a point to your insults?"

"Considering what lies ahead, it's for the better. I doubt the old you would've survived." Jasper disregarded the pain as he balled his hands into fists. Any more patronising statements and he would let them fly right into Griffin's jaw. He might break his wrist, but it would be well worth it to wipe that look from his face. Griffin stared down at Jasper's fists and added, "I know you don't trust me."

That's an understatement, Jasper thought. A reddish glow crept into his cheeks. He lowered his head, letting his brown curls fall in front of his eyes. "No."

And I'd rather not be having this conversation either.

Griffin pulled out a brand-new pair of glasses similar to the ones Savara's uncle used to wear that were taken from him during the kidnap. These weren't as feeble or wiry, though still equally round.

"What's the occasion?" Jasper asked sceptically.

"Consider it a peace offering." For someone as eloquent as Griffin, the words seemed to be getting caught in his throat.

"What do you want?"

"I know you wish to protect her," Griffin continued. Jasper looked back at him, a crease forming between his eyebrows, but he kept his mouth shut as he waited for Griffin to get to the point—a cue not misread. "If you hadn't realised, she is special… in more ways than one." His tone softened. "She has a part to play in future events, as do we all, but I want to make sure that she survives it. In the end, we both want the same thing."

"Is that supposed to endear me to you?" Jasper growled.

"No," Griffin assured him in his same steady, cocky tone. "I'm going to be honest with you because I need your help, and I know you won't give it unless I am. It's why I brought you here in the first place."

Jasper raised an eyebrow but maintained his silence. *What could this asshole possibly need with me?*

He figured Griffin was using Savara—and he'd told her as much—but he never thought for a second that Griffin would have plans for him too. Although, in hindsight, Griffin was too calculating to have let even someone as inconspicuous as him slide through the cracks in his plans.

"If what you said in the woods was true—"

"You think I'm lying?"

"No, but if what you said is true, that would lead whoever they were into the Harri capital of Idune, and if there are Argia captives among them, I can only assume they intend to start a war within the city." Jasper could tell the words rattled even Griffin to speak. "I didn't realise it before we visited the palace, but after seeing it for myself, and considering what you've told me, I believe the attack will be another distraction for something even more sinister."

"Don't get me wrong," Jasper began. It pained him to speak. "I'm," he considered his choice of words, "glad, I guess, that you're *trusting me* with all of this, but I don't understand. We aren't friends, and you know this. So why?"

Griffin sighed. "The world is shifting. Spirits that have long slept are waking up, and part of it is because of her. Her soul belongs to those spirits."

"If any harm comes to her—"

"I am seeing to it that it doesn't," Griffin interrupted. "But I will need your help." He pulled out a book from under his cloak and rested it on Jasper's bed. "You like to read, I gather. Something we have in common."

Jasper's eyes widened as he stared at it. Even before he took hold of the book, he knew how rare it was. Everything, from the feel of the embossed, worn leather to the elegant, handwritten, ink-splotched flourishes that lined the pages, was familiar. Jasper's mind had already set itself on figuring out where Griffin had found it.

"Where did you get this?" he asked, recognising it as a twin to the volume he'd taken from Hyrum. "And what do you want from me?"

"In my tent, there is a library. All the questions you have, about this world and these people, you will find answers to these books. They're yours, on one condition."

Of course, with Griffin, there were always conditions.

"In that collection, there are a series of journals written in an ancient text that few alive can even begin to grasp. Brass tells me you might be able to read them. My father was in the process of translating them before he died." Griffin turned away as he mentioned his father, but Jasper caught a glimpse of the soft frown on his face. If he didn't think of him as an arrogant, manipulative dick, he might have even felt sorry for him. He was happy to know that everyone, even Griffin, had someone who ruffled their feathers.

"Will this help her?" Jasper asked, worried by the way Griffin's tone had softened. He'd unconsciously stopped on a page with a picture of the divination symbol scrawled across the top righthand corner. Sprawling letters of a different tongue trailed down the rest of the page.

"I believe so," he replied, but Jasper could sense the doubt in him. Griffin dipped his head tentatively and made for the door, stopping at the threshold. He waited, as though once again measuring his words, before adding, "You love her."

It was barely a whisper, but Jasper would've heard it from miles away. He didn't reply. He didn't need to. They both, it seemed, already knew the truth.

"That's good. She'll need it. It just might be the thing that saves her." He bowed his head and set off into the dawn, leaving Jasper alone with his thoughts.

He didn't know how to interpret Griffin's last words. It seemed they'd made a truce, for now. It also meant he intended to put Savara in danger. Savara was more than capable of getting herself into trouble, she didn't need Griffin to help her along.

Jasper had never prayed before. He'd never been to church, and he wasn't fond of the idea of some grand entity watching over everyone's suffering for its own entertainment. Despite this, he rested the book on the bedside table and clasped his hands.

"I've never asked for your help before. Hopefully, that means I'm long overdue a favour. I don't even know if you're listening, but in case you are, please watch over her. She has no idea what she's gotten herself into. And though I am going to protect her—you know I'd give my life for her—I just don't know if I'll be enough. I'm worried about what this world has in store for us… for everyone. Please, whoever you are, wherever you may be. Please watch over us all…"

Jasper had never thought much of his voice. It wasn't loud or imposing. It wasn't a voice that people usually paid any attention to. He'd gotten used to people not listening to him, but that night, he hoped that someone out there was.

CHAPTER 27

A MYSTERIOUS LETTER

SAVARA HAD SPENT the beginning of an uncomfortable night waiting to hear about Jasper's condition. She'd chewed her nails down to stubs, but that didn't last long. When she bit and began to bleed, she resigned herself to twirling hair around her fingers and inadvertently pulling out a few strands in the process. Outside, chirping crickets counted the uncomfortable seconds by. An eternity had passed since they had rested Jasper onto the medical bed and Brass had set to work.

They all waited there at first, but between her nervously questioning whether he was alright and Griffin pacing around the room, Brass thought it was best for everyone to leave, get a mediocre night's sleep, and let him work in peace. Brass was the only one who seemed to maintain any semblance of level-headedness, and she was grateful for it, even if his one-word reassurances did nothing for her nerves.

"Are you alright?" Griffin called from the door. Aside from the bags forming under his eyes, physically, he looked like he always had, but Savara could feel the strain in his muscles to keep moving, the nervous energy in his veins. She knew he would sleep just about as well as she would—if they ever got to sleep.

"If I said yes, would you believe me?"

"No," he said with a half-smile. "The day didn't go how I imagined it would."

Savara let out a nervous laugh as tears filled her eyes. "I'd be more worried if it had." She'd spent the last hour or so replaying the scenes in her mind, everything from the burning corpse in the alley to seeing Jasper dangle over Sebastian's shoulders. Each time she revisited the incidents, she trembled. Her left side ached from stress-induced intestine bunching just below her ribcage.

She knew the events of the day had taken their toll on her physical appearance as well, which seemed to be why Griffin refrained from sudden movements and loud noises. He inched closer, actively keeping the distance between them alive, though, she didn't know if it was for her benefit or his.

"Would you like to talk about it?" The softness in his voice sounded genuine, but being Griffin, she knew there was something more to it.

"About what?"

"What happened earlier?"

She hugged her knees into her chest and sniffled. "What's there to say?" Within the span of a single day, she'd found out that she was both a princess and a daemon, she'd been kidnapped and made a deal with the devil, and somehow worse still, she'd unconsciously almost killed two people, her best friend included. What was she supposed to say? Sorry for being born this way? Sorry for having messed up this world she remembered nothing of?

"No one is blaming you for what happened," said Griffin. It didn't matter what anyone else thought; she blamed herself. "…in case you needed to hear that."

Savara shrugged. She didn't feel like speaking, much less to him. She could almost feel the question forming in his mind. Could she control it? Her power? And how would that be useful to his cause? The answer to the first was a resounding *no*, and as for the second… What use would it be having someone around you couldn't even trust to not kill you?

To Griffin's credit, he didn't ask. He turned and headed for the door. As he reached, his hand balanced on the edge of the mesh hesitantly. She heard the tug of the heavy fabric, but she didn't hear him leave.

"I can understand you not wanting to talk to me," Griffin mumbled. "…but you should talk to somebody." He worked the same hushed tones that rang of innocence and kinder words to reassure her, but those weren't the things that ended up convincing her. His drooping shoulders, the way his cloak hung on him like a much heavier weight, the way his blue eyes had paled. As for what he'd said, she had no one to talk to. Who would be able to understand her trauma? Who would be able to look her in the eyes after hearing of the voices in her head and the murderous intent in her hands?

No one.

He didn't bother looking back as he crossed into the night, but Savara knew that if he had, she would've seen a frown on his typically unmoved face. She watched him go, even down to the last second it took for the mesh to sweep closed behind him. In the remaining silence, she questioned if it was really an act at all.

***

GRIFFIN PONDERED HIS next move, still shaken by the day's events. Brass had already kicked him out of the medical tent on account of his constant busybody pacing, and Savara didn't want to talk about *anything*. She looked even more ruffled than he'd imagined she would. He felt sorry for her. Everything had been thrust upon her so suddenly, and she scarcely understood it all.

But he had to do it.

He had to bring her back to see just how important she was. After what she'd done against the man in the alley, and after what she'd done to Jasper, he knew he was right to have done so.

For the moment, he decided it was best to head back to his tent. He needed to consult his books for information on the stones. The earlier he started, the greater jump he would get on *them*. But who were they? Though the legends surrounding *them* were many, the ones with any true insight were few and far between. He had hoped Savara might have clued him in, but she wasn't about to figure herself out anytime soon, let alone the history of an entire exiled nation.

And they aren't alone either, Griffin remembered. Jasper had mentioned a man with lightning in his fingers. *That could be Alexei,* he thought. That bastard always did have a way of making the most out of other people's suffering. He was discharged from the Izar ranks because he was unstable, to begin with. *But Alexei doesn't work for free. Whoever hired him must be working with deep pockets and deeper ambitions.* Griffin knew quite a few people who fit that description, but none coming from the northern territories.

He continued down the path towards his tent, wrapped up in his thoughts when he noticed that Storm had planted herself rigidly in front of his tent. A vicious scowl marked her face. Instead of her usual kohl, worry lined her eyes. She must have seen Sebastian and his injuries. Nothing else, despite her efforts to deny it, would have troubled her this way.

"Let's go inside," Griffin said. "I'd rather not be overheard."

She followed him in silence, but the second the mesh swept closed, the cork in her anger popped. "She almost *killed* you all, Griffin," Storm growled.

"*Almost* being the operative word, Storm," he replied as he searched the many shelves for one of the strange leather-bound books his father was always fussing over. "She's just as much a threat as I am," he added uninterestedly.

The book must be here somewhere... He continued to shift around the many volumes in the library.

"You forget how much of a threat you can be," Storm scoffed as she paced around the room, her vibrant red braid swinging back and forth like a pendulum with every irritable step. "Besides, from what Sebas says, her powers aren't... normal." Griffin didn't contest her. The next thing he heard was a loud wooden thud. He turned around to see yet another knife embedded into his beloved old table. "What is she, Griffin?"

It was no use hiding anything from Storm. One way or another, she'd find out, and he knew that if he willingly told her, the subsequent blow wouldn't be as hard. No one would rest easy until she did, and besides, Storm was exponentially more valuable in the loop than out of it.

"One of *them*." Griffin saw all the emotions play out on her face as she tried to process the information: confusion, denial, anger, fear, and finally, hesitation. He'd felt the same before he realised what she was.

"One of *them?!* And you're okay with that?" she yelled. "Do you know how dangerous it is to keep her here? What if she goes wild—"

"She's not a zoo animal, Storm, and she's certainly not being *kept* here against her will," he said, returning to his book search. "And yes, I'm fine with her being here," he added, disregarding her harsh comments. *Finally,* he thought as he plucked one of the dustier volumes from the shelf.

Storm stood with her arms crossed and a downward curl to her lip. "You have the bad habit of overlooking flaws in some that pose great threats to others."

That caught his attention. Griffin raised his brows. "If I didn't, there are a lot of people that wouldn't be here, Storm." Not just a lot of people, *she* wouldn't be there, and she recognised it too, biting her lip to keep whatever opinion she was forming in her mouth. "Besides, you need her here as much as I do. Without her, we stand no chance."

Storm turned the idea over in her head. "And how are you so sure she's on our side?"

He wasn't. He could only hope. But he knew she wouldn't accept that as an answer. "Her eyes speak a language you and I are both *intimately* acquainted with. Revenge." Griffin waited for her shock to dissipate before adding, "*They* killed her family. You know as well as I that revenge is a powerful motivator."

"You and I also know that revenge can drive people insane," Storm retorted, looking more troubled now, realising as he did just how dangerous someone seeking revenge could be, especially when that someone had been burdened with powers that seemed to be out for blood.

"Which is why we must tend to the better parts of her character and not feed whatever violent tendencies she might have inside," he urged.

"Fine, but I'm not pretending to like her," Storm huffed.

Griffin raised an eyebrow at her and smiled. "I'd never ask anything less of you." He knew she'd grow to like Savara in time, or at the very least, not dislike her so vehemently. For now, acceptance—especially from Storm—was as good an achievement as any.

"By the way," Storm added, raising her nose pointedly, "you have a letter," she said as she tossed the small brown envelope onto the table. Such a simple thing, and yet it rattled him to his core.

Griffin blinked twice to make sure it was real. It didn't fade. He glowered at the unopened message that bore his name, turning it over in his hand incredulously. "Where did you get this?" he asked, remembering the last time he received a message like this one.

"A mole," she said, curiosity tingeing her voice. "It appeared at the bonfire."

Griffin ripped it open, scanning its contents before casting it out of existence. He pulled a piece of parchment and a quill from atop one of the book piles and began to scribble. His letter was no more than three lines, but the seriousness of them was clear. He shoved the parchment into an envelope and scribbled only the address of the recipient. "I have to see to the human about other matters," he said finally. "I need you to ensure this letter gets to her safely."

"Lady Amaia?" Storm read, contorting her face as she looked up at him. "May I ask why you've chosen now of all times to contact old family friends?" she asked as she watched him pour and seal the blue wax over the envelope.

"No."

Storm studied the envelope. The scrunching of her brow told him she wasn't exactly happy with any of his decisions, but she held her tongue. She bowed her head, ready to leave when he called to her again.

"And do me a favour… Train the human. We're going to need all the help we can get."

"I just hope you know what you're doing, Griffin." Storm sighed and marched out into the night.

He waited until he was sure she was gone and then some before whispering, "So do I…"

Griffin grazed his hand over the mark Storm had so gratuitously left in his father's table. He shook his head and smiled, thankful that he would never have to find himself at the other end of her sword.

Despite her temper, she had the good head not to damage any of the papers scattered across it. Maps and letters and everything in between lay strewed across the wood. Griffin sifted through the pile until he found an envelope similar to the ominous one he'd just received. He plucked it up uneasily, guilt riddling his intestines as he flipped it over. The sprawling cursive name had long since faded and its contents reeked of age.

And to think I'd thought this was only a power grab, Griffin thought as he contemplated the letter dated almost a decade ago. Not even he could have imagined the extent of his mistake. The ink now looked more grey than black, but the words were still perfectly legible:

Be wary of things that move in the dark. They plan on ousting the fires.

~ a friend

Back then, he'd already known of the mafia's intent. Big Tog, as he remembered, had always spoken of a day when the mafia would take control away from the palace. Back then, the threats had always seemed more for show. After the attack on Osiir, he'd wrongfully assumed that it was Big Tog finally making good on his years of empty words from the underbelly of Osiirian society, but nothing about that attack was befitting a man of his character. Big Tog would've waved banners throughout the Argia nation, letting them know he was in charge, and forcing the people out onto the streets in fake parades. In contrast, no one heard of the attack on Osiir for days, long after the rivers of blood had dried into the streets. Not even Big Tog had spoken up back then.

That letter had only been the beginning, and he'd been too blind to realise it.

After his father's death, when Griffin began sifting through the mess of papers and stacks of books that should have belonged to someone with more standing than his father, he found a strange note from none other than the queen herself. Her daughter—the child he remembered attending a five-day funeral for—was alive, cast off to a world beyond this one, and needed additional protection from what she only referred to then as *the dark*. The news had rattled him then, and he could only imagine how it had affected his father.

Griffin cursed himself now for having not realised all of the strange coincidences that led him here, but he would not make the same mistake twice. He had schooled his features into mild intrigue with Storm in the room, but he had recognised the envelope, the signature, even the ashy smell of the parchment. His very core stilled as he ripped it open— as it should have many years before.

The seconds ticked by, empty but not hollow, as he read and reread the letter. He wished he could say the words came as a great surprise to him, that the piece of paper hinted at something he couldn't have dreamed of in the worst of his worst nightmares. But he would be lying. This new letter only confirmed his fears.

Griffin tossed it back onto the heaps of papers, glowering briefly at the whorl of shadows at the top of the map before slipping one of the many his father had worked himself to death trying to translate under his arm. His father, as much as it pained him to admit, was always three steps ahead of the world, and he felt like a failure in comparison. Long gone, yet Griffin tried desperately still to climb out from behind his shadow. He cast the thoughts away, along with the feeling of disappointment they brought. He had work to do.

With any luck, the human will be the one to translate it, he thought, the book weighing down both his mind and his arm.

He set off into the dark for the second time that night, hoping the irritating lump of bone and skin in the medical tent turned out to be as valuable as a loaf of bread in a famine. Great coincidence that he'd agreed to let him come, but after everything he'd been through, Griffin realised he wasn't a firm believer in coincidences.

CHAPTER 28

DECISIONS

THE APPRENTICE MOVED through the grand corridors with ease, taking comfort in the echo of his footfall on the marble floors. Above one hand, a bulb of blue light bobbed, illuminating the space in front of him. The other hand, the damaged one, remained hidden in his pocket, toying with the little stone that cost half a village to take. His fingers grazed it, tucked away between the folds of the burgundy silk lining, avoiding the spattering of blood on its surface. He considered it now, the only source of true warmth in the darkened castle. This time, he didn't smile.

He'd known the cost of his actions long before the rivers of blood had settled under the Osiirian sun, long before the queen had taken to insulting him, long before he'd bound his soul. It had been longer still since he'd given a damn. Originally, he'd thought it was for a greater good. Part of him still thought so, and not just *that* part. Besides, it was as close to a choice as he'd ever been given. Looking back, he still wouldn't change a thing.

The world had been made imperfectly. They were simply setting it right.

The Apprentice questioned his master only once, right at the beginning, when he'd been ordered to kill for the first time. The experience forced him to question if they weren't just out to watch the world burn. He didn't make that mistake again. He didn't know why they had to do it back then, he doubted they even could. He wasn't yet able to see. Now, with the little stone in his pocket that gave truth to the legend, he knew.

And yet, as he neared the chamber, his heart quickened.

The first time it happened, he thought the thing inside him had launched an attack. After so much time spent with the simple echo of a heart, he'd forgotten what it felt like to have it beat properly in his chest. If the day in the palace had taught him one thing, it was that the thing inside him could be bested; he just had to find out how. For now, he had to play along, allow it to continue its murderous crusade; only now, with a new foothold on his own heart, it would be that much harder.

His pace slowed as he reached the door. The blue light disappeared from his palm as a frown grew on his lips. *It's time.* The Apprentice smoothed the elegant black blazer on his torso and ran his hands through the tendrils of midnight he called hair. He had become a creature of the night, just like the ghosts that haunted these empty halls. Even the darkness retreated around him. This darkness—*regular* darkness—was nothing to fear. On the contrary, it was something beautiful, gentle. Something that heals the wounds time leaves behind, where traumas can be forgotten for a night, the body can rest and rejuvenate, and the world stills for a moment's breath. Darkness is beautiful.

I am a different kind of darkness.

Great oaken doors lined with spirals of silver stood before him. A cruel cold emanated from them that made even the fire in his pocket shiver. The doors had no handles. Usually, this would mean they weren't meant to be opened, but if his time in the dark had shown him anything, it was that everything can be opened, some things just demand a higher price. One of the curls of silver in the embroidered door had been sharpened to a point. He raised his thumb to it and pressed, letting the blood trickle into the wood. The thing inside him rattled to life again with the pain. The faded colour of the oak brightened as it absorbed the blood. With a sinister hiss, the doors slid open.

It was too late to reconsider the gravity of his actions; he was no longer the one making decisions. The flame in his pocket shook, finding synergy with the powerful thing sitting at the end of the room. Plum-coloured eyes glowed through the darkness, sparkling as they sought out the orb.

"You have returned," the voice called to him.

The Apprentice stepped forward into the single streak of moonlight that filtered through the window. He took a knee, his hand tentatively hovering over his pocket as he thought of all the lives that this crusade would take. With a heavy sigh, he dipped his hand into the pocket and brandished the stone towards the shadow.

A sinister laugh rumbled through the hollow halls. When The Apprentice looked up again, he found the plum-coloured eyes but inches from his own, staring at the orb. The man's feet made no echo on the marble floors, a testament to how much he'd lost in his banishment. Shadowy fingers wrapped around the orb, plucking it gingerly from The Apprentice's own. A wicked grin spread across the shadow man's face as he contemplated it. Holding it seemed to fill out the hollows in his person, but The Apprentice knew better than to think this man was whole.

The shadows pooled around him, clinging like the lost souls they were to a hollow and insubstantial vessel. The Apprentice stared up at the face of the man who commanded the darkness as a burning sensation flowed into one of the gemstoned slits on his back. It reverted to blood and trickled down his spine. The Apprentice let out a sigh of relief.

Six more and I'll be free…

His master smiled, but the tone of his voice made even the darkness shiver as he said, "And so, it begins…"

CHAPTER 29

TRAINING

THOUGHTS NAGGED AT her through the night. Her eyelids hung like weights, slowly slipping from her grasp, but she couldn't let them close. Not now, possibly not ever. It was all too recent: the kidnapping, the forest, and the two almost-murders her hands had longed to commit.

Not my hands, she reminded herself. These hands may have looked the same, but they weren't hers. These were cruel, foreign, and unforgiving. How could they be her hands? *Not my hands,* she realised, *the hands of whatever's inside me.*

* * *

"WELL DON'T YOU look like chilli flakes on a chocolate sundae," Sebastian remarked as he sauntered through the door. The injuries from their kidnapping made his usual summer breeze walk slightly off-step but, considering what she'd seen of his back and bruises, he played it off well. Savara almost couldn't believe how well he looked, but of course, this was Sebastian. Even a bad day for him looked better than the best days of others.

"What's that supposed to mean?" Savara grumbled. Her eyes stung with the bitterness of a long night of little sleep.

"Well, miss *Right Side of the Wrong Bed*, it was supposed to be a compliment."

"…I don't think you and I have the same idea of a compliment."

"Not my fault you have no taste; that's my favourite topping," he laughed. His melodically warm and infectious laugh had gained a hiss to it that she imagined came from bruised lungs. She rolled over to the far side of the bed, turning her back to him. That marked laugh of his would be yet another haunting reminder of everything that had happened. She could feel his searching gaze on her spine. "Have you spent the whole night like this?" he prodded.

"I couldn't sleep…" she mumbled as she stared at her hands beneath the sheet. The image of them covered in spidery red veins had burned itself into the backs of her eyelids. If she allowed her eyes to linger too long on the thought, the vision returned, along with that sickening restrictive feeling that took over her body.

"I see that," Sebastian said as he sat himself down at the edge of her bed. "It's been a week since… you know."

A week, five hours, and twenty-seven—no, twenty-eight minutes. How could she forget? The many nights had dragged into one excruciatingly long one, whose little pockets of sleep were marred by nightmares that kept her up for another thirty-six hours. And in all that time, she'd seen Jasper once and Griffin in passing. If it weren't for Brass' occasional check-ups, she would've been entirely alone.

"Listen," Sebastian began. "How about, instead of wasting away to sleep deprivation, you come training with me?"

"I think I'd rather be buried alive," Savara replied, hugging the blanket closer, though she'd be lying to herself if she said she wasn't partly touched by his offer.

"That's not really on my itinerary right now, but if you'd like I can call Storm for you. I'm sure she'd be eager to oblige."

"Please don't," she groaned.

The last person Savara wanted to see was Storm. She knew Storm would find a way to blame her for everything that had happened, and her subsequent wrath would make hurricane destruction look like gardening.

"Good, so you'll come then? It's better than wallowing in self-pity, and maybe I'll even let you land a hit on me."

"Will it get you to leave me alone?"

"Possibly, though, who's to say *you* won't end up glued to *my* side?" he teased. Savara sent a wild pillow flying, which Sebastian caught all too easily. "Not to be a bad cough about it, but *this*," he added, tossing the pillow back at her, "is exactly why you need to train."

He was right, of course. Savara hadn't the faintest idea of how to hit or where to strike. The attack in the alley and subsequent kidnappings made it clear that learning to fight was a necessity. There were things in this world that would eat her alive without blinking. Since she wasn't about to use those powers again, defending herself the normal way was better than nothing.

* * *

SEBASTIAN HAD BECOME her shadow over the past few weeks. Any time Savara thought about sneaking off for a moment's peace, he would find some way to keep her on her toes. After suffering through various fruits to the head, a face full of mud, and a swollen shoulder from a flying chair she "should've dodged easily," she was finally beginning to get the hang of it.

Savara learned to punch on sandbags which left her knuckles bloody and swollen, but her blocking and dodging still had room for improvement. Despite it all, she continued. If she was going to survive in this world, let alone avenge her uncle's death, she needed to push on.

Since the day in the forest, Jasper had taken to spending long hours in Griffin's tent. Savara couldn't understand it, considering they'd fought like cats and dogs at every point before then. She'd even seen him hanging about with Storm on various occasions, though he always looked the worse for wear afterwards. She missed talking to him. Jasper had been her only friend for the better part of a decade. But things were different now. He was different. Being here had practically made them strangers.

As for the rest, Griffin spent most of his time in correspondence with strange people with even stranger names. Storm hated her, so her company was out of the question. Brass would occasionally ask her to tea, but Savara found she was usually too anxious for the kinds of calm and quiet teas that Brass enjoyed. Simon kept to his animals, which only left Sebastian. He somehow always managed to keep her busy. She didn't mind though. His constant company was the only thing keeping her sane, which was why she happily suffered through the growing number of bruises on her arms and thighs, and even a limp that had only just healed.

THIS MORNING'S TRAINING session brought her back to the clearing where they'd been attacked. Skies that looked like they were holding out for rain hung above. Sebastian strolled into the centre and dumped a heavy sack onto the ground. Swords, knives, daggers, spears, scythes—all sorts of sharpened weapons fell from the sack.

"Pick your poison," Sebastian called to her with more energy than she'd ever had on a good day. It didn't matter which weapon she chose; he could best her with them all. While Savara looked them over, he etched a large circle into the ground. "The object of the game is to stay in the circle."

"Is everything a game to you?" she called back, rolling her eyes as she picked up a katana. The hilt was wrapped in royal blue silk, the collar holding the blade a glittering gold. The edges seemed blunt enough that she wouldn't get hurt too badly when he landed a hit. He mostly reserved landed hits for hand-to-hand combat, that way she'd learn without needing too much medical attention—or so he claimed—but the last time they'd sparred, he told her she was beginning to get too comfortable. Today she'd have to keep her guard up.

Savara walked into the centre of the circle brandishing the blade. Sebastian raised an eyebrow and smiled, digging out its twin from the bag. Red silk and a silver collar, just as blunt, but in his hands, twice as deadly.

"That's Storm's favourite too," he said, and with a snap of his fingers, the etched circle caught fire. Dancing flames created a wall around them. "Try not to get burned," Sebastian added with a wink as he took up his stance. He always let her strike first.

Sebastian dodged her first few slashes with tiresome ease, even having the audacity to yawn. Savara huffed and swung with more force. This swing met steel, splitting the air with a metallic tang. At the other end of the blade, Sebastian grinned.

Now, they would fight.

The blades whistled through the air, clinking when they met each other. He pushed her to the edge a few times, letting the flames lick her boots. Savara pushed back, focusing more on how not to get burned rather than where the next hit would come from. She tripped over a stone and fell with a hard thud onto her back. Pebbles dug into the patches of skin between her clothes. Regrettably, she'd made the mistake of looking back at the flames rather than at him and turned to find his sword inches from her neck.

He stared down the sword at her. "Never lose sight of the blade," he said, relaxing his hold on it and offering her his other hand.

"I'm not a fighter," Savara reminded him as she dusted herself off.

"You certainly won't be until you start considering yourself one," Sebastian replied. He took a few steps back and waited again for her strike.

"As if thinking myself better is going to make me better," she moaned.

"It certainly won't make you worse," he said, flicking her blade away with ease. "Again."

The sun made its graceful ascent into the sky. They'd been at it for hours and all she'd gotten out of it was a twisted ankle, a scorched wrist, and dirt in uncomfortable places.

"How is it that you—" Savara bobbed, narrowly missing what would have been an actual slice to the forearm, "barely grip the thing and still manage to—" she jumped and landed hard on the dirt, "land almost every hit?"

Sebastian laughed as she pushed herself to her feet. "Believe it or not, there's a genuine art to sword fighting… like painting. Actually, the people to be most wary of in a fight are those who grip their swords like paintbrushes."

The earthy, grainy taste of dried dirt filled her mouth. Savara gagged, coughing up as much as she could before wiping her dusty lips. That's what she deserved for talking when she should've been paying attention. "And why is that?" she asked, still unable to remove the taste of earth from under her tongue.

Sebastian winked and readied himself again.

Fine, don't tell me, Savara thought. *Paintbrush…* She slackened her grip and focused on the tip of the sword, rather than the handle. In her next swing, Sebastian dodged, staring incredulously at the spot on his shoulder that the sword would've slashed through.

"I did it!" she beamed. Her pathetic stance could be corrected another day. For now, she was happy to finally be able to keep on her feet.

"Impressive," said Sebastian, clearly just as surprised as she was that she'd grasped the concept so quickly. "Let's see if you can do it again."

Another hour of whistling swishes and clanking steel passed by. The air was starting to feel like water to her aching muscles. Savara imagined that even something so trivial as brushing her teeth later would be a task.

"So, what's with you and the human?" he asked. She knew he was trying to distract her now that she was slowly getting the hang of it.

"Nothing. We're friends," she replied, striking again. Another metallic clank echoed through the air.

"I don't know of any friends that would jump worlds for me," Sebastian smirked.

"You can't have many real friends then," she returned, huffing as best she could to keep the air in her lungs. "What about you and Storm?"

Sebastian faltered. He missed his step, opening his stance too wide. She landed a blunt blow on his arm and looked just as surprised as he did about it.

"You finally got one," he said with an evasive laugh, ignoring the comment that had made it possible. "I think we can probably head back. I'm starved. Plus, I've been listening to your stomach all morning," he added as he packed up the supplies.

Sebastian was quiet for most of the walk back, but she could tell something was eating at him. Savara wondered if she'd crossed some unspoken boundary, cursing herself for alienating the only person that could stand to be in her company, when he suddenly slowed his pace. The camp was only a few paces away.

"Is everything okay?" she asked.

"She's a case of her own," he mumbled finally. A bright red blush crept over his nose and onto his cheeks beneath the beard.

"Storm?"

He nodded guiltily.

"Have you two ever…?"

"No. I tease her now and again but that's as far as it goes." Sebastian looked longingly towards the camp and sighed. "Just don't mention this to her, please."

"Why? Are you afraid of her?"

Sebastian bit his lip. "Not exactly…"

"Don't worry," Savara assured him. "I wouldn't. I couldn't even if I wanted to. She doesn't like me, remember?"

"Good."

Savara rested a gentle hand on his shoulder. "I bet she holds her swords like paintbrushes," she mocked.

Sebastian raised his eyebrows playfully. Along with the blush, a grin spread across his face. "No," he said, his eyes burning with something deeper than admiration. "She becomes the paintbrush."

CHAPTER 30

TRADING IN BLOOD

JASPER PULLED THE glasses from his face and pinched the bridge of his nose. The migraine was getting worse. He stood up, stretched his back, and walked over to one of the improvised tables for a drink. He knew the ins and outs of Griffin's tent almost better than Griffin himself and could navigate the stacks of books that lined the floor on instinct alone. Above him, the holographic stars of the roof twinkled.

He'd spent the past few weeks attempting to translate the journals with annoyingly little progress. It had taken him an entire week to realise the pages had been coded with cyphers, and two more to crack the first one. Between this and training with Storm, Jasper had little time for anything else, which proved convenient as Sav had been avoiding him ever since the attack. He knew better than to confront her. She would come to him in her own time. Right now, she needed to heal. He only wished he could be the one to help her.

The mountains of books surrounded him like soldiers readying an attack. The challenge was proving difficult even for him. Each one held pages of warped symbols and jumbled words that haunted him at every waking hour.

There must be something I'm missing… Jasper rested the glass down on another pile of books, about to return to his makeshift desk when a voice startled him from behind.

"How is it looking?" asked Griffin.

"Shit!" Jasper jumped, accidentally knocking over the glass. It shattered instantly as it hit the floor. "It's just you. Not much better," he admitted. "I can't seem to crack them. These books are making a mockery of me."

Griffin frowned. He'd been gone for a few days, off on another one of his secretive excursions, but he looked as though he'd hoped Jasper had made more progress. "Is there anything I can do to help?"

"No," Jasper said with a sigh. "Not unless you have a magical magnifying glass that can translate text automatically."

"If I did, do you think I'd have you holed up in here?" Griffin smirked, trying to make light of the situation.

Possibly, Jasper thought with his own little smile. Or at least the Griffin from before their kidnap would have for sure. That Griffin probably would've locked him in a barn somewhere and thrown away the key.

"Do you want my answer?" Jasper laughed, enjoying the excuse to diffuse the tension. Somewhere in the mountains of paper and ink lay the secret of Savara's nature, and finding it was of the utmost importance.

"How is she doing?" Griffin asked, plucking the thought from the top of Jasper's mind.

"I haven't seen her since," Jasper said guiltily. "I figured she needed the space." He stooped down to collect the shards of broken glass. "Sebastian tells me she seems okay. He's been training her to take her mind off everything."

"I'm surprised at how okay you are with them spending time together," Griffin remarked.

Jasper hid his frown under his mess of brown curls. He didn't *love* the idea of them spending so much time together. Sebastian was one of those people Jasper used to resent with every fibre of his being—devilishly handsome, unapologetically flirtatious, with a charm that flowed like a waterfall—but he cared more about Savara than his own damaged ego. He couldn't understand what she was going through, he wasn't from this world, but maybe Sebastian could.

"She needs him more than me right now. I remind her of… *that*. Besides, this research will help her more than anything else."

Griffin stooped down beside him and rested a hand on his shoulder. "Believe me, you have nothing to worry about."

"Ouch!" Jasper yelped, raising a bloodied thumb in front of his face. He plucked the shard from the wedge it had created in his skin, letting sticky red droplets slide down his wrist and fall where they may.

"Are you okay?" Griffin pulled a cloth from one of the random tables and handed it to him. "I'll clear the rest of this up."

"Wait!" Jasper shot a hand out and dragged Griffin back down to the floor. "Look…" he said, pointing to where the blood had fallen onto an exposed sheet of paper. It curled around the indents of the handwritten pages and glided across the page, soaking into the old sheets of parchment. "…the letters are changing," he added. The sweeping black scripture began fusing with the red of the blood, reorganising itself into new words. "This is incredible!"

"This is dangerous," Griffin said, an acute hint of worry tingeing his voice. "I don't understand how such a thing was created. It defies all the natural laws."

"Welcome to the club. Your world defies all my laws too, and yet here we are," Jasper mocked. He was about to press his bloodied thumb onto another page when Griffin grabbed hold of his wrist.

"What do you think you're doing?" Griffin hissed.

"Did you not just see what happened?" Jasper asked as he pulled his hand back. "We've cracked it!"

"You just traded blood for information," Griffin growled. "Don't you see a problem with that?"

"I see a way to save the woman I love," Jasper retorted, turning back to the newly legible page. "I'll bleed myself dry if it'll give us the information we need."

Both men stared down at the page with varying degrees of intrigue and dread. The sprawling script at the title had formed various e's and a series of r's before settling on the phrase: *The Legends of Iturri.*

Griffin blanched. The next words he spoke rang soberingly clear through the tent. "Nothing good is traded in blood."

CHAPTER 31

A DEVIL'S DUE

AFTER ANOTHER GRUESOME day of training, Savara found herself back in the comfort of her tent. The full moon had risen high into the sky outside. A hot shower had removed all the dirt from her hair and skin, but the bruises on her arms and thighs remained fresh and rosy.

Savara dug into the chest of clothes for something warmer as the autumn nights were slowly fading into winter ones. A surge of energy hit her fingers as they grazed something in the chest. Savara jumped, startled by the sensation. Savara rummaged through it in search of the source.

Oh, the package, she thought as she pulled it from beneath the pile of clothes. It buzzed in her palms, the lettering still shimmering silver, the twine still intact. She rested it on the bed beside her and stared at it, wondering if to open it, yet still unable to bring herself to.

"What are you?" she asked the strange little box.

"You make a habit of talking to inanimate objects?" asked a raspy voice from behind.

Savara jumped again. She hadn't realised she was no longer alone. She'd smelled the ash and initially imagined it was a waft from the bonfire, but the scent of cheap cologne that curled the hairs in her nose was unmistakable. The man leaned casually against one of the support beams of the tent, apathetic, but patiently so. Strands of straight blond hair hung like curtains in front of his face, parting in the middle to allow access to the cigarette in his hand.

Savara leapt to her feet, grabbing the lamp at her bedside, raising it to throw. "Who are you and what are you doing in my room?"

"Testy," he sighed. "And futile." He put the cigarette to his lips once more and sparked a flame between his fingers.

Argia, she realised. Suddenly the lamp didn't seem like such a great idea. The gasoline in it would only give him fuel. She rested it back down and steadied herself on the bed. "All I have to do is scream and someone will come running," she hissed.

He took another long puff of his cigarette and contemplated her. "I know," he replied with the casual elegance of kings. "I wouldn't if I were you."

"And why is that?"

"Not tired of the face jewellery then?" He bobbed and lifted his head, pushing the hair away from his face, exposing two piercing citrine-coloured eyes.

Savara touched her fingers to the protruding rubies in her cheeks. She'd almost forgotten they were there. "Big Tog sent you…"

"Took your time, but we got there in the end," he smirked. "I got a lot of shit to do before the night is out, and I'd rather not be stuck playing courier. You're coming whether you want to or not, so decide now whether it's in chains or on your own two feet." He flipped his wrist and stared at a sparkling gold watch. "And I'd hurry if I were you. Big Tog doesn't like to be kept waiting."

She'd given her word—no, her soul—despite what Griffin had told her, and now, the time had come to make good on it, but something told her that she was making good on a very bad thing. She pushed off the bed and made for the door, tossing the strange package back into the chest and slamming it shut.

His sinister lips curled up into a smile. "Atta girl," he said, flicking the cigarette to the floor before escorting her out.

"How are we getting there?" But the answer jumped out at her before she got out the last word.

Stallions. Two blinding stallions with manes of glittering flames. They moved like gasoline on water. As they shook their heads, the scent of smouldering cinnamon surrounded them. Savara stepped up to them cautiously. She had never seen two more beautiful creatures in her life. They bowed as she neared. Savara bowed back, thinking it rude not to.

"Cute," the man said as he helped her onto one and hoisted himself onto the other. They rode off into the night, galloping as fast as the wind, unaware of the smoking trail they'd left behind. The mares' manes lit up enough of the ground in front of them to see the trail, but not so far as to see their surroundings. It didn't matter; they had no time for sightseeing.

BIG TOG'S HOUSE was much simpler than what she'd imagined a mafia boss' house would be. It was a white, blockish structure with thin slits for windows that looked almost fort-like in nature, surrounded by a garden of lilies. The man warned her not to touch any of them, nor even to get so close as to sniff one, going so far as to drag an insinuating finger across his throat. They were Big Tog's prized possessions. Savara shuddered, wondering why she'd agreed to come in the first place. The stones on her cheek vibrated. *That's why,* she remembered.

The man sparked up another cigarette and rang a hanging bell.

"Those will kill you," Savara said, brushing away the clouds of smoke.

"I'd be surprised, I'm counting on my job killing me first," he laughed.

The door opened before she could speak. The thin man standing in the doorway with the devilishly curled ram horn hairdo brandished an eager smile.

"Welcome," said Big Tog, wiping his hands on a tea towel. Savara caught glimpses of his rubies from beneath the cloth. "Just in time for dessert. My wife makes the most delicious pavlova," he added a little too loudly.

Savara looked at the table behind him, covered in food and surrounded by smiling faces, and frowned. "Can we make this quick? I don't want anyone to realise I'm gone."

"Hmm…" was his only response, but he invited her in, nonetheless. He paused briefly to kiss the woman she imagined was his wife, excusing himself from the rest of the dinner party, and led her into the study. The room hadn't changed since she was last here, but it did feel better to come without the bindings. Big Tog shut the door, locking out the noise and laughter in the other room, and smiled. "My wife's pavlova is shit. Too much egg, not enough sugar. Bless her soul."

Savara blinked awkwardly, unsure how to respond without incurring his wrath. She decided on a non-committal nod, which Big Tog seemed to accept with ease.

He leaned against his desk, contemplating her as she shuffled awkwardly to one of the comfier chairs in the room. She was cautious to choose one without holes in the armrests. She was tired of being bound.

Savara gazed around the room, nervously avoiding his gaze. The last time she was here, she'd arrived as a captive and was too scared to truly take in the room. This time, she got caught up in the simple elegance of it, helped in part by the light of the many shifting sconces. It reminded her of the palace, and he seemed all too ready to be a king. Portraits in gilded frames lined the walls, an intricately woven but plush rug covered the floor, an eye-catching collection of large crystal figurines in the shapes of various animals sat at one end of his desk, and tall stacks of paper balanced out the other end. On top of the piles, Savara spied the same knife he had tried to use on Griffin being used as a sinister paperweight, easily within range if his temper took a turn for the worst.

A clock at the other end of the room sounded, marking the lateness of the hour.

"What are you?" Big Tog said finally, taking cue from the chimes that cut through the silence.

"Excuse me?"

"A witch? A curseling?" he prodded unrelentingly.

"A what?" Savara asked again.

"Hmm… I had to be sure," he said, relaxing his shoulders and lowering the veins on his hands. He folded his arms in front of him and pushed out his haughty, squared chin. "So," he began casually, "my boys tell me your fighting skills are… improving."

"How did you know—"

"I have eyes and ears everywhere," he said, waving a nonchalant hand. The way he studied her like an animal in a zoo made her shudder. "But they do not see you use your powers. Why?"

"What do you care?" She glared back, weary of the grin curling on his face.

Big Tog laughed with a timbre that raised the hairs on her arms. The laugh sounded as though it should've come from someone twice his size—the man he might have once been, judging by the portraits on the walls. Face to face with him now, gaunt, and rigid, with shadows filling the hollows of his face, Savara found the overall effect even more sinister. His hairstyle under the low lighting alone brought out the devil in him.

"Can it be? You fear your powers?" he asked, stalking around her as he did once before, only this time without the knife in hand. He contemplated the gemstones poking out from the skin of his palm with a curious fondness.

Savara touched the matching set on her cheek guiltily, afraid to give anything away that he could use over her. She had already bound her soul, wasn't that enough?

So what if I'm scared of them? Anyone in their right mind would be. At least now I can fight...

"You will suffer greatly if you choose not to use them," Big Tog added. From his mouth, it sounded awfully like a threat. He took hold of her jaw and ran his thumb gently over the gems on her cheek. "You do remember our deal?"

Savara's lips formed a frown between his fingers. "How could I forget?"

He grinned his trademark toothy grin. The gold sparkled in his mouth, reflecting the light from the room. "I grow fond of that fire in you, my little duck." He lifted her hair from her ears. "In case you haven't noticed, I like things that burn."

She tugged her face out from his grasp. "What do you want from me?"

"What are you offering?" he said as he ran his tongue over his golden incisors. The muscles in her body seized up at the thought. He laughed at her discomfort. "I kid," he laughed. "I will tell you in time, but first we get acquainted." He summoned one of his maids who brought with her tea, lemon tarts, and a large decanter of something dark and viciously alcoholic. "Wife may have me on diet during the day, but she goes to bed too early to control me at night," he winked as he took a seat in front of her.

Savara accepted a glass tentatively, all too aware that his charm had its limits. Big Tog walked the thinnest of thin lines like an experienced trapezist. In one moment, he could be pleasurable and easy to laugh with, in the next, holding still-beating hearts. Savara reminded herself that he was only so accommodating because she was his plaything. The moment that changed, she could easily find herself on the other side of the line.

"Now, my little duck, about those precious powers of yours…"

Savara had known the question was coming. Could she control them? Last time, he'd scared her into using them, or rather, scared them out of her, but that wasn't control. Her powers seemed to be an entity all their own, she was merely a host who occasionally managed to halt their destruction. She explained as much to him, but he said those were only excuses she'd made for herself to not have to take responsibility for her actions. Savara let him believe he was right—for all she knew, he might well have been. Something also told her it would be prudent not to contradict a mafia boss.

"Give me your hand," Big Tog said, extending his own to collect it. She raised an eyebrow as she rested her hand in his. He interlaced his fingers between hers and kissed each one with care. Savara shifted uncomfortably at the brush of his lips. Suddenly, he closed the grip on her hand and squeezed tightly.

"Ouch," she said, and then repeated more prominently when she realised he wasn't stopping.

It took her a moment to distinguish pressure from heat, but eventually, the smell of burning hair was unmistakable. Savara tried to pry her hand from his—from the flames that enveloped them—but his strength was no match for her, not even with the adrenaline coursing through her veins. Savara's pupils widened as she struggled against him. Boils grew on her charring skin. She shrieked. Tears fell in waterfalls from her eyes, but he regarded her with nothing more than apathy. When he figured he was reaching a limit, Big Tog let her go.

"You do not respond to pain," he said simply, reaching over for a shot of the dark liquid.

"What was that for?" Savara whimpered, unable to stop her arm from shaking. It hurt to move her fingers. It hurt to touch them. Her falling tears stung the curls of burned flesh.

"Piece it back together," he replied indifferently, throwing back the shot and munching down on a tart.

"What?" she cried.

"The flesh. Piece it back together."

"I can't."

"You have not tried."

"I don't know how to use my powers," she bawled, the pain in her hand becoming too much to bear.

"You remember what it is to have an unburned hand," he said. "Imagine that. Piece it back together. Or don't and let it get infected." Big Tog licked the last of the tart from his fingers and reached for another one.

Savara stared down at the blackened remains of skin and the patches of visible bone. Her whole body shivered in pain. How would she ever fix it? As the question popped into her mind, she sensed a low rush of power curling around the charred flaps of skin. It hovered around the wound, answering her call, waiting for her to want it—for her to ask it to heal her. With tears in her eyes and a sudden cold in her body, she willed her skin closed.

It stung as though it were being burned all over again. Slowly but surely, the fibres of skin began to stitch themselves back together, covering the white of her bones.

Her blood began to follow the usual path through her hand. It took her over two hours to set it all back together.

In the meantime, Big Tog had taken to recounting various highlights of his past and how he'd worked his way up from street urchin to the most feared man in all Osiir as he gobbled down the rest of the lemon tarts. When the final skin fibre snapped back into place and her last tear had long since dried, Savara held her hand to the light and gasped. She studied the shadows cast by her fingers over her freshly restored skin. It looked as good as new, as though she'd never been burned.

"Not bad." Big Tog grinned as he downed another shot of liquor and passed one to her. The liquid burned its way down her throat and into the pit of her stomach. A new wave of shivers rushed through her body, crashing into the old ones like clashing currents in a swelling ocean.

Despite the initial shock and disgust of the pungent beverage, Savara beamed. She hadn't realised her powers could be used for something other than killing. This new skill had opened her eyes to a new world, one where she wasn't the monster the world claimed she should be. She wondered what more she could do, thinking of ways she could use her powers to help people rather than hurt them.

But Big Tog watched her with that same hungry look in his eyes. Little fires burned in them as gazed upon her like a child with a new toy. His help had not come from a place of generosity. He expected something in return. "Now," he said in a voice laced with charm and persuasion. "About our deal…"

CHAPTER 32

A NEW DIRECTION

DESPITE WHAT GRIFFIN had told him, Jasper was not going to give up. The information was there, right in front of him. He was sure of it. He couldn't just forego the chance of finding something because he didn't understand the consequences. That's how science worked. It's true, this world had a morbid twist to it. He'd never imagined he'd have to pay for discoveries with blood, but that only confirmed his theory. Whoever had written these books and infused them with this perverse magic was hiding something important.

Every good vault has an even better lock, he thought. Griffin had underestimated how much he cared for Savara and how far he was willing to go to keep her safe. He'd prick his finger over every page of every book in this damned library if it meant protecting her from whatever in this world was out to get her.

Jasper picked up the cane he'd taken from Hyrum and pulled at the gorilla's head, unsheathing the blade hidden within. He ran his thumb over the edge of it, wincing at the sharp burn of the metal in his skin.

"Here we go…" He picked up the book, smudged a bloody thumbprint onto the page, and watched as the jumbled words transformed before him.

* * *

BIG TOG SUMMONED one of the maids again, this time whispering a task in her ear and sending her on her way. He dug into his desk and pulled out a small. He regarded it fondly. Black ink on white paper, marking out the artistically softened features of a man with whom he shared various features—chiselled jaw, charming smile, fiery eyes. The man looked to be a fair bit taller than Big Tog and several years younger as well.

"My son," he said, handing her the sketch.

Savara couldn't understand how or why, but something told her she'd seen this man before.

Big Tog plucked the knife from his desk and toyed with it as he spoke. "We are not so different, my little duck. I once felt lost in this grand expanse of world. There was even a time when the darkness called out to me too, though, not the way it does to you, I imagine." His lips curled into a vicious smile that made her bones tremble. "I was young and foolish in those days. I would've given my soul to anyone who promised to pick me out of poverty. When the darkness called, I answered. I promised something I hadn't yet had in exchange for my rule of Osiir: able-bodied soldiers who could fight with fire." Her mind suddenly travelled back to the night in the forest when Jasper spoke of caged Argia headed into battle. "I got what I had always wanted, control of the city and a life free of poverty, through what I believed to be a steep but not unreasonable cost. Only, it wasn't mine to pay. Not yet. When the darkness returned, it took what I had promised, and more…"

"Your son," she realised.

"…is *kanala*, brilliant in battle and destined for greatness." Big Tog unhitched a heavy breath. The grandfather clock at the end of the room punctuated the silence between them. Finally, after a long train of thought, he spoke again. "I know what you are, child. There has not been one like you for an exceptionally long time. Many have forgotten your kind entirely. Only those who have seen the darkness, as I have, remember to fear it."

Echoes of the screams from the night in the forest swelled in her head, similar to those of her nightmares. The sensation appeared too readily in her palms, of slow beating hearts and a thirst for blood and chaos. She frowned as she gazed upon her hands, slowly losing faith in the idea of using her powers for good.

"You have a gift," he added, relishing the word. "You should embrace it."

Some gift, she thought, remembering the version of her that used to spend entire afternoons with Jasper on the beaches back home, waving twigs in the air like wands. This magic, *real* magic, was not nearly as fun as her books had made it out to be.

In the past few weeks, she'd discovered she was an orphan (officially), a princess (and sole heir to the Argia throne), a bad friend (considering that Jasper had hardly looked at her since she'd almost gotten him killed), and last, but not least… a Blood Daemon. Maybe she'd only convinced herself she was a good person to avoid having to see the truth. She hurt people, her friends, her family, innocent people. Maybe she felt like an outcast for so long because she was trying to be something other than her nature. Maybe she was a monster.

"Before I tell you what you must do, I have one final surprise," he said. As he spoke, a knock came from the door. A young, scrappy-looking boy no more than sixteen entered the room, held by the collar by the same man who had brought her here. "Thank you," he added. The man bowed. Savara noted a distinct look of disappointment on his face as he departed. "Do you know why you are here, my boy?" Big Tog asked. The boy shook his head nervously. "Good." Big Tog turned to Savara and beckoned her over. "Feel for his heart," he said. "Use those beautiful powers of yours as you did on my men."

Savara recoiled. "What do you mean?"

"Feel for his heart. Make him walk." Before she could voice her doubts, he added, "I have seen it done. Make him walk."

Her nerves tensed at the malice in his tone. She did as she was told and called out for her powers. They were slow to rise, but eventually, she managed to coax them out until she could feel them extend past her body and over to the boy.

Savara focused on the accelerated beating of his heart and willed him to step towards them. To her surprise, the boy's legs obeyed.

Big Tog nodded as he looked at the boy, whose eyes had widened with fear. "Brilliant!" he exclaimed, and for a second, Savara smiled, until she heard his next words. "Kill him."

The young boy's face blanched, his feet frozen in place as his knees trembled.

Savara's control faltered. She gaped at Big Tog, whose face lacked the emotions needed to be human. "You never said I'd have to—" she stuttered.

"Kill him," Big Tog repeated irritably.

But Savara refused steadfastly. Big Tog shook his head. He took her hand, lacing her fingers between his own, knife in hand and aimed at the boy's chest. Savara tried to pull away, but he was too strong. Her muscles trembled under his force. Just as the tip touched the boy, the thing inside her roared to life.

In her palms, once again, she felt the lives of the two people around her. Every breath, every heartbeat, even the space their souls occupied in their bodies. It was intoxicating. Savara successfully stayed Big Tog's hand, as she had done with Griffin, but when her power began to call for blood, she hesitated.

In that brief moment of doubt, the knife plunged into the boy's chest and deeper still into his heart. His trembling body slunk to the floor; his face whiter than the marble tiles around him. Savara dropped to his side. She clutched him. Held him close. Attempted to warm his already freezing body. To keep the spurts of blood from escaping his chest.

Big Tog simply moved to the desk and cleaned his knife.

"Why?" Savara demanded, but Big Tog wouldn't answer. She begged and pleaded with whatever was in her to save the boy, the way it had patched her hand, but the thing inside wouldn't answer. With a few more violent tremors, the life of the young boy vanished. "Why?"

"To understand the contours of your *special* powers."

"Why did you have to kill him?"

"He was a rat. I have no sympathy for rats," he offered when the body had grown cold. There was no remorse in his words. "Besides, if you were stronger, you could've stopped me," Big Tog said candidly. She finally understood why Griffin had wanted to protect her from him. He was a killer, a psychopath, a true monster. "This was a free lesson, my little duck: those you don't kill get a second chance to kill you."

"You monster," she snarled.

He only shrugged.

Instantly, the thrum of power returned to her hands with a hunger. Savara turned her blood-marked hands on him, shaking as she lost herself. Tendrils of lavender whipped themselves around her. She breathed heavily, intimately aware of all the life around her. Big Tog's, his sleeping wife, the various guards he had stationed around the house—even his precious garden of lilies. Savara screamed as tears pooled beneath her chin. The tendrils charged forward, tossing Big Tog over his desk, sending papers and ledgers flying in all directions. A crystal turtle-shaped paperweight landed heavily at her feet, shattering as it struck the ground. Shards of glass strewed themselves across the floor around her, like painfully sharp confetti for a distinctly macabre parade. Big Tog groaned from the other end of the room.

What have I done? Savara stared down at her trembling, blood-marked hands. She slumped to her knees.

The light from the sconces evaporated. The random sheets of parchment drifted gently to the floor in her wake.

"So beautiful…" Big Tog twisted to his feet and replaced a stray hair into his curling ram horns. "Do you not see? You can grab hold of life, control it, break it, with no need for the mess of blood. You can become its master."

"I won't… That's not who I am."

"You were blessed for a reason. What more glorious reason is there than that?"

"I don't kill. It's not in me to—"

"Say what you will, my little duck, but the same world that made me made you," he said as he brushed the dust off his suit. "As for our deal, hear this now and hear this good. The shadows have taken the missing Argia to Idune, and among them, my son. Bring him back. But before you do, you will find the Prince of Shadows, and you will take his life, just as I have taught you. Only then will you be free of the stones."

The rubies burned cold in her skin, finally filled with their deadly purpose. A promise made and a soul bound was now a sentence to be upheld.

"I would never have agreed if I'd known I'd have to—"

"Kill someone?" He glared at her with no signs of his former charming self. "You think you are the only one who has made a deal with the devil?" he growled. "One way or another, we all do… and the devil always demands his due."

Tears streamed down her flustered cheeks. She had no idea how she was going to bring his child back, let alone kill whoever the Prince of Shadows was, but now her life depended on it.

"Why me?" she whispered, the emotions having swallowed her voice.

His smile drooped. "You are the only one who can." The grandfather clock on the other end of the room chimed four. "The sun is almost up. They will begin to notice your absence."

Savara didn't thank him for his time, or his obscure lesson about her powers. It was the exchange of services, his in sharpening her sword, hers in wielding it for him. She mounted the horse, teary-eyed and trembling, and rode back with his second in command the way they'd come. She offered to go alone, but the man refused. She was now valuable property—Big Tog's valuable property. He was there to make sure she arrived safely.

Suddenly she remembered Big Tog's initial threat of killing her himself if she failed. What she now understood made the threat much more deadly: the deal they'd made, at its morbid core, was his blood for her own.

Near the end of their journey, the horses stopped suddenly, whinnying wildly, falling short of knocking her off.

"What's wrong?" she asked, but the answer screamed back at her louder than any voice ever could. Billowing clouds of smoke rose above the treetops. The moonlight disappeared behind a dark cloud of black smoke. She jumped from the horse and ran as fast as she could back to the camp. Animals ran past her in the opposite direction, ones she recognised from the stables. Her heart pounded like the hoofs of the stallions she'd left behind. She picked up the pace, once again feeling the sour taste of fear on her tongue and hoping she wasn't too late.

* * *

THE APPRENTICE SIPPED his jasmine tea, watching the goings-on from the small café in the upper levels of Idune. The people here were just as idly ignorant as the ones in Osiir at how the world moved outside their precious gates. They continued about with their shopping and their outdoor martial arts lessons, completely unaware of the wars being waged just beyond their borders.

The waitress dropped off another sweet cake to accompany his tea. She smiled sweetly, but he knew she would soon forget his face entirely.

The knife at his side hummed.

The time was coming for their world to shift. He knew what had to be done, and what would happen when he did it, but that didn't make it any easier. The Apprentice released a breath and took another sip of steaming tea. He decided to enjoy his last few moments of peace in this frivolous town. No matter what happened on the day of the solstice, nothing was going to stop him.

CHAPTER 33

ONE LITTLE SPARK

ALL AROUND HER, tents were alight with blinding red flames. People scrambled to the safety of the forest. Some of the Argia attempted to control the fires, but they were too powerful. The best any of them could do was channel the flames away as others escaped out into the cool night air.

Savara's heart raced as she rushed to find her friends, jumping over rows of flames, and dodging the fleeing people. Some even tried to pull her along with them, but she shrugged them off and continued.

"Storm!" she called to the flaming redhead running past her. "Where is everyone?"

"Where have you been?" Storm shouted back angrily. "You've had half the world losing their heads looking for you!"

"I—"

"Never mind. I'll deal with you later," she hissed, marching off in the direction of the next burning tent. Ash fell from the skies like blackened snowflakes in a toxic blizzard.

"I'm sorry," Savara called as she tried to keep up with her. "Let me help you."

"You want to help?" Storm spat, attempting to waste no more time with their conversation. "Fine, get the rest of these people out of the tents."

With the help of a few Argia soldiers, they managed to clear the first quarter of the camp.

"Who's still missing?" Savara asked.

"Sebas went off looking for your human friend, and neither of them is back yet!" Storm yelled. She slashed frantically through burning timber and canvas, moving on to the next tent with increased urgency. Her eyes grew watery with each one she didn't find them in. She pressed on, carving easily through the sides of the tents with just a flick of her sword.

Savara struggled to keep up. "We'll find them," she called out to her.

Storm spun around with a fury, tears lacing the rims of her eyelids. "We'd better find them, or I swear on all Iturri, it'll be your neck at the end of my sword," she said.

Savara gulped and nodded, unable to voice her understanding. She followed Storm through the burning maze, passing the rest of the group who were all busy with their sections of the camp. Brass and two other Zerua sent air currents through the pathways, blowing away the smoke and allowing people to escape the tents. Griffin directed everyone to the safety of the forest. There was still no sign of Jasper or Sebastian.

"Jasper!" Savara cried; her voice drowned out by crackling fires. Just as she was about to lose all faith, they found them, in the last tent, inches away from being consumed by the flames.

* * *

STORM SLICED THROUGH the mesh with ease, sending plumes of smoke billowing through the opening. Her heart skipped a beat as her eyes met his. The world around them was consumed by flames, but his eyes still glowed brighter than anything she'd ever known.

How dare he get himself into such a mess, Storm thought.

Sebastian held back the encroaching flames as Jasper struggled to free his leg from under one of the fallen support beams. She and Savara worked quickly to lift the beam.

"Take your friend and go!" she yelled to Savara.

"But—"

"Now!"

Savara nodded. She and Jasper limped through the slit, but Storm stayed behind. She'd seen Sebastian struggling with the fire. She heard the crackling of the beams overhead.

"Anika, go!" he called to her. "The flames are too strong."

Another menacing crack sounded above them. Storm shot a glance upwards, noticing the last support beam was about to break.

"Sebas, don't be stubborn. I'm not leaving you," she replied between smoke-filled coughs that left her light-headed. She knew it was now or never. Storm rammed into him with all her might, pushing both their bodies through the slit, landing with a hard thud. The tent came crashing down behind them, sending the scent of charred wood and cloth billowing into the night sky.

The world evaporated around them, consumed rapidly by the vicious flames, but in her mind, time stood still. Her head rested on the hollow of Sebastian's chest; his quickened heartbeat echoed her own. She pushed herself upright, coming to rest in a compromising position on top of him.

"I like a woman on top," he grinned. By the hiss in his voice, she knew he'd bruised his ribs again.

"Don't get comfortable," she scoffed, contemplating bruising him more as she made to stand. She couldn't believe that, even as flames danced and clouds of smoke swallowed the air they breathed, Sebastian found time to make a joke. Suddenly, the smirk disappeared from his face. Sebastian pulled her in close and rolled over her. "Sebas—" she yelled, interrupted by a subsequent blast overhead.

Storm closed her eyes. The brightness of the blaze seeped through her eyelids, glowing first a hot white, then orange and red before eventually settling on black. A tear streamed down her cheek from the intensity of the moment. When she heard his heavy breath again, she knew it was over. Storm opened her eyes, finding him staring back at her, relief plastered across his face. She couldn't believe it; he'd done it to protect her. He'd shielded her with his body, extending his hand out to block the crashing wave of flames above them.

Sebastian held her gaze for what felt like an eternity. The water lacing his eyes highlighted the gold in his irises. The wind tousled his hair around his cheekbones.

"Sebas…"

A smile tugged at his lips. "Taking turns is fun too," he added with a wink.

Storm shook her head. "Get off of me!" she spat as she kicked him backwards. She stood up, dusting off the dirt and ash that now covered every part of her body. Sebastian rose beside her, ignoring the charring in his arm and the soot that coated his body. His eyes fixated on her alone. "What is it?" she hissed, eyeing him cautiously.

"Your hair…" he said, reaching behind her and holding up the braid that still clung to her head by half as many strands as before.

Storm reached back and dragged her hand along the tangled red braid. She frowned, reaching the part that had been chomped on by the flames. With a swift flick of her sword, she chopped off the length of it that hung below her shoulders and left it lying limp in his hand.

"Keep it, waste of time to maintain anyway," Storm replied as she turned back to the rest of the group, her new bob ruffling freely in the smoky breeze. Out of the corner of her eye, she spied Sebastian contemplating the length of her hair. She knew she shouldn't bother with him, but the way he gaped at the braid left her wondering. "What is your problem, Sebas?"

He grinned mischievously at her before tossing the charred red braid to the fire. "I love a woman with short hair."

*　*　*

THE BRILLIANT ORANGE of the dawn sky was marred with heavy plumes of ash and smoke. Savara and Jasper, along with the rest of the camp, had taken refuge in the forest in whatever manner of shelter they could hassle together. Thankfully, no one was badly injured, but no one slept the night, either.

For a long time, neither spoke, letting the moaning of the wind speak for them. Savara stared out at the dying embers of yet another ruined home, hugging her knees into her chest. Everything she did ended in disaster. Tonight was no different.

"We should never have come here," she mumbled.

"Sav, what's done is done. It's not your fault," Jasper replied as he stroked her back.

"But it is…" She raised a hand to her gemstoned cheek. She still hadn't told him about Big Tog and the soul bond, and after the night's incidents, telling him was truly the last thing she wanted to do. How could she tell her best friend that she'd killed someone? That she would have to kill again or be killed herself?

"Sav?"

"I made a deal I shouldn't have…" she sighed. Savara bit her lip as she turned to him, his sad, brown eyes pleading with her, longing for the communication they once had. She longed for it too, but this world had changed them. She'd come seeking answers, but the more she found out about herself, the less she felt she knew. Jasper knew nothing, but he had a right to. Maybe they could salvage whatever was left of their friendship.

The story trickled from her lips in non-specific details at

first, but when it grew time for her to explain her gems, the words poured from her in floods. The pressure of the secret had built up inside her and now, burst open like a broken dam. Everything from their time in the palace to her encounters with Big Tog. Fear flashed through Jasper's eyes as she told him of the boy she'd inadvertently killed.

Jasper recoiled from her. "You never told me."

"I couldn't. I didn't want you to… fear me…"

"Sav, how could you even think that?" he said with an edge to his voice she'd never heard before. "I don't understand why you would keep this from me."

"I only wanted to keep you safe." She frowned. They both knew it was a lie. The real reason she'd kept quiet was that she didn't know how to tell him—the person who gazed at her with awe in his eyes—that she was a monster. "You don't know what this world is capable of," she stuttered. *Or what I am*, she wanted to add but couldn't.

"Because I'm human?" Jasper growled. "That's it, isn't it? Being human just isn't enough for you…"

"Jasper, how could you say that?"

"It's the truth, Sav. Admit it. Being human was never enough for you, not even when we were home."

"That wasn't my home, Jasper."

"Do you hear yourself?" He clenched his fists. "It was the only home you'd ever known, or have you forgotten that too?"

"I haven't forgotten anything!"

"You've forgotten me!" he yelled, sending birds flapping into the precarious dawn. "You go off with Sebastian every day, pretending to learn to fight when really, you just want to avoid anything that makes you think of home. I'm the one who spends my days searching through towers of books to find something that might help you. Something that might save you from whatever's inside you. So what if I'm just human? I'm the one who's been there from day one…"

"I…" Savara whimpered, tears brimming in her eyes.

"But that was never good enough… *I* was never good enough." A silence set in heavily between them. After a few seconds, Jasper stood up, turning his back to her. "I must be an idiot for caring about you as much as I do."

"I never meant to hurt you," Savara whispered.

"You did a great job of that. The worst part is, I have always been there for you. I have never judged you. But you *still* felt you had to hide this from me."

"Jasper, don't go," she pleaded. "Please, don't go."

He unclenched his fists and sighed. "Some things, Sav, you don't get to choose."

Savara's heart dropped with each step that carried him further from her. There was nothing but distance between them now. Her eyes followed him until he disappeared behind a pile of smoking wood that somehow seemed less scorched than she did. As her anger and fear grew, the thing inside her grew too. Restless and hungry. Hot tears streamed down her pallid cheeks.

What have I done?

Savara dug her nails into her palms, trying to suppress the menacing rush of power growing within. Her nails punched moon-shaped holes in the skin, but the pain was nothing compared to the vicious battering of her powers. They lusted for use, hammering her very bones. She feared they might break her. She couldn't let them.

I'm not a monster...

Savara repeated those words over and over until the voices in her head stopped trying to contradict her. When the violent feeling finally died down, she let out a warm cloud of breath in the chilly morning air. The blood trickled from her palms, but it was a small price to pay for keeping a lid on whatever monster lay in wait beneath her skin. She focused on the slits in her palms, willing the skin to stitch itself back together as it had with Big Tog, but this time, it didn't respond.

Fine, she thought, feeling utterly defeated.

Savara sat alone, entombed in her own misery until the cruelty of the wind that wrapped her shoulders became too much to bear. Its sad song highlighted only her sorrow. She'd done it this time. The damage she'd done tonight was irreparable. Jasper was not coming back.

The thing inside her had quelled for now, and there was no use freezing in place. Savara sniffled and wiped the tears from her cheeks, leaving streaks of black ash in their place as she set off for a new place to wait out the cold.

She made her way over to the pile of charred wood that was once her tent. The roof had collapsed, and everything had fizzled up with it. There hadn't been much to the little tent but at least it had been her own. In it, she wasn't a missing princess or a bloodthirsty daemon. She wasn't the person that snapped at her friends or killed on command. In it, she was just Savara, something she hadn't been since she jumped worlds.

And now it's gone...

She nudged the debris with her feet, searching for some semblance of the person she was before life fizzled up in her hands. The wreckage around matched the one inside her. The ash reminded her of every shifty shadow, every lonely night, every cold-sweat-inducing nightmare. If she closed her eyes, she was back in the square, surrounded by violent flames and streams of blood. If she listened hard enough, she could hear the screams of townspeople as they begged for their lives. Every morbid detail came back with terrifying clarity. Maybe, just maybe, they weren't nightmares at all…

Suddenly, her foot hit hard metal with a clang. Savara furrowed her brow as she stooped down to brush off a layer of ash from whatever the flames had left standing. Her chest? She opened it, careful not to burn her fingers on the warm rims, unsure how it had survived the blaze. In the centre, still bound by brown paper and twine, she found the strange parcel—eerily untouched.

"This is all your fault, isn't it?" Savara growled at the little package. "None of this would have happened if it weren't for you." She dragged another charcoal-stained finger across her cheek, sweeping away her tears as she plucked it from its resting place. She carried it towards the edge of the line of cinders that was once the camp. "Because of you, I'm twice an orphan," she hissed, entering the part of the forest that light recoiled from. "I'm stuck in this world where I have to kill or be killed…"

The contents of the box rattled in her hands, resonating with her words.

"Because of you, I became a monster…" The hand holding the package shook violently at her side. The acceptance of her nature brought no catharsis. "I didn't want any of this!" she wailed into the dark.

I've lost everything… my home, my family, my friends…

Her world had dwindled to a series of traumatic flashbacks that endeavoured to attack at her most vulnerable, all because of the stupid package. Resignation caressed her spirit, but there was no love in its touch. Only the promise of more bloodshed.

"Fuck you, and fuck this," she hissed at the little box as she hurled it into the depths of the forest.

Savara slumped to her knees and began to sob. Her uncle, gone; Ms Short, gone; the family she once knew—all gone. Her best friend, her new friends… what more did she have to lose? What more did this world insist on taking?

Her own heart had been so used to receiving sensations from others that she'd almost forgotten she too could feel— could hurt. Life had insisted on breaking her, taking away more and more of her until it finally did. She didn't wonder if she'd ever recover, the innocent part of her that believed in recovery was gone.

Savara had no idea how long she'd been crying, only that the cold had set in around her. The cold of night. The kind that loomed in the darker depths of the forest, to which not even the daring sun beyond had access. Soon, the chill took shape, gripping her shoulder beneath a firm hand.

"You're not done yet," said a voice she was tired of hearing but still couldn't place.

The scent of night flowers filled her nose. A new shadow loomed over her in the already darkened wood. She stared with water-logged eyes at a soft face framed by curling tufts of ebony hair that made his midnight-coloured eyes glow in comparison. She knew this face. She didn't know how, but she knew it.

"I am," Savara wept, pulling her gaze from him. "I'm done. I can't do this anymore. I can't keep hurting the people I love. I can't keep pretending I'm okay. My heart feels like it's about to give out all the time and I can't keep pushing..." She sniffled. "I want it to give out. I can't hold on any longer."

"You're stronger than this," the voice replied with care. "Besides, it's not your time."

Upon hearing that phrase, Savara wondered if this entity, who had been chasing her all around Visanthe, wasn't Death himself. "Make it my time," she whispered. "Please."

"I see..." The chill around her disappeared for a second. When it returned, she heard something drop at her feet. Death stooped beside her again and ran a cold finger down the side of her face, scooping up her tears. The sensation of his touch lingered long after he'd removed it. "The world has not yet ended, princess, and you are not yet bested." Death sighed as he stood. "We will meet again soon," he added before evaporating into nothingness.

When Savara finally looked up from her knees, she noticed a lingering cloud of sparkling black dust hovering beside her. Beneath it, where Death had stood, the little brown package had returned; this time, with a strange silvery card attached to it and a single word scrawled across it: *Idune*.

CHAPTER 34

LETTING GO

BY MORNING, THE once vibrant camp was nothing more than ashes and rubble. Griffin wandered through the remnants of the paths, kicking charred bits of wood with his feet, and stomping out the occasional lingering flame. Brass walked beside him silently though Griffin could sense him waiting for an opening to speak.

"Out with it," he said finally, tired of feeling the heaviness of Brass' gaze on his neck.

"Your father's camp…" Brass commented.

"Was just a camp," Griffin replied coldly.

"Are you sure?"

Griffin remembered few things fondly about the time his father had spent here. After inadvertently showing Savara the one memory, the rest had come back to haunt him, as though they had been lying in wait.

Just as well it got burned down, he thought. If someone hadn't, he might've.

"Very."

Brass nodded. "Who do you think started the fire?"

"The mafia," Griffin replied, watching the horizon for any new signs of trouble, but the world had stilled since the flames.

Brass furrowed his brow. "They have never given this kind of trouble before…"

Griffin's eyes came to rest where Savara and Jasper were talking heatedly. "We've never had someone like her here before," he said, frowning as he watched Jasper storm off, leaving Savara in tears. Griffin watched as she stared at her palms, a breath caught in his throat, wondering what might happen in her anger. He'd seen her powers manifest before out of fear. He unconsciously readied himself on the balls of his feet, in case he'd have to stop her, but was relieved to see her drop them and hug her knees. He needed to check on her once they'd finished their rounds. Guilt tugged at him.

The two men walked a ways further in silence. Most of the people at the camp had fled during the night. Thankfully, no one died and not too many were injured, but the loss of the camp meant they would have to seek out other refuge.

Somewhere safe from all of this, Griffin hoped, but he knew that no one in Visanthe would be safe with the shadows lurking.

"What do we do now?" asked Brass as he stared out at the various mounds of ash.

Griffin knew Brass had always been fond of the place, especially coming from somewhere that forced him to be something he wasn't: a killer. When he still lived as one of the guards of the Zerua king, Brass was the most stealthy and effective of all in the king's party. But Griffin had seen the pain such a life brought him with his own two eyes. He wasn't born to kill; he was made to. And now, he would spend the rest of his life healing those in need, saving lives to atone for the ones he'd been forced to take.

When Brass first came to the camp, Griffin had promised him that he would never again have to take up that deadly mantle. Their friendship began as an escape, but since then, had become a brotherhood. However, with the camp burned down and the shadows on the rise, Griffin worried it would be hard to keep his promise.

"I don't plan on rebuilding," Griffin replied as he stared up at the sky.

He had always been able to read the stars, find guidance within their brilliance. A younger him used to think they simply watched and mocked the lives of those on the ground, but he'd since learned to heed their warnings. The stars were the record-keepers of time. In time, all things would eventually come to pass. There was no use in fighting it. And, for a time, this brought him comfort.

But not now. The stars above had long gone, and this dawn sky held no wisdom, only warning. And he'd already received all the warnings he could handle.

"Griffin!" Savara called as she rushed towards them. A quiver played at her lip; a small thing tucked beneath her arm.

"Are you okay?" he asked, noticing her ash-lined cheeks.

"I…" Her eyes fell to the ground, unable to hold his gaze. "This is all my fault."

"What do you mean?"

Savara hesitated, letting the words hover on the tip of her tongue. "I spoke to Big Tog last night."

"You what?" he growled, clenching his fists at his sides. He'd warned her of how dangerous he could be, and still, she'd gone back. Her impulsivity was dangerous. Griffin didn't realise just how much until now. She could've gotten herself killed, Big Tog could've kept her as leverage, or worse… "Savara, I told you—"

She tensed. "I know." Her hand floated up to where the rubies marred her cheek. "I had to…"

Griffin's heart sank as he stared at the stones glowing red under the rising sun. If he'd been more careful, she never would've made the soul bond. If anything, this mess was his fault.

"He knows about the stones," Savara added, her voice hoarse from a long night of crying and a lack of sleep. "And he knows *they* are planning an attack. They have a whole army of Argia soldiers headed for—"

"Idune," Griffin interrupted. The skies had been warning him as much for some time, of a possible shift in rule, but he never imagined it would be brought on by violence.

Savara pursed her lips and nodded. "I have to be there when it happens. Big Tog's son is there amongst the captured soldiers. I have to bring him back and…" she hesitated.

Griffin knew there was more to the story, whether Savara was going to tell him or not. If it were only a matter of finding his son, Big Tog would've flooded the streets of Idune with his underlings. No. This reeked of something more sinister.

If Big Tog knew about the stones, there was a chance he knew who was looking for them, too.

Idune was known to all as the unconquerable city, but after decades of peace and parties, Griffin doubted they were prepared for the kind of fight that awaited them. Worse still, he knew that if Idune fell, the rest of the world would too.

"Brass," he said, turning to his dearest friend, "I need you to salvage whatever mode of transport we have. We are leaving for Idune as soon as possible. You and Simon stay close but keep out of the fight. I promised you wouldn't ever have to see this kind of violence again. I still intend to keep my promise."

Brass bowed and made for the others, but Savara lingered.

"I'm sorry about the camp," she whispered, twiddling with a strand of hair between her fingers.

Griffin dropped his shoulders. It wasn't her fault, no matter how much she blamed herself, but she knew he wouldn't believe her if he said so. Finally, he sighed as he returned his gaze to the smouldering ashes. "It was just a camp."

He could hear her open her mouth as if to speak again but she must have thought better of it. Instead, she left him alone to his thoughts.

The curious letter whose twin predicted the downfall of the Argia glowed vividly in his mind. Last time, he'd ignored the warning. This time, he would not be so foolish.

Night spreads across the earth, shadows climb the walls.
~ a friend

Griffin stared down at the charred tent that once belonged to his father, where something glinted from within the rubble. He brushed away the debris and stooped down to pick up a still-warm, charred silver locket. He opened it. Inside, the pictures of his mother and father were surprisingly intact. His eyes glazed over as he contemplated it, wondering briefly whether to throw it back into the smouldering ashes before ultimately slipping it into his pocket.

The wind that howled through the forest spoke of change, carrying something slightly grimmer than the cold. He'd felt this kind of air before and knew what it meant. Death was lurking nearby, waiting for his next prey.

CHAPTER 35

THE GATES OF IDUNE

WINTER HAD ARRIVED earlier than expected. Even the temperate climate of the Harri territories had dipped, spreading worry through the homes of unprepared farmers whose crops would not last if temperatures kept dropping. This new cold brought with it the whisperings of trouble. Grey clouds sat interlaced on the distant horizon, slowly creeping towards the capital city of Idune.

In contrast to the Argia territories which had been mostly clustered around the main city of Osiir, the Harri territories were pockets of autonomous townships, tribes, and the occasional urban hubs. Unlike the Argia, whose element was sparsely available and very much feared, the Harri's element of earth was abundant. The people's reverence of Iturri and the earth around them was on display everywhere in the form of monuments and temples, even the occasional ceremony.

Savara stared out the window of the rickety carriage, entranced by the great wall rising from the horizon. Jasper sat at the front with Simon, discussing the curiosities of the Harri people. Storm and Sebastian rode on stallions beside the carriage, each one avoiding the other's gaze but subtly wishing to be seen. Griffin and Brass opposite her, discussing the subtleties of their plan. Occasionally, he'd ask her how she was feeling, and she'd give a non-committal nod in response. He seemed to accept this as her being okay. In reality, the situation and her task weighed on her more than she could say.

They dropped Brass and Simon in the last town before Idune and prepared themselves for the task at hand. The rural farm towns, impoverished villages, and miles of withering crop fields that they'd passed nearer to the Argia territories gave way to suburban metropolises lined with orchards and greenery that had yet to die in the curious cold front. Crops, however, weren't the only things troubled by the cold. None of them had slept properly since the fire, and Savara doubted they would anytime soon.

All roads merged into one as they neared the great stone wall. It extended for miles in each direction, wrapping in half-lunar fashion around the foot of an equally impressive mountain range. Behind it, a river flowed into the city from higher altitudes, helped by an extensive network of aqueducts that looked like they'd sprouted straight from the ground. Golems carved in perfect detail out of shining black granite towering almost twenty men high lined the great wall. Their carved clothes belonged to the Terra Army of old, even authentically equipped with sheathed long blades. They shined under the heavy mountain sun as they stood at attention, protecting their great homeland.

Suddenly, the carriage jumped. A long rumbling sound echoed for miles as the ground beneath them shook. Savara poked her head out of the window, wondering what caused the abrupt stop when she found herself staring at a large granite foot.

"Halt. Who goes there?" said a booming voice from high above. One of the golems had pushed itself off the wall and blocked their path.

From inside the carriage, it was impossible to tell where the voice was coming from. Even as she stepped out, it took her a while to notice the tiny man standing inside the cavernous mouth of the golem.

"We come in peace," Griffin called back to him. "We have valuable information for the council."

"The council?" he spat. The man made a series of forceful-looking movements from within the mouth of the golem. In response, the towering structure extended its arm to the ground beside the carriage with a loud thud. The man stomped down the arm and halted in front of them. He was taller than Griffin by an inch or two, and his stature was just as robust as the golem he controlled. He crossed two muscled arms over his armoured chest as he gazed down at them all. "Who do you think you are, demanding such an audience?"

"Guests of the Lady Amaia, third in command of the High Council of Idune," replied Griffin, unfazed by the man's imposing nature.

The man grumbled and stomped his foot, simultaneously catapulting himself onto the wall in a feat of great acrobatics. He spoke heatedly to one of his colleagues atop the wall before leaping back into the golem's mouth. The golem lifted its foot, unblocking their path. The guard then signalled to his companion, who followed suit. The two guards slammed their arms to their sides, causing a part of the wall to crumble, and leaving enough space for them to cross into the city. No sooner did they pass through than did the gates reform behind them. The sound reverberated through the mountain range as he called out to them, "You will be watched."

"Why the need for such protocol?" asked Jasper.

"There are people here who don't believe *they* have returned," Griffin replied. "They see only nation-on-nation violence. Some on the council would rather see people like us hanged than go to war, so be careful."

Savara looked out the window at the mix of fancy shogun-style and traditional wood and granite-style housing that lined the cobblestone streets. Scattered evenly throughout the city, she noticed grass patches and rock gardens that allow residents to practice their skills. Children trained in martial arts in the open-air temples, some even managing to manipulate the earth: raising it, lowering it, shaping it, and hovering it. Carts with stone wheels moved of their own volition beside them and followed curving roads deep into the mountains.

Blissful ignorance, she thought as a crease formed on her brow. *And nothing like Osiir.*

Arriving at their designated lodging quarters, they found their guide: a young soldier, waiting on the balls of his feet in a uniform he hadn't grown into yet. "We are proud to welcome you to the capital city," he said with a voice that was just beginning to drop. "I will be your guide during your time here." His youthful eyes glittered with pride. "I was told Lady

Amaia has invited you all to dinner. You will find the appropriate attire in each of your wardrobes." He guided Savara to the female quarters, where she and Storm would be staying, separated by a wooden wall. "I shall collect you promptly in an hour," he added with a bow as he led the boys to their quarters on the opposite side of the courtyard. Storm glowered at her for only a second before slipping into her room.

"Not like I asked to be neighbours with you," Savara whispered—in case Storm had extraordinary hearing. Her eyes followed the boys down the stairs and across the courtyard, hoping to meet eyes with Jasper, but he dipped into his room without so much as a glance in her direction. They hadn't properly spoken since their fight and Savara wanted nothing more than to fix things between them, but she didn't know how. She hoped that she was wrong—that being human was enough—but a sinking feeling in her gut told her otherwise.

The plain wooden furnishings of the room reminded her of the old family house sitting a world away. She remembered sprawling out on the bed, basking in the sunlight that filtered in through the windows as she allowed herself to be consumed by endless amounts of books about magical places and fantastical worlds. In those days, magic had seemed exciting. Nowadays, she knew better. She almost laughed at how innocent she'd been.

Savara walked over to one of the open windows and rested casually against the sill. Children played, musicians practised, and happiness thrived behind the protection of their great wall. To them, Idune was a paradise. Only she and Griffin knew that Idune was a stronghold waiting to fall. Big

Tog had warned her as much when he demanded she return his son—among other things. This city was vast, more so than Osiir. Savara feared she wouldn't find him before the attack, and the idea of waiting ate at her nerves.

At least she would have dinner to occupy her time.

CHAPTER 36

DINNER

SAVARA RINSED HER skin under steaming water to rid her body of nervous energy. Outside, dark clouds loomed on the horizon. She could sense them stalking towards Idune, the same way she'd sensed the storm back home. The same way she'd always known when a storm was brewing. Was this a byproduct of her powers? Or a testament to her intuition? Either way, she knew not to ignore the feeling.

The first knock at the door came from a young parlour maid waiting to brush through the knots in her hair and paint her face. The plan originally was to tie her hair up, but when the girl recoiled at the sight of the rubies on her cheek, Savara realised it might be prudent to keep something in front of her face, lest others react the same. The girl applied a gentle smattering of makeup to her hollowed cheeks and the bags under her eyes, and stained her lips a bright red, matching the colour of the stones almost exactly. The girl then opened the wardrobe, revealing a flowing green gown, which she helped Savara into silently before bowing out.

This was the dance of royalty that Savara had imagined in Osiir. Nameless people to wait on her and whose encounters left her more distant, more alone than she'd been before. She knew it wasn't the life she wanted. She wanted the life she'd had, missed it with every fibre of her being. She couldn't cry now, though. The young woman's handiwork would go to waste.

Savara twirled around in front of the mirror, letting the setting sun reflect off the glittering emerald embroidery. Unlike in Osiir, wearing this dress did not make her feel like an impostor. This dress fit her better, and, more importantly, had no connotations of royalty. It was simply a dress. Savara wrapped her arms around her torso. She could allow herself to feel good for at least a night. After all, this might have been a dream of hers, once upon a time.

As she imagined her childhood, filled with similar dresses and attending balls and galas, a second, gentle knock sounded at the door. The young soldier from before, wearing a black suit and jade bowtie, bowed gracefully.

"Are you ready?" he asked, offering her his arm.

Savara took a last glance in the mirror and nodded. Besides, her stomach was beginning to rumble, and they had been promised dinner. A simple, strangely elegant dinner. She took hold of his arm, allowing him to lead her down to one of the open-air carriages on the streets where her companions were already waiting.

Jasper's jaw hung open as his eyes followed her down the stairs. Griffin pushed it closed and bowed, nudging him in the side to do the same. Savara bobbed her head and smiled nervously. She may have looked like the royal she was supposed to be, but she still didn't feel like one.

"You two clean up well," she said, staring at them in their matching moss-coloured tailcoats.

"You look…" Jasper gulped. "I mean…"

Savara took hold of his hand and squeezed. Neither knew where to begin or to say what needed to be said, but the gesture bridged the gap between them. There was still a long road to be walked, but at least they were back on track. Jasper smiled awkwardly, his eyes glittering to the point of forming tears. In his smile, she saw the world they'd left behind, the one that didn't care if she was a princess or a daemon. For a second, she let herself indulge in the memory, imagining the world didn't depend on how well they could hide in plain sight—how well they could be sheep among wolves.

Sebastian appeared behind them, having added a large, blooming rose to his tails, and made a show of bowing exceptionally low as he winked at her. She laughed. He could always be counted upon to ease the tension. Finally, Storm arrived, fuming as the soldier led her to the carriage, looking like a goddess in green and white. She was complaining about the lace flowers covering her dress when she caught sight of Sebastian. He scrambled up from his bow to meet her, taking hold of her hand, and kissing it as one would a queen.

"You're looking like a vision, Stormy my dear, but you shouldn't have gotten all dressed up for me," he smirked.

"Watch it, Sebas."

"You don't have your knives tonight, Stormy, but I still have my fire," he whispered in her ear.

"I don't need my knives to strangle you," she whispered back. She breezed past him and climbed into the carriage. Sebastian bit down on the mischievous grin forming at his lips and crawled into the carriage at her side.

The carriage was designed to look like an elegant minecart with a half-roof and a driver's perch at the front. The body was made of stained wood and velvet, but the wheels were made of solid stone. The young soldier hopped into the driver's seat and Jasper scrambled in beside him, ready to probe him with questions about the city no doubt. Griffin led Savara into the final row of the carriage where they shared a look of apprehension as they took their seats. The soldier began moving his hands in a circular motion, sending the carriage lurching forward abruptly before gliding up the street.

Jasper marvelled at the ingenuity of the Harri. He prodded the soldier about other technical applications of their powers, who in turn looked as though her were about to push Jasper out of the carriage.

Savara watched the interaction fondly, admiring curious spark of his. She wished they would talk again like they used to, but she knew it would take more than a hand squeeze and an apology to repair what she'd broken. She turned instead to the world outside, watching as night began to settle around them.

On the pavements beside them, streetlamps began to come to life. People in uniform worked quickly, stomping on the ground to lift them, sparking rocks together to light the fuses inside, and stomping back down to ground level. This great dance of lifts and drops accompanied their journey en route to one of the grander houses at the edge of the neighbourhood.

Griffin, who'd maintained a semblance of calm throughout, frowned as they drew near.

"Have you been here before?" Savara asked.

"A lifetime ago," he offered. "Our gracious hostess was a friend of my mother's once upon a time…"

Savara pursed her painted lips. Griffin looked worried. She'd come to realise that the things that worried Griffin should worry them all.

The carriage slowed to a halt in front of the grand, two-storey house at the base of the mountain. Wooden columns wrapped in ivy and rose sprouted like trees from overflowing flowerbeds, supporting the structure. A neatly curved stone pathway bled onto an imperfectly cut rock staircase, which in turn gave way to paper doors. Groomed topiaries mixed with wild bushes, river stones with paper lanterns, and lots and lots of glass. Everywhere, fragile met firm; danger met delicate. It looked like a symphony brought to life.

They were led into a large parlour with flutes of something akin to champagne in hand by a kindly manservant, who assured them their hostess would be down soon, before dismissing himself to attend to the other guests. Jasper was instantly swept up by the daughter of a visiting minister and some of her friends. Savara frowned but made no attempt to save him. She figured he'd have more fun with them than with her. Besides, she had a different task that night. It was a long shot, but if she kept an ear out and her eyes open, she might be able to find news of where Big Tog's son was hiding.

"When she said she'd invited us to dinner, I didn't expect…" Savara mumbled to Griffin, as she gazed around at the crowd.

"Neither did I," he replied tensely. "It's either a good way to dissimulate our presence or to keep us from causing trouble. Knowing her, it's probably both."

Savara sensed the nerves trickling from him, despite his usual rigid façade. His anxiety ate into hers so much so that the drink in her hand began to shake and spill. She lifted it to her painted lips to avoid more spillage when Griffin rested a hand on her arm.

"Be careful. It's stronger than what you might be used to," he whispered.

Savara knew it was best to heed his warning but, between their combined nerves and the sweet scent that seeped from the glass, she was enticed into sipping. A hot shiver rushed down her throat, warming her body and dizzying her mind. The curl of power around her steadied, quelled by the strange beverage. It was a good thing she didn't plan on using her powers, otherwise, their sudden suppression would be cause for concern. She wondered if the effect was unique to her, or if the drink itself had special, numbing properties. And if so, why?

A band struck up a chord in the far back of the room. Savara swayed lightly on her feet, loosened by the drink. Couples all around the room joined hands and began to twirl around the dancefloor, the greens and reds of their outfits looked like freefalling leaves in the autumn wind.

Suddenly, she noticed Griffin's hand extended in her direction.

"I didn't picture you as a dancer," Savara said.

"I've got a few surprises up my sleeve," he replied. "Besides, I'll get a better view of everyone from the dancefloor."

Savara looked down at his hand hesitantly. "I don't know how," she whispered.

"You don't have to," he said with a smile. "I'll lead."

Maybe it was the drink or vibrant energy around them, most likely the combination of the two, but she took hold and followed him out onto the dance floor.

"How are you feeling?" he asked, drawing her in close for a dip.

"Nervous…"

"I know, you've been stepping on my feet," he said, turning her cheeks red. "And otherwise?"

"Oh…" Savara cast her gaze to the ground as he spun her out. Nerves had been eating at her since they hatched this plan. Guilt, too. What if she couldn't control her powers? What if she made things worse, again? "I'm afraid. What if the world is broken beyond repair and it's all my fault?"

"The world was broken long before you," Griffin said as he snapped her in for a rhythmic embrace. His dark blue eyes glittered inches from her face. Despite how well he hid it, Savara sensed the rippling of his own worry in the air around them. "Let's hope no one else has to lose their life to fix it."

The song ended, but she was still caught in his embrace. She wanted to tell him she believed him, that she trusted they would fix it. But that would've been a lie.

"I'm going to go find out where our hostess is," he added, planting a kiss on her forehead before disappearing into the crowd.

Savara stayed behind, contemplating the dancers gliding around the ballroom. Some of the guests glanced back at her, their heads tilting curiously as they caught sight of her gemstoned scar. She brushed her hair in front of it and made to blend in with the crowd unnoticed, but someone had already set his sights on her.

"Don't they all just look ridiculous?" said a strangely familiar voice. The voice, which rumbled low like tides against a cliffside, belonged to a man with ebony black curls and a matching suit. The air around her cooled as he neared, as though she were being blanketed by the night. She avoided his prodding gaze. "They dance around as if there's nothing more important than this…pretentious display of ill-gotten wealth."

"Harsh tone for a guest, wouldn't you say?"

The man laughed, the timbre and warmth of it raising the hairs on her arms. "Let's just say I'm happy to point out the obvious."

"That feels cruel," she replied, wishing to be free of the conversation.

"Perhaps…" She could hear the smirk in his tone. "And you? Should you not be dancing with the rest? Or are you as cruel as me?"

"I'm not…cruel," she lied. Her stomach churned in response.

"Yet, you linger in the shadows. Is it for fear you might be seen? Or fear that you won't?"

Suddenly, it clicked. She remembered the chill, the voice, even the scent that wrapped around him. Her heart began to race. She scanned the room for Griffin or anyone who might save her, but none of them were anywhere near her. She was alone, standing beside a man who she was certain was Death himself. Yet, this man, whoever he was, felt too alive to be the same Death she'd seen in her uncle's eyes. He had a static about him that rippled through the little distance between them. A danger about him, too. His energy tugged fiercely on hers. It was all she could do to avoid his gaze.

"This feels like a dream..." she replied instead, hoping the answer would allow her to remain on the outskirts.

"Well, if it is your dream, I must say I'm glad to be included. Although, you could've perhaps picked a more intimate setting."

"I—"

"I'm kidding," he added with another gentle laugh. "Actually, I was hoping for a dance, and thought if I rattled you first, you might not be so averse to it." He extended a hand towards her. In his palm, she noticed a star-shaped scar. "I promise it won't be worse than looking like a lost puppy all night."

"You want to dance with me?"

"As fetching as you are standing like a statue, movement might suit your needs. Consider it an offering of help. In case you were afraid of wandering eyes, a moving target is harder to see."

She studied his hand carefully. It wasn't a terrible idea, and yet, she found herself looking for an escape. Something about being alone with him set her nerves on edge. Maybe he wasn't Death, but he wasn't a saint either. That much she could tell by his energy alone.

"Besides, people tend not to notice me. You might find it to your advantage."

This was true. The people around them seemed to look the other way as soon as their eyes landed on him, as though redirected by an invisible force. Savara chewed on the inside of her cheek as she contemplated his offer. As much as she didn't want to, she found the prodding gazes of the crowd to be motivation enough to move. She accepted his hand at first but whipped her own back as soon as their fingers met. The blood drained from her face. Savara stared at her palm, waiting for the sharp tingling in it to die. Whether it was because of him or not was beside the point. The thing inside her had awoken.

"Is something wrong?" the man asked innocently.

"No…" she lied.

The flesh of her palm still bore the marks of her fingernails. It buzzed with that sinister energy she'd learned to fear—the kind that meant her powers were waiting. They pushed against her skin like a second heartbeat. The thing inside her was hungry, the dulling effect of the drink having worn off. Savara took a deep, steadying breath, hoping to compose herself before the man grew suspicious—if he wasn't already.

"It's nothing," she lied again.

Savara accepted the man's hand, this time prepared for the wave of energy that flooded through her body. She focused on keeping her powers at bay as he promenaded her to the centre of the room. She kept her eyes on her feet, hoping he wouldn't see through to her fear.

The man was patient with her. His fingers wrapped around her hand and guided it to his shoulder. His hand rested on her lower back, his touch sending shivers down her spine. When she'd adjusted to the new sensation, she noticed a new lightness in her body. A weight had lifted, from her heart, from her mind. For a moment, she felt more energised than she had in years.

But the thing inside her was hungry, the effect of the drink having worn off. Savara turned her focus to keeping her powers at bay, lest they be released upon an unsuspecting party. Whether her partner noticed her tension or not, he did not let on.

By the second song, Savara had all but forgotten the crowd of people around them. Even her powers had settled in the arms of the stranger. And in his arms, time stilled. The scent of night flowers spilling from him was like a remedy to an illness she hadn't recognised she had. Despite the crowd, Savara felt as though they were the only ones around for miles.

"I can't recall the last time I've enjoyed a party like this one," he remarked, pulling her in gently after a spin.

"I…" She caught herself before letting slip the fact that she had *never* been to a party like this, afraid of what kind of conversation might follow. "…can't either."

Then, slowly, the atmosphere around them began to change. Unlike the last few vibrant songs, the next was low and sultry. Classical elegance, tinged with an air of desert mystique, thanks to the addition of a simple Cajon and tambourine.

They danced in perfect harmony, despite her lack of practice. His touch had become a source of comfort. He moved as though he already knew her rhythm. As though it were second nature to him. Following his lead, Savara fell into a pleasant daze, aided by the strange energy engulfing them both. The music blocked out the din of the public, his presence shielded her from its gaze. The world might have ended in that moment, and she wouldn't have noticed.

Over the course of their dance, her eyes had drifted away from the crowd and landed squarely on him. His suit, his chest, his chin, his eyes…

They pierced her being, connecting to the light inside her. Even as her feet settled to a halt, she found herself a captive of his gaze, hardly noticing the song had long ended.

But then, he released her.

"To think I was about to leave when I saw you. A gift wrapped in paper and twine, almost too good to open…"

Suddenly, the illusion shattered. Her breath hitched in her chest, replaying his words in her head.

"What did you say?" she whispered, unable to find her voice.

"Thank you, Savara," he said with a bow and turned on his heels. She furrowed her brow, staring at him as though only now seeing him for the first time. He paused amidst the crowd, briefly turning back to her. He winked, his sad blue eyes glowing brighter than anything in the room. She frowned, watching as he disappeared into the crowd.

The music and laughter came crashing back into her, no longer held at bay by his presence. By the time she managed to process the encounter, he'd disappeared entirely. She almost chased after him when Griffin returned with another drink in hand and a much stiffer expression.

"Who were you talking to?" he asked.

Savara opened her mouth to reply, scanning the room for the man in black who had seemingly vanished without a trace. He was nowhere to be found amongst the patrons. He'd vanished as though he'd never been there to begin with.

"No one," she said with a sigh. Her heart quivered at the lie.

"You look like you've seen a ghost."

"You have no idea…"

Another sultry song began to play. People continued to dance at first but soon peeled away in favour of watching a single couple in the centre of the ballroom, whose passionate energy seemed to engulf the room.

Sebastian and Storm danced around each other like a pair of vipers, eyes locked as they twisted shoulder to shoulder. She was swift and light-footed, teasing like the breeze that lifted skirts. He was sultry and intense, with all the charm of slow-burning logs in a fireplace. With each gentle twirl, she fanned his embers, coaxing out the flames within. Some of their movements were so provocatively tight that, at points, it was hard to tell where he ended, and she began.

Savara marvelled at the sight of them two moving together with such feeling and harmony that they could've been mistaken for the most passionate of lovers.

"I thought she hated him," she whispered.

Griffin chuckled. "When one pushes, the other pulls. It's all a game they play with each other," he said as he regarded them fondly. "One day, they're going to wake up and not know the difference between game and reality." He looked down at her and smiled. "For the time being, I find it entertaining to watch them bicker now and again," he concluded in time with the song.

Uproarious cheering and applause filled the room. And just as Griffin had predicted, no sooner did the song—their false pretence for civility and possibly sentiment—end, did the battle begin anew. But now was not the time for lovers' quarrels. The clock struck twelve, sending the sound of heavy copper chimes reverberating through the house.

Lady Amaia descended the grand staircase with four manservants in tow, holding the train of her glittering red gown and the draping green sash she'd slung over her shoulders. She beamed, displacing the slender gold chains connecting her nose to her ear—the same kind that lined her wrists and layered her neck. Applause sounded for their gracious hostess and, after the typical speech that required time but lacked depth, for the commencement of the meal.

CHAPTER 37

LADY AMAIA

WHILE MOST OF the guests shuffled into the dining hall, a few stayed back to exchange brief hellos with the lady of the evening. Griffin waited patiently at the door for her to make her rounds before confronting her, but it seemed she had other plans.

"Griffin, my child!" Lady Amaia called to him in an overly flamboyant way that made him wonder whether he was truly the intended audience. "How you've grown," she said, pinching his cheeks with henna-stained fingers. "Your eyes are just as beautiful and blue as your mother's."

"Thank you, Tante. You're looking as young and radiant as ever," he replied quietly, kissing her jewelled hand. Lady Amaia had a way of never quite ageing or doing it so slowly and gracefully that each decade that passed treated her more like a single year. Griffin was unaware of her age, only that, however old, she didn't look it—and enjoyed hearing about how she didn't. "When you invited us to dinner, we were under the impression that—"

"It would be more intimate?" She dropped her tone as she pretended to fiddle with her piercing. "Believe me, if there were any other way. It seems you are not our only guests this season…"

Her eyes hinted over at another part of the room. Griffin followed her gaze to where a man with all the genuine facial features of a fox spoke casually with visiting young duchesses. The man cast a slow, calculating glance in their direction, all the while maintaining his polite conversation. Malice glinted in his eyes.

We aren't the only ones being watched, he realised. His chest tensed as he wondered if their messages had been intercepted. "I see…"

"Oh my! This necklace is such a dreadful thing. Keeps coming undone," she blurted out for the world to hear. "Fix it for me, my darling," she added, turning her back to him.

Griffin obliged, believing for a moment that she'd been telling the truth. Yet, when she turned, he found it perfectly clasped. In fact, he found no clasp at all, rather an elegantly carved stone resting at the nape of her neck, connecting all her golden chains. Being *kanala*, she could clasp and unclasp it of her own accord with the wiggle of her pinkie finger, if she so wanted. She didn't require his help any more than he could give it.

He rested his hand on her shoulder, but before he could speak, she rested her hand over his.

"Lean in and listen," she whispered instead. Griffin did as he was told. He played along, pretending to fiddle with it as she continued. "I'll be quick. I received your last message, but I believe it was opened before reaching my hands. I don't know how you know about the stone, but yes, it is safe. As for what you said about the shadows, I'd like to believe you, but…" She made a disapproving noise. "They were exiled. There's no way they could've escaped."

"Tante, they have the stone of Osiir. They plan to attack Idune using Argia soldiers."

She was silent for a moment. He noticed her back tense at his words. Lady Amaia was one of the strongest women he knew. He'd never seen her afraid of anything—except this.

"Griffin, my child, it is not safe for you here. People these days talk of war with the Ur. If what you say is true, I feel we may be in for troubling times indeed." She let out a heavy sigh. "The council will not take this news lightly, especially when your word goes against his…"

Lady Amaia adjusted her chin, hinting at the man she'd pointed out earlier. As if summoned by the thought of him, the man bowed out of his own conversation and made his way towards them. A look of arrogance and intrigued plastered his face.

"Who is he?" Griffin managed to ask before the man arrived.

"General Dhoot, war hero and up-and-coming politician, though he's more tyrant than hero…"

"Looks like you could use some help with that, young man," said the general, his voice echoing over their intimate conversation.

"Thank you, my child," Lady Amaia announced, turning back to face Griffin. "This thing is dreadfully cheap. I shall have to get a better one made." She pulled him in close and whispered, "Be careful." She planted a kiss on his cheek, leaving a bright red lip print just below his eye. When she turned back to face the general, she was a mask of calm and composure, as though their conversation had never happened. "General Dhoot, what a pleasure it is to see you again," she said, forcing his name from her lips as though wringing dirty water from a sponge.

"The pleasure is all mine, my lady. You are looking as radiant as always," he replied, lifting his pointed nose before kissing her bejewelled hand. "And who might this be?" he added, his pointed snout and sharpened incisors on full display.

"My nephew," she replied. "He and his friends have decided to grace me with their presence this evening."

"How…quaint." He and Griffin exchanged scrutinising gazes before bobbing their heads respectfully. "Permit me to escort you to your seat, my lady," said General Dhoot, offering his elbow to her.

Lady Amaia nodded and bid Griffin a pleasant dinner. Griffin bowed in return. He watched as General Dhoot escorted her to the high end of the table. The general made a point of glancing at the clasp of her necklace. He scowled, turning back briefly to Griffin with narrowed eyes before taking his own seat.

Uneased riddled through him. Despite all his precautions, his letter had been intercepted. And if what Lady Amaia had said about the Ur was true, there would be more than one war on their hands. He inclined his head politely to the general, who had not let up his gaze. He was careful with his expressions, making sure not to give anything away, or make another enemy just yet. Already Griffin knew the general was going to be trouble. Lady Amaia's warning would not gone unheeded.

Griffin peeled away, concerned that they'd walked into a trap. He searched the crowd for Savara, needing to make sure she was safe and that her powers were under control, now that there was a new threat so close.

She waited at the edge of the room, looking as though she'd lost something. When he asked about it, she'd lied and said it was nothing. As they sat down to eat, she stole the occasional glance around the room, a crease deepening at her brow. She searched for someone in the many seats of the exquisite oaken dining table. Every time he caught her eyes darting around, he'd follow them to where they'd last settled. Each time, he found nothing out of the ordinary. Judging by her frown, so had she.

THE FIRST COURSE did justice to all the stories he'd heard over the years of Lady Amaia's parties. Delicate lamb chops dressed in raspberry sauce, thinly sliced sweet potatoes glazed in spiced cinnamon and butter, garlic chips, and salted asparagus dip. The main course far exceeded all expectations. Dishes burst to life, literally, of every colour under the sun. Blackened meats that, when cut, exposed flesh of red and blue; from inside thin bread domes, multicoloured vegetables poured out, shining as if they'd come from a painting. And, of course, drinks were never lacking. For dessert, a replica of the Great Wall, done in a tiered sponge of every flavour from coffee to lemon. When the last set of dessert forks was cleared, trouble began anew.

"A toast!" came the announcement from the far end of the table. General Dhoot stood up with his glass raised high and his pointed nose even higher. "To our most gracious hostess, the lovely Lady Amaia."

"Here, here!" came the kind replies. Glasses raised and many nodded agreeingly, some even clapped, but Lady Amaia herself was not impressed. She raised her glass and nodded slightly, the shock and suspicion in her eyes only visible to those who truly knew her. Griffin lifted his glass in agreement, though, he too sensed something was wrong with the auspicious show of appreciation.

"May she continue to do what is good and just," General Dhoot continued. "And may the country thrive at her helm." Emotion swelled like a rising tide over the dinner table. Lady Amaia's smile vanished. She knew as well as Griffin did that something sinister waited just below the depths of these profound statements. And almost in confirmation, through the applause and cheers, a single voice distinguished itself.

"And to you, General Dhoot, hero of the North. May you and your army be forever strong."

"Here, here!" the room erupted once more.

General Dhoot lavished in their praise, bathing himself in adoration. He looked over to Lady Amaia with a rotten grin curling at his thin lips. She smiled sweetly in return, though her eyes were as cold as the buckets of champagne that rimmed the table.

Griffin's grip tightened around his glass, realising now the extent of the trouble they faced. The entire council… They would side with him.

"What's wrong?" Savara asked in whisper, having noticed his apprehension.

"We're being toyed with," Griffin replied, glowering in General Dhoot's direction. The cocky general cast a lazy glance over towards him, brandishing pearly white incisors that glittered like knives under the shifting light of the hall. The man had all the tells of ambition. Dangerous, costly ambition.

"Why?" she asked.

Power, he thought. Power was always the end goal. Everyone wants to be in control; some just go to greater lengths and higher heights to attain it. Much less an idea than an entity all its own, preying on the weak and feeding on the desperate. It kills as well as any creature of flesh and bone.

"There are two kinds of power in this world, Savara," Griffin mumbled. "Respect, which comes at a price to you, and fear, whose price is paid by others. Respect is earned only through your own suffering and humility, but fear is gained through deception, manipulation, and—on occasion—blood. Sometimes, the difference between them is so fine that they can be mistaken for each other, but if you look closely, you can see where the past leaves its mark."

The kind of power the general sought may have looked like respect to the untrained eye, as evidenced by the elitist applause from around the room, but Griffin saw through his façade. The general was no saint, and the wicked, arrogant grin plastered across his face was something born of spilt blood.

Griffin had been so ravelled up in his thoughts that he almost didn't notice the small note in his lap. The manservant who refilled his drink had let it subtly slip from his jacket. He unfurled it slowly in one hand and casually reached for his drink in the other, letting his eyes dip to the three scribbled letters on the otherwise empty paper. *ORI.* He glanced briefly across the room, catching the expectant eyes of Lady Amaia, who nodded before returning to other affairs.

"Sebastian," he whispered across the table. "I need a smoke." Without question, Sebastian excused himself.

Savara caught Griffin's arm as he was about to leave. "I didn't know you smoked," she said.

"I don't," he replied in a whisper and slipped out into the night alongside his friend.

THE COOL AIR from the tops of the mountains swirled around them, a refreshing change from the heat of the dining hall.

"Should I be worried about your taking up of bad habits?" Sebastian asked.

Griffin curled the little note around a cigarette and passed it off for him to light. "Not if my bad habits keep us alive," he replied. He took a long pull from the cigarette and handed it back.

Sebastian nodded and followed suit. "You know, Grif, it's days like these I wonder why we don't just leave it all behind, let go, let someone else fight..." he said through a heavy puff.

The pair looked back at their friends through the windows. Griffin noted that, even walls away, Sebastian and

Storm had a way of finding each other's gaze. Storm turned up her nose and ignored him, though Griffin saw the relief drape her shoulders. Sebastian looked on in reserved awe, the way he always did behind her back.

The answer was as obvious as the lovestruck daze in his eyes.

"Because we care," Griffin replied.

After letting the words sink in, Sebastian turned back to him and nodded, a blush creeping into his cheeks. Neither made to speak, letting heavy, smoke-filled breaths fill the space between them. To any wandering eyes, they simply looked like two people sharing a smoke in silence, watching the slow ascent of the moon.

CHAPTER 38

A FINAL SUITOR

SAVARA FOUND HERSELF waiting alone for the rest of her party to be finished with the night's revels. She could no longer stand to be in the company of people who saw nothing but the stones on her cheek and mumbled of her strangeness despite her being in earshot of their conversations. Savara held tight to a flute of champagne and strode out onto one of the many balconies of the house. The night, as much as it scared her, had always welcomed her. Maybe, deep down, she'd always known she was a creature of the night. The stars glimmered, reflected in the bubbles of her champagne, reminding her there was always light somewhere. She stared up at them, hoping that they would bring her comfort, the way they used to a world away.

A final man strolled up to her, leaned himself over the railing, and contemplated the stars at her side. An older gentleman, with a salt and peppered beard that reached past his neck. Each step he took towards her shook the small, wooden balcony. He wasn't large by any means, rather stocky, and well-built despite his advanced age. Savara sensed a strong energy radiating from him; her powers sensed it too.

"Fine night for stargazing," he said.

"I'm not one for parties," she replied before he got the chance to mention the strangeness of her solitude. In the dim light of the balcony, she let her hair fall over her face, hoping to hide the stones on her cheek.

"I can't say I enjoy them either," he admitted gingerly. "Though one must make sacrifices in the name of the position they hold. Don't you agree?"

"I suppose," Savara said as she turned to him.

The man's eyes fell on her—one the colour of jade, the other the colour of moss—as he bowed his head respectfully. Savara flinched at the first sight of the man's different eyes, a movement he took note of and grinned.

"Forgive me," she apologised, trying to pull her gaze from his jade eye, which glowed vibrantly under the light of the moon.

"Feel free to look," he said, gesturing to it. "A battle scar from forgotten times."

Savara nodded, but for the rest of the conversation, she endeavoured to keep her own eyes elsewhere. "I was told Idune has been blessed with many years of peace."

"Yes, well, we are fortunate that our people are strong of both heart and faith."

Savara smiled politely, but the way he stared at her set her bones on edge. His gaze was too harsh, his demeanour too unassuming. In that way, he almost reminded her of her uncle. She wondered if he could sense the energy inside her, just as she had in him.

"You are not from these parts, are you, child?" he added when the silence between them grew awkward.

"No," Savara replied curtly, gulping the wildly intoxicating beverage to stifle the nerves creeping over her shoulders. "I'm not."

"I don't mean it in a bad way, my dear. Simply an observation." When she hesitated, he added, "The customs of royalty are different in other nations. Ours are slightly more relaxed, seeing as our monarchy disintegrated many years ago, before even my father was born. I can understand that they might seem trite to those of more upkept households."

"I wouldn't know," Savara said, though his insinuation of her noble birth rattled her. How did he know? Had they met before? The man wasn't exactly forgettable, neither was his strange eye.

"No?" The man raised his heavy brows. "My mistake, then." He smiled and returned his gaze to the stars. "Curious, aren't they? They say our people are descended from the stars. I've never been one to entertain myself with grand thoughts as these, but in my advancing age, I've come to appreciate them more."

"How so?" Savara asked, peering behind to see whether her friends were ready to leave, but not wanting to seem rude in the man's presence.

"A single star is all it takes to light even the darkest of nights. For an old man whose heart still quickens when the sun goes down, this simple fact brings me comfort." He chuckled softly. "It is as with people. In moments of ease, few of us realise our own importance. It is only when the night comes, during the moments of absolute darkness, are we tested in our ability to shine."

Savara frowned. His words reminded her of her quest for meaning, the one which had brought both her and Jasper to this world and very nearly got them killed in the process. She turned back to him attentively this time. Worry traced the crease between her brows. "Do you really believe that?"

The man nodded. "I do, my dear."

Savara raised a hand to her cheek, grazing her fingers over the gemstoned scar. "How do you know when your night has come?" she asked.

The man took his time, contemplating her words with care. "I suppose there is no true knowing when our night has come. For some, it might be a noble death in battle; for others, it might simply be a conversation. Something trivial yet destined to spur on another, the way an established tree leaves fresh seeds or an old flame lights a new one."

As Savara was about to prod further, Jasper appeared at the entrance to the balcony.

"Sav, Griffin says it's time to go," he called to her, eyeing the man cautiously.

Savara nodded and turned back to the man. "Thank you," she said as she bobbed her head.

"May our paths meet again," the man replied, his eyes following her into the house and then through the garden below.

CHAPTER 39

A WOLF AMONG PORCELAIN CATS

DAWN HAD NOT yet broken fully, but already rays of sunlight crept over the mountain range, staining everything in the valley an unfriendly shade of vermillion. Even the clouds glowed with the warning colour. A deafening silence echoed within the walls of Idune, taking up residence in the frigid air. Most of the townspeople would not be up for another hour or so. Those few that were—bakers, street sweeps, and lamp extinguishers—kept their noises to a minimum as they readied themselves for the day. For the moment, all was eerily quiet in the Harri capital city. Underground, a different scene was taking place.

Below the vast mountain range, a secret gathering was about to begin. The grand chamber of the High Council of the Harri—almost too grand for the peasant lifestyles they claimed to live—was abuzz with activity. The chamber itself was older than all its occupants combined and reserved for only serious occasions, of which there hadn't been any in over a decade. The halls echoed with the ghosts of council members past. Many of today's occupants were obliged to sweep the ancient dust and cobwebs from their seats before taking them. But that didn't bother them so much as the reason they were there, to begin with. This morning's matters had everyone on edge.

The walls of stone and marble curved in on themselves to form chapel-like ceilings, leaving just enough of a gap in the centre to allow light to flow in from above. Tunnels let in the clean mountain air, and an aquifer somewhere deep below brought their water. Candles flickered in sconces along the walls, sending shadows dancing and reflecting vivid colours off the various precious metals and crystal-work that adorned the room.

The five council members—one head for each of the industries: mining, building, military, education, and farming—sat at the front, looking troubled and lacking sleep. Behind them hung a great golden gong, whose echoing metallic sound signalled the beginning, end, and order of the hall. Before them sat the rest of the court, important members of the militia, some governing members of other Harri townships, and finally, their visiting guest.

The meeting had been convened last minute at the request of Lady Amaia, with no more than a slight indication of war within the city. This was, to them, a ridiculous idea. Idune was and had always been the unconquerable city, but the gravity of such a situation had to be taken with the utmost seriousness.

The meeting started just as calmly as the day but quickly escalated into something more.

"Council members, we beseech you. War is coming," said Griffin over the murmurings of the hall.

"Why should we trust them?" shouted a man from somewhere in the stands. "Suppose it is they who seek to destroy us?"

More shouts went up until the whole chamber vibrated with the sounds of their voices. All eyes turned on Griffin with a sour hatred. He stood firm, unshaken by their glares; after all, he'd endured much worse than the hatred of a ruling class.

"My people," said Lady Amaia, "we are not convened to judge the man before us. We are here to judge the severity of the situation."

"Even if what this young man says is true, we do not need his help. Our army is stronger than any other in existence!" called a man from the back. "No creature of flesh and blood can come close to our wall."

"I am inclined to agree," Griffin replied, keeping his attention on the five leaders before him. "However, these creatures are not of flesh and blood, but rather of ash and shadow. They prey on the mind, feed on fear, and are—as we have so far confirmed—indestructible."

His words echoed through the now silent hall. Eyes had gone wide, cheeks had paled. Some shifted in their seats, unsure how to feel about the news.

Griffin cast a glance over the sea of hollow faces, searching for some sign of defiance, but none appeared. They looked like fine porcelain dolls, decorated with all the airs of "expense" and "class," and just as hollow.

How easily broken, he thought, resisting a frown.

"Preposterous," said a woman near the front. "No creatures of such nature exist." Though, by the purse of her lips, Griffin could tell she was unsure herself. She waited for one of her many porcelain companions to come to her aid and speak up, but not a soul stirred. Their sceptical eyes simply followed her as she rose, spoke, and sat shamefully once more.

"And why would such creatures be spearheading an attack into our lands?" asked Lady Abeer, the eldest of the council of five.

"My lady," Griffin said with a respectfully low bow. "We have reason to believe that, not unlike the attack on Osiir, *they* are responsible."

At first, his words echoed in the silence of the hall as people processed them. Then, mumbling swept over the room like a dense fog. Some people exchanged grave looks, others were noticeably flabbergasted, and the younger of the present company was lost entirely but copied the expressions of their neighbours.

One thing was clear: the mention of *them* had everyone in the hall trembling.

"This is nonsense!" shouted Lord Aito, the warrior lord. His tone was accusatory. "This man is an Izar looking to take control over us, as they have always tried to do."

More hands went up in protest, and so did the voices. The house became a kennel of barking dogs, and Griffin a cat in the centre. He took a sharp exhale and watched onward stoically as the council exchanged their looks until the gong sounded once more.

"Quiet!" screeched the frail voice of Lady Abeer. "We have a question from the back."

"Thank you, my Lady Abeer," the woman said, clearing her throat of both nerves and phlegm. "Yes. How can you, boy, stand here and claim *their* existence, and that of the army, when it is *your* people who, for years, have attested to *their* extinction?" she asked, throwing as much spite into the word *your* as she possibly could, trying to mask the hesitation innately placed on the word *their*.

"I was unaware of their continued existence until recently. It seems there was never an extinction, only imprisonment," Griffin replied.

"My Lady Abeer," called a middle-aged general from one of the foremost rows. "As you already know, in our great nation's history, there has never been such a war to cross into our city. Even if there were to be an attack on Idune, they would never break past my guards. What these people suggest is simply ludicrous."

Griffin didn't need to turn around to know who this attack came from. The familiar piercing glare of fox-like eyes prickled on the back of his neck. He turned, as a matter of courtesy alone, to meet the same malicious grin from the previous night.

General Dhoot.

"You would say that, you arrogant fool," came a voice from the other side of the room. This too was a voice Griffin recognised, though it had been years since he last heard it. "Is it your position or your lust for power that has made you dismiss any possibility of failure?"

A man not much older than himself, with dazzling lime green eyes and a thick head of neat, black curls descended into the pit of wolves. Griffin didn't bother to hide the surprise in his eyes. He smiled, accepting the pat on the back from an old friend.

"Sergeant Isaac. What a pleasant surprise," he said, clasping his hand over an equally firm and steady one. "How are you, my friend?"

"Actually, it's General now," the young man replied. "It is good to see you again, Griffin."

"My apologies, General. And congratulations," Griffin said, adding a pat on the back.

General Isaac nodded politely. "We shall have more time for pleasantries later. Are these dogs giving you trouble?" he added in a whisper.

Griffin frowned. "We've come to warn the council of an attack, but by the look of things I'm afraid my word is not worth as much as it used to be."

"I see." General Isaac cleared his throat as he turned to address the court. "My ladies and lords, members of parliament, this man has helped our nation on many an occasion. During the great battles of San Bartoleme and Guienne against the invading Ur forces from the east, and the battle of Madera against invaders from the west. He knows of our strengths, and more importantly, our weaknesses. If he comes here to warn us of an attack, having risked his own safety, I can assure you it is not to stir up trouble, as some of my comrades so callously put it. I will vouch for this man, and on my head be whatever punishment lay ahead."

Once again, the hall erupted in complaints and criticisms. Masked by the general confusion and uproar, the two friends spoke in confidence.

"There was no need—" began Griffin, but General Isaac held up a hand to stop him.

"I will explain everything once we are away from prying eyes and ears." He clapped Griffin lovingly on the back. "It truly is good to see you, my friend."

"On another note, you wouldn't happen to know what ORI stands for, do you?"

General Isaac pursed his lips as he studied his friend, his eyes riddled with concern. "You have gotten yourself into real trouble this time…"

"Nothing I can't get myself out of, I hope."

General Isaac shook his head and laughed knowingly. "I hope you're right. ORI?" he repeated. "It's not a what, it's a who," he said as he directed his chin towards the councilmember sat squarely in the middle. "Iturri spare your soul, my friend."

The councilman had watched Griffin like a hawk ever since he'd first set foot in the chamber. The weight of his gaze alone was suffocating. The man's eyes—one moss-green, the other a vibrant jade—hadn't once lifted from him. Judging by his scowl, he was fed up of the in-fighting. He stroked his beard once before standing.

"Silence!" he shouted, his booming voice reverberating through the hall. "Approach the bench, young Izar."

Griffin shuddered like the walls around him. Perhaps Isaac was right, he was in trouble. Griffin stepped cautiously towards the bench, hyper aware of the many eyes on him.

When he'd stepped up to their platform, Lord Ori slammed his fist against the desk. Around the six of them, the floor rose to become a wall of thick stone that prevented even the most astute listeners from overhearing.

Griffin's shoulders stiffened. He'd trapped himself in with warriors who, aside from Lady Amaia, were not partial to him or his cause.

"Speak, young Izar, in confidence," said Lord Ori.

"My lord." Griffin bowed low enough that his neck peeked through his clothes, hoping such an act would at least curry favour. "I bring news regarding the massacre of Osiir."

"Was it not an insurgency then?" said Lady Amaia with a furrowed brow.

When they'd met before, Griffin had wanted to mention the massacre. He hadn't expected to be ambushed by an entire party. Osiir had played a large part in both of their lives and had thus been a source of shared trauma. Perhaps it was wrong of him to have kept the secret, but he'd had little choice. Especially now with the likes of General Dhoot sniffing around.

"I am afraid not, my lady. The attack came from other parties... *They* are back, and they are after the stones."

For a long time, no one spoke. *They* had not been mentioned between these walls in a long time... Not since Savara's divination. And it had been longer still since anyone had spoken of the stones.

"The stones are a topic of myth and legend," said Lady Abeer finally. Her voice was soft and sweet, though Griffin could tell that even she was teetering on anger.

"You cannot be serious, boy," stammered Lord Aito, sending angry spittle from his lips with each sharp word. "How dare you come here and make such claims!"

"Never has such a serious accusation come to the ears of this court," added Lord Andor soberly. Though his voice fell calmly and smoothly from the lips behind his beard, his fingers tapped relentlessly on the desk.

"I mean no disrespect, my lords and ladies," Griffin assured them. "Nor do I make such claims without reason. I have seen the palace for myself. The Argia stone is gone. Who else would have use for such a thing?"

"And how do we know that you did not take it for yourself?" Lord Aito replied. "How do you even know of the existence of the stones in the first place?"

"How dare you accuse him," chided Lady Amaia. "He has come here of his own volition looking to help us, the penalty of death hanging over his head, and you will not even consider the possibility that he is telling the truth?"

"No. I will not," he retorted. "This all sounds like a great work of fiction invented by a child still clinging to the death of his hysterical father."

"And your denial makes you sound like a pompous fool afraid of a fight," Lady Amaia scoffed. "When, sir, did you lose your spine?" Lord Aito's face was livid, the building rage turned his cheeks a plum purple, but Lady Amaia's challenging glare silenced whatever qualms he had.

Griffin understood that Lord Aito said what he did out of fear. He might have been right to question, but he appreciated Lady Amaia's unwavering support.

"I know of the stones because my father was entrusted

with protecting them. Or at least, one of them. A task that was passed down to me after his untimely demise."

The council members shifted uncomfortably in their seats, awaiting Lord Ori's verdict, though he seemed to still be processing the news. When he finally spoke, his voice was less than reassuring.

"You are certain it is *them?*" asked Lord Ori.

Griffin nodded. "Yes, my lord. My companions and I were attacked in the forests outside Osiir by creatures our lands have never seen. Shadows brought to life. I fear they will do the same here."

"How is it you found out about this supposed attack on Idune?" Lord Ori prodded.

"One of my companions overheard their plans to burn through the city using *kanala* Argia captured from the previous attack on Osiir," Griffin replied. "My lords and ladies, I beseech you. I have seen these creatures with my own eyes. They alone are enough to sound the alarm bells."

After a heavy sigh, Lord Ori turned to the council. "If this young man is right, and *they* are after the stones, we may already be too late."

THE HOLLOW SONG of the wind filtering into the chamber echoed above them all. By the time the walls came down, the council was ready for war. Instructions were given with conviction and taken without question. Even General Dhoot agreed to prepare his soldiers. The once brave and boisterous crowd shuffled out of the hall in silence. Their shallow airs were no good in a time of crisis, and they knew it.

Griffin sought out General Isaac to thank him for his help in convincing the council. Without him, his pleas might've gone unheeded, or worse. He found him at the entrance to the hall, already involved in a heated conversation. Griffin lingered a few steps away, not wanting to interrupt, but seeing who was involved, couldn't help himself from eavesdropping.

"When all this is over and done with, do you truly think these people will judge you well, General Isaac, for working with an Izar?" said General Dhoot, glowering at his young comrade as he fixed his glossy black hair into place.

"I will be judged for aiding in the defence of my proud homeland. How will you be judged, *General?*" General Isaac scoffed in response.

At this, the older general merely smirked. He fiddled intentionally with a medal of leadership pinned to his breast pocket, nestled between two others, as he stared down at his companion's comparatively bare chest.

"I will be remembered exactly as I plan to be—as I should be. As a hero." He brushed an invisible layer of dust from his uniform, and with it, the remnants of their not-so-cordial conversation. He raised his pointed nose and disappeared down the hall, hands clasped behind his back, exuding the lackadaisical arrogance of a cat finished with its most recent toy.

"Is it just me or is there something wrong with him?" mused Griffin.

General Isaac frowned. "Whatever he may be, he is nothing if not loved by the people."

"So I noticed…"

General Isaac turned to his friend with a sobering caution in his eyes. "Be careful with him, Griffin. I say this as a friend, I wouldn't be at all surprised to find out that he has his dirty little hands in all of this." For a split second his eyes widened like glowing green saucers before he dipped into a ceremoniously low bow. "My lord."

Griffin turned to find Lord Ori standing expectantly behind him. He too dropped into a bow.

How did he manage to sneak up on me? Am I losing my touch? Griffin wondered.

Lord Ori inclined his head and cleared his throat. "General Isaac."

The young general, understanding his presence was not wanted, got to his feet, and bid the two of them a good day. He flashed a final warning glare at his old friend before disappearing down the hall.

"Young Conroy, a word if you will."

Griffin bobbed his head courteously. His actions betrayed no hesitation, knowing all too well that when a legend wished to speak, he'd do best to listen.

Lord Ori strolled towards the deeper parts of the mountain without so much as a glance in his direction. Each step took them further and further from whatever comfort public spaces could provide. Griffin followed him through the many cavernous halls in silence, until they reached a place where not even the echoes of their footsteps could escape.

CHAPTER 40

LORD ORI

THE WALLS SEALED themselves shut with an echoing roar, trapping them in a tomb of stone. When the last trace of outside light died, a new one came to life. Crystals glowed around them, washing the shadows away in an emerald wave of light. Behind these, Griffin spied streaks of magma burning too far off to provide any comforting warmth. Where the previous room had been filled and felt hollow, this one was hollow but felt suffocatingly full. In place of cobweb-covered gemstones and ornamental metals, this room contained nothing but a polished dirt floor. The other room held pretence. This one held power. Tangible purpose.

Through the vast emptiness surrounding them, the lord began to speak.

"You do realise that withholding information from the

council in a trial is a felony," said Lord Ori. His booming voice shook small pebbles from their notches in the walls.

"I do, my lord," Griffin replied, knowing better than to lie to the great and powerful head councilman of the Harri Provinces. "I do so not without having weighed the consequences."

"This information must be valuable, then."

"It is, and I am told you are the only one I should trust with it."

Lord Ori stroked his peppered beard as he paced about the floor. His steps were unhurried, but the floor trembled all the same. His bare, calloused feet had a distinct earthquake-provoking quality about them. This heaviness and power extended to the rest of his body as well. Griffin watched carefully for any signs of trouble. He'd heard enough stories of the old lord to know that caution was wise in the presence of someone who would just as readily crush him under rubble as he would shake his hand.

"Help you? I thought you claimed to be helping us?" Lord Ori shook his head in amusement. "What is it a young Izar like yourself should seek from an old Harri like me?"

"Answers, my lord," Griffin replied, cautious of his reactions. If Lord Ori so wanted, he would be buried under a mountain's worth of rock before he could blink. Griffin cast a glance around the room, searching for signs of shaking pebbles and trembling walls. For the moment, all seemed stable. Lord Ori paused his pacing, waiting instead like a dormant volcano. Griffin cleared his throat and spoke once more. "Regarding long forgotten things."

"Long-forgotten things are most often found in the realm

of your people, not so?" The lord raised the bushy black eyebrow above his jade eye. "They have stripped the lands bare of anything that might have caused them difficulties in their leadership."

"The Izar are not aware of these activities, nor of the information I am about to share with you. They are the strict business of the Ris."

"The Ris?" Lord Ori replied, curiosity tainting his voice. After a moment of silence, he laughed. The sound bounced around the room, causing the walls to vibrate. "It has been quite some time since that name has been spoken within these walls. I believe the last person to speak it was your father, long before you were even thought of. He had a knack for landing himself in these… inconvenient situations. A trait passed down I see." Noticing Griffin's discomfort, he grinned. "So, to hide from the Izar, to be on the heels of war, to invoke the stones, and above all, to come asking favours of me? You have quite the mess on your hands, young Conroy." He stomped on the ground and raised a stool of rock to sit on as he contemplated Griffin's request. "Lady Amaia is fond of you. Or at least sympathetic to your plight."

"Yes, my lord."

"She was fond of your mother, from what I remember." Griffin nodded, unable to bring himself to speak of his mother and hardly wishing to remember her. "The world was a much simpler place back then. No mafias, no uprisings, no lack of morality. People prayed to the spirits and worked for their bread. There were still wars, of course, but over much more trivial matters. Which village should get which plot of land, which man should take which wife, which brother should be king…" He sighed heavily. "The legends, contrary to popular belief, did not have as much bearing over the world as they do now. Do you not agree, young Izar?"

"I do, my lord."

"I have seen many things in my life, young Izar. Many of which I could have happily lived without seeing. I must admit, however, that I never thought I would live to see the day that history repeated itself. I must truly be old." He let out a bittersweet and sobering laugh. "I imagine your father told you of the last time the stones were a topic of discussion."

"Not in detail, but I am familiar with the story."

Lord Ori frowned. "Then you will also be familiar with the ending." Griffin nodded. After an extended period of silence and introspection, Lord Ori cleared his throat and contemplated Griffin's eyes. His glare had a tangible force to it, like rods poking into the skin. "Sometimes the answers we seek bring us more pain than comfort, and sometimes the road to answers is paved with more questions. I suppose that is the beauty in it all… in this wonderful game we call life. At the end of the day, to live is to survive, and surviving is nothing more than living to see another day. Are you sure you wish for answers, young Izar?"

"I'm afraid, my lord, I have no choice," Griffin replied, meeting his gaze without hesitation. "There is one in my company with whom I believe you are already acquainted. You may hesitate to remember her, given her nature. It is she that urged me to make this journey, and on her behalf that I seek your help."

"And who might that be, my boy?"

"Princess Savara, daughter of Queen Anissa of Osiir, last heir to the Argia throne."

Lord Ori blanched, a deafening silence settled between them. The seconds ticked by as the councilman processed the information. Judging by the fear on his face, Griffin realised he too had withheld information.

"I must admit, part of me was still clinging to the idea that you might be pulling an old man's leg," he replied finally. "To call upon the council, to invoke such a name… You really are telling the truth."

Griffin nodded.

"Hmm…"

Suddenly, Lord Ori slammed a fist into the wall of solid rock behind him. Griffin's heart skipped a beat, fearing that he'd made a mistake in trusting the lord. Fearing that his life was over, and that he would be forever entombed in these walls. Instead, the shockwave created a tunnel which bore straight through to the other end of the mountain. At the end of the tunnel, Griffin spied a glimmer of daylight. He unhitched a sigh of relief.

"I had hoped, for many years, that this day would never come. The Argia princess, the shadows…" Lord Ori gazed through to the world beyond, a sad smile gracing his face. "I suppose it is fitting such questions be brought to me, as I was the final one to lay judgement upon your friend. Come, child. Fate has requested our presence at the turning of an era; it would be wise of us not to keep her waiting…"

CHAPTER 41

THE BLACKENING OF BLOOD

JASPER HAD MANAGED to salvage a single book from the flames that devoured Camp Saar. The strange, leather-bound volume that lusted after his blood sat at the foot of his bed. It called to him. *More,* it whispered, sending chills down his spine. He made no move to collect it, and hadn't, since their arrival in Idune.

He ignored the calls, staring instead at the spiderweb of blackened veins beneath the skin of his wrist. Jasper hadn't noticed it before, the slow turning of his blood. It started as a smudge, something akin to a spot of spilt ink below his palm. He'd tried scrubbing it for almost ten minutes before realising he would scrub off the skin before the spot.

Since then, he'd taken to wearing longer sleeves. Luckily for him, the weather had been unusually cold for the region—so he was told—and his change in attire raised no eyebrows. Twice more he'd slit his thumb and spilt the blood onto the curiously cyphered pages before he realised that the stain was spreading. As much as he hated to admit it, he knew Griffin had been right in his warnings, but he also knew he had to continue in spite of them, owing to the importance of what lay inside.

He passed his hand over it wearily. For now, it had stopped spreading, but there was more he needed to learn from the book. How much more was still a mystery and, having become acquainted with the strange volume, he figured it might bleed him dry before he got what he needed. He continued to stare at his blackened veins, knowing it would only be a matter of time before it began to spread again.

A knock at the door startled him. Jasper rolled his sleeve down quickly to hide his veins. "Come in."

"Human," Storm called, leaning up against his doorframe.

"I have a name, you know."

"That's good for you," she said, waving her hand in the air, ignoring him completely. "I need your help."

"We've been training together for at least a month, Storm," he growled. "Don't you think it's about time you learned it?"

"I know your name. I'm just waiting to see if you survive before I decide to use it," Storm replied matter-of-factly. "Now, are you coming?"

"Give me a second."

Storm nodded and closed the door behind her.

Jasper stared down at the book at the foot of his bed. Its incessant hissing prompted him to open it once more, against his better judgement. He could almost feel it smiling back at him as he held it, knowing that it was about to be fed. The book fell open to the last page he'd unlocked. Under an ornate diagram depicting seven evenly sized spheres were the words:

The Seven Stones of Cartha

Jasper unhitched a breath and reached over for a knife on his bedside table. He twirled it between his fingers tentatively. Somehow, the book knew blood was near. The splotch on his wrist began to itch. Curiosity bubbled inside him.

Just one more, he thought. *Where's the harm in one more?*

Outside, Storm banged on the door. "I don't have all day, human!" she yelled.

"I'm coming," he called back, knife in hand, still deciding if to give in.

"Hurry up!" she growled.

Jasper scurried to the door, leaving the book alone and wanting. He was proud of the restraint he'd shown in the face of temptation. His breath, along with the hissing, eased the further he got from the book. He opened the door to find Storm tapping her foot expectantly.

She scanned him from head to toe, arms interlaced in front of her. "You forgot your sword."

"You never said I needed it."

"What purpose would you serve me without it?"

Jasper groaned. "Okay, give me a second."

He ran back into the room, grabbing the curious cane that had once belonged to Savara's uncle, which held a hidden blade beneath the golden gorilla's head. His eyes passed over the book once more, the knife glinting beside it.

"To hell with it," he whispered to himself as he reached over and grabbed the blade. The book purred like an innocent cat as the shapes on the page began to tangle with the spilt blood to form words.

Jasper darted back towards the door with subdued enthusiasm. He would come back to find the newly translated page whenever Storm decided she was finished with him.

She took one look at him, noticed the blood dripping from his thumb, and said, "You're bleeding."

"Paper cut," he lied.

Storm looked past him to where the book lay open on the bed. Her cheeks paled. She opened her mouth as if to say something before apparently thinking better of it. She pursed her lips instead and stared at him, trying to figure out what it was he had done.

"Am I interrupting?" Sebastian growled from behind her, narrowing his eyes at Jasper.

"No…" Jasper frowned, keeping his serious gaze on Storm, urging her not to pry.

"Something's happening at the gates," Storm said finally, speaking this time to Sebastian. "And next time I knock," she added with a not-so-gentle punch to his chest, "answer the damned door!"

"Should we not get Griffin?" asked Sebastian, rubbing the spot she'd slammed a fist into.

"And Sav?" Jasper asked.

Storm shot a glance towards the other end of the building. "I couldn't find either of them."

"Have you looked—"

"In the rooms? Yes. No sign," Storm replied flatly.

"And you aren't worried?" Jasper asked. "She could be hurt, or in trouble, or—"

"Contrary to what you must believe, human, I am not, nor will I ever be your lover's keeper," Storm hissed.

"She's not my—" he began, but the intensity of her grimace silenced him.

"Besides, considering they're both gone, I see no reason to fret. They must be together," she added as she turned away. The short strands of brilliant red hair swished behind her as she strode off in front of them both.

Sebastian fixated on him, his jealous eyes searching for an explanation.

"Nothing happened."

"Swear?"

"Swear."

"Then what has her so ruffled this morning?"

"I have no idea," Jasper replied, but something told him that her glance at the book on his bed hadn't helped.

They followed Storm out into the courtyard where a cart was already waiting to take them to the gates of Idune. Jasper stared at Savara's empty room. He hadn't had the time or the guts to speak after their fight, and even if he had, he feared too much damage was already done. Jasper frowned, wondering where in this crazy world Savara had gone, and what sort of mess they were in now.

CHAPTER 42

CHASING RABBITS DOWN HOLES

SAVARA WOKE TO the feeling of being strangled, somewhat relieved to find that her sheet had pinched itself under her pillow and curled around her as she tossed and turned. Sadly, this understanding did not help her to close her eyes and drift off once more. Griffin was right to have warned her about the drinks. She was wrong to have ignored him. She hardly remembered leaving the party, let alone having undressed and planted herself in the bed. Now, with a blinding pulse in her brain and a strange dream on her tongue, she wondered if she would ever get back to sleep. She'd lived this night before, many times in the creaky old house that held more secrets than cobwebs. Never had she imagined she would relive it a world away.

A cold breeze sauntered in from the mountains beyond her window. The last of the stars still held tight to their positions in the sky, but day would soon break that hold. She contemplated closing it and attempting to sleep for what little night remained when a faint noise came from outside that sounded like her name.

Curious, Savara got to her feet and strolled over to the window. Below, she spied three men in heated whispers. She knew it was wrong to eavesdrop. She almost returned to her bed when she heard her name again.

"Who are we looking for again?" asked a grunty-looking man with a five o'clock shadow that had turned into a ten o'clock one everywhere but the top of his shiny bald head.

"The Argia princess," replied a twiggy one. "She's supposed to be travelling with that Izar that's always stirring up trouble."

"Why don't we just catch her now and spill her guts?" asked the first with a yawn.

"No!" urged the third man, one who looked entirely out of place with his polished attire and glossy black gloves. "Bring her to me. There will be no spilling of blood."

The three men cast their gazes upwards to the balconies. Savara ducked to avoid their line of sight but not before having met eyes with the latter. The one that looked like the fashionable embodiment of trouble itself.

"Up there," he called. "Someone is watching."

Her heart pounded heavily in her chest as she scrambled for a hiding place. The only way out was also the only way in unless she planned on scaling two stories and a mountainside. The wardrobe was too shallow. The bed too high off the ground. They'd spot her instantly in the bathroom. Her heart raced as her feet padded across the floor, still searching for safety. She tapped urgently on the wall that separated her and

Storm, hoping the flaming redhead might come to her rescue, but there were no sounds of life from that room at all, not even Storm's usual snoring.

"Please…" she pleaded to the dark, unaware that it was listening. Savara dropped to her knees beside the bed, preparing herself for the inevitable, when she heard a pebble fall from the wall. Two more followed. In response, she turned to find a pair of blindingly blue eyes staring back at her expectantly from a newly formed hole in the wall beside the bed. There they were again, the eyes that chased her, belonging to the man that saved her. Savara gasped, but the man put a slow finger to his lips and shook his head.

"Come with me," he whispered and stalked back into the dark of the tunnel.

Savara didn't have much time to think as she darted over to the tunnel. Heavy footsteps began climbing the stairs outside, drawing closer with each second that ticked by. The rock wall sealed itself shut as soon as she crossed inside. Little specks of bioluminescent moss came to life in the dark, casting their glow over the walls like tiny green stars.

"How is this—" she began, but he cupped his hand over her lips and tapped his ear. His hands smelled of night flowers, a scent she'd curiously grown fond of during her time in Visanthe. In the silence of the tunnel, the only sounds she could hear were those of their combined heartbeats and worried breaths. Then, from beyond the rock, the sounds of muffled voices appeared. The stranger plucked a small pebble from the wall, revealing a peephole that would be lost from the outside. The pair stood in wait, listening as the three men scoured the room for the girl they'd seen.

"She's not here," growled one.

"She was just here!" hissed the other. "She didn't just disappear."

"What if she did… what if she turned herself into a spirit…" the first whispered fearfully as he scanned the higher corners of the room. His companion whacked him over the head.

"Don't be doltish. She probably just slipped out the window." The second cupped a hand over his eyes and gazed out the window at the mountainside. "I don't see how she would've managed that one though… But we need to leave. Boss said not to be seen. Sun will be up soon."

Giving up their search, the two unkempt men departed. The final man, the most elegant of the three, crossed paths with them on the way out. He stayed on, pursing his lips as he scanned the room, clearly unconvinced by Savara's disappearing act.

The stranger prickled at the sight of the polished man. The man on the other side of the wall removed his gloves.

Savara hitched her breath, watching as streaks of blue lightning danced over his fingers.

The stranger stiffened, pushing Savara further into the tunnel. The next thing she knew, the blue glow of lightning was seeping through the cracks in the wall, and the man before her was blocking any stray surge with his hand. When the light died once more, the stranger pressed a shaking finger to his lips until he was sure the man on the other side had gone.

"Who were they?" Savara asked, taking his hand to steady herself.

"Bad news," he replied, patting away the thin layer of dust that coated his otherwise impeccable blazer. He glared at her with those midnight blue eyes that had chased her all around Visanthe. Dense energy radiated from him. It had a strange duality to it that made her heart ache. Tangible lust and distant longing bundled into one. She'd noted as much when he'd asked her to dance, and when he'd saved her in the forest…

"Who are you?" Savara asked.

"Probably best you don't know," the man replied.

"I'm tired of not knowing," Savara groaned as she dusted herself off, the echo of footsteps her only reply. She turned back to where the man had been moments before, finding the tunnel suspiciously empty. She stood alone, the bioluminescent moss her only company.

Savara knew she should look for Griffin, explain what had happened, and ask the guards to search for the intruders, but she couldn't stop thinking about this strange man. There had to be a reason he'd always shown up when she'd needed help. She figured he must know something about her. If not about her powers, then at least why the world seemed out to get her.

It was only a matter of time before Savara found herself feeling around in the dark, following only the echo of a haunting stranger into the deeper parts of the tunnels, unaware that the darkness around her had begun to smile.

CHAPTER 43

A MISSING PIECE TO THE PUZZLE

THE MOUNTAIN'S CHILL seeped into her bones. The path, rough and gravelly beneath her bare feet. But not even that deterred her. She balanced herself against the cave walls as she descended, chasing after the man whose eyes had followed her throughout Visanthe. Whose voice had brought her back from the brink of collapse. The man who'd saved her life. And yet, she wasn't even certain he existed.

For all she knew, she chased after a ghost.

With another shaky step, Savara lost her balance, tumbling deeper into the darkness. Pebbles attacked her back, rocks scratched at her arms. She reached out her arms to steady herself, but this far down, they were made of a slippery, polished, black granite that was impossible to cling to. Losing all notion of up and down, Savara wondered how much further she would have to fall.

Then, out of nowhere, the cold of the cave gave way to a refreshing springtime warmth. She hit the ground with a loud thud, a cloud of loose dirt billowing around her. Savara coughed out whatever had managed its way into her lungs as she got to her feet. She shielded her eyes against the blazing mountain sun above, wondering where in the world she'd ended up now.

Around her, the world was surprisingly green. A plush patch of grass surrounded by little pockets of bubbling magma and rimmed by fields of crystals glimmering in the morning light. The vibration of everything—from the walls that stretched high above to the tiniest blade of grass below—told her that this strange place was alive. Even the heat of it was unlike anything she'd ever felt before.

Iturri. The word arrived in her mind all on its own. It buzzed around her invisibly, tingling the little hairs on the nape of her neck and pulsing at the base of her spine. There was power here, more than she could have ever imagined.

"What is this place?" she whispered.

Suddenly, a wall of stone crumbled away beside her. Savara jumped. Two figures emerged from the resulting tunnel, an elderly Harri gentleman with a salt and peppered beard that Savara vaguely recognised, and behind him, a young Izar she knew well.

"Griffin?" she called as she moved towards them, all but forgetting the man she'd chased here. "How did you find me?"

"I didn't," he admitted, inclining his head towards the elderly man.

"You..." she said, remembering the lines of his face and the unmistakable glowing eye from the previous night's dinner. She'd been too preoccupied with hiding her own energy back then to focus on his, but in the solitude of the garden around them, she realised he was much more powerful than he'd let on that night. His spirit hummed with the same force that governed the garden, only magnified. Distilled in his person. It was something dense, harmonic, and somehow, grounded in nature. Savara retreated a step, remembering his prodding questions from the previous night, and worrying what kind of conversation would've led him and Griffin to this place.

The man contemplated her as he had the night before, this time, however, he looked to be waiting for something. Recognition, possibly. When none came, he pursed his lips and cleared his throat.

"Princess Savara, of the house of Orrin," he said as he clapped a hand over his chest and bowed. "I am Lord Ori, and your friend tells me you need my help."

Savara's eyes widened. She raised her brow at Griffin, who shot her a reassuring nod. Her powers curled in her palms, just beneath her skin. The air around this new gentleman buzzed. Whoever he was, she sensed he was powerful. Dangerous in his own right. Yet, it seemed that Griffin trusted him—mostly. She wasn't sure Griffin trusted anyone fully. She bit her lip as she bowed to the man.

"Forgive me, sir, for not having introduced myself when we met," she said.

"Do you truly not remember me, then?" he replied with a subtle frown. "When we spoke at the party, you were truly oblivious?"

Savara's heart sank. He already knew her somehow. Had their entire conversation been a test? Why could she not remember him? Unless… Suddenly, it dawned on her. Back at the party, he'd mistaken her for royalty. But then, it wasn't a mistake, was it? He'd known. He'd known her from that part of her life. He'd remembered her where few people did. He was part of it somehow. Part of the reason she'd lost her memories. No wonder he'd come up to her so cavalierly…

"I lost all memories of my childhood… But something tells me you already knew that," she replied.

Lord Ori gave away nothing as he asked, "What are you suggesting, young princess?"

Savara cringed at the title—her title. Even now, even after all she'd discovered, it still felt wrong.

"You can tell him," Griffin chimed in when she made no move to respond.

She didn't trust this man, not as much as Griffin seemed to. He was respectful to her now, now that she was no longer a child. Now, she was something to fear. And judging by how he'd first gazed upon her, he knew it, too. Nevertheless, she obliged, recounting all she'd uncovered about herself since her return—all but her Arima blood, though she supposed he already knew as much, and, of course, how she'd gotten her gemstoned scar. When she explained what she knew of the imminent attack on Idune, Lord Ori broke his semblance of calm. Something in his energy shifted, imperceptible to all but her, thanks to those same fearsome powers of hers.

Savara purposefully neglected to mention the visit from the strange men, or the reason she was in the garden, to begin with. She said nothing of her saviour. His identity was still a mystery, and if she was being honest with herself, she wasn't entirely sure he existed at all.

"May I see your hand?" was all Lord Ori asked of her after her tale.

Savara pursed her lips as she stared down at her palm. She contemplated it briefly before handing it over to him. Her heart echoed in her ears, afraid of what he'd see. Would he be able to see the darkness in her? The bloodlust? The life she'd taken?

Lord Ori raised her wrist to his all-jade eye. "I thought I might not see a mark like this again in my lifetime…" he said solemnly. "I almost hoped I didn't."

Savara withdrew her hand, holding it close to her chest. "What does it mean?"

"War, my child. It means war."

Lord Ori stomped a heavy foot on the ground, shaking the walls of the sanctuary. He thrust a fist towards the opposite end of the garden, opening a new tunnel through the mountain.

"Young Conroy, follow that tunnel and find your friends. Have General Isaac give word to the rest of the court to evacuate everyone who is unable to fight. We are no longer safe within these walls." Griffin bowed and made for the tunnel. "And hurry, before he paces a hole in my floor!" Lord Ori called out.

Savara watched Griffin for as far as the tunnel would allow, until he was swallowed by the darkness. When the rock closed behind him, her fear began to rise.

They were alone, and this time, if something happened, she would have no one to save her.

Lord Ori stomped his heavy foot again, this time raising two stools from the rocks buried deep within the ground. He sat cross-legged on one, motioning for her to do the same.

Savara hesitantly obliged, careful not to lower her guard too much.

A crease formed at his brow as he said, "I am sorry for your many struggles, young princess. I had recognised you the other night. I said nothing because I wanted—I needed to see if you remembered. If the charm had worked…" His echoing voice softened. Shame rippled in the air around him. "That night, in your eyes, I saw old decisions that have haunted me for years come back to life. I was there the day it happened. The day you were chosen."

"What do you mean chosen?"

Lord Ori let out a resounding sigh before recounting a tale of his own. Savara listened with bated breath, barely able to contain her horror. It was a tale so intimate that, despite not remembering it for herself, it had her holding back tears. It was the tale of her divination…

THE WORLD STILLED as the crowd waited for the young princess to slide the rings on her finger and receive her judgement. An eerie chill danced around them all, despite the flickering flames of the amphitheatre. He was not the only one who had sensed something wrong. The other leaders shifted on their pedestals, their troubled eyes darting back and forth to one another, wondering how they would react to whatever was about to happen. And when it finally did—when the rings broke away, revealing the mark of the Arima—they knew their fears were not without reason.

Poor child, Ori thought even then, scarcely past infancy and now marked by infamy. There was no way for her to know what her divination meant, not only for her kingdom but for the world at large. Not many alive would even remember the truth. Their existence had been blurred into obscurity, but the leaders were well-versed in such legends and legacies. Poor child looking back at her mother for clarification and wondering why the world had suddenly stopped. Her heartbroken mother, however, would not meet her eyes.

The crowds were swept away and hurried off to finish the rest of the festivities as the leaders gathered for the grimmest of meetings. What to do with the child was decided that same night. They had to act fast before the news reached the rest of the world. Things of such a nature tended to spread like wildfires when left unchecked, and this news was not something that could go unchecked.

What to tell the crowds was an issue to which each leader threw in their two cents. That very night they came up with the idea that the child should be killed off—not physically, but rather tucked away from society. Memories were wiped and chronologies altered.

Those brief minutes marked by her divination were erased from the minds of the masses through a gentle rain—courtesy of the leader of the Ur. To the public, the child existed no longer. Killed off much earlier, tragically, but sympathetically. But such a divination meant greater actions would need to take place. Old prophecies were rearing their ugly heads, and they, the leaders, would've been foolish to ignore the warnings…

"NO ONE MEANT for you to get hurt," he added finally, but it did nothing to console her or stop the tears from streaming down the sides of her cheeks.

The sky shifted quickly above them from the brilliant mountain blue to a swirling vortex of blackened clouds, traced by streaks of lightning. Harsh mountain winds flooded through the city, sending leaves from the still-green trees rushing through the streets. The burning scent of ash followed, dragged down to the ground only by the sudden rain. Moments later, the sun was swallowed whole by the clouds. In the distance more shadows gathered.

CHAPTER 44

THE PRINCE OF SHADOWS

SINISTER CLAPPING BROKE the silence. It came in slow and monotonous, echoing throughout the sanctuary.

"What a lovely story," came a voice, echoing from one of the large tunnels.

"That voice…" Savara stiffened.

But it wasn't just any voice. It was *that* voice, the one she'd only ever heard in her mind. It echoed through the cavernous chamber, the mere sound of it curdled her blood.

"Who goes there?" said Lord Ori in his earthquake-provoking growl. "Whoever you are, you are trespassing on hallowed grounds."

"Ah, Ori, still as uptight as ever. Nice to see some things don't change," the voice called again.

The energy around them shifted. Savara sensed violence brewing in the air. Her powers tingled in her palms, resonating with the energy of the voice, as though they were one and the same. She turned to face it. Her heart sank immediately.

A pair of midnight blue eyes dulled slightly by a swirling dark haze appeared from the darkness. Paled, olive-skinned hands appeared next, traced by blackened veins. They continued their slow clapping. The voice which followed rang out as cool as clouded sky but was stained by the malice of its words. When the man's full body appeared, he left Savara speechless.

It was him, the man that had saved her on multiple occasions, only he didn't look like he had the previous times they'd met. The energy surrounding him was dark and twisted. His ebony curls shifted despite a lack of wind, seemingly defying gravity. It gave him the appearance of being trapped underwater. And that voice… It wasn't his at all. This one belonged to her nightmares.

Savara clenched her fists, preparing herself to attack when Lord Ori rested a firm hand on her shoulder.

"Hallowed grounds as these are not sites for violence," he said, narrowing his eyes on the man. "Or possession."

The clapping finally stopped. "I agree," said the young man in the sinister voice.

Something evil hung in the air between them. It sought out the thing inside her like a bear sniffing for its next prey. She felt it approaching, invisible, but dangerous, nonetheless. Savara tried to remain calm, to keep her powers under control, but the sensation kept prodding at her.

What had happened to the man who had saved her? And what did Lord Ori mean by possession?

But before she could linger on the questions, the man pulled out a dagger. Lord Ori stepped in front of her, using himself as a human shield. He had the constitution of a bear, and yet, Savara feared for him more than she did the man with the sinister voice.

The dagger glinted under the light of the magma in the walls. It was a twin to the one she had seen in Griffin's tent in almost every way, save for the colour. This one glowed a hot white in the spirit-tinged air of the sanctuary.

When she looked back at the man, she noticed his eyes had hollowed. In a single fluid motion, he sliced through his palm as though it were butter. The cut was deep, but he didn't flinch. His face remained expressionless as he took the knife in his bloodied palm and stabbed the ground below his feet.

The earth trembled.

The dark red fluid traced the engraved hilt as it seeped down into the grass. The strange shadowing of the man's eyes and veins flowed with it. The muting of the colours of his person disappeared into the soil. His skin and eyes regained their crispness. His face remained hollow as he avoided her gaze.

Purposefully hollow, she realised, taking an uneasy step backwards.

The skies above them rumbled. The earth below them shook. Beyond the cavern, a storm approached.

* * *

"LOOKS LIKE ONE hell of a storm," Sebastian said as he looked over the brim of an ever-steaming teacup towards the darkening horizon and then back to Storm. "And the weather seems rough too," he added with a smirk.

"Sebastian, is it really the time for jokes?" Jasper asked, questioning his unusual cheeriness given the circumstances. From where they stood, high up on the great wall of Idune, the wind raged like the unforgiving ocean thrashing against a cliffside. His bones quaked. Horrors waited beyond the clouds, horrors that even the sky feared.

"Ignore him," Storm growled, her eyes fixed on the whorl of shadows inching ever closer to their perch. "Sebas is just asking for a fight."

"Begging and pleading, Stormy, my dear," Sebastian grinned. "You in an obliging mood?"

"I'd carve your heart out if I got the chance."

Sebastian purred. "I love it when you talk dirty."

"Sebas, if you had half the brains you think you have, you'd have twice as much as you do now," Storm spat.

"Very funny Stormy, my *darling dearest*, but I only need one brain cell to know that the blush creeping over your cheeks means—" The words caught in his throat.

In the time it took for Storm to draw her sword, a hummingbird would have barely beaten its wings. She slashed cleanly through the teacup with a swiftness and precision matched only by the wind itself. The base clattered to the ground far below them, along with the rest of the tea. The handle dangled precariously between his fingertips.

Sebastian's eyes widened in awe, but Storm remained entirely unfazed. Her gaze never once lifted from the shadows, despite the obscuring strands of brilliant red hair carving around the harsh edge of her cheekbones. The sword hung easily at her side, a single drop of tea gliding gracefully down its blade.

"I wouldn't finish that sentence," she hissed before returning to the expectant army below.

"How many times have you used that one?" Jasper asked when Storm was well out of earshot.

"Not as many as you'd think, and hopefully more than I should've," Sebastian replied.

Jasper raised an eyebrow. "You do know she'll kill you one of these days, right?"

"Is that what you think?" Sebastian laughed. "If she wanted me dead, I would've been dead years ago."

"Then why do you continue to push her?"

Sebastian stared down at Storm as she exchanged words with a soldier on the ground. The smile that spread across his face was unmistakable, as was the glimmer in his eyes. Storm glared up at them briefly and frowned before resuming her conversation.

"I guess I just know great ways to waste a good cup of tea." Sebastian shrugged and tossed the remaining bits of porcelain to the stones below, their clank and smash engulfed by the howling air currents around them.

* * *

A PLUME OF dust swirled upwards from the ground around the knife. Eyes as red as rubies pierced the cloud. A man stepped out of the vortex of smoke looking more fleeting than whole. He was barely substantial, something akin to a shadow.

"Stay behind me," Lord Ori whispered to Savara.

This new man inhaled deeply, letting the crisp mountain air fill his mostly solid lungs. His charcoal suit shifted like the dust that comprised him. Pearly white teeth and ruby-red eyes stood out against the rest of his shadow-tinged body. Their vivid contrast further highlighted the viciousness that Savara sensed in him.

"A wonder it is to be whole again," he said with a satisfied laugh as he relished in the sensations around him. "My, my, Ori. It has been a while," he continued. "I'd like to say you're looking no worse for wear, but lies have never been my strong suit…"

"Adrius," Ori spat. "How is this possible?"

The man glowered at him. "Come now. You didn't expect them to get rid of me? You know as well as I that every land demands its leader, and no man is above the will of Iturri…" He held his hand up to the light, contemplating his new form as he spoke. "That little Izar wretch might have stripped me of my body, but she could never take my soul." He raised his chin proudly. "If you remember correctly, souls are *my* realm."

This new man, whoever he was, was the true owner of the voice that had tormented her for the past few years. That same voice chilled her blood and rattled her bones, echoing throughout the sanctuary. It felt like sacrilege, his presence here. As though his arrival had taken some of the power she'd original felt buzzing around her.

"Why have you come back? Why now? If you were so confident you could, why wait this long?" Lord Ori prodded.

"Timing is everything," he growled, casting his attention towards Savara. "The divination of our little friend here meant the time was finally right." He addressed her directly, his eyes twinkling with hunger as they beheld her. "I believe, Princess of Flame, you have met my apprentice. I apologise that it has taken me so long to formally introduce myself—

something I now intend to rectify. I am Adrius," he said as he executed a perfectly respectable bow. "The Prince of Shadows."

This is him, she realised. The true owner of the voice from her nightmares.

"Leave her out of this," Ori retorted, still protecting her with his body the way a father might—the first time anyone had. The gesture, little as it was, made her feel as though she wasn't alone.

The Prince of Shadows scowled at this. "She is the root of this, whether you wish to accept it or not."

As the two men bickered, Savara's skin prickled with the sensation of being watched. She turned to find The Apprentice staring intently at her from the other end of the chamber. The intensity of his gaze burned her skin.

Savara frowned at him. Time and time again, his eyes were the ones she'd met as she was led out of trouble. But now, they were the ones she'd followed into it. She wondered what he could possibly be thinking. In her mind, she cursed him for having led her here. He must have known she would've. Had he simply saved her from one threat to deliver her to another? Or, if he had truly been possessed, was even the person who had saved her at all?

She brushed off his gaze as she turned back to the Prince of Shadows. He looked much younger than Lord Ori, but his soul was much older. Though she hadn't directly tried to use her powers on him, his energy engulfed the room. It was powerful, more so than anyone she'd met in Visanthe. And it was darker too, infinitely so.

"What do you mean?" she asked, surprising both The Apprentice and Lord Ori with her boldness. "Why was my divination so important?"

The Prince of Shadows contemplated her with a sinister grin. "Shall you tell her, Ori, or shall I? If anything, it's poetic, you taking away her memories before and now being the one—"

"I told you to leave her out of this," Lord Ori snarled. His hands balled into tense fists as he slid his foot back into a fighting stance. "This conversation ends here. I'll make sure of that."

"I thought hallowed grounds were not stages for fighting?" the Prince of Shadows mused.

"For you, I will make an exception," Lord Ori retorted.

Shards of rock met tendrils of shadow. The once peaceful garden grew angry. The chamber buzzed with an energy that felt like the collision of worlds. It made her knees buckle. All she could do was watch the battle. Nothing was out of reach. Nothing was off-limits.

The elderly Harri lord moved with force and prowess, launching rocks from all corners of the sanctuary, and hurling them like bullets toward his attacker. The Prince of Shadows hardly moved at all, letting his dagger-like tendrils carve everything in their path. To Savara's dismay, he even seemed amused. Like Savara, The Apprentice watched from the sidelines, dodging the occasional flying rock. His eyes flicked from her to his master. When he was sure that only she was watching, he mouthed the words *get up*.

Savara narrowed her eyes at him. He mouthed the words again, urgency lining his eyes, but it was too late for her to heed the warning.

The Prince of Shadows raised a hand in her direction, sending two stray tendrils after her. Her heart raced, forcing the adrenaline through her veins in hopes of getting her moving again, but to no avail. Savara sat paralysed with fear. With a vicious slash, the tendrils pierced the ground beside her. She shielded her eyes. She pleaded with the thing inside her to make an appearance.

Please, please, please… she begged, searching the darkest parts of her soul in vain. The rumbling of the ground beneath her terrified her. The next thing she knew, thick vines began wrapping themselves around her legs, strapping her to the ground.

"I can feel your fear, princess," called The Prince of Shadows. "I can sense your doubts… You're worried about becoming a monster?" The corners of his mouth tilted upwards. "Oh, princess, how naïve you are…" The next wave of his fingers sent Ori flying into the solid rock wall before slumping to the ground.

"No!" Savara cried, reaching her hand out towards him.

Finally, they appeared. Her powers. Her palms tingled, radiating energy like heat from a fire. It reminded her of the attack in the forest, how she'd taken control of her own light. Her subsequent movements came from somewhere deep inside her soul, somewhere she hadn't been privy to before. Savara motioned a hand towards The Prince of Shadows, sending tendrils of lavender light in his direction.

Last time, she'd tried the same on a disembodied voice. This time, at least, she had a target. She felt for the contours of his soul, trying like she had with the child in Big Tog's study, but found only endless depths of darkness. Grasping at him was like grasping at nothing. She wondered if there was anything truly alive in him at all.

The Prince of Shadows, with a dark energy of his own, clamped down on hers and smiled.

"Finally, it begins."

* * *

SHADOWS BEAT DOWN on the city of Idune like a tsunami dragging an island to the darkest depths of the sea. Buildings burst into flames. People fled their houses in flocks. Screams littered the ashen air.

"Storm!" yelled Jasper as he stabbed at the shadows. "Behind you!"

She slashed at the anthropomorphic cloud, deterring it rather than vanquishing it. "They aren't dying! What are these things?" she called back.

"They're not good," he replied, hacking at the air around them with much less grace. "Don't let them touch you." His limited knowledge of fighting showed but wouldn't stop him. He'd cut through thousands of shadows if he had to. The lives of his friends were on the line. His life was on the line. Her life.

"How are we going to get rid of them if we can't kill them?" Storm yelled back.

"We're not…"

Suddenly, a wave of living targets appeared. They marched in unison, arms poised to fight. They jabbed in time with their steps, sending a wave of brilliant red flames across the floors.

"That's more like it," Storm said.

Jasper looked across at the sea of blank faces. There was something almost inhuman about the way they moved. No soul, no life. It was almost mechanical in nature. One particular face caught his eye. A middle-aged man whom he recognised from his capture outside of Osiir approached him.

"I know you," he said, but the man didn't register his words. "Storm! Those are the captured Argia. Don't hurt them!" Jasper called to her. "You're Thomas, right?" he asked, but the man continued to approach, arms readied for an attack. "I don't want to hurt you," he continued, but the man's expression was unchanging, fixed, like a statue. The man waved a hand in the air, sending out a trail of flames towards him. Jasper jumped just in time.

"I don't think they can hear you," Storm hissed.

Worried she was right, Jasper regarded the man's eyes with a pleading gaze. The humanity he had once known had been obscured entirely by the shadowy black dust. "They're in there somewhere," he replied. "They have to be…"

Just as the man was about to dole out a lethal dose of fire, Storm sliced through his chest, leaving a jarring streak of spurting red liquid across it. "They're possessed," she said firmly. "If you don't want me to kill them, don't let them get so close."

The man coughed violently as the blood spurted from his lungs. Fear filled his eyes briefly before he crumpled to the ground. With two more painful coughs, he was gone. His body stilled and grew cold before being consumed by another wave of flames. There was no time to mourn the man's tragic and dehumanised death. The flames and shadows raged on around them, dancing together in a dangerous harmony; the kind which toyed with the fine line between life and whatever lay beyond.

CHAPTER 45

THE EARTH STONE

THE PRINCE OF Shadows brushed off her attack easily, as though it had been nothing of consequence. He sent a wave of shadows her way, capturing her the way she had intended to him. They stunned her momentarily. For a second, her vision blipped.

By the time Savara recovered from the shock, it was too late. She'd been freed from the stun, but she was the only one. The Apprentice stood behind Lord Ori, pressing the knife firmly to his throat.

"Stop!" Savara screamed. She aimed a hand at The Apprentice, ready to unleash her powers in all her anger, control be damned. But then, the Prince of Shadows caught hold of her wrist. Something about his hold strangled her powers, cutting them off at the source. She panicked, feeling her powers wither beneath his touch. "No…" she whispered, trying to grasp at them even as they slipped from her fingers.

"That's enough for today," he told her. This was her only warning. She knew, should he wish it, he could've stopped her heart then and there.

Instead, the Prince of Shadows brushed a cold, bony hand across her warm, fleshy cheeks. She shuddered again. He was a thing of nightmares—his voice, his army of shadows, his domination over souls. He was the embodiment of everything she'd ever feared.

He was worse than Death.

He stared at her hungrily, contemplating the stones that marred her cheek.

"So, you've bound your soul? You must kill to save yourself…" He spoke as though he could read the story of their deal in the red glow of the stones. "It's eating at you," he added, relishing in her discomfort. "I can take it away, you know?"

He ran his finger over the gems. For a moment, they disappeared. Her heart lifted, finally free of the weight of the task. It felt like finally coming up for air after a long stint under water.

But something about it didn't feel right. It wasn't freedom, at least, not the kind she wanted. It was yet another trade, like she'd made with Big Tog. A cage for a cage.

Savara pulled away from his touch, the stones immediately returning.

"Let him go," she whispered, fighting against the heavy call of murder that accompanied the stones. Her knees buckled, but she wouldn't let herself fall. She couldn't.

"I'm afraid I can't do that, princess," he replied, his voice cold and resentful.

The Prince of Shadows nodded to The Apprentice. Before Savara knew what was happening, The Apprentice raised a hand, enclosing them all in a field of blue light. The sound of thunder high above disappeared, yet the storm raged on.

"Take me instead!" she screamed, fearing the worst. The Prince of Shadows furrowed his brow. "It's me you want, isn't it?" she said, this time with more resolve. "You've been chasing me around Visanthe. Let him go, and you can have me instead. I'll go willingly…"

"You?" The Prince of Shadows let out a rumbling laugh that ground at her bones. "You think your life is worth that of a seasoned general? A little girl who can hardly use her powers in place of the leader of an imperial court. Do those lives equate to you?"

"No, but…"

"This isn't a question of life and death, my child. It is about the end of an era. And not even you can bargain with that…" The Prince of Shadows released her, knowing she was too broken to move. He stalked around the hall, letting his voice carry throughout the chambre. His steps were graceful—*he* was graceful, like the night itself made living. "I know you feel it too. The prodding in your soul. The hunger. That constant wondering at why you came to be…" The Prince of Shadows beamed as he prowled around her. "You and I are cut from the same cloth, my dear. And do you know why?"

Savara shook her head, unable to speak. Unable to deny his claims. She'd known it, deep within her soul. Something was coming to a close, and there was little she could do about it. She'd thought seeking out her purpose might have quelled these fears, this overwhelming sense of dread which lingered in endings. But she was wrong…

"The world does not make many like us. When it does, we must heed its call."

"I am nothing like you," she spat, fighting the heat rising in her cheeks.

The Prince of Shadows grinned.

"No?"

With a wave of his hand, he cast a whorl of shadows out into the centre of the chambre. On command, The Apprentice projected images into the swirling mass— violence, death, her friends beyond the sanctuary.

"Have you not marched your friends into war so that you can find out about that pathetic past of yours?"

"Jasper!" she screamed into the cloud. A circle of flames had engulfed both him and Storm. She hadn't realised the war continued beyond these walls. "Don't hurt him," she pleaded.

"You mistake my goals, my child. I do not wish for death and destruction. I too wish for that naïve idea of peace. But… There is power around us, in the hidden contours of this world. Trapped. I know you feel it too, for we are the only ones who can. It is in our nature—our *blood*."

Savara watched the cloud with bated breath, knowing she would be of no use to them here. The Prince of Shadows was right. She'd endangered them all in her selfishness. She couldn't defend them, let alone herself. She watched as the fire encroached upon her friends, cursing herself for her uselessness. When the Prince of Shadows drew close once more, she no longer recoiled.

"In turn, there are those in this world who believe themselves worthy of controlling this great power. They believe themselves greater than spirit. Great enough to capture it, to lock it away." He rooted himself beside her, his voice darkening as he spoke. "This world was never meant to be divided. This great separation has caused people to forget what they are—what we are. They exile and abandon instead of choosing to learn, to understand. They toil away in squabbles over an ability as trivial as breathing… But if they can't appreciate their own precious little lives, why should we?"

He curled his fingers, directing the shadows through the whorl of clouds. They slithered like serpents across the floor, sharpening into tendrils as they aimed for Jasper and Storm.

"Stop," Savara begged, though her voice had lost all force. She was utterly powerless against the Prince of Shadows here. If he had any better nature to appeal to, she had yet to see it. Her last hope, her only hope, was the plea. "Please, don't hurt them… I'll do anything."

The Prince of Shadows stayed his hand; the shadows hovered in place. "Anything?" he repeated with a vicious smirk.

"Don't listen to him!" yelled Lord Ori from the other end of the chamber.

"We will not hear from you," the Prince of Shadows replied. A stream of shadows whipped from his hand and gagged Lord Ori. The Apprentice pressed the blade deeper into his throat until a small trickle of blood appeared at his collarbone. "There is more to our story, princess, and I believe it is time I reveal it. What was done to you was done to me, many years ago… Have you not wondered why, after all these years, you were the only Arima divined? Why they cast you aside? Exiled you to the human world? Why you are all alone in this world?"

"I…" But what could she say? She'd spent many a lonely night feeling like an outcast in her pretend home, only to find that she'd been exiled from her real one.

Tears fell in streams through the crevices in her gemstoned scar and down the sides of her chin. The Prince of Shadows had plucked the feelings straight from her soul. All her longing for connection, all her pleas for love and acceptance. Even now, even after all her friends had done for her, she could not stop the depression from resurfacing.

"They fear us, my dear. Would you like to know why?" He cupped her cheek in his hand, the gesture something almost loving. But this man, this creature, felt no love. He was a heartless shadow, a deliverer of pain. And yet, Savara could not help but wonder. "If you give me what I want, I promise to show you the truth. No more lies, no more secrets. You will finally understand the reason behind your precious life. You shall know of the purpose to which you so readily and unwittingly cling."

Her heartrate picked up, the sound of it echoing in her ears. Truth. Truth from the last person she'd expected, but the only person who truly seemed to understand her. Maybe he was right, they were one and the same. She'd come all this way looking for answers… What choice did she have?

"No one gets hurt," she replied, a severe frown marking her face. "I'll help…but no one gets hurt."

"Good girl." The Prince of Shadows winked. "Deep in your heart, you know this is the right thing to do," he said. Savara was going to be sick. "Now, your friend over there has something I need, and he knows exactly what it is, don't you?" he called to Ori, who bobbed his head, careful not to accidentally cut himself on the blade. "You give it to me, and I will call off the attack below. We'll leave just as easily as we came. No more unnecessary deaths."

"You want the stone…"

"One stone for thousands of lives," he replied. When she didn't initially react, he added, "Come now, Savara my dear, you don't want all these deaths on your hands." He returned to her, lifting her hands gently in his own. "How would you sleep at night, knowing that it was your fault that all those people lost their lives? That you could have spared them the horrors but chose not to?"

"But—"

"And how much better would you sleep if you finally knew who you were? The reason for your divination, princess. I can tell you." He grinned as he brushed her hair behind her ear and began to whisper. "Tell Ori to hand it over, and I promise you will finally understand what beautiful role you play in this world."

She gazed over at Lord Ori and his captor. The Apprentice looked away; his eyes were, for once, unable to meet hers.

"You swear it?" Savara replied tentatively.

"I swear on my life, my soul," he said, moving in front of her and bowing his head ceremoniously low. "Princess. No more unnecessary secrets. No more unnecessary deaths."

With the same polished dagger that brought him to life, he carved an "X" into the spot where his heart might have been, as a sharpened shadow slit her other cheek. Their wounds glowed viciously red with unspoken purpose before hardening into crystal.

Savara found it uncomfortable that he so quickly bound his soul to his word, wondering what fearsome thing he had in mind. But as their souls were now bound, she had no choice. She could already feel their sickening prod to fulfil his request. She treaded softly past The Prince of Shadows and bent down before Lord Ori.

"It's okay," she whispered. "Everything is going to be okay. I promise everything will…"

Resignation set in across his face as his jaw slackened under the light gag. She knew he didn't believe her. There was little more she could do to console him. He reached a heavy hand up to her cheek. In his touch, she sensed fear, pain, doubt. She felt his resolve and hope fade, leaving behind only an empty acceptance. She knew there was nothing more to say. He reached the same hand up to his face and removed his jade eye, placing it gently in her outstretched hand and closing her delicate fingers over it. This was his apology.

Life beat inside it. It vibrated in her palm, humming softly, speaking to her in a tongue she had yet to learn. Savara frowned at it. For that moment, time stood still. She forgot the war raging on around them. For a moment she felt only peace.

Then, that moment ended.

The Prince of Shadows hovered over her in wait.

"Remember your promise," she growled.

"I am a man of my word, my dear." He bowed again with an outstretched hand. "A stone for the truth, and no more unnecessary deaths."

Prying her fingers from the crystal proved to be no easy task. When she managed to open her hand, a sickening weakness rushed through her body. Savara reluctantly placed the glowing jade crystal in his ghostly palm, careful not to take her eyes off him for a second.

The man turned it over in his hand and inhaled deeply. His eyes sparkled like red stars in the night sky. It didn't seem like the power of the stone weighed on him as it had on her, but there was a change in the quality of his features. The hollowness in him began to fill.

From within the cloud, Savara noticed the shadows on the battlefield subside. They slithered down from the bodies of their captives, disappearing into nothingness. Her spirits lifted when Jasper's face appeared, albeit concerningly burnt and bloodied in places, but alive. The possessed Argia seemed to be waking up too.

He'd kept his word; the fighting was over.

A look of relief crossed over Lord Ori's face, for he too knew his people were safe. And yet, as she glanced at The Apprentice, she found his features riddled with concern. She'd seen his eyes glittering on the darkest of nights, giving her safe harbour in the worst of her nightmares. His voice alone had brought her back when her body was overrun with shadows. Now it looked as though he couldn't stand the sight of her.

"What about me?" she asked, regaining her voice. "You swore to tell me who I am, and why I have these powers," she demanded of the Prince of Shadows.

His red eyes sparkled as he contemplated her, taking interest in her newfound determination.

"You wished for the truth… We have been gifted with powers that few can comprehend. We can tap into the energies of the world and those around us. We are required for a functioning world, but because of this, they *fear* us." His voice became a vicious growl. "They locked us away, exiled us, but they never understood that we too were made with a purpose, that we cannot be restrained…" A satisfied smile grew on his lips as he spoke. "Your divination was a sign that the world is ready for a change, that we are once again needed. The end of an age is upon us. You see, we are the signals of change, the conduits of spirit itself… The harbingers of death."

"What does that mean?" she hissed.

"Tsk, tsk, princess. A deal is a deal." The Prince of Shadows took one last deep breath of mountain air before turning to his apprentice. "You heard her, no more unnecessary deaths," he said, throwing him the crystal before disappearing like a shadow in direct sunlight.

Three things happened at that point in such a tight interval that no one could properly say which came first: the scream, the rain, or the blood.

The curtain of light came down around them, bringing the darkness into the foreground. A spark of lightning struck the peaks above, sending debris clattering to the floor. The waiting clouds finally burst.

All in an instant, The Apprentice caught the stone, slit Ori's throat, and held it under the fresh fountain of blood. Its jade light glowed vividly through the hot red mass. Savara let out a blood-curdling scream. The Apprentice looked up at her horror-ridden face briefly and stifled a frown before vanishing in a cloud of dust as his master had before him.

Savara rushed over to help, but she knew there was little she could do. She pressed her hands firmly over his throat, hoping to stop the bleeding, but to no avail. Plastered across Lord Ori's face was terror in its purest form. His face, frightened, pleading with her to keep Death's spindly fingers from taking hold. The great Lord Ori shuddered as any mortal would in the hands of Death himself, all the while gaping like a fish on land and choking violently on his blood.

But Death will always follow its harbinger…

"Help!" Savara screamed, though her voice came out feeble through the stream of tears. "Help!" No one came. "Please work," she pleaded with eyes closed. "Please!"

Savara dug deep inside of herself, begging whatever unholy thing lay inside her to fix him. She could feel her powers fluttering in her palms, hovering just shy of his body, but they refused to go any further. They wouldn't work their magic on him as they had on her hand. His body spoke a language her powers couldn't understand. She tried with desperate force to coax them out, but they never crossed the threshold. Under the streams of spurting blood, her hands trembled.

The rain poured down around them. The cracks of thunder echoed through the sanctuary, drowning out the sound of her sobs. Droplets mixed with tears slid down her flustered cheeks. Beneath her palms, she felt his spirit fade. She wanted to hold on to it—force it back into its container, keep her promise to him that all would be well—but it was no use. Beneath her palms it pulsed in and out, the gaps between growing longer and the pulses fewer before the stillness finally set in.

As the rain dripped to the ground from his body and hers, their pasts dripped away with it. Their hopes and triumphs, their pain and fear, they all seeped deep down into the soil, catching on stones and mixing with the rest of the raindrops, only to flow down a drain somewhere.

CHAPTER 46

SPILT BLOOD AND STOLEN STONES

BY THE TIME Jasper arrived, it was too late. Lord Ori's lifeless body lay strewn in a pool of his own blood, slowly polluting the rainwater and staining the green grass below red. Savara hovered over him trembling, unable to move her hands from his throat, still hoping to stop the bleeding. Jasper pulled her up from the floor and held her tightly in his arms, struggling against her kicking and screaming.

"Get off me!" she wailed.

He whispered to her, hoping to soothe her torment. "Sav, it's all over."

But Savara couldn't hear him. She buried her face in his chest and, still trembling violently, let out a sob of defeat. "It's my fault," she stuttered. "It's all my fault."

The storm raged on above, ousting fires, purifying the air, and washing away the suffering.

The day's trauma had ended just as suddenly as Lord Ori's own life. Terra soldiers swarmed, pushing past the pair of them with all the force of a mudslide towards their leader, and somewhere between them, Griffin forced himself through to her.

"What happened?" he yelled at Jasper, seeing that Savara was coated from head to toe in blood.

"I don't know."

Griffin's frantic eyes followed the Terra soldiers to the other side of the room, catching a glimpse of Lord Ori's corpse. "Take her to her room. There's nothing more to be done."

* * *

IT SEEMED ALL too soon to be convened in the hallowed chambers again. This time, however, the halls were empty, save for Griffin, the two generals, and the remaining four council members. Emptiness, guilt, loss, and fear had set in over their honourable faces. The whites of their eyes were stained red from the tears. Hands balled in fists shook in anger and futility.

There was nothing more to be done.

"They were already inside," General Isaac said with a quiver in his voice. "Somehow, they were already inside." He clutched a traditional Terra soldier helmet under his right arm to keep himself from trembling.

"So, it is true, then?" asked Lady Abeer in her usual gentle voice. A deep frown set in across her wrinkled face. She looked more frail than usual. "The world is at war with the shadows…"

Griffin nodded. He tried his best to pay attention and respond to the council members, but in his mind, he replayed the day's events over and over, wondering where his plans had gone wrong, cursing himself for having underestimated their enemies.

"We shall have to ascend someone tonight," reminded Lord Aito. A burn mark ran up the side of his torso, peeking out from under his armour-plated tunic. He too had been in the battle.

Before tonight, Griffin had wondered whether he or any of them remembered what it was to fight, to be at war. Back when the world was less at peace, and his stomach was half its current size, Lord Aito had been a soldier—*a warrior*, Griffin recalled. The kind that spat on the corpses of his enemies and paid for blood with blood. Griffin saw it in his eyes now, the thirst for the battle, the rage pushing at his fists. Tonight, Lord Aito remembered what it was to fear.

Tonight, all of Idune remembered.

Lady Amaia shot him a chastising glance. "Can we save politics for tomorrow? Our friend is dead."

"Amaia, you heard the child. We are at war!" he shouted. "We need to protect ourselves." Unable to contain the trembling in his hands, Lord Aito slammed a great fist onto the stone table, leaving an imprint for all to see. Lady Amaia stood up just as forcefully on the opposite end of the table. The sound snapped Griffin out of his daze.

"Children, please," said Lady Abeer. "Amaia, someone will need to inform Yensa. I'd rather his poor wife not hear it as gossip." She turned to the two lords and spoke again. "As for the two of you, we shall need to inform the ministers. Send out messengers as soon as we are finished here. Aito is right. We will need to ascend someone this evening; otherwise, I'm afraid our enemies might take advantage of our circumstances." Finally, she turned to Griffin. "You are free to stay, to heal, to regroup, but I am sorry to say you will not have our support once you leave. We have a duty to our people, as you will understand, and as such, we must protect our homeland."

"I understand, my lady," Griffin replied with a bow.

The meeting adjourned not soon after.

"We did everything we could, General," said Griffin to his friend as they exited the halls.

"I understand," sighed General Isaac. "Believe me, I am just as surprised as you are. How is your friend?"

Her petrified, hopeless eyes flashed through his mind. "She's in shock. I should get back to her."

General Isaac took his hand and pulled him back. "I warn you, there are some here that will take advantage of the current situation." General Isaac made sure no one else around was listening before he continued, "Motivated only by their own political success. I tell you as a friend, Griffin, I believe it is best you make haste to your next destination. Do not heal or regroup here."

"Thank you, General Isaac."

"And Griffin," he added, "should you ever need assistance, know that there are those within the Terra Army that remember you fondly. You will count on us should the need arise." He held out a bear-sized paw which Griffin gladly took hold of.

"Thank you again, my friend."

***

"LET ME HELP you with that."

Storm huffed. She knew it was him even before his smug face appeared at her door. "Sebastian, so help me Iturri—"

"I come in peace," he said with his hands raised above his head. His golden curls hung loosely over his shoulders. Parts had been tinged orange from the fight. She didn't know what bothered her more, the fact that even after a battle he still managed to look like a fallen saint or that it didn't bother her half as much as it should have.

He's wearing that stupid face again. The half-smile and glassy eyes told her he was worried. *Does he think I'm some sort of helpless creature? That I can't take care of myself? How dare he,* thought Storm.

His concern irritated her more than his presence. She could run him through with her sword without mercy or remorse any day she pleased. Her eyes fell to her arm, charred in places, splintered in others, dangling limply at her side. She'd have to swap to her right arm for a while; the wounds would take some time to heal.

Maybe on a better day, she frowned as she unhitched a sigh. *At least the blood isn't all mine.*

"I didn't say come in," she growled as he strode up to her.

Sebastian took the cloth without asking and began to soak it in the water. She watched hesitantly, knowing she should kick him out before he got too comfortable, but she couldn't bring herself to be rid of him.

The veins in his arms bulged as he wrung the cloth free of water. Under different circumstances, he would've made more of a show of it, but then, under different circumstances, she wouldn't have let him near enough to notice.

"Careful. My right arm works just fine," Storm scoffed.

"I'm sure." Sebastian warmed the cloth in his hands and moved to dab it on her forearm.

"Ouch!" She flinched, raising her other hand to strike.

"It's easier to clean with warm water," he said, resting his hand lightly on her thigh. "Calm down."

Storm bit her lip and braced herself for the pain, but Sebastian was gentle with her in a way she never imagined he could be. He kept his head down, keeping the towel warm between his fingers, but he must have sensed her watching because a smile curled on his lips.

What a self-obsessed ass, she thought as she turned away.

Silence fell between them, hanging expectantly in the air, but her pride would not move her to speak. She could handle silence; it was better than having to deal with any smug comments. The sound of the drops of bloody, dirt-tinged water returning to their basin each time he wrung out the cloth was enough to fill the void. Eventually, however, she was unable to resist peeking over her shoulder.

Stupid hands, she thought as she watched them dab the cloth on her wound with care. *Stupid arms*, though she remembered how they carried her off the battlefield, how they held her the previous night. She remembered their intimacies, though she'd never admit it to him. It was better he think that she'd forgotten everything in an alcohol-induced haze than for him to know she remembered. But she remembered everything.

Her eyes had rested on him longer than she'd intended. Finding his two glowing, glassy eyes staring back at her startled and embarrassed her so much that she kicked him off the bed.

"That's it. I'm fine." She blushed, trying to hide it under the new length of her brilliant red locks. "Get out!" she yelled.

"You're insane," he retorted.

"I can do the rest myself," she said dismissively. And then he laughed. "Of all the—"

"I know," he replied, rubbing the part of his chest that had made contact with her boot. "I didn't offer because I thought you needed the help."

"Oh?" she spat, keeping the redness in her face hidden.

"I offered because I *wanted* to help."

Storm glowered at him, wondering why he would ever *want* to help her. *Maybe he'd inhaled too much smoke and wasn't thinking straight.* He blandished that horrible smouldering look of his—the one that women drooled over. *I hate that look…*

"I'm sure there are other damsels in distress that need your help," she replied as she turned up her nose.

"Possibly."

Storm rolled her eyes. "They're probably half as injured and much less capable…"

"Probably."

"…Fine."

After a long pause, Sebastian relented. "Fine," he sighed as he moved for the door.

"Don't." The word slipped out before she could catch herself.

"If you want me to stay, you'll have to ask."

Storm bit down hard on her lip. Sebastian waited for another second, staring at her with a forming frown, before returning to the door.

"…stay…" she growled finally.

"Nicely."

"…please."

Though he didn't reply, his smirk spoke volumes. Sebastian picked up the rag again and began to dab her wounds. This time the silence between them nagged at her. To have him there, the bane of her existence tending to her like she was helpless, irked her immensely—and he knew it. A small part of her thought it was sweet, but she had no time for sweet. *Those things are the first to be ripped from you in this cruel world,* she remembered. But when his rugged fingers grazed her cheek, brushing the strands of hair that hid her fluster behind her ears, she realised it was too late. Somewhere between loathing him and the thought of losing him, she realised she might sort of like him. She readied herself to push him away when he rested his hand on her leg again.

"There's blood on your forehead," he said calmly. "I'm just trying to clean it. That's all."

Storm turned up her nose but allowed him to dab at the wounds. She tried her best to avoid his gaze, but her treacherous eyes seemed to seek out his. She couldn't believe that, even after a battle, his eyes still sparkled like a thousand suns. Charred in places and covered in soot, and yet, his attention belonged only to her.

He touched the cloth lightly to her head. "You know," he began, "this might be the longest you've gone without threatening me."

"It's the longest you've gone without being insufferable." She turned to swat him across the face with her good hand, but he caught it mid-swing and gazed into her eyes.

"I was going to say, it's nice."

She pulled her hand from his, unsure of what to do next. Both held their tongues, unable to muster the courage needed to open their mouths and speak their minds. The seconds that ticked by stretched like minutes, spreading out between occasional stolen glances and silent sighs. Finally, he dropped the rag back into the basin.

"Well, you're all cleaned up," Sebastian said, moving to stand.

"Sebas, I—" Storm began, unsure why she had decided to speak even as the words left her lips. She knew she had to say something, or else risk looking like a fool—and she wasn't a fool. She sighed. "You could've let me die back there."

Sebastian thought about it for a second before nodding. "…I could've."

"But you didn't…"

"No."

"Why?"

Sebastian scratched the back of his neck shyly. The move itself seemed too uncomfortable to be casual. "You could've let me burn back at the camp."

"I know…"

"But you didn't."

"…no."

"Curious, isn't it?" He bit his lip to stop the grin from spreading across his face. "You should get some rest. Griffin says we'll be leaving during the festivities."

He was already halfway to the door when she regained her voice. "Don't tell me what to do."

"Stormy, my dear, I wouldn't dream of it," he replied with a wink and closed the door.

Her heart seemed to echo in the lonely room.

Storm picked up a knife from her bedside table and threw it with her right hand. It embedded itself square in the door where his face had been moments before. She waited for her accelerated pulse to steady, to regain her composure, but she knew it was already too late.

He's done it, she thought with a frown, slowly beginning to realise that he'd broken her.

CHAPTER 47

A DARKER GAME AFOOT

SAVARA REPLAYED THE day's events over and over in her head as she sat alone in her room.

Jasper had offered to take her over to Brass, who'd returned just in time to tend to the wounded, but she declined. She claimed she had no injuries worth looking at, despite her obvious trembling. He'd led her away from the scene and allowed her to break down in his arms. He assured her that there was nothing else she could've done, that none of it was her fault, that she was safe, but he didn't get it.

She wasn't safe anymore. No one was.

She'd forced him to see to his injuries, not wanting to tell him she needed to be alone. The memory of Lord Ori's panicked face was etched into her mind. She'd cleaned the blood from her palms and changed her clothes, but she still felt covered in it. Hot, sticky, and falling over her in showers like the ones that rained from above.

"I felt him die," she said into the emptiness of her room, echoing the words she'd said earlier to Jasper. "I felt his life in my hands. Every beat of his dying heart, every worry on his mind. I felt every piece of him slip through my fingers."

When she told him, he'd pulled her in tight, trying to hold every inch of her shattered soul together. "*I can't let that happen again,*" she'd whispered. "*You won't,*" he'd replied, but his unsteady heart hadn't been sure, and neither had hers.

"You sure do love a pity party," said a voice from beyond the walls.

"What are *you* doing here?" she scoffed as the man who she now knew as The Apprentice appeared from the same hole as he'd done earlier. "Come to finish me off?"

"What resignation…" He crossed his arms, drooping his head so his irritating midnight blue eyes were obscured by the waves of black hair. "Suppose I did, princess? You don't seem to be running."

"I'm tired of running."

"You could've fooled me. You've holed yourself up in this room, thrown yourself a spectacular pity party I might add, instead of healing with your friends. Sounds like running to me."

"What do you care?" she yelled.

"I don't," he shrugged. "I just figured it would take more than that to break you."

"You don't even know me."

"I know a lot more than you think, princess."

"Whatever. Besides, didn't you hear? I'm the harbinger of death. I could probably kill you without even leaving the bed."

The Apprentice shook his head and smirked. "I don't think you've quite figured out what it means."

"I don't know what to think anymore," she said as she buried her face in her knees. "I came here searching for something that might bring my life meaning… something that would make me feel like I belonged somewhere, but everywhere I go I feel like an outcast, and on top of it, these stupid powers of mine only bring death and destruction."

"I'm going to stop you right there, princess," he began, holding up a scarred palm to silence her. "Life, despite what any of those do-gooder friends you have there might tell you, is inherently meaningless."

"Thanks."

"Curb the fire, I was going to say… the moments that fill it are not. Stop looking for meaning in life. If you must, look for meaning in moments."

"Sage advice for a killer," Savara replied, refusing to admit aloud that her mind had already begun to repeat his words.

"Who said I couldn't be multifaceted? Besides, I'm not a fan of letting my past define me." He grinned at her as though they shared an intimate bond.

"Have you come just to insult me?" she growled, narrowing her eyes into dagger-like points as she glowered at him. The Apprentice ignored her and stalked over to her wardrobe, opening it wide but blocking her view of within as he rummaged through one of the boxes. "Hey! Do you have any sense of boundaries?" she called out to him again irritably.

He turned back to her with the package in his hand, contemplating the intact wrapping and still-bound twine with a furrowed brow.

"I'm surprised you haven't opened it," he said, rattling the package before placing it into the pocket of his crisp black coat. "I'll let you get back to sulking. Maybe we'll see each other again when you decide to stop reacting to life and start making something of it because, if you haven't realised, princess, only you can." He winked as he climbed into the tunnel, letting the shadows swallow him whole.

Savara blinked. Blinked. Shook her head and blinked again. She had a hard time believing what had happened, even though she'd seen it with her own eyes. She glared at the hole in the wall, her jaw slackened in disbelief, as she turned his words over and over in her mind.

Every time she thought she understood the world around her, something like this would happen to warp understanding entirely. The question forced her to recall the faces of all those she'd lost, how they'd lived—and died—and wonder where the meaning in their lives had been, and if, as he'd said, it existed at all.

Savara stood at the edge of the hole, flustered and furious. She was tired of all the games. Tired of everyone else being one step ahead of her. If life was truly about moments and not meaning, she knew her moment was waiting somewhere at the end of the gaping tunnel. Harbinger of death or not, as she clambered through the hole, she took comfort in the fact that she was no longer waiting for answers. She was going to get them.

* * *

"GRIFFIN."

Griffin couldn't remember the last time Brass said his name with such tension in his voice. That tone he reserved for things that he knew would bring about trouble. He turned to find his friend bobbing casually behind him, but his frown told Griffin something was gnawing at him. Something of the most pertinent and important nature.

"Is everything alright?"

Brass glanced around quickly before replying, "I think there's something you need to see."

He reluctantly agreed to follow him down to the holding cells where they'd put the Argia they'd managed to rescue from their possession. Some of the men still trembled, traumatised by the day's events. Others had even refused to sit in unlit cells, huddling themselves next to whatever source of light lay in the room for fear that the shadows might return. The elderly tried their best to calm their young comrades even though they themselves were still admittedly spooked. None of them had gotten any sleep. Griffin feared none of them would. He knew that would only push them closer to insanity.

Brass stopped in front of one of the furthest cells in the room and tapped lightly on the bars. "Are you still awake?" he asked politely.

The man stirred. He looked to be the only one who hadn't had a problem with the darkness or with sleep. He rolled over on the bed, brushed the tangled blond hair from his eyes, and stood up. His step was pained and off-beat, like a clock that tocks faster than it ticks. Even still, as he reached the bars and stepped into the low lighting of the hallway, Griffin realised why Brass had been worried. The broad shoulders, the cut of his jaw, even the glow in his amber eyes was unmistakable. His hair had seen too much sun, turning his curls from strawberry blond to a vicious gold. His face, though marred with an unpleasant mixture of mud and blood, still looked as fierce as the day Griffin had last seen him.

Griffin could hardly believe his eyes. "How many people know?" he asked under his breath.

"No one yet," Brass whispered back nervously. "I thought I should tell you first…"

"Keep it that way," Griffin added forcefully as he turned back to the man in the cell. If Brass hadn't confirmed it, he would've thought it was all a strange dream. Granted, it was a dream he'd had before but never like this. Especially under the circumstances, there would be no happy reunions. "Does anyone else know who you are?" Griffin asked in a faint voice. The last thing he needed was the rest of the world to find out. He would have a bounty on his head the minute they left Idune, or even before.

The man shook his head. His glittering trellises bounced the way his mother's used to, swishing and bobbing just above his shoulders. Griffin searched his eyes for some sign of recognition, some sparkle of a shared past, but this man's eyes were coloured alone. He looked empty but not hollow, as though it were something he could choose.

"Do you know who you are?" Griffin asked again.

The man nodded simply. Griffin knew if they spent any more time down here, people would get suspicious. But how could he leave? The one person he'd spent an entire life trying to forget—believing he was dead—stood before him. Nothing made sense anymore.

Brass, having noticed the war going on in his head, jumped into the conversation. "What will you tell her?" he asked.

Griffin hadn't thought about Savara during their time in the prison, but Brass was right. He would have to think of her sooner or later. This news was too big to be kept a secret, especially from her. Even if no one else were to know, she had the honest right to. For the time being, however, he ignored Brass' question. Good as it may have been, he had his own to ask.

"Why didn't you come back? Why didn't you let the world know?" Griffin prodded. The words came out too desperately. What he meant was, *Why didn't you let me know?* After everything they had been through, he couldn't believe—no—he wouldn't believe that this man would have left him in the dark.

The man cleared his throat. "I didn't know then. I didn't know anything then. The shadows brought back the memories."

The man's voice had all the qualities of golden honey. Sweet and heavy, with a slight accent he must have gained in the Red Desert. But there was no mistaking him. Everything from his frame down to his tongue betrayed his birth. His tall stature and chiselled jaw were stolen from his father, no question, but in everything else, he was the spitting image of his mother, the Queen of White Fire.

* * *

"GET BACK HERE with that!" Savara called into the darkness of the tunnel. "You murderous, self-obsessed, narcissistic—"

"Not the nicest way to speak to the person who saved you…multiple times," he reminded her, his voice echoing off the walls in all directions.

Savara followed it to a dim light at the end of a different tunnel, which she was surprised to find opened out into a clearing in the forest at the edge of the great wall. He leaned casually up against a tree, turning the package over in his hand as he waited for her to arrive.

"We need to stop meeting like this," he added.

Savara stormed over to him. "You lying, double-crossing piece of shit!" She let a clenched fist fly, hitting his jaw with as much force as she could muster.

He looked as though he knew it was coming but allowed it to happen anyway. The second time she swung, however, he caught her arm and turned her around with the left-over force from the blow. "Once is enough."

A fire raged inside her, forcing the blood to her cheeks and the power into her palms. The Apprentice cast two beams of blue light around her wrists, binding them together to prevent another strike to the face.

"You killed him," she hissed, trying to wriggle herself free. "You deserve more than one small fist to the jaw."

"You mean the Harri lord? Really, princess, I don't see why you're getting so worked up. You knew him for all of what, five seconds?" The Apprentice replied as he waved an apathetic hand in the air.

"That's not the point! He had a family and friends and—"

"And so does the rest of the world, princess," he interrupted. "You complaining is not going to bring him back to life either."

"You killed him after your master said not to. Or do these blood pacts mean nothing?"

"The *soul bond* you made was between you and *him*. Besides, *you* agreed to no more unnecessary deaths. It's not my problem if you aren't careful with your words."

Savara's blood ran cold. "What do you mean?"

He twisted her into his arms to better meet her eyes. The scent of night flowers danced in the silence that settled between them as he regarded her. "Wording is *everything*, Savara."

"You mean to tell me," she began, straining her throat with the grim, memory-laden words, "that Lord Ori's death was somehow *necessary*?"

The Apprentice held his tongue, but the shrug that followed told her she was right.

"There never was a hope of saving Lord Ori," she whispered. Under the darkened canopy, the shaky reassurance she'd found when chasing him down began to buckle along with her knees.

Some people's purpose is just to die, Savara realised, but her stomach curled in on itself at the thought. *It was all for nothing...* She swayed where she stood, unable to balance herself, but The Apprentice tightened his grip and steadied her with unexpected care.

"You don't look well..." he said.

"What do you care?" she sniffled. Her mind still spiralled with the idea that death in itself was a purpose—the purpose.

"Can I help it if I find your bitterness endearing?"

"Just... give me back my package and leave," she mumbled.

"Hmm…" The Apprentice raised a tentative hand to her face, and though she initially recoiled, she allowed him to brush the stray lock of hair from in front of her eyes. The feeling of his fingers grazing her cheek lasted long after his hand dropped back to his side. "You mean *my* package."

"Yours…?" She furrowed her brow.

"And I don't think so. I gave it to you once, you didn't open it, you didn't want it, you didn't even look at it. I'm taking it back," he replied, a coy smile tugging at his lips as he spoke.

"But I thought…" She fumbled for the words as her mind searched back for the record of that day, for the face through the window she couldn't quite see but eyes she would never forget. "You were there," she realised. "You were in the café the day my uncle was killed. You were the man that the waitress was talking about… The man in the glass. Why?"

He scratched at the side of his neck guiltily. "I thought it would be safer in your hands than in mine… but now I see you're not looking to stick around much longer, what with all that moping and moaning. I figure I should take it back, find a new hiding place and someone else who needs it."

"Why would I need it?"

He snapped his fingers and released her from the bindings before flinging the package to her. "You tell me, princess."

The strange box buzzed in her hands. The brown paper had been scorched in the fire, and what once spelt out an address—coincidentally, the one she'd been staying at during her stint in Idune—was now completely illegible. The twine unravelled easily between her fingertips, revealing a wooden box lined with carvings of stars and planets and other things Savara had no names for. However, it was the contents of the box that rattled her to her core. She'd almost dropped it when she realised what was inside.

"Where did you get this?" Savara asked hesitantly, staring down at one of the legendary stones. Judging by the swirling shadows contained within its glass walls, she guessed it belonged to the Arima—the *Blood Daemons*. That, and the fact that the tiny orb seemed to be calling for blood.

"Now she's interested." He grinned. "Let's just say I have sticky fingers."

"What do you expect me to do with it?" she stuttered, hearing a voice that she imagined belonged to the orb ringing in her mind.

Similar to the one that Lord Ori had, this orb had a spirit of its own and seemed to be calling out to whatever lay inside her. This time, however, the two things spoke of life and death through feelings rather than words.

"Don't know and don't care, just try not letting you-know-who get his hands on it," he replied, turning away from her, and pulling out a strange, golden object that looked extraordinarily like a pocket watch, but wasn't.

The orb thrummed with a power palpable through the wooden case. Savara closed it, unable to bring herself to break the hold it had on her any other way. "Aren't you his obedient, murderous little lapdog?" she asked, still reeling from the orb's grip on her mind. "Why would you want me to have this if he needs it?"

"Is that what you think?" The Apprentice asked as he turned back to her, placing the golden object in his coat. "That I go around killing people for the fun of it?" Disdain set in on his face. "Maybe if you ever got past your languishing in self-pity and that shameful need to feel good and accepted, you'd have realised that I am the only reason you are standing here today."

"You're the one that got me into this mess," Savara hissed, anger beginning to bubble inside her.

"I got you out of a much bigger one you had no idea you'd stepped your arrogant little foot into," he barked.

"And you expect me to praise you for that?"

"At the very least, you could say thank you."

"Thank you?" she spat. The fury glowed in her eyes as clear as the stars above them. "Why would I ever thank a *monster* like you?"

"Monster?" The Apprentice gritted his teeth in anger. "Oh, believe me, princess, if you could be so lucky to have me as the only monster in your life. Don't forget, I know what that thing is inside of you. I wouldn't be so quick to label others as monsters if I were you."

Savara stared down at her trembling hands. The power had crept into her palms without her notice. It flurried between her fingers expectantly. One outward flick of the wrist and they'd seek out whatever semblance of a soul he had left in him and crush it. She balled her hands into fists, digging her nails into the moon-shaped scabs she'd made the last time she'd been this infuriated.

He's right, she thought, but she'd never speak it aloud.

Noticing the blood trickling from her palms, The Apprentice frowned. "I shouldn't have come back."

"So, why did you?" Savara snarled.

"I needed…" he hesitated, casting a glance around the empty forest before continuing. "I needed to see for myself."

"See what?"

"The state you were in…" he whispered.

Savara frowned. "It was you who saved me in the forest outside of Osiir," she said, offering a measly olive branch, but The Apprentice held his tongue. "I recognise your voice… and your eyes." She waited. "Are you going to tell me why? Or just stand there in silence?"

"Just be happy *he* needs you alive, princess, or I might have left you on that floor," he replied, though she knew by the way he avoided her eyes that it was a lie. After having spent so much time with Griffin—the master of half-truths and evasion of the straight-forward—she knew when there was more to a story.

"Why send the shadows after me if he needs me? Didn't he know they'd hunt for blood?"

"The shadows are a pack of hungry dogs, and a hungry dog knows no master beyond its stomach."

"So, your saving me wasn't even a choice of your own. And here I thought you might have been capable of some good. Now I see you were just following orders—something you seem to be very good at, despite what they may mean for the lives of others."

"Spare me the hysterics, princess. We all become killers eventually." He inched towards her, forcing her back against the tree. "At least I treat life with dignity, and if I kill, I kill with reason."

"You wouldn't know dignity or reason if they bit you in the ass."

"Is that so?" he growled, glaring at her as though he were deciding whether to kill her in that moment. Their bodies drew close like magnets pulling one to the other.

"You've proven yourself a cold-blooded killer…" Savara hissed, wanting to remind him that he had Ori's blood on his hands.

"Go on…"

She stepped forward in challenge, eyes locked on each other unrelentingly. They'd come so close that their breaths were sharing breaths.

"With no heart and no soul…" she continued.

"How kind."

"You're mocking me."

"I'm discovering myself."

"Are you proud? Of the suffering you cause? Of your heartlessness?"

In the silence that settled between them, she could hear the faint beating of his heart in the gaps hers left empty.

"You have no idea…" The Apprentice frowned and took a step back, pulling at the magnetism between their two souls. "I don't know why I still bother to check on you."

"What's that supposed to mean?"

"Not that it's anything to you, princess, but I have my reasons for keeping you out of trouble."

"And, of course, you won't be sharing those reasons, will you?"

The Apprentice grinned. "You're catching on."

Savara let out an exasperated huff. "Do you enjoy tormenting me?" she hissed.

"If I said I didn't, would you believe me?" he mused. Savara grimaced at him. "Lighten up, princess. Considering what's coming, you'll need the diversion."

"What do you mean?" she asked, initially defiant until she recalled his earlier words. A sobering realisation took over.

"What you said before of unnecessary deaths… Are there more to come?" The Apprentice pursed his lips, refusing to speak, but the answer was written across his face. "You don't have to do this."

"I have no choice…" he said.

"What about not letting your past define you?"

"It's not my past that worries me."

Savara bit down on the anger, realising all questions pertaining to the future would be ignored or avoided. "Why did you really come here?" she prodded instead.

"You're annoyingly persistent."

Noticing a ripple of embarrassment from him, she added, "Humour me."

The Apprentice took his time in forming a response. "They say souls like yours attract the broken," he replied finally, gazing at her with eyes still fraught with storms.

"Souls like mine?"

He looked as though he were about to clarify when a twig snapping somewhere in the distance startled them both. "Fuck…" he mumbled as he pulled out a handful of familiar black dust, about to toss it when she caught hold of his hand.

"Where do you think you're going?"

"I'm late for another appointment."

Savara gaped at him incredulously. "You're just going to leave me here?"

"You're a big girl now, princess. You made it perfectly clear you don't need my help," he scoffed.

"Is this all just some game to you?"

"*Life* is a game, princess. One great, big, meaningless game. And we," he gestured ceremoniously between them, "its sentenced players, are all losers from the moment we place our piece on the board. The sooner you learn that the better." The Apprentice frowned as he threw the dust to the floor, disappearing in a cloud of sparkling smoke, but not before a final warning. His words rang clearly through the small patch of forest. "Welcome to Visanthe…"

Savara wished she could wail after him, but the noise returned, reminding her she was not alone in the forest. She regarded the spot where The Apprentice had stood, hoping he might come back, but he was gone. Her heart trembled as she wondered what would become of her. The vaguely familiar snarl of an unpleasant voice from behind meant she would soon find out.

"Well, well, well. What do we have here?"

Before she could turn to see her new company, someone clubbed her from behind. The last thing she saw before the fall was the shine of polished black boots, and a streak of blue lightning above. Before her eyes, the world faded to black, as though it were nothing more than a dream.

Enjoyed this book? Here's a teaser of the first chapter of the second book, **Visanthe in Ruin**, available now in eBook, paperback, and hardcover!

CHAPTER 1

UNWELCOME WATERS

THE SHIP ROCKED GENTLY with the twilight currents, a sensation that had lulled most of its occupants into a pleasant, dreamless sleep, but the young human aboard this galleon of magical beings was too agitated for even the most nightmarish sleep. As a result, Griffin found himself at the receiving end of the agitated lecture. Thankfully, he hadn't been able to sleep either; otherwise, he would've contemplated murder.

A headache had been brewing in him ever since they'd left port. No amount of meditation or water had yet been able to quell it. To make matters worse, the human came in with a fury.

"You promised you would find her!" Jasper yelled, sending resting gulls flapping from their perches atop the crow's nest into the night skies. The starlight danced across their feathered backs as they circled and settled once more into their nests.

Griffin rubbed his temples. "I know what I said," he hissed, trying not to wake the whole ship or whatever sea monsters he'd been told lived in these dark waters. "But the situation required a different approach."

"What about your friend in the army?" Jasper prodded. "He must know something."

"General Isaac is unavailable for conversation," Griffin sighed, remembering the conversation they'd had after the battle. Jasper didn't need to know of the mess they'd left behind or the threats mounting against them. He'd only insist on them turning back and searching for Savara themselves. But there were bigger problems at hand that demanded their attention.

Griffin downed another glass of water and an awful-tasting syrup that Brass had made for him once he'd told him they would be embarking on their journey by way of water. It had the double effect of soothing his stomach from the swaying of the ship and taking away any stress-induced migraines that reared their ugly heads.

"We can't just sit on our hands and wait. We've got to do something," Jasper scoffed.

"What makes you think I haven't?" Griffin growled as he crossed his arms over his chest. The move had the unintentional effect of reminding Jasper what had happened during their time in the Harri territories, though he knew Jasper was the last person who needed reminding of anything. Griffin's burns from the battle in Idune had all but disappeared, leaving only light patches of scarring on his forearms. It had been a gruelling fight, but in the end, they had all made it out relatively unscathed. The physical scars would fade eventually. The mental ones concerned him.

It had only been a fortnight since the battle and the group was still worse for wear. Storm was bound to using her right arm for the time being, but she'd be better soon enough. She was too stubborn to let the injury stop her. Sebastian had been spared from any great injury, though he spent most of his mental energy worrying about Storm's condition and annoyed at her refusals of his help. There was Lance, his childhood best friend whom he'd once thought…

No. Griffin forbade himself from finishing the thought. *No more wishful thinking.* Eventually, they'd have to speak. Maybe not of their shared past, but at the very least of what future lay ahead. Right now, the thought of him would only bring on the desire for a drink, and that would do no one any good.

And then there was Jasper, the painful human whose voice was, at present, only adding to the throbbing in his head. Jasper kept himself up most of the night worrying about *her.* Griffin wouldn't admit it aloud, but this was something they had in common.

"Yes, but—"

"Your feelings for Savara apart, we do have other matters to take care of. Do we not?" Griffin reminded him.

They'd made a deal. First, they would find a way to restore her memories, then they'd save her from whatever mess she found herself in. If the information in the bloodthirsty book was to be believed, they needed Savara to remember the time before her divination. Until then, she was relatively useless, which also meant she was safe.

Jasper pressed his glasses to his nose and stared at the ground, the anger in him subsiding, replaced by something of a more sober nature.

"Yes," he mumbled, the word barely a whisper. He tugged at his sleeve, holding back words Griffin knew he'd never speak without help, but with another heavy exhale, he instead turned for the door.

"How is it?" Griffin asked, tone softening to put Jasper at ease. "Your… condition?" His eyes hitched on the black veins tracing the length of Jasper's arm, the ones he'd tried to hide under his long-sleeved tunic. Griffin had seen those marks before, though it hadn't occurred to him when he began seeing them on Jasper that they were of the same origin. His father's arms were riddled with them in his lifetime.

It was those books. Whatever knowledge they contained came at a deadly price. If Griffin had put the two together sooner, he might have worked harder at dissuading Jasper of their charm.

Jasper tucked his arm behind his back guiltily. "I've had better days."

"If it becomes too much…"

"I'm fine, Griffin," Jasper hissed. "Don't forget, I'm not doing it for you."

"I haven't forgotten anything, but you will not be able to protect her if you cannot protect yourself," Griffin replied.

Jasper avoided his gaze, but Griffin knew his words had landed. Jasper's dedication to his friend was admirable. A small pang of guilt appeared in his chest. If he were in Jasper's position, nothing and no one would sway him. He knew that his words, and what little guidance they might offer, would not be enough to convince Jasper otherwise, but they might give him pause for the time being.

"I left Brass in Idune to see what he can find out about her disappearance," Griffin added, hoping to lift his spirits, even if only slightly. "If there's something to be found, he'll be the one to find it." Jasper nodded, his frown lifting as he headed for the door. "It's probably best to leave that book alone for now. It's already taken enough of you…" Griffin called out to him. All he saw was the back of Jasper's head, but Griffin sensed his apprehension at the words. Jasper's pause lasted only a moment. In the next, the door closed heavily behind him, leaving Griffin alone to his thoughts.

The slivers of moonlight danced across the wooden floor, shifting with the soft currents beneath the ship. Griffin strode over to the porthole at the far end of his room, opened the latch, and poked his head out. He took a deep breath, letting the sea breeze fill his lungs. Its salty scent brought him back to the shores of Yozora where he'd spent the better part of his winters training to be the soldier his father would be proud of.

The royal guards had never been known for their compassionate training methods, but compared to the time spent with his father, even the days in which he'd been stretched out and pushed to his breaking point seemed like bliss. Now, many years later, he was thankful for their strict and torturous methods of training. At least he was prepared. There was a war coming, and not everyone was going to make it through, but Griffin would be damned if he didn't do everything in his power to keep his friends safe.

Jasper cared about Savara the way he cared about his friends. Griffin knew that, if it came to it, Jasper would lay down his life for her. It was admirable of him, endearing even. Jasper was a curious creature; so very human, and yet, so readily adapted to Visanthian life, as if he'd been bred for it from the beginning. Griffin shook his head, entertaining himself with the idea that he'd even begun to care for that powerless lump of skin and bone.

As he stared up at the night sky, his mind wandered back to their final night in Idune and the grave conversation he'd had with General Isaac, the one he neglected to share, knowing it would only make Jasper worry more.

* * *

"They are elevating General Dhoot to the Council," said General Isaac. He'd schooled his features into indifference, but the tension in his voice said otherwise.

General Dhoot, the commander of one of the largest divisions of the Harri army, was nothing but trouble. Griffin had sensed as much from their previous encounter. Bloodlust and a desire for power lingered beneath his polished exterior.

"They can't be serious," growled Griffin. "Have they skimmed over the other possible successors? Lady Amaia couldn't have agreed—"

"Lady Amaia has less sway with the council now that Lord Ori, may he rest in peace, is no longer at its head."

Griffin narrowed his eyes at his friend. "And who is?"

"The leader of all Harri armed forces himself, Lord Andor." General Isaac admitted. "Considering that the world may very well be at war, the council, and the people, thought it best to have a more… militaristic leadership going forward."

"They can't possibly believe that General Dhoot has the best interests of the nation in mind," Griffin scoffed.

"That, my friend, is exactly what they believe." General Isaac bit his lip. "He has more sway than anyone because of his popularity with the aristocrats—and plebeians, I might add."

"I'm sure there's someone else who could serve as a military figurehead…" Griffin thought aloud, continuing his incessant pacing across the floors of the darkened war room. "What about you? Couldn't you—"

General Isaac raised a hand to interrupt. "Thanks for the vote of confidence, my friend, but I am being reassigned."

"Reassigned?"

"To head up the troops on the western front and keep the peace on the border with the Argia. After the attack on Idune, people fear there are more fires to come and think it's best to keep relations with the Argia *contained*."

"They're moving you from the capital?"

General Isaac frowned, no longer able to meet his eyes. "I'm afraid so…"

"I'm at no loss as to who might have suggested such a thing," Griffin growled, halting his steps as he processed the gravity of General Isaac's words. "That means they are taking you out of negotiations?"

"Correct." The pair exchanged a nervous glance before General Isaac added, "If news gets out to General Kyara of the Ur that we have lost Lord Ori, we might have a full-scale invasion along the entire eastern border."

"She wouldn't risk her army for a tiny plot of land. Not when she knows of the Harri nation's strength."

"She would, knowing how that might favour her in trade, and if the only person who was able to reason with her is now dead." General Isaac stiffened. "If word gets out of Lord Ori's death——"

"I am afraid, my friend, it is no longer a matter of if but when."

General Isaac blanched. "Well, then… when word gets out," he corrected, "there will be nothing and no one to stop her."

Ever since Griffin took Savara to the palace at Osiir, he'd known that her memories had been tampered with. His own, too, if the lapsus at her divination was anything to go by. He had already planned to make a trip to the Ur islands. Somewhere in Solia, there was an old Ur woman who had been long branded a witch for her ability to turn a potion. Maybe it was worth it to pay a visit to Iliso, and hope, for everyone's sake, that General Kyara was in the mood to listen to reason.

"Thank you, my friend," said Griffin with a heavy sigh. "You have given me much to think about." He turned for the door, readying his mind for the journey ahead of them, when General Isaac called him back.

"I know that look, Griffin," said General Isaac, his voice serious. "Do not get yourself involved in this war."

A smile tugged at Griffin's lips as he cocked an eyebrow. "I have no idea what you are talking about."

"You forget, we were sparring partners for over two years. I know your planning look intimately," General Isaac reminded him, a wry smile tugging at the corner of his mouth. He pulled a piece of parchment from a pile on the war table and began to scribble. When he finished, he clapped his hand on Griffin's back and handed him the note. "If you do somehow manage to get yourself into trouble, I'll be positioned at this station."

"Should I take offence to your surety at me landing myself in trouble?"

General Isaac laughed. "You also forget, it seems, the many times we spent cleaning the floors of the kitchens because of your landing us in trouble."

"How could I forget? I'm still picking the grime out of my fingernails." The two shared another laugh before Griffin added, "Thank you, my friend."

"No, thank you. It is twice now that you have saved my life, and I am not sure how much of these debts I will be able to settle."

"If all goes well, you will take them to a distant grave."

General Isaac nodded.

Griffin slipped out of the room without so much as a goodbye. He pocketed the piece of parchment and made off to find his friends. A war between the Harri and the Ur would be a problem, but if the final goal of the Arima lay in collecting legends, no nation would be spared from the bloodshed.

If you enjoyed this book, please feel free to leave a review of it on your favourite sites. These reviews help small-time authors like me reach new audiences and are much appreciated!

Stay up to date on L. M. Sanguinette's new releases and giveaways by signing up for her mailing list or following her on social media. Find all the links at the page below:

https://linktr.ee/lmsanguinette

OTHER WORKS

Also available in hardcover!

POETRY COLLECTIONS

COMING SOON...

Of Arrows And Roses (A Visanthian Novel)

ACKNOWLEDGEMENTS

I don't know if I could have ever imagined the amount of work that went into writing and publishing a novel before this. When I was younger, I dreamed of becoming the kind of author who got to simply tell stories and not concern herself with the ins and outs of how those stories reached the public. I now know how naïve that sounds, and because of this, I'd like to give a special thanks to all the people involved in turning this book from a simple story thought up on a whim over seven years ago into something that I hope will touch the hearts of many people around the world.

First and foremost, I'd like to give a big thanks to my editor and guiding light during this process, Cara Flannery. She took what was much like an unbaked cake in story form and turned it into a multi-faceted wedding cake, and I couldn't be more grateful. Her words of support and gentle nudging in the right direction have made all the difference in the finished story and made it one that I can be especially proud of.

Secondly, I'd like to acknowledge the work of the brilliant cover artists that have given their input on this book. For a story with so much character, I struggled for many months to choose the right cover. This was a huge problem because many people (contrary to what we are taught) *do* judge a book by its cover. From the get-go, I knew I needed something that would stand out on the racks, but I couldn't pin down a design. That's where the designers from MiblArt came in and saved the day. Tania and her team were a major help in creating something I knew would catch people's eyes, without giving away too much of the story. I'd also like to thank my incredible cartographer for the wonderful depiction of Visanthe.

Next, I'd like to thank two authors who, despite their flourishing and hectic careers, have always managed to find the time to give me advice and support on this new journey. C. N. Crawford, author of *City of Thorns*, and Bethany Atazadeh, author of the Stolen Kingdom series, have been so kind and generous with their help and support that it would be remiss of me not to mention them.

Finally, this book would never have been completed without the constant love and support of my family and friends who, since the very first moment I decided I wanted to be an author, have inspired, and motivated me to pursue my passions. Some of whom became beta readers, editors, and people to bounce my ideas off. I could never have reached this point without them, and I am so grateful that their constant support has produced something that they too can be proud of.

ABOUT THE AUTHOR

L. M. Sanguinette was born on a small island in the Caribbean, where the palm trees watched over her like giants and the sea crept up to her feet to say hello. Ever since she was little, she surrounded herself with tales of fantasy and magic, hoping that one day, she too would be involved in a story like the ones that captured her imagination.

Years—and many rewatching's of Avatar the Last Airbender—later, she is happily living in the worlds that her mind created, filling her bookshelves with more books than she will ever read, and practising her own version of magic.

When she's not sitting at the computer, she can be found snorkelling near forgotten shores, twisting from silks that hang from the ceilings, or in one of the many hidden coffee shops of Madrid, conversing with the spirits of the old city and dreaming up new adventures.

9798986891002